FRACTURES

FRACTURES

Lamar Herrin

THOMAS DUNNE BOOKS

St. Martin's Press

New York

THOMAS DUNNE BOOKS.
An imprint of St. Martin's Press.

FRACTURES. Copyright © 2013 by Lamar Herrin. All rights reserved. Printed in the United States of America. For information, address St. Martin's Press, 175 Fifth Avenue, New York, N.Y. 10010.

www.thomasdunnebooks.com
www.stmartins.com

Design by Phil Mazzone

Library of Congress Cataloging-in-Publication Data

Herrin, Lamar.
    Fractures : A Novel / Lamar Herrin. — First Edition.
        pages cm
    ISBN 978-1-250-03276-8 (hardcover)
    ISBN 978-1-250-03275-1 (e-book)
  1. Families—Fiction.   2. Upper class—Fiction.   3. Inheritance and succession—Fiction.   4. Hydraulic fracturing—Fiction.   5. Domestic fiction.   I. Title.
    PS3558.E754F73 2013
    813'.54—dc23

                                                                2013023588

St. Martin's Press books may be purchased for educational, business, or promotional use. For information on bulk purchases, please contact Macmillan Corporate and Premium Sales Department at 1-800-221-7945, extension 5442, or write specialmarkets@macmillan.com.

First Edition: November 2013

10 9 8 7 6 5 4 3 2 1

For David Polk and Joe Survant,
Kentuckians, landmen and rivermen alike,
old friends

PART ONE

THE JOYNERS

1

On an April day in 1970, when most of his fellow architecture students were taking their spring break, Frank Joyner drew a Gillette razor blade across his left wrist with one express purpose in mind: he wanted to see if, when the blood appeared, he was willing to let it flow, or if, in fact, he wanted to live. On hand he had a stack of gauze pads, an Ace bandage, and a leather belt he'd tested on his forearm and then punched a new hole in that could serve as a tourniquet. In an anatomy book he'd checked out of the library, he'd read that the veins running down his wrist would yield, if cut, a dark blood, which would only ooze out, and that gauze pressed down beneath an Ace bandage would be sufficient to stop it. Flanking the veins and deeper set were the radial and ulnar arteries, and these would yield a bright red blood in a pulsating flow, which would take a tourniquet, in addition to the gauze and bandage, to stop. The arteries brought blood from the heart, oxygenated to that brighter red as it passed through the lungs; after its long, wearying trip through the body, the veins brought the blood back.

He'd intended to cut to the deeper and thicker-walled arteries, so that he would know, know for sure, but had in fact cut only to the depth of the veins, which had yielded a slow, blanketing flow more plum-colored than red, and which he'd contemplated for a while—impossible to say how long—before sighing deeply and applying the gauze and Ace bandage. He was twenty years old. Of course, he accused himself of cowardice in not cutting deeply enough to reach the arteries, but he also commended himself for not wasting time. He didn't need the brighter, more youthful blood to tell him what the darker, more trav-eled blood had already made clear. He wanted to live.

Within an hour, maybe sooner than that, he'd gone back to work on a model for an airport terminal, which, of all the models he'd made or drawn (the use of a computer eluded him throughout his career), he had never forgotten. In the diagonals of its ramps and roof-pitches it had achieved the effect of a plane rising, in a long, graceful ascent, off the face of the earth.

Suicides had run in his mother's side of the family. His grandfa-ther, while still a young man, had jumped into one of the many gorges left by the retreating glaciers in their small Northern town. This was in 1930, when such acts were not uncommon. Fortunes had been lost, lives ended. But two weeks later, Frank's great-grandfather, a small-time dairy farmer who had never had a fortune to lose, hanged himself from a rafter in his cow barn, and that was the suicide that his great-grandson brooded over. Shame or sympathy for what his own son had done? Or the powerful pull of his example? A seed long dormant that with the son's leap into that gorge had suddenly burst into life, and, hence, death? Or perhaps his great-grandfather had longed to kill himself for years but had refrained for fear of inflicting shame or a sympathizing pull toward extinction on his son.

Meanwhile, the women in the family had resisted and survived. The grandmother continued living in the country house that her dead husband had built when he'd been a wealthy man. She raised her fam-ily there, one member of which, Frank's mother, chose for her husband a man who had been witness to the bitter, Christmastime butchery of the Battle of the Bulge and who had vowed if he survived to live the most uneventful life he could. Surely, he'd known the history of self-destruction in his wife's family, but he'd married her anyway, and together they'd lived long enough to die of natural causes, a triumph that perhaps only Frank, their son, fully understood. With the blood oozing darkly over his wrist from a cut as thin as a hair, he'd understood the meaning of life was to prolong life for its own sweet sake. There was beauty in the blood, and faced with the world's ugliness, the temptation to generate more and more beauty out of oneself was strong, but that was a form of narcissism that left nothing behind. It amounted to an erasure.

The scar was his, his alone, which he rarely saw himself, covered as it was by his watchband and a sprinkling of black hairs. He doubted anyone else had seen it, either. Frank Joyner was now sixty years old. No recluse, he lived in his grandfather's country home, on land that had once included his great-grandfather's dairy farm, a hundred acres of long, natural shelves left by the retreating glaciers, and full of their till. He walked his property almost daily, both its pastures, which a farmer hayed for him, and its forests. As an architect, he was all but retired. His real occupation now was taking care of his grandson, Danny, a sixth grader, eleven years old. In half an hour a school bus would leave Danny up the hill at an intersection of roads, and today Frank would walk up the hill, not to meet his grandson and walk him home, but to observe him as he got off the bus with other classmates and to see if what his grandson had told him was true: that he was being harassed because of some comments his grandfather had made to a local newspaper reporter when asked about the natural gas drilling that was about to take place in their county and that every farmer Frank knew had leased his land for.

In answer to the reporter's question Frank had posed one of his own: Did the young reporter know that their town had once lain under a mile of glacial ice, and that since the last ice age, some ten thousand years ago, the land had been rising at the rate of two centimeters

a year? Rising to meet us, he'd added, and until it had risen to its full
height, didn't she think it was best to leave it alone? He had said this
without thinking and not really intending to be taken seriously. More
than anything else, he had probably been flirting because the young
reporter was pretty. But it was true. The geological process was called
isostatic adjustment, and the land had eighty meters to go before it had
risen back to where it had started from and an isostatic balance was
restored. Days when he was out walking, he could talk himself into
believing he felt that two-centimeter lift under his boots.

He looked at his watch. Only today did he slide the band back and
search out the scar, its pallor almost undistinguishable from the un-
derside of his wrist. He remembered the sting of the razor opening the
veins as if it had just happened. He remembered the extraordinary
quiet and the sweetness of the blood's flow. The scar was another way
to tell time, he understood. Forty years and counting. Parents dead
and gone. A wife who'd become an ex. Three children. And their children. One of whom, his daughter's, was practically his. A community.
His most notable architectural accomplishment had been to save his
boyhood school from demolition and to convert its classrooms, offices,
and gymnasium into a building of apartments, restaurants, and shops.
His admirers. His grateful and his disgruntled tenants. He and his
family had lived on the top floor of the restored school building, in a
penthouse-size apartment that had once housed classrooms for the
eleventh and twelfth grades. A lifetime. Considered geologically,
barely a blink.

A November snow had fallen, covering the paths through the trees
and the wiry undergrowth. But he knew where the paths were, and
when he was unsure, he knew to follow the tracks of the deer. There
were other fresh tracks, too, rabbits and squirrels and the light, scam-
pering prints of the chipmunks and the always precise paw prints of
the foxes, not to be confused with the larger and more trampled prints

of the coyotes, who moved in packs. The wild turkeys left behind the sharp-angled, carefully etched prints of a cuneiform text, something you might expect to see carved on a Babylonian temple, and on occasion he'd seen bear tracks, flat and five-toed, remarkably humanlike except for the narrowness of the heel. He'd not yet seen a bear; they had only recently returned to the county. But the split-hoofed deer tracks were everywhere, along with their berry-size droppings, and he'd learned to trust the deer and the slender and sometimes sinuous paths they took through the undergrowth.

Sooner or later on his walks, he'd sight the deer and the flaring white of their tails as they broke and bounded before him. It was a game of tag, of catch-as-catch-can. The hunters no longer nailed planks up the trunk of a tree and across adjacent limbs for their perches. Now they had assembled units, made of iron, the ladder topped by the seat with its footrest and safety rail, the kind you find in roller-coaster cars or baby car seats, which were also useful for steadying your aim. He had not been a hunter. He understood that the deer herd had grown out of all proportion and had to be thinned, but when deer-hunting season had been extended a week, and then two, those were weeks when he couldn't be wandering through the woods or fields.

He didn't wander, not really. He was deliberate in his pacing and extraordinarily aware. He heard the crunching give of the moss frozen under his feet. He paused and heard the wind in the ticking treetops and a swishing, murmuring sound that was as close to human speech as the natural world was going to get. He overlooked the trash that neighbors whose property adjoined these woods had dragged out there and allowed to molder, directing his attention instead to the snow hanging in the feathery white pine limbs and to the short-needled tracery of the hemlocks. Following the deer tracks and the paths he knew as well as they, he had no sense of himself as a crusader, none whatsoever. What holy city did he hope to take back? If he was perfectly honest with himself, during these walks in the woods the last thing he wanted to see was a holy city, a city of any sort, anything

man-made rising out of the ground to block his path. A disillusioned
architect, keeping his eyes off the trash and deer hunters' perches and
the logging roads that snowmobilers used, too, so that he could see
what? A world freshly covered in snow that up till now only the animals had visited? He had family and he had friends and he had a
woman friend, who also happened to have been a tenant of his, but it
was only when he was out in the fields and woods that he fully understood what a lonely man he was, and only there was his loneliness
something like his ticket of admission.

He was standing in a field of young spruce and dogwood thickets
when the school bus pulled up at the intersection and the children began to get off. Two girls got off first and hurried up the street with
their candy-colored backpacks already on their backs. Three boys got
off after them, swinging their backpacks, and one of them clearly
made a provocative remark, for the closer of the two girls turned and
spat something back at the boys, who in response swung their backpacks more wildly and called after the girls in chorus. Then Frank
saw his grandson Danny get off with his jacket open and his shirt
untucked and his backpack slung over one shoulder. His head was
bare, his straw-colored hair flat and long, his face leaner and longer
than his grandfather knew any other face in his family to be, and if
his mother knew who the boy's father was, she wasn't telling. Jen
(who had a softly modeled face, hazel eyes shading to green, and hair
the off-luster brown of the dogwood branches) had left with a man, a
bluegrass fiddler, and come back a year and a half later with a baby
and let it be known that the fiddler was not the father. There'd been
a banjo player and a bass player in that band, too, and she had more
or less discounted them. Of course, there'd been other bands, but all
she would say she never actually said, just left implied: that the only
thing worth saving from that time on the road had been this boy. Six
months ago she'd asked her father if Danny could live with him for a
while, while she checked something out. Good for Danny, good for
him, and an absolute necessity for her. She hadn't been gone long,

but when she came back, Danny remained with his grandfather. Did he mind?

Danny came off the school bus walking down the road and away from the boys, who, yes, heckled him after having gotten no satisfaction from the girls. Frank couldn't make out the words, just the jeering tone to their voices and something spent behind the tone, as if they'd said all this before and could only repeat themselves now. That seemed to anger one of the three, who shouted words that Frank could make out: "More money for the rest of us! D'you ever think of that?" Then a bellowing "Duh!"

Moving on a parallel course through the fields and woods, Frank made no attempt to keep up with his grandson, who would be up in his room when his grandfather got home, perhaps playing a video game or reading one of his sorcery books, but just as likely lying on his bed and staring at the ceiling and thinking powerful thoughts. When the thoughts got too powerful to bear, Danny would go down to the basement and attack a skateboard ramp he and his grandfather had set up. Frank's grandfather Jonathan Coldwell had built his house well, but no one in the midtwenties had anticipated the reverberating volleys a skateboard could produce when unleashed against a loosely built ramp.

Frank emerged from the woods and crossed a last field, one of his own. The field fell off, the snow coming in drifts to his boot tops, and he had before him the valley the glaciers had gouged out, which, seven miles farther north, would become a long and precipitously deep lake. Behind the ridgeline across the way he could see another ridgeline, and the suggestion of yet a third. As you flew over the land, the undulations from one valley to the next could have a lulling effect, but down in them, where the streams bit deep into the sedimentary rock, the gorges were carved at times lethally clean. You went down far enough and there was, of course, that Devonian shale.

The farmer who hayed the field for him was late in getting in a last row of baled loaves. They were huge, cylindrical, as dark and shaggy as some wintering beast. Frank was leaning against a bale of snow-topped

hay as his grandson disappeared inside the mud-porch. For just a moment the choice was between this valley, overflown by the crows and
the white-breasted goshawks and even, on occasion, by bald eagles,
and the house he'd retreated to, which had brought with it this land
and all that might be drilled out of it.

And the boy.

Did he mind?

Gerald, Frank's older son, lived in California. Once a year, he and
his Ohio-born wife brought the girls back to visit both sets of parents.
Mickey, Frank's youngest, had lived in a number of states, but always, it
seemed, within driving distance of his hometown. It was Mickey who'd
asked his father if he knew what "compulsory integration" meant. He'd
admitted he didn't, only that it sounded like one of those bloodless
euphemisms the Pentagon was so fond of during the Vietnam War.
No, Mickey maintained, it meant exactly what it said. His father and
his land would be compulsorily integrated into the gas-drilling
scheme, whether he liked it or not. Down went the drill, as far as two
miles, he'd been told, and then out went the drill, and although the
vertical drilling might take place on Farmer X's property, the horizontal drilling could easily pass under yours. Hence, you were integrated.
Legally. Compulsorily. The only difference was that Farmer X got
paid. Just so his father knew what he was doing. Mickey could care
less, he was just passing on information, although Mickey continued to
hover nearby.

Jen was presently at home. The child of his he'd spoiled because she
was the child he'd had the most abiding trust in was for the moment
close at hand.

Did he mind?

His grandson was neither up in his room nor down in the basement. He was sitting at the kitchen counter, having finished a glass of
milk and a granola bar his mother had brought out a supply of. But he
was waiting for his grandfather.

"C'mon, Granddad, gimme a break."

"I was taking a walk."

"Yeah, right. See anything interesting?"

"I saw you."

Danny finished his milk. Deliberately, he cleared away his crumbs, creating a space on the countertop. He gave to the crumbs the same cleaving sort of attention as when he looked his grandfather directly in the eye. "So what are you going to do?"

"What do you think I should do?"

"Fuck 'em."

"Remember, we had a deal, Danny. No cursing unless it's absolutely necessary."

"Screw 'em."

"More of the same."

"Then don't do anything."

"This is not a game, Danny. You understand that? It doesn't make any difference what we do. That boy was absolutely right. They'll get rich and we won't. That's the only difference."

Danny flinched then, as if he'd been stung, or betrayed, and Frank went on to impart some grandfatherly wisdom. "Remember, there's such a thing as a dry well. There's such a thing as a bust. Sometimes fortunes are lost before they're made. They might start drilling and—"

His grandson stopped him then, without cursing, just ending Frank's easy-come nonsense. "Mr. Valenti says there's enough gas down there to supply the whole country for ten years!"

Mr. Valenti was his grandson's sixth-grade teacher.

2

J EN WASN'T AT HOME. IN FACT, SHE WASN'T EVEN CLOSE BY. SHE'D GONE to a city almost two hundred miles away to break it off with a man she'd been keeping up a long-distance relationship with. The man was waiting for his divorce, and she'd been waiting to see if it would all go cold for her or deepen into something she was willing to fight for. This man ran an alternative grocery store that had caught on, allowing him to employ a number of like-minded people, all of which—the store, the people, the vision—she admired. The woman he was divorcing himself from didn't. This was a way of life she cared nothing about, but as the store prospered, she was determined to get some of that alternative money, which she could spend as easily as money flowing by on the mainstream. That was the gist of it, according to Robert, who was tall, long-faced, gentle, with large, never-aggressive hands, and he was slowly becoming obsessed. Since he was tied up with the store and his wife's maneuvering, Jen had driven the last few times to see him, and the last couple of visits they hadn't even made love.

She'd ended up spending more time in his store—because she liked the place, the smells, the friendliness, which was never overstated, over-extended, or too chatty for its own good. It became clear to her then, while Robert made himself available to everybody except her: he had heart to spare but no resources. This last time she drove down to see him she practically hounded him into bed, where she pressed him for some mind-clearing sex and ended up scaring him more than a little. Which was what she'd expected. Robert, she said, without meaning to be mean, and if to hurt him, only a little, in a bracing sort of way, I'll be rooting for you, but I'm not going down with the ship. If one of us gets away, let's make it me. Then she asked him to say good-bye to the three people down at the store she liked the most.

Partway back home (hardly a home, rather a small apartment her father had set aside for her in his old school building), she stopped at a roadside tavern and had a brandy. It was cold. She was cold inside, her chills coming in shudders. Shudders of remorse or liberation? A guy sitting at the bar hit on her, and she came close to taking him up on it, but only after making some nonnegotiable demands. As long as he didn't say another word, and as long as he didn't lay a hand on her. Only if, only then. But the cheap, roadhouse brandy burned that non-sense out of her, and she got in her car and, steering by dead reckon-ing, made it back to her town. She emptied her mailbox and picked up the newspapers delivered in her absence. The only page she read was the first of the second section, where the local news was printed. She was drinking a chamomile tea, to settle her stomach and her nerves, when she came on the comment the pretty young reporter had teased out of her father. Except she didn't hear the flirtation, only the bad at-tempt at poetry, or the windiness of a man seduced into saying the most wrongheaded things. The earth was rising up to meet him. The earth would not look kindly on those seeking to hold it down. Still, she gave a single, hooting laugh.

With her nerves and stomach only partially settled, she walked down to the art gallery on the basement floor of the old school build-ing to tell the woman she worked for she'd be on the job the following

morning and all mornings thereafter. This woman, Luisa Bowen, had
been one of her father's first tenants and had known him as long as
anyone else in town. Consequently, she knew more than her share
about his daughter and her tribulations. You're saying it's over, Luisa
said, and Jen said she was saying just that. Then she apologized for
taking such long weekends and leaving Luisa a bit in the lurch. The
fact was the gallery (which was also a sort of Latin American jewelry
store) had never done a lot of business, whether anyone was on the job
or not. Luisa couldn't afford to pay much, but Jen worked there because the art was lovely to look at and the light entering from the elevated windows (the space had once housed a locker room, she believed
her father had said) was never harsh and was frequently restful, and
just down the hall was a little restaurant whose lunch specials gave off
wonderfully rich aromas. The downside of all this was that Luisa, a
caring, straight-spoken woman, mothered her more than a little, which
meant that Jen had two mothers in the same building. She was the
landlord's daughter, and the other mother figure, more discreet than
Luisa, it was true, was Helen Gobright, who was seeing her father and
shared some of Jen's concerns. Helen lived on the second floor, Jen on
the third, and Helen was concerned that Frank had it in him to become a hermit out there in his grandparents' house, precisely the reason (one of the reasons) Jen had persuaded her father to let her son,
Danny, live with him for the summer. The summer had extended into
the fall, which also concerned Helen and, if she was being honest with
herself, Jen, too.

Her own mother, her biological mother (as if Jen could see right
into their similarly coded cells), lived out in the suburbs in a ready-
made house her ex-husband would abhor and, while never disowning
any of them, not one child or grandchild, allowed herself to be entertained. Basically, Jen saw her mother when she was summoned.

She expected a summons. She hadn't checked her phone messages
yet, only seen that the red light was blinking. If her mother had read
the same comments she had in the local paper, Jen expected one of

those calls to be from her, insisting that they talk, which would lead to the further insistence that Jen talk some sense into her father, since she was the only one in the family he would listen to. Marjorie Joyner, née Rawlings, might not need the money the gas companies were paying, but other members of this family did, and comments such as the ones her ex-husband had made had ceased to amuse her. The message would more or less say that.

Jen's father *did* confide in her, so Jen might possibly know more about family affairs than even her mother did, who made it her business. The problem was her grandmother Jane's will. When Jane had died, she'd left the land and the family house outside of town to her only son, giving her two daughters, Carol and Sharon, certain sums of money instead. But in leaving her son the property, she expressed in her will her desire that he take care of it and share its benefits with his sisters. What had she meant by that? Hard to say, since she'd also gone on to mention a land-trust organization in the area and to suggest that she would not be averse to seeing the property end up in their hands. Reading between the lines, it was pretty clear that Jane, a sweet woman who'd been no sentimentalist, knew her daughters had no attachment to the house or the land (Aunt Carol had married quickly and gone to New York to live, then had remarried and settled in New Jersey; while Aunt Sharon had ended up down South in one of those North Carolina cities, Raleigh or Greensboro or Charlotte, Jen was never sure which) and that her son, Frank, for better or worse, would always stay close to home. Since both daughters had married well, neither had objected when Frank had decided not to sell the house. He paid the taxes, and then when he'd decided to rent the house out, he'd shared the benefits with his sisters down to the dollar.

When he did move out there himself, no one had thought it would be for any longer than an interlude. But an interlude between what and what? His wife had left him and, "accepting a ride" with a male friend of hers (that had been her mother's sly-faced euphemism), had traveled to California, ostensibly to visit her older son and his family ("ostensibly" there was a fine, upstanding excuse for almost any activity, Jen knew that as well as her mother). When she'd surprised a lot of people by coming back (Jen not being one of them, having left and come back many times herself), Marjorie Joyner had settled for that modular house on the outskirts of town, where she could keep an eye on things and even make a downtown appearance now and then.

Then there were things her mother didn't know. Her younger son, Mickey, was a tall-tale teller, so the chances that he'd actually been busted for cocaine use and spent a week in county jail were slim. Or that he was, if not gay, then gay enough to put himself at risk from AIDS, which his sister discounted, if not entirely. She and Mickey held late-night phone conversations, and with her little brother, for all his exaggerations, there was usually a grain of truth. He taught history in high school, and perhaps he did stay one step ahead of scandal by changing jobs a lot since he'd already held three. Their mother knew only that she had a prosperous son and a wayward son and a seemingly promiscuous, unwed mother of a daughter, and an ex-husband who had taken early retirement and retreated to the rural sidelines just as the game was heating up. But since she did not get along with her ex-husband's sisters, Carol and Sharon, Jen's mother did not know where the current trouble originated.

That was information Jen was not ready to share. Aunt Carol's first husband, and the father of her daughter, was a man named Wilson Michaels, who practiced criminal law in New York City. Jen wasn't sure how, but Michaels had learned of that solicitous clause in Jane's will and had, in the name of his daughter, been pestering his ex-wife over in New Jersey to get her brother to sell, if not the land, then at least the house, insisting that the dribs and drabs those rent payments amounted to were a joke. Ex-spouses with joint custody of children (a problem Jen would never have) were known to pester a lot. Even though Carol might have agreed with her ex, she found him infuriatingly small-minded and ended up defending her brother when the issue came up. Then the landmen for the natural gas companies began to lease property all around her backward brother's hundred acres, and did she know what the lease payments alone were going for in that area of the state? Wilson Michaels would tell her. As high as five thousand dollars an acre, which, times a hundred, came to half a million. Once the gas was pumping, the royalties were going for 12, 15, up to 18 percent. These were enormous sums, in case over there in New Jersey she couldn't figure it out, so enormous that even the portion that would correspond to his daughter would be enormous, too, and what did she propose to do about that?

According to Jen's father, Michaels claimed to have seen the will and declared that the clause in question was perfectly valid in a court of law. Aunt Carol claimed that her ex-husband could not have seen the will unless she had shown it to him, and she'd never done that, but he was a smart and mostly unscrupulous lawyer, and she wouldn't put it past him. And anyway, anyway, once in her life she was prepared to say he might be right. She had her daughter, whose name was Brenda, to think about. Aunt Carol had proposed a family reunion, from which Wilson Michaels would be excluded (but not the sisters' current spouses, men who had nothing in common with big-city lawyers), in order to come to a sensible decision about leasing the property. Jen's father had, in turn, consulted his lawyer, who told him that he had the law on his side, but that judges could make curious decisions if the courtroom got emotional, and appellate judges were always reluctant to overrule. Best to keep it out of court. Could the land be divided, say, twenty-five acres for each of the sisters and fifty for Frank? The lawyer claimed to have known of a case in a nearby state when a gas company had leased and then drilled on as few as sixteen acres. If they were convinced there was gas down there, they could drill on a dime.

Her father's lawyer was the same man who had, many years before, rescued the old Deweese school building from demolition for Frank and two other investors by selling the town board on its historic significance and the revenue it would generate, and by extracting from the state a grant for restoration funds. Frank and his investors had gotten it for a song. Then the lawyer, Ray Whittaker, had taken his friend and ex-schoolmate Frank aside (for Whittaker had attended Deweese, too) and worked out a scheme with local bankers to buy out the two other investors (out-of-towners, both) so that by the time the building was redesigned, rebuilt, and open for business, although the town board had some input on how it was to be run, it essentially belonged to Frank Joyner. Jen had spent her teenage years in that huge, top-floor apartment. Her brothers had fought it, but she hadn't because she thought it conferred on her a certain oddball glamour, something she could show scorn for and luxuriate in at the same time. She and her brother Mickey had called it their penthouse, where they were "pent" up, as in a "penitentiary."

She had to laugh. It was a deeply mixed laugh, full of a begrudging admiration and not a little disbelief. Clinging to the old homestead, saving it from what? Those avaricious gas drillers and their contaminating ways? Her father had already saved his old school, for Christ's sake! He could return to his fourth-floor apartment (and it really was a lovely place, with its multileveled living room and a wall of windows in the kitchen to catch the morning light) and get his lady friend, Helen, to move in with him. Jen would, too. And Danny. Why not? Drill, baby, drill! they were clamoring over most of the county, and why not let them? They were going to anyway. What this old school building, converted into quaint restaurants and shops and apartments, really resembled was a fortress. A massive, dark brick place with a battlement-topped tower and old quarried tiles on the hall floors. Impregnable. Im-fucking-pregnable. Incapable of being impregnated. This time Jen poured herself a glass of burgundy and began to play back her phone messages. Her mother's was the first. Followed, more mockingly aghast, by her second. The last and most recent was from Jen's ex-boyfriend Robert, telling her how sorry he was and asking if there was any way.

3

In a county just across the state line, a tank truck delivering water to a Conklin Natural Gas Company drilling pad killed a dog and badly injured the boy the dog belonged to. The road was a narrow farm road, the outsize truck was barreling along, and the dog was crushed. The boy, who was knocked into the roadside ditch, unaccountably survived, although it was not known for how long. The driver did not stop, and later when he was detained (the boy's horrified mother had witnessed the entire event), he claimed that he'd never known, had never felt a thing. Local reporters remarked on how large and powerful these trucks were and how much noise they made and led viewers and readers to believe that such a thing was possible. Truckers driving trucks that large and loud might never know if they had killed a dog or a boy as they barreled along.

If it had not happened to a boy out with his dog, the network news programs might not have picked it up. But the confrontation between a Norman Rockwell vision of the country and a heedless rush to energy exploitation was too good to pass up. The major networks sent their reporters and camera teams to the site. The nation saw those loud, smoking, outsize trucks and the narrow country roads. The drilling pads were frequently located close to the road, leveled out into terraced plateaus. Clearly, there was something mysterious about them, as if those elevated pads were stages for some primitive, priestly rite. Truncated Aztec pyramids and their human sacrifices came to mind, except the bulldozed and then grassed-over terraces were actually attractive to look at and clean to the eye.

The trucks weren't. Compared to the drilling pads, the trucks were like some common industrial denominator, utterly incongruous in this remote, bucolic terrain, a standing offense to the eye, ear, and nose, and deadly to children out with their dogs. TV cameras took footage of the trucks as they filled their tanks at a nearby river, and then more footage as they returned from the pads and discharged the water they had taken on at the site. Only that discharged water might well contain chemicals, whose names the gas companies were unwilling to disclose, and other dangerous elements, even radioactive ones, such as radium, which, until drilling had begun, had been safely out of reach a mile beneath the earth. Or those same chemicals and elements, subjected to the intense pressure of the hydrofracking, might have migrated upward through strata of sandstone and limestone and entered aquifers and, hence, private wells. A homeowner might turn on his tap, hold out a match, and watch his water blossom into a vaporous methane flame. It had happened. It looked wondrous. Homeowners with their wells so contaminated didn't seem to tire of demonstrating it, and a reporter with a gift for comparisons soon dubbed them modern-day alchemists. Another reporter with a sense for the language pointed out that *hydrofracturing* was a cunning misnomer since, as a fracturing agent, water—*qua* water—had never been the issue. No one disputed that natural gas was a desirable transitional fuel, only half as polluting as oil or coal, or that the country possessed it in abundance. The question was the price. When it became known that the parents of the boy whose dog had been killed and whose life hung in the balance had leased their own land and were waiting for the pad to be built, the question took on an accusatory edge. Was it even worth a dog's life? Belonging to a dear, freckled-faced boy? The TV viewers were left with images of those grossly oversize trucks, those country roads, and those elevated pads whose drilling towers shone as brightly as Las Vegas casinos into the night, and from whose tops flew American flags.

Mickey Joyner had seen the drilling towers and seen the casinos and considered the comparison apt, in the sense that both were garishly out of place and as American as the boy with his dog. The towers—*derricks* would be the right word—could be found within ten miles of the town where Mickey Joyner taught American history to high school boys and girls. They weren't closer because the county the town was located in, invoking a zoning regulation against rural industrialization, had decided to hold the gas companies off, although pressure had been intense to let them in. Adjoining counties were reaping huge benefits in increased taxes, commerce, and employment, and Mickey's county was still subject to the truck traffic. The trucks were everywhere. The gas companies had reached agreements to keep the roads they used in good repair, but all that meant was a motley run of patches up and down roads that hadn't seen fresh asphalt in decades. You could take an afternoon drive in the country where Mickey lived, lie down to sleep at night, and behind your closed eyes see trucks thundering down on you, shouldering everything else off the road, the fresh rectangular patches of asphalt separating you from them resembling an advancing bar code where the price of your life was written and its expiration date. But the derricks belonged because in the accelerated rush to exhaust the country of its resources, incongruity had never been an issue; things such as boys and their dogs, or secluded homesteads out beside unpolluted streams, were mated to the land only in postcards. The country had been surreal from the start. You didn't need to be stoned, and Mickey wasn't much anymore. It was always out there, wild stuff, unimaginable stuff, things like these long, erect, pumping pinnacles of light, or, when he'd driven out to California that summer and visited his brother, those Las Vegas casinos in constant eruption against the desert darkness.

In America, he told his students, everything was outsize, everything was out of place because "place" was never intended to last out the day. It was nothing to be ashamed of, he'd say if he could see the sensitive ones squirming. It was who we were, who we had been. It testified to the indomitable, questing energy of a people. Think of the land rushes, the gold rushes—we weren't a people to sit idly on our hands. Or he'd tell them about the town he came from, which had been settled by soldiers on land tracts awarded for service in the Revolutionary War. Within twenty years most of those settler-soldiers had roused themselves and moved on, leaving only the sedentary behind. It was okay. Get up and go. Consume your way across the country. Scorched earth—the way Sherman had marched through Georgia. Sherman through Georgia? They'd forgotten who General Sherman was? Tell me we don't have to go back to the Civil War again!

His students liked him. They picked up on his mockery. They assumed American history could be read this way. And they remembered more often than not. American history was peopled with heroes who could also be the objects of some heckling fun. But when he left to go visit his brother, Gerald, in California, he really thought he might be gone, too. He'd changed teaching jobs twice already and assumed he could find another if he had to. Except for his students, who would have moved on to other classes anyway, no one would miss him if he didn't come back. Mr. Joyner was not a joiner. Nor was he exceptionally given to joy. He might slip himself a mickey every so often, but his sister exaggerated that out of all proportion. Or maybe he did. He didn't mind telling stories on himself that weren't exactly true. Or, said another way, he'd tell the stories to see what tug toward the truth they might contain.

He'd told his sister he'd spent a week in jail; he hadn't—during a traffic violation the cops had caught him with pot and held him overnight before releasing him, uncharged, except for the speeding ticket, the next morning. Without really exerting himself, he could talk his way out of fixes or jams if he had to. Out of sheer curiosity, he'd talked himself into a one-night fling with a man he knew, one night, which, as he'd told his sister about it, somehow got extended over months, with the perils of AIDS like a minefield you had to dance through. The truth he was being tugged to was that he could elaborate a lifetime out of a day, but that he needed that day, in such and such a place. He was not a fantasist. He was a historian, who knew no history was complete without its counterhistory. He'd read Edgar Allan Poe's "The Imp of the Perverse" and talked himself into believing that if the upstanding, the unimpeachable, the widely applauded, didn't tempt you into the twisted, the blatantly wrong, and the universally condemned, none of it made sense. He was his own standing joke, whose only talent, in addition to amusing students into remembering a portion of what he said, was to occasionally amaze himself. He'd done that? That silliness?

He was a dilettante. He fooled around.

Of his girlfriends, only one stayed in his mind for any length of time. She'd checked his groceries through at the local supermarket, and her name, as her name tag indicated, was Cheryl. He'd said, This town is small. Why do I only see you here? She'd told him to hang on, and five minutes later, minus her supermarket smock and name tag, had walked out into the parking lot. She had a slow manner, large bones, and large brown eyes. She never got mad or even cross with him, only puzzled sometimes, and then her eyes would blink longer than usual and she'd turn away. Her mildness and her air of undisapproving disengagement led him to wonder if she had been, was, or was about to become a member of some cult or evangelical sect. She never initiated their lovemaking, but when he did, she yielded to him gladly. Only at the end, with uncharacteristic urgency, did she demand her due. She began to unnerve him a little, as if, behind that slumberous facade, she were really poised and waiting until he went entirely off guard. To do what? To leave town, it turned out. Weeks later he got a postcard from another town. It spoke about a new job, new surroundings, and, seemingly, a step up on that ladder toward her future she had once talked about but he hadn't taken seriously enough to believe was real. No word about abandonment or betrayal. A smiling circle of sunshine at the end.

He took her lesson to heart. Time to move on. But her real lesson he missed entirely and only learned later, from the vantage point of another town. What it came down to was that she enjoyed her own company and he didn't. What had seemed like dullness or indifference was really the happiness of being who she was, especially when faced with the unhappiness of a man hard-pressed to live inside his own skin. It was such a simple truth and, really, without parallel: self-love—unquestioning, unwavering, and urgent only at the end. What could be simpler? What could be further removed from his habitual mockery? But how could he love himself? But how could he not and go on drawing air better breathed by others? He laughed it off, but it wouldn't go away. What was there for Mickey Joyner to love about himself? His students liked him because he was clever and quick and said shocking things. Teachers who said those things over and over ended up hating the sound of their own voices. Cheryl was all of a piece, he was in smithereens, but, really, wasn't one of his smithereens more interesting by far than her all-of-a-pieceness? He'd lie in bed at night, and the image that began to appear in his mind was of those tall, overlit derricks and of that drill bit spinning down. Through earth, water, and various strata of rock before reaching the shale, in its narrow band, perhaps no more than one or two hundred feet wide, where the bit made its veering turn, headed out on the horizontal, and, with a pressure that might, a mile above it, blow a concrete cover off a well, began to spew a lover's mix of water, lubricating chemicals, and sand into the cracks.

He was doing it to himself. Every time he lay in bed at night and tried to explore himself, he ended up in the pull of that image. Down and out. Plumb your depths and, then, swing wide. Compulsory integration. He was all for it. Just don't destroy the planet in the process.

And, please, slow down the trucks and keep little boys and their dogs behind closed doors.

He drove to California—the river, the plains, the mountains, the desert, the beach. His older brother, Gerald, lived in one of those sagebrush communities built on the side of a mountain a short way south of Los Angeles. The way Mickey saw it, his brother's house could be burned down in a fire, washed away in a flood, buried beneath a landslide, and the remains even blown away in a Santa Ana wind once the other elements had had their go at it. It was not something you brought up. Nothing in Gerald's demeanor, or his wife's or that of his two young girls, indicated that anything except more sunny days were in store. That same unflappable demeanor had allowed Gerald to live on top of the Deweese school building, even though Mickey knew Gerald didn't like it, while Mickey, younger and more easily deprived, had complained bitterly. The irony, of course, was that Mickey would end up teaching school, as if he had been fatally infected in the Deweese, while Gerald . . . well, this was one thing Mickey had always felt about his brother. He was beyond irony, out of its reach. There was no comeuppance he had in store that would be ironically apt.

Gerald was the tallest in the family (Jen was tall for a girl), with the squarest of shoulders and nothing at odds or out of balance in his face (Mickey had a small and sometimes twitching mouth). He wasn't entirely sure what Gerald did for a living, something in telecommunications. Mickey was there for ten days, and on none of those days did his older brother bring aggravations home from work. If he suffered aggravations, which Mickey seriously doubted, he managed to jettison them as he wound up the hill.

Mickey spent some time with his sister-in-law, Sue Ann, his height, the sculpted cheeks of a jogger, with an even pacing and extraordinary assurance to her movements, even when her six- and eight-year-old daughters were causing havoc in the house. She asked him what he would like to do, and he said, because he'd never been in the Pacific Ocean before, the beach. He tried to bodysurf the waves, and his nieces laughed at him when one flipped him over and he emerged trailing amber-colored strands of kelp. He sat on the beach with Sue Ann and asked her if that vast expanse out there reminded her at all of the cornfields of Ohio, which was where she'd come from. Did she miss it? She said she didn't think about it much, her life was out here now, with her husband, her daughters, and her house. They had visitors from back East—Mickey's mother had been one of them—and that was always nice, especially for the girls, but, well . . . and she sat up straight on her beach towel and made a subtle shrugging motion with her shoulders and back, masterful, really, as if to say, that was all behind them, back there, a continent away. Before them, the ocean, and she raised her face to its wind and light.

The evening came when he and Gerald stood on his brother's patio and gazed out over the cactus and sage, and palm and eucalyptus trees, and the squat, gnarled trees that must have been mesquite. The ocean lay on the horizon, the rose-tinted orange of a sun that refused to set. A California evening. The forces of nature at peace. Pacific. Gerald said, "How are you, Mickey?" His voice was maybe an octave lower than the one he'd used to exchange pleasantries in up to then. He added, "Where do you go from here?"—meaning not the Grand Canyon, or Yosemite, or other natural wonders of the West.

And Mickey, almost as a courtesy, in deference to the way things had always been, said, "I was hoping you could tell me."

Gerald held a pause. The evening was languorous—but this was a pause of another sort. "If I told you I always thought you were the smartest of the three of us, would that surprise you?"

Mickey gave a quiet, sober laugh. "You know what I've discovered? I don't have it in me to be a pioneer."

"A pioneer?"

"I mean, intelligence aside, I can't do it alone anymore."

Gerald drew breath to answer his brother, then quietly let it out. After a moment he placed his wineglass on a nearby table. His other arm he placed around Mickey's shoulders, and they stood like that, facing west, in the distance, at the limit of sight, that ribbon of ocean, slightly duskier now.

Finally Gerald said, "Wasn't there a girlfriend?"

"I don't mean *alone* like that."

"How do you mean it?"

"I mean, left to myself, I can't seem to see my way clear."

"Well, maybe not a girlfriend, Mickey. But a wife, a family . . ."

And with his free hand Gerald motioned back behind him, toward his house, even though there was a hesitation to his movement, a misgiving, as though he sensed he shouldn't be offering himself as an example like that.

"I've missed you," Gerald said. "It's the one drawback about living out here. We don't see each other. We start heading off in different directions, then when we do get together . . ." He stopped, perhaps hoping that Mickey would finish his thought.

But in that vein Mickey had nothing to add.

"And Jen," Gerald continued, "Mom and Dad. Dad—"

"Dad's an interesting case," Mickey broke in, and he slipped out from under the older man's arm. "He was lucky, and then very smart. He found something he could devote himself to, an old building, without a single graceful line, that was about to be torn down. But he'd spent his boyhood there, and boys don't have many graceful lines, either. Believe me. They live in perpetual slouches, even the ones who sit in the front row and make a show of taking down every word you say. But Dad found a way to make the boy in him sit up straight and win the world's applause. It's been a shelter for him. Notice that I didn't say *womb*."

"I remember you hated it."

"Well, that's true, too. I wasn't a man who'd been a boy there. I was a boy who belonged somewhere else."

"And, if I'm following you, you're looking for a connection back to wherever that was."

"Let's stick with Dad," Mickey said, "because look what happened.

He dragged all of us there. You took it in stride, Jen went back and forth, it's true, I rebelled, and Mother bided her time and then went off with another man and left him—"

"We don't know that," Gerald reminded Mickey, authority tempered with forbearance in his tone. Gerald's tone. It almost made Mickey want to reach out and cuff his brother on the shoulder.

"What don't we know?"

"That she went off with another man."

"Granted. Only that another man was driving the car when she left him."

"What's your point, Mickey?"

"That it worked for him. It served its purpose—"

"The Deweese did?"

"Yes, and when it didn't any longer, he went out and found another shelter."

"You mean the Coldwell house?"

"*And* the hundred acres. The old homestead. Some place to . . . *consolidate* your life." Mickey chose his word carefully.

And here stood his brother, on a hillside, before a house that could be burned, flooded, buried, and blown away on a meteorological whim. Gerald said, "I worry about Dad out there."

"Why? Why in the world would you do that? I remember reading a writer once who said you never forgot the places where you ran as a boy. It's true, you know, Gerald, even though I can't remember a single one of mine. And then here come the gas companies throwing their money around, and here come the farmers lining up to sell out. One of them, the Yapletons, trace their lineage back to the tract settlements after the Revolutionary War. All under attack, all sold out. Dad holding the fort."

Gerald looked off toward the horizon, where the last sunlight was, indeed, about to die out, then back to his brother. He did not disguise his disapproval, only measured it out. "I think it's a little more complicated than that."

"Of course, it is," Mickey quickly conceded. "Sure it is, I know that, Gerald. I'm only saying Dad keeps finding a way. And there's Danny. Jen's put him out there for a reason, you know. It has nothing to do with gas money or anything like that. She has faith, even though we both know she's made some crazy decisions in her life. But, then, who hasn't . . ."

Gerald hadn't. By any rational estimation he'd chosen right, he'd chosen handsomely—just look at the results.

"I mean," Mickey tried again, "if you can't find it in yourself when you lie down at night, you'd better try to find it in someone else. Dad makes me smile. You do, too, but Dad makes me smile a lot. I'm out of here tomorrow."

"Why tomorrow?"

"You've seen one beautiful sunset . . ." Mickey waved a dismissive hand at the horizon.

"Stay a while longer."

"What's the point?"

"How often do we get to see each other?"

"Every summer you've been decent enough to come back." Mickey hadn't meant that sarcastically. Gerald was the most decent man he knew. Maybe decency itself was the question. He touched Gerald's shoulder, as though to bridge a gulf. He allowed his hand to linger. He experienced an old, familiar warmth, faintly parasitic. "Why'd you move out here, Brother, so awfully far away? Putting a desert, the Great Plains, and one hell of a mountain range between you and us."

Gerald drew a breath, which, just in the deliberate way he drew it, told you it was going to be wasted. Of course, it would help if Mickey didn't know his brother so well. "It's a good job. Sue Ann and the kids like it here. It's a pleasant place to be. Anything else you read into it—"

Mickey laughed. "I do at my own peril. I know, big Brother, about my own peril."

"Well, that's what you do, isn't it, Mickey? Read into things?"

"And can you believe it? They pay me for it! Of course, not as much as they pay you."

"Stay another week. Sue Ann and the—"

But he cut his brother off. "That was emotional blackmail you were about to commit. 'Don't deprive Sue Ann and the kids of the chance to get to know you better.' I love you, Gerald. I won't let you do that to yourself."

Mickey gave his brother a prolonged hug and, the next morning, followed him into Los Angeles, where, after honking his good-bye, he entered the area of Beverly Hills known as the Golden Triangle, the most expensive residential property, he'd heard, in the country. If it was indeed a triangle, it was located between Sunset Boulevard and Wilshire, with, maybe, Canon Drive connecting the two, and, back when the major studios controlled the movie business, had been home to the most venerable of the stars. Mickey wasn't looking for them. They were all dead, anyway. A whole generation of them—Gable, Cooper, Stewart, Lancaster, Peck. He simply wanted to see, before he turned around and went back home, the most desirable residential property in the country, where only the few who could afford it wanted to live. He was disappointed. He would have to have been. He got out of his car and walked the streets as the lone pedestrian. It was still early. The hired help were arriving in their Hondas and Toyotas. A few luxurious cars were visible in carports or parked up the circling drives. The narrower of the streets passed under a tunneling of palm fronds. Everything was quiet. The alleys, which he hadn't expected to see in California, alleys where people back East hid their trash from public view, and their bad behavior, were clean, wide, and orderly, the trash cans ranked according to size. The houses themselves were large, of course, but of no dominant style. They might have a Spanish flavor until you came to the Elizabethan or the French Provincial. The lawns were manicured, the bushes all trimmed. There were no gaudy flower displays, and he supposed the trellises of something like bougainvillea would be located around back by the pools. The dominant odor was of sprinklers watering perfectly seeded lawns and the aged and exclusive scent of boxwood bushes in close trim. On the street, a trace of high-octane gas but of no burning oil.

He saw no one (except arriving gardeners, arriving maids) until, as he walked down a sidewalk on the way back to his car, a short, burly figure in a white terry-cloth bathrobe walked down his drive to re-trieve, of all things, his newspaper. Whoever he was, he had a tan as dark as a coconut shell and a head of hair like some wavy, fibrous growth. He walked with a sailor's rolling swagger. Not until he growled, "Good morning," did Mickey recognize the actor Peter Falk, who, along with the others, had been thought dead by now, thought dead by Mickey as he returned the greeting. He stopped and looked at the ac-tor squarely, as if to make sure, and Falk glanced back over his shoul-der as he retreated up his drive. He gave a gruff shake of the head.

Expect the surreal in this highly excitable country of ours, except that Falk had already been replaced in Mickey's mind by his father as he came out to retrieve his newspaper from its container beside the road. Not that his father and Falk looked anything alike. Mickey's fa-ther was tall, almost as tall as Gerald, of angular features and exposed, watery eyes. He was a little bent in the back, Mickey assumed from bending over his drawing board all his professional life, but, it oc-curred to Mickey then, standing in the Golden Triangle, occupying for the moment a pricey piece of land, what his father really looked like was not an architect but a farmer, who for years had been digging into hard, rocky soil. It was true, his father had always seemed like bedrock America to him, more venerable than any of the stars, the flip side, since every side must have its flip, of someone like the wisecracking Lieutenant Columbo. But both still very much alive. Very much alive.

PART TWO

CHILDREN OF THE WORLD

4

Sunlight filled the room, and it sounded as if the whole world outside were running with freshly melted snow. A steady drip was coming from somewhere, and while he lay in bed, a last clump of snow fell from the limbs of the white pine overhanging the deck, but mainly what Danny heard was a chorus of running-water sounds, from the faintest trickle to the torrent rushing down the ditch in front of the house. It was Thanksgiving Day. There was no school bus to catch. The house would fill up with family for the midafternoon meal—his mother was coming, his uncle Mickey, he believed, and other uncles and aunts—but for the moment the house was quiet, and it was just his grandfather and him.

He listened to the sounds melting snow could make outside his window. When he finally did get up, he thought he might see grass in the large lawn below his east window. He saw enough grass that as he stood there, the patches seemed to enlarge. Before he stepped away from the window the grass was general, and it made more sense to say he saw patches of snow. The sun passing through the window warmed him so quickly it might have been July.

He didn't hear his grandfather, which surprised him since his grandfather was an early riser. But then he realized the water was making too much noise.

He went into the bathroom. Water was running down the little kitchen side roof directly beyond the commode. The window there gave him a view of the valley, which was shimmering with so much reflected light. He turned the latch on the window, and it opened on a spring. The air was cold, of course, since he was out of the sun, but the water noise was so loud he couldn't hear himself pee. He closed the window, flushed, and, turning to the lavatory on his left, threw water onto his face. The boy he saw in the mirror seemed like a boy left over from another day, alien to the way he felt now. For an instant he was actually surprised by the anger he saw in that alien boy's face. The world was awash, and here was this kid who refused to get in the flow. Then he smiled at himself, and the kid gave up his joy-begrudging anger and smiled back.

His grandfather didn't have to call him to breakfast. Danny bounded down the stairs and entered the kitchen. "Isn't this amazing, Granddad!"

Frank said, "It'll be soggy going if you get out in the yard. Be sure to wipe your feet."

"It's like summer!"

"Except it's not."

They ate their breakfast at the counter, perched high on stools. The water dripped in a steady syncopation onto the kitchen sill and coursed down the ditch outside.

"Those first Thanksgivings were freezing cold," Danny informed his grandfather. "The Pilgrims might have starved to death because their crops hadn't come in yet, but the Indians helped them out. Am I right or wrong?"

"That's the way you see it in the picture books."

"Then when their crops did come in and the Pilgrims had enough to eat, they slaughtered the Indians. Which means Thanksgiving means giving thanks for generous, gullible Indians who hung around long enough to get themselves killed."

"Is that something Mr. Valenti told you?"

"No way! I figured that one out for myself!" Danny got off his stool and came around and gave his grandfather a half hug, half-cuffing slap on the shoulder. "Don't worry, Granddad. No Indians left. It's gonna be a great day!"

Jen tasted the gravy, the stuffing, the cranberry sauce. The smell of the turkey cooking would be left behind in Helen's apartment, and that Jen counted a real loss, to eat Thanksgiving turkey cooked somewhere else. But Helen knew her kitchen and didn't know Jen's father's and would do this only if she could do it well. Helen's daughter, Cindy, would not join them, even though she lived in a city a short hour away, not if her mother was celebrating the day in another man's house after her husband (and Cindy's father) had just died (it had been two years). Jen would do what she could. The turkey was moist—it couldn't be better. Perhaps warming it up in her father's oven would release enough of the smell into the house. What Jen could do nothing about was her aunt Carol, who was coming and bringing her current husband, George, and her daughter, and Jen's cousin, Brenda, from the preceding marriage, and Brenda, recently divorced herself, would be bringing her own daughter, around Danny's age, whose name Jen had forgotten. Jen knew what all that meant, just as she knew that even though Mickey had said he'd be coming, he probably wouldn't show.

From behind, Jen wrapped her arms around the older woman's waist. "You're wonderful to do this, Helen. You really are."

Helen put the spoon she held onto the stove and placed her hands over Jen's. "It's always a sentimental time. You're over him now, aren't you, sweetheart?"

That was an open-ended question, and for just a moment Jen began to run through the men she'd gotten over in her life. The problem was she'd been thinking of her father and thinking of her son. Helen didn't give her time to arrive at the right man. "Robert," Helen said. She had a low-register, melodious voice, always a little mournful.

"It just makes me sad. If he were a bastard, it'd be different. There's a little part of me that thinks I deserted him in his hour of need. It's his wife—"

Helen squeezed Jen's hands, signaling her to leave it at that. "That's because he's not over her yet."

"Now there's an understatement if I ever heard one!" And in the same freewheeling tone, Jen was about to go on about how hard it was to get over any of them, impossible, really, the way they attached them- selves to you, even the worst of them, the real bastards, the best argu- ment for a nunnery she knew. But she didn't go on because she caught herself in time. You got over them if they died in your arms and you buried them, as Helen had her husband two years prior. The regrets then were of an entirely different sort, part of the human condition, an argument not for a nunnery but maybe for jumping into a gorge, since they had them close by.

Gently, Jen worked her way out from under the pressure of the older woman's hands. The bastard—the bitch—was Helen's daughter, Cindy, to treat her mother this way. At bottom, Cindy, whom Jen had never met, was accusing her mother of something resembling prosti- tution. Sleeping with her landlord, she was surely getting a big chunk off the rent, maybe even getting the place for free. Jen didn't know if Helen was sleeping with her father or not. She had never said and her father had never hinted at it. Jen devoutly hoped so, but she also hoped it didn't have to all get entangled that way. Perhaps just a deep, abiding, loving friendship, companionable to the last hour, as if sex ever got you anything more than a moment's reprieve. Helen's apartment was much larger than Jen's, with the sort of tall, triply sectioned windows bored students used to gaze out of and dream. As far as prostitution went, it was Jen who got her apartment free. She'd rather ask Helen if she was sleeping with her father, and how many times a week, than ask her how much rent she was paying.

"It's perfect, Helen, believe me, couldn't be better," Jen said.

"Your father deserves it."

"Dad *does*, but I'm not sure about some of the other people who are coming. And Mickey. You've never met Mickey, have you? I didn't mean him."

"Frank talks about him a lot. They talk on the phone. Occasionally, he'll quote me something Mickey said."

That surprised Jen more than she was willing to admit. "He will? Quote Mickey? You're sure you don't mean Gerald?"

They began to make the trips down to the car it would take to bring Thanksgiving to what everybody in the family still called the Coldwell house, even though Jonathan Coldwell, soon after he'd built it, had bequeathed it to his descendants. Once Jen's father had gotten control, he'd rented it out to a succession of tenants until he'd gotten ready to occupy it himself. So much transience, and then this hunkering down. If she was being honest with herself, she didn't know why she had asked if Danny could live out there for a while. It wasn't to give her free rein in her love affairs—if anything, Danny could have provided her with a shield from some of those. And it wasn't so that he could have a boy's life in the country. He was a town boy, a kid on the streets. Not many country homes had a skateboard ramp in their basement, for Christ's sake! She thought it had to do with the hunkering down. If her father was going into hiding, she'd need more than just an excuse to visit, she'd need a conduit, some access to an intimacy that would have to do, exclusively, with the three of them. Helen gave her another conduit, into another sort of intimacy. Jen did not let a thought escape her, or its counterthought. She had access. She was not shameless. She was grateful. She did not pry. She gave thanks and observed from close range.

. . .

When his mother drove up with his grandfather's friend, Danny was standing with this second cousin he'd just met, observing the torrent of water rushing down the ditch in front of the house. They had just seen a dead bird pass, and then a dead frog, and his second cousin had not been much impressed. Her name was Cynthia, and Cynthia and ditch water did not go together, Danny had quickly surmised. He had told her about his skateboard ramp and was about to take her down to the basement and perform for her when his mother drove up.

Jen hugged her son before turning her attention to his second cousin. When she got set to introduce Helen, she had to frankly admit she had forgotten Cynthia's name, and the way Cynthia grinned at that and spoke her own name, with a bit of a tease, as if she were playfully holding something back, endeared her to Danny even more. Which Jen picked up on at once. Cynthia was a little charmer, who, under her down coat, Jen could see, was already rounding out. Then as if to give Jen, and not Danny, an eyeful, she took the coat off and folded it over her arm and raised her face and budding breasts to the sun. This was the girl whose sweet-talking, tough-talking big-city lawyer of a grandfather was out to drive her father, Jen's, to the wall. Jen told Cynthia what dish to bring in from the car, and she told Danny, and among the four of them they took Thanksgiving dinner into the house.

No one was there. They had all gone outside to sit on the back deck, under the towering white pine. It was that warm. The house blocked the north wind off the deck. The view was to the southwest, looking out on the valley, which was the reason Frank's grandmother had had the deck built, with a continuous bench along the perimeter. For two years she took her morning coffee there, in her all-but-windproof pocket, gazing off to the valley, listening to the chuckling coo of doves in the pine above her, receiving visits from her children and her grandchildren, one of whom, the quietest, the most puzzled but most patient, was her grandson, Frank. Then she'd died.

Jen's aunt Carol was there, with the fleshy face of the women in her family and a naturally friendly manner as if nothing was preying on her mind. Her second husband, George Miller, had a way of sitting back, standing back, always seeming a little removed, and he was there. Carol and George, between them, had had a daughter who was not there. But Carol's first daughter and Jen's first cousin Brenda was, although she gave the impression of not wanting to be. She kept glancing off through that break in the foliage to the valley as if she were plotting an escape. Mickey, of course, to no one's surprise, had not arrived.

Danny and his cousin Cynthia came out, neither in a deck-sitting mood. Danny said, "When are we eating? I want to show Cynthia my ramp."

Jen and Frank exchanged glances, that furious and futile-sounding clatter in both their heads. Jen deferred to her father. Frank said, "Not now, Danny. We're almost ready to sit down."

But before they did, Carol said the one thing so far that came anywhere close to the real reason behind her family's visit. She breathed down the sun-warmed pine scent and the false spring coming out of the ground and to her brother said, "I can see why you want to keep this just like it is, Frank. It's a sort of a fantasy world out here." She emphasized the word *fantasy*. To her husband, Carol added, "It's the exception that proves the rule, isn't it, George?"

Neither her husband nor anyone else understood exactly what she meant.

Carol had her soft side, unshared by her daughter Brenda, who was supposedly in pain from her recent divorce. That had been the pretext for the visit, to allow Brenda to take solace from her extended family. She gave a disgusted little laugh under her breath, and George gave a thoughtful, under-his-breath hum.

After that they did sit down, and before the turkey could be served—but not before it had been carved—Mickey arrived.

He had grown a beard, an unluxuriant, patchy black, which hid his weak chin and took attention away from the finicky movements of his mouth. His fine hair was beginning to thin. His attention seemed bolder and more concentrated than in years past, but teachers had their ways to command a class, and Mickey was always a bit onstage. His sister knew that, offstage and brought to a halt, Mickey ran the risk of making a real wreck of his life. Frank knew Mickey was the most vulnerable of his children and, for that reason, the one who would be called on to live by his wits, wits he, as father, admired. That Mickey had become even a high school historian struck Frank as bizarre since Mickey would seem to be the last person to stand reflectively back from anything. Gerald had a more equable, worldly outlook, and a much longer view. Maybe for that reason he'd gone to live in California, so that he could see his family from a continent's perspective, while Jen, up close, could master all the minutiae put before her as long as she wasn't under the influence of some all-absorbing man.

At the head of the table, Frank, instead of saying a blessing, invoked the memory of his grandmother, who'd raised a large family, which included Frank and Carol's mother, practically by herself. But the remarkable thing about his grandmother, Frank said, was not just her positive attitude but its special quality, which had made a lasting impression on the boy now become a sixty-year-old man. He called it her resoluteness, her "measured" resoluteness. It was as if every morning his grandmother tallied up her life, weighed its pros and cons in some scale, then came down "those" stairs and went into "that" kitchen and began to prepare the meal that would take her family one day further ahead. Even as an old woman, when her family was all gone and he was just a boy come to visit, she did that. Down those stairs and into that kitchen. She'd been an extraordinary woman, who while others were giving in to panic had held on to what counted. In her case, her family, this land, and this house. Then Frank sent his grandson Danny a private glance. That was probably what Thanksgiving was all about, he said, finding someone to give thanks to in this matter of staying alive and well.

Once the grandmother's memory had been laid to rest, the family ate and talked mainly about what lay on their plates and, with eager exclamations, asked for seconds of. Mickey, in an effort to catch up, seemed to engage Carol's family in conversation one by one, steering clear of politics and the single big issue about which he could have held forth, and talking instead about his teaching and George's insurance business (Mickey's grandfather Arthur, the one who'd survived the Second World War, had sold life insurance). Cynthia he could talk to as if she were a favorite and slightly rebellious student. With Brenda his tone became solicitous, verging on a pep talk, until she'd had enough and asked him how *his* love life was going. Mouthful by mouthful, Frank kept coming back to Helen, singing her praises. Danny and Cynthia exchanged a lot of covert glances, with abbreviated head movements and held-in-check grins, a sort of code Jen assumed she could crack if she wanted to make the effort. Mostly she smiled and observed and, a couple of times, when everybody else was caught up in somebody else, thought about Robert, what kind of an alternative Thanksgiving he was spending, with that bitch dreaming up new ways to turn the screws.

Mickey, making maybe the biggest socializing effort of his life, wondered, since he'd missed it, if they couldn't have dessert and coffee out on the deck. Frank stepped out there, stood facing east and west, then came back to report that the weather had turned, the sky was clouding over, and the temperature had dropped maybe fifteen degrees.

Taking advantage of the momentary breakdown, Danny asked his grandfather if he and Cynthia could be excused. Something about a maneuver he wanted to show her on his ramp, a "tailslide" that he claimed made little noise, and even though Frank warned him that the basement would be damp from the melting snow (but, so far at least, the sump pump had not come on), Frank went ahead and gave permission. Shortly after they'd left the room but before the tailslide began, Carol finally brought up the matter of the gas lease. Saying, "Frank, the last thing I want to get into now," she allowed that they could only talk about it provisionally, anyway, since for any final decision Sharon would need to be there, "but I don't see how we can put this off any longer," which caused her husband, George, to lower his head and grunt his assent and her daughter Brenda to sit up straight at the table with an avid flair to her nostrils. Carol concluded by admitting she'd consulted with Sharon about this and could assure him they spoke with one mind, and then she performed an astonishing piece of stage business, so astonishing Jen took one look at her father and had to fight hard not to laugh. Carol reached into the pocket of the tweed jacket she wore and pulled out her mobile phone, which she laid beside her plate. Somewhere in North Carolina (Raleigh? Greensboro? Charlotte?), Aunt Sharon would have pulled out hers.

Frank said, "What do you want to know, Carol?"

"If you're willing to talk about leasing this land. From what I'm told, they're paying five thousand dollars an acre now."

"That figure might be exaggerated. Told by whom?"

Everybody at the table knew told by whom. By a bullying, big-city lawyer whose name Carol didn't want to mention.

But Brenda did. "By my father," she declared proudly.

"Are you, Frank?" Carol softened her tone.

"Willing to talk?"

"Yes."

"Always," Frank said.

Then from directly underneath them, from the very foundations of the house, it seemed, came the reverberating clatter of a tailslide perfectly pulled off or a tailslide that had crashed and burned. For the first time since he'd been there, George Miller sat up straight in his chair. "What in the world was that!" he exclaimed, genuinely alarmed.

"My grandson showing off for your granddaughter," Frank said, although Cynthia wasn't George Miller's granddaughter, not quite.

Jen released a long-held breath, looked over at Helen, who had worked so hard, and almost cursed. Instead of serving as a tension breaker, Danny's skateboard performance seemed to add to it, and Carol hastened to get in, "Don't ever think I'm unaware of the beauty of this place, Frank. Don't ever think that. I have my sentimental side, too."

"I know you do, Carol."

"When I looked out over that valley, I saw what our grandmother used to see. I see what you see, Frank. Maybe it's a shame there's going to be gas drilling out there, but my whole point—and it's Sharon's point, too—is that it's going to happen whether we like it or not, so we might as well share in the benefits. Is that unreasonable?"

"Unreasonable? No, I would say you have the reason all on your side."

"It's not *my* side, Frank," Carol insisted in a sympathizing way, pleading with him to see the light. "It's really the country's side, too. This is our chance to get our 'energy independence,' Frank. I think of those people out there in . . . I don't know where, somewhere . . . in Wisconsin, say, or up in Maine. They don't have what we do. They share their . . . I guess their cheese and their lobsters with us so maybe it's time we shared our natural gas with them." She lowered her head and sank a bit in her chair. She was uncomfortable in this role. She didn't try to hide it. Her current husband started off on a line of argument known by all, that as far as polluting the environment went, natural gas versus oil or coal . . . but everybody at the table extended their sympathy to Carol, whose hand reached out and covered her cell phone in that moment, as if she were apologizing for its presence and wanted to sneak it back into her pocket. Then she seemed to brighten. Something had occurred to her. "It's what you said, Frank. It's like our grandmother, who came down those stairs and went into that kitchen every day of her life. We have something we can give the rest of the country so that *they* can give thanks to us. It would be wrong of us not to give it. It would be . . ." She paused to search for the word, and Frank supplied it.

"Ungracious? Un-American, Carol?"

"Well, it would be, wouldn't it, Frank?"

In that moment Danny tried his second tailslide, a thunderous attempt. The house shook. Frank walked to the basement door and called down to Danny to hold off, that he'd tell him when, and when he came back to the table, Carol seemed to be trembling with the aftershocks of Danny's effort. Frank put his arm around his sister's shoulder and led them all into the living room.

There, seated across from each other on matching sofas, Brenda tried to engage Jen, cousins a generation removed from their softhearted parents, but Jen wasn't interested. As children they'd visited back and forth, even occupied the same bed, but Brenda was still working off the bile from her divorce, which she seemed to be spitting out with each word. And there was the hint of a threat, too. To the effect of, take my mother, take me, or you get my father. If we don't get past all this sentimental shit, the hammer comes down. Jen's chief memory of Brenda's father was when Jen had been taken for visits there before the marriage had broken up, and one day Brenda's father, this Wilson Michaels, had returned home from court triumphant. He'd told Brenda to plant a congratulatory kiss on one of his cheeks and Jen to plant one on the other. She remembered the swelling fullness of the cheek, the aggressive smell of some aftershave, and the smell of the Scotch he was using to celebrate with, but what she really remembered was the gleam in his eye, which seemed to have rolled unnaturally down in its socket to regard her as she carried out his command. The eye was burning like some angry, old planet, and the gleam was so mischievous it was terrifying. You've got one chance, little girl, to give me my kiss, or I'll be licking my chops with you, too, just the way I did with that judge and jury and poor schmuck of a prosecutor. George Miller seemed to be reading Jen's mind when he said the best thing for everybody would be to keep this out of court. Or perhaps he was being protective of his wife, for whom the prospect of her ex-husband storming around a courtroom would be a nightmare. But Jen was no longer thinking of Wilson Michaels. She was thinking, I haven't heard a sound from Danny and his nubile little cousin now for . . . how long?

Mickey said, "Maybe before you make any final decisions, everyone here should take a trip down where I live and see what's going on."

Everyone knew where Mickey lived and knew the high points of what was going on.

Carol said, "Is that poor little boy going to live?"

Mickey said, "The last I heard he will. But they doubt if he'll ever walk again, or run with his dog. But, now that I think of it, he no longer has a dog."

Carol said, "It's so sad."

Brenda cast a scornful look at the ceiling, as if to say, On the scale of sadness . . .

Helen, apparently, had not heard. A boy? A dog? She looked at Frank, who drew and released a deep breath, instead of shaking his head.

Helen looked at Jen, who was only half amusing herself wondering, had she ever seduced a boy anywhere near Danny's age? In fact, she wasn't sure if a boy Danny's age could do the deed. How old do boys have to be? A glance at Cynthia and you knew that young lady would not be content to play doctor.

Jen said, "I assume the driver was never prosecuted."

Mickey said, "For?"

She hated it when Mickey or anybody else played dumb. People were dumb enough already. "Hit and run! What else?"

"He hardly ran. He was going to a drilling pad a few hundred feet up the road. What you have to get in your mind is there are drilling pads with their derricks at every turn in the road, and the trucks are everywhere. Boys with their dogs or little girls out picking spring violets are things of the past."

Brenda made a contemptuous sound, Aunt Carol sighed heavily, the phlegmatic George Miller began to fidget, Mickey turned his attention to his father, and Frank touched Helen's hand, lightly, but with a clear message: *Patience.* Danny and Cynthia came up the basement stairs and kept going, up the second-floor stairs to Danny's room, where they closed the door and put on music loud enough to cover any other sounds. The only sound that got through was that of a piece of furniture—a chair, his desk?—knocking against the floor or a wall. Were they dancing?

Danny had been so anxious to see *her*. Then little Cynthia had come along, brought by her ax-grinding mother. Whoever Brenda had divorced should be lifting a glass in thanksgiving now.

Jen discovered she was jealous, that was all. She gave a quiet, gasping laugh, but loud enough, it seemed, so that everyone looked at her. They had stopped talking about gas-leasing and gone on to sleeping arrangements for the night. It was getting dark out—she hadn't noticed. Frank had urged Carol and her family to stay there, with him, in the Coldwell house, in two empty bedrooms with the beds already made. But Carol had had to admit that they had already checked into a motel. Which meant that the battle lines had been drawn. Family with room in their house did not allow other family members to sleep in motels. But, pleadingly, Carol had said that was the way it was going to be.

It had been then that Jen had laughed. Only jealous, that was all! Almost charming, that stage she'd come to in the mothering of her son. Jealous of a sexually precocious little cousin. Jen smothered a second laugh. That was all.

Well, that was enough, goddamn it!

Mickey and his father stood at the base of a towering silver maple that grew on the downslope from the house. It flared skyward, and with the leaves fallen and each branch and twig a distinct silver-gray in the early-evening light, it was like a tree of deliverance, it was a chalice lifted to the sky. Any of a thousand different routes offered escape from earthbound affairs.

"Don't do it," Mickey said to his father.

"Didn't you tell me it didn't matter, anyway? What was it you called it? They were going to get you whether you leased or not?"

"Compulsory integration. Make them compel you then, but don't willingly put your pen to the paper."

"Tell me why, Son. Give me a reason Carol and Sharon will understand."

"Radium, strontium, barium, all radioactive, plus whatever 'lubricating' chemicals the gas companies are putting in themselves. Surely benzene, for starters. Slickwater, they call it. Ninety percent of what they pump down there comes back up, and they call that flowback fluid. Thanks to Bush and Cheney and that crowd, utterly unregulated by the Safe Drinking Water Act. They were dumping all this into the rivers. Now they take the wastewater to treatment plants to be neutralized, but since we're not talking about shit here but some private formula of chemicals the gas companies refuse to reveal, the treatment plants are putting it back in the river as lethal as when they got it."

"You could have said this to your aunt. Why didn't you?"

"I'll tell you what else is coming back up. A salt sludge so corrosive they were using it on the roads to get rid of ice, until it began to eat away the pavement, too."

"Why didn't you?"

"Land leasers are getting sick. Not from the water—they're smart enough not to drink that anymore. Something's in the air, some chemical equivalent of pollen that's causing these asthmalike conditions no one has any idea how to treat. They're wearing gas masks while they're counting their dollars."

"Son," Frank said quietly, and directed Mickey's eyes up the center of the tree, where the last light of the day—this blessedly warm day of Thanksgiving—lay along the branches and twigs. The cold of the season was in the damp ground, which rose up their pant legs.

In a musing tone, anecdotal, as though he were about to tell a joke, Mickey continued, "There's this old guy living out in the woods in a cabin he built himself. The farmer over the hill leases his land. The drillers send their graders in and build a road. For twenty, thirty years, however long, the old guy's been taking a shower in springwater that flows down the hill. A clean old guy. Built his own shower, too. When the graders are through, the springwater comes in muddy. He waits a week, a month, and when he complains to the landmen, they slap the old-timer on the back. No chemicals, just some mud after decades of springwater so clean it'd make you want to be a hermit, yourself."

"Tell Carol that, Mickey."

"Landmen," Mickey went on in the same musing tone he might have used to attract his students' attention when he wanted to give the impression of holding off his rage, "they stride out over the land. They take its measure and decide its worth. Did you know that two miles straight down the land still belongs to you? You own a little wedge of the earth's molten center, too, and they'll tell you how much that's worth. The sooner you sign on the dotted line, the sooner you can add it all up and head down to Florida. D'you ever read *Hamlet*, Dad?"

"Many years ago."

"I remember one line. Nothing to do with 'To be, or not to be' or 'the play's the thing.' I remember Hamlet looking at his brother-slaying uncle and saying, 'A man can smile and smile and be a villain.' "

"So he can, Son."

"Don't do it."

"I guess Carol is right. We'll be looking out on that valley and seeing drilling derricks whether I sign or not."

"Commit the symbolic act."

"You teach history," Frank said. "Tell me one symbolic act that changed the course of history."

"John Brown's raid on the Harpers Ferry arsenal."

"That's not very symbolic, even though it might have speeded up the Civil War. Brown killed and got killed. If I'm not mistaken, Robert E. Lee captured him."

"That's an A-plus, Dad." Mickey applauded his father. "Here's a better one. Henry David Thoreau spending a night in jail for failing to pay taxes to finance the Mexican-American War."

"It didn't stop the war, though, did it? And we got pretty much what we wanted, which included Texas."

"Trick question, Dad. Thoreau wrote an essay about that night in jail called 'On Civil Disobedience.' A little over a hundred years later every kid in the sixties read it, went onto the streets, and the Pentagon did not invade North Vietnam, only bombed it, which meant the Soviets and the Chinese stayed put. The correct answer to the question is that Thoreau's night in jail saved us all from World War Three."

Frank had been a kid in the sixties. He'd done his share of on-campus protesting, sit-ins, and the like, but he had never read "On Civil Disobedience." In high school in the Deweese he'd had a nature-loving English teacher and had read *Walden*. It was probably the first house-building book he had ever read, and could it possibly be that his interest in architecture began with Thoreau's cabin? He didn't think so. He'd have to think on it some more, but, standing under that soaring maple with his son, he remembered Thoreau as a lonely man, perhaps a morose man, who finally ended up feeling disaffected from even the animals that lived around him, yet the animals and maybe the fish in that perfectly clear pond of his were the only family he had.

Frank reached out and gripped his son by the back of the neck. He might have instructed Mickey to reach out and hug that tree, except that tree-hugging was precisely what he didn't need neighbors to drive by and see him or his children doing. But Mickey had to get his strength from somewhere.

Then he pulled his son to him, but that was not going to be enough.

In the sixties—it had been 1970 by then—Frank had made the decision to go on living, but that didn't mean he had strength to spare. He'd been a kid back then. If they were talking about symbolic acts, that letting of his own blood was as close as he'd come. What could he have been thinking? Had he been depressed? Had some twenty-year-old girl thrown him over? Had some studio professor devastated him with a review? Suicide ran in the family, and he wanted to see if it ran in him? That had been what he'd told himself, but with all that blood-stopping paraphernalia he'd had on hand, he could accuse himself of playing at it; he'd been a sophomore and had made it into a sophomoric game. "Give me a little time, Son," he whispered into Mickey's ear.

Was Mickey coming with Jen and Danny to go see their mother? Surprisingly, he was. On the way Jen told him to expect more of the same on the drilling issue, with the difference being that their mother thought she was speaking on their behalf, her poor disinherited children. Mickey said he didn't know about Jen—actually, he did—but he could sure use a few thousand bucks. How about Danny? Get himself a world-class skateboard ramp and not something he'd built with his own hands out of scrap lumber lying around. Jen wanted to know if her brother was serious, and Danny had pretty much figured out his uncle was as serious and unserious as he was going to get. Kids know—especially kids thrown back on their own devices when it came to entertainment—the kind of games people play with themselves when their tolerance for boredom is low. Danny could play those games as well as anyone else, but on this leasing issue the other kids had been harassing him about, he didn't want to play. "No fuckin' way!" he told his uncle, which caused his mother to fake a little gasp.

Mickey told Jen it looked as if some of the old man was rubbing off on the kid and asked if she was sure she wanted to keep him out there. And that was Uncle Mickey keeping up the game. But when his mother directed the question back to him—"Danny?"—her voice had a smiling front side and a serious back side, and Danny had a decision to make. He did his best to toss it off: "I'll stick around a while longer." Uncle Mickey laughed under his voice, and his nephew knew it must have been because of his grown-up tone. Well, what did his uncle think? All this drilling into the earth was kids' stuff? Mr. Valenti had told them the Nez Percé Indians never even plowed the land for fear of inflicting pain on Mother Earth. What did Mickey think drilling holes two miles down was going to do?

Then, before they got to their mother's house, Jen told Mickey about the article in the local paper and what their father had said. Uncle Mickey gave a kind of cheering laugh and then cursed. *That* was what they'd needed to tell Aunt Carol and her ball-busting daughter and her decent-enough husband! The earth was rising up to meet us after ten thousand years! We should be sweet-talking and not pounding holes into it. We should be whispering sweet nothings into its cute, cavernous ear.

For some reason his mother said, Goddamn it, Mickey!

Marjorie Rawlings (although she'd kept her married name) had had a brother who'd died and another who'd moved as far away from their father as he could get and was still kicking around in some Southern state, the last she knew. From an early age, Marge had stood up to her father and won his admiration, while her mother had never stood anywhere but on the sidelines. Marge had worked in Pop Rawlings's bar and without exactly giving it a feminine touch had somehow softened its tone. She had her defenders and admirers, and before anybody got badly out of line, a voice at the back of his head said, How is this going to look in Marge's eyes?

Jen was a lot like her mother in that she was not afraid to take a stand—relished it, at times—in defense of her softer side. But what Marjorie knew, she knew dead, while her daughter never ceased to sort through her jumbled emotions.

With Mickey his mother struck a perpetual wait-and-see pose. What have you brought me this time? She expected improvements, which was her way of indicating how far Mickey had to go (in that respect, her older son, Gerald, was a bastion unto himself). The beard was a joke. Too often men grew one when they didn't want to face the world.

As for Danny, it was as if his illegitimacy and his mother's secrecy in that respect was his grandmother's private delight. Danny could be moody and try to make up for it by pleasing too much, but he had that ace in the hole. No one knew who he was.

Marge thanked them for coming to see her in her little prefabricated home that was as clean as Pop's Place had been when it opened its doors each day. The worst use—and abuse—had been washed off, but not all of it. Her home smelled of cigarette smoke and the air-freshener she treated it with when she knew any nonsmokers were coming. That didn't stop her from smoking in their presence, however, and squinting at them through narrowed eyes, which could give her a shrewdly appraising look. It also kept most visits short.

Jen had not brought her food from Thanksgiving dinner. Her mother would not have expected it and would not have accepted it if her daughter had. Marge wanted impressions, information, gossipy speculation, hard, cold facts if they were available. How Marge knew just who had been present at the Thanksgiving dinner in the Coldwell house Jen did not know, but Marge knew. Had any progress been made on the land-leasing issue, or—on a raspy laugh—was their father still waiting for the ground to rise up and give him a big hug?

Above all, Marge did not want to be made a fool of. She'd been fool enough to marry him and stay with him all those years. Frank Joyner, the architect, a quiet civic sort of hero, with some peculiar tangents, it was true, and Marjorie Joyner, who could play proper when she had to, who was self-possessed enough to occupy a number of roles, but who couldn't avoid a certain swagger in any of them.

She didn't want money, she claimed, all she wanted was for her husband—*ex*-husband!—not to embarrass them all.

Her daughter advised her to see the humor in it.

Marge said she would if she hadn't been married to the man.

"You get a divorce," Jen contended, "and it's as good as standing up in the town square and proclaiming that, from here on out, the man speaks for himself."

"You stand up! I'd rather find a hole to hide in!"

Everybody laughed, except Danny, whose grandmother almost always entertained him.

"Granddad's right!" he declared. "You can't be digging holes that deep down in the earth. No one knows what's down there!" That, of course, was Mr. Valenti speaking. "There might be . . . radios down there!"

Now they all laughed at Danny. His uncle told him he meant "radioactivity," and Danny had the good sense to laugh at himself.

It was a tension-breaker. Marge offered her visitors something to eat or drink, which received laughing protests, all except from Danny, who had been skateboarding and not sitting around a table, after all, and his grandmother told him he knew where the cookies were. It was only natural that while he was out of the room, Marge would ask her daughter how much longer she planned to keep him out there with Frank. As small as her place was, Marge had room for him, if it was a matter of finding somewhere to put her grandson up, and that offer was only natural, too. If you thought about it, boys were in short supply in the Joyner family, and Marge had raised two. She gave Mickey that narrow-eyed, appraising look of hers that everyone expected to erupt in a howl of mockery, but never did. "And then," Marge went on, "you've got that huge apartment sitting empty on top of the Deweese— you and Danny could live there—unless that's where Frank's got one of his paramours installed. No, now that I think of it, the lady's got an apartment of her own. . . ."

Marge trailed off. Jen refused to bite. Danny came back in eating a peanut-butter cookie his grandmother had made especially for him.

"Enough said," Marge said, sitting back and allowing her cigarette smoke to stream before her eyes.

Mickey came out of his slouch. Who had the key to that apartment, he wanted to know, what they'd called their penthouse, when they'd played at being grand? Jen did. And she knew her mother did, too, even though she wasn't entitled to it and, for that reason, would never give it up. Mickey said that was where he wanted to spend the night, back in his old room, where twelfth graders had once counted the days until their misery came to an end. He made a gesture of supreme pleasure unto himself, a little fist pump of delight.

Once at the door, though, he changed demeanor completely. He stage-whispered to his mother, "Lay off of Dad, Mother. He has a serious decision to make."

But no one stage-whispered like that unless they wanted to be laughed at again. So his mother did, and at his father, too, guilty by association to have such a laughable confederate as his son.

Night had fallen while they'd been inside. An overcast sky, a wind rising, and the temperature dropping by the minute. There was a streetlight, and if they'd stood there an hour longer, they would have seen the snow come back, riding that rising wind. That earlier interlude on the deck, which Mickey had missed, overlooking the valley, which that morning Danny had seen shimmering with reflected light, might or might not become the stuff of family lore when Thanksgivings past were recounted. It might be the family would choose to forget it, unreal from the start and shameful in its long-standing consequences. The Indians fed the Pilgrims and then the Pilgrims cast the fiendish Indians down to hell. Only Danny felt a grown-up sense of satisfaction at how things had turned out. His cousin Cynthia would never see another tailslide like that, and for better or worse, the battle lines had been drawn. Before he'd let them drill a hole in his grandfather's land, he'd lie down on the spot and dare them to drill through him. All his schoolmates would be counting their grubby dollars, and he would be lying on the ground, defiantly, entirely in the right, as the trucks and drilling gear departed and the ground in gratitude gave him that two-centimeter lift. He really couldn't wait.

She didn't even bother to put on her nightgown. Fully clothed, Helen lay on top of her bed until she couldn't anymore, then she got up and drove from the Deweese through slanting snow to Frank's house, to which she did not have a key. But through a living-room window she could see firelight flickering on the walls. The door had yet to be locked for the night, and she walked in and sat beside Frank on one of the two sofas. More relieved than surprised, he said, "You've come back. How nice," and took her under one of his arms.

They sat like that, speechless for a time, watching the fire burn down as the snow began to cover the ground it had given up only that morning. The house was quiet. The boiler was not firing, and Danny lay asleep upstairs, his skateboard where he'd left it at the foot of his ramp. Helen was near tears. As close as she got under Frank's welcoming arm, she knew herself to be an outsider. She was not thinking of her dead husband. In moments like this, her loneliness never wore his face. Impossible to say how, but she sensed a similar sort of loneliness in Frank.

She felt for him deeply, as she knew he felt for her, but there was a limit to what they could do for each other. She might have been stationed on one side of a gorge, he on the other. They could make reassuring signals to each other. On good days they could even read the expressions on each other's face. Some days shouting didn't make it across, but on others, days of a blessed calm, a whisper did. It helped her to see it like this.

The fire burned down. On the hearth she could see the splinters and little scraps of bark where the last log had lain before Frank had tossed it in. The sound from the fireplace was a succession of soft, muttering pops while, from above, the wind made its way down the flue. The smell in the house, once you got beyond the burning wood, was of the Thanksgiving dinner that had been eaten here, without the oily residue of the turkey, of course, which had been cooked elsewhere. She said, "They're good people. Brenda's been hurt so she's taking it out on the world. Carol has to play the part, but she really wishes it would all go away. I wouldn't want to have your decision to make, Frank."

He responded with a grateful sound in his chest, for her interest, her nearness. He nudged her still closer, placed his large hand on her head, and absently smoothed back her hair.

Danny turned over in his bed, a sound they heard all the way downstairs. The wind picked up outside, a high blow to the quiet, trailing whistle coming down the flue. Still, the boiler did not fire. Frank's breath was pensive, if a little labored. He sounded tired.

She said, "Don't you want to go to bed?"

He made a deep, humming consent in his chest, still stroking her hair.

"I want to sleep here tonight. I hope you don't mind."

She heard him say, "Danny," under his breath, and she said, "I know."

He didn't look at her as he spread out the ashes on the fire and closed the glass doors. He went through the house, locking doors and turning off the remaining lights. She waited for him at the bottom of the stairs, as empty-handed as she'd been when she'd suddenly walked out of the Deweese, where she'd lived for these two years that she would never have been able to measure on the calendar. She had more space than she needed there, and a golden light in the autumn afternoons. The nights she had spent here in the Coldwell house had been when Danny was off with his mother; the other nights she'd spent with Frank in her apartment, which, of course, was his, his vision, beginning with the designs he'd drawn to convert spacious but graceless classrooms into living quarters that were not cast adrift but belonged. The "vernacular," he'd called it. How to convert structures we hardly saw anymore, they were so much a part of our lives—a train station, a grain elevator, a barn, a warehouse, a school—into places to live. He'd talked about it as if he were talking about healing a wound. She'd understood him to mean we abandon our buildings at our peril since they carry off with them so much of who we are.

He put his hand on the small of her back. The door to Danny's room was directly above them. A carpeted runner ran up the center of the stairs, and she allowed him to guide her out ahead. Once upstairs, to reach Frank's room they had to double back, and once inside, the carpeting gave way to less sound-absorbing rugs. The room was cold.

The day's abnormal heat, and then the fire he had made, had thrown the thermostat off, and Frank invited her to place her hand on the cast-iron radiator. It was as cold as cast iron could get, and only after she'd touched it and looked up at him did he smile in such a way as to include her, too. They were in this together, this world of cold radiators. She'd left no nightgown or pajamas here. Frank turned back the bedcovers for her, and she stripped down to her bra and panties and slipped inside.

All she had wanted was to sleep at his side. She'd had a choice when her husband, Paul, had died; she could have found a place close to Cindy to live and shared her loneliness with her daughter. Cindy's marriage had broken up years earlier; they could even have lived together. Cindy was no longer her father's daughter and Helen was no longer his wife—they could have mourned father and husband side by side. But Helen decided to stay in town and ended up doing the opposite of what Frank's wife had done: from the suburbs she moved to the town's center in search of some company. She found Frank's daughter and then she found Frank. But it was not as if Jen had fixed them up. Every tenant should know her landlord—it was one of the oldest relationships in the world, which they'd joked about. He was the lord of the land and she a mere peasant, who was allowed to occupy her apartment on his lordly sufferance. But even as they joked, she was aware she filled a vacancy in the Deweese that his wife had once occupied; it was real what had happened—Marjorie Joyner had moved out, out to the suburbs, and Helen had moved in. It had the feel of chess pieces being rearranged. It had the feel of fate. Even though by that time Frank had gone out to the country to live. But he came back. He wanted her to feel comfortable there. If there was anything he could do. And his solicitousness became a form of tenderness she responded to with genuine surprise as they regarded each other from opposite sides of their personal divides. You nice man. You very decent and nice man. While her daughter, Cindy, with no one there to cushion her loss, met her mother's good fortune with scorn.

"Frank," Helen whispered. She couldn't hear his grandson Danny's breathing on the other side of the wall, but she could hear every other sound he made. Through a scant barrier of plaster and lath, their head-boards joined.

"I know," he whispered back, and then he held her until they were warm.

They were no longer supple twenty-year-olds, but somehow—surely she couldn't do it again—she was out of her panties and off with her bra, and Frank was out of his pajamas and soundlessly inside her, while Danny slept on. The sound was outside—the wind blowing snow—and the sound was of an agitated Danny perhaps doing tailslides in his sleep, while she kept mouthing her landlord and lover's name silently in his ear—Frank, Frank—and he responded no more audibly that he knew, he knew. Making love with an eleven-year-old boy not a foot from your head had a curious effect: it drove her sense of intimacy deeply inside. In there, the warmth that she and Frank created be-tween them seemed more lasting than cast iron. She wanted to sleep and awake to it and had convinced herself that she could, even as it began to crest as if on some subterranean wave, and near tears again, she breathed his name. He knew, he knew. The wave broke, as it would have to, and she was done, while Frank kept reaching out for her, reaching out for her, until he, too, gave way, and they were back where they'd started, in each other's arms on opposite sides of their gorge, sharing some strange warmth rising up from below that would last the night, although not as long as cast iron. She did hear the boiler come on before she slept, a rumbling sound that softened into a whoosh as hot water moved into the pipes and spread through the house. She listened to the warming water. Their radiator made a tingling sound of welcome. They would not be cold when they woke up the next morning. Still the day for it, she gave thanks for that.

5

Most of what Frank had learned about his father's role in World War II he had to deduce, or read for himself. His mother did tell him that she almost broke up with her teenage boyfriend because he seemed so desperately eager to leave her and go off and fight, and so desperately anxious that the war would end before he got his chance. But he made it under the wire, turning eighteen in the summer of 1944 and arriving in Cherbourg, France, in the late fall. Still, he thought he'd missed it. The Allies had Hitler on the run, and most people were predicting—and Eisenhower had bet Montgomery as much—that the war in Europe would be over by Christmas.

Christmas found Arthur Joyner in Paris, held in reserve. His buddies luxuriated in the reception they got from the French, especially the French girls, but—and on this score Jane Coldwell, his stateside sweetheart, needn't have worried—Arthur Joyner was not the luxuriating sort. Christmas bells had already begun to ring when, on December 16, with his back to the Rhine, Hitler disregarded the advice of his generals and counterattacked through the hilly region in Belgium known as the Ardennes. It was the bloodiest battle of the war for U.S. forces, fought in the coldest temperatures and the heaviest snows, and the bodies of the fallen froze. Once again, Arthur Joyner missed it. His battalion was called up to relieve forces from Patton's army, which had already recaptured the key crossroads town of Bastogne, and although German snipers were still active in the forests when Arthur Joyner marched through, he never felt personally under fire. But what he saw and the atrocities he had described to him by Belgian farmers and townspeople made him vow never to lift a violent hand against a fellow human being for the rest of his life. He might have dreamed of battles and daring deeds, but his American sweetheart was right: he was no soldier. He should never have been in such a headlong rush to leave her side. And, yes, she wanted him back.

All his father told Frank, his firstborn, was "It was unspeakable, regardless of what a monster Hitler was, and I never intend to speak of it. I can't stop you from reading about it in books, although I wish you wouldn't. I don't want you to think of your father in that way."

But, of course, Frank did read about it—in book after book. And they all said the same thing. It was Hitler's crazed last attempt. He took kids out of school and middle-aged men out of breadlines and threw them at his enemies. In the first days they pushed deep into the Allied lines—they created a "bulge"—and then they were overwhelmed. In snow up to the waist the battles raged back and forth, and what Frank Joyner was sure his father had seen and never forgotten marching to the relief of Bastogne were fields and forests full of frozen remains. In a desperate attempt not to freeze, the Germans had stripped the American corpses of their clothing, and then the counterattacking Americans had stripped the German dead of theirs, so that the remains that Frank Joyner was sure his father had seen belonged to neither one side nor the other, but to the disposable human race. The naked corpses humped up like manure under the snow, like refuse, like offal. They became human remains only when a hand reached out, some joint—an elbow or a knee—poked through, or the frost-rimmed round of an eye met his. Nothing looked deader—less likely to have ever been alive—than the gray of their frozen flesh, and later when it came time for Arthur Joyner to settle on a profession, he didn't have much choice. Life insurance. The one thing we had worth insuring. Our only defense—really no more than a feeble protest, perhaps only a futile recognition—against how easily it could be taken away.

This his son deduced. His father was a walking oxymoron. He was resolutely mild. He was fiercely temperate. He couldn't be roused. He'd provisioned himself for a lifelong siege, and he'd done it, his walls had stood till the end. With him he'd had his wife, and she, of course, had had to deal with violent death long before her husband. She'd been a little girl when her father had killed himself, but old enough to detect something just as unspeakable—something unspoken—in the voices around her. Two weeks later, with her grandfather's death, the voices might have hinted at some horrible curse. Frank was convinced she had clear memories of both her father and grandfather, if only by the way her face tightened when she shook her head that, no, she was too young, she didn't remember a thing. Once, he thought, she had slipped up. He remembered a particular picnic. The family went on picnics with an almost religious regularity, the preparations precise and the execution orderly and almost always free of fuss. He didn't remember their ever running to get out of sudden rain. He didn't remember either of his sisters sulking if they didn't want to be brought along. All of them seemed to understand that going on a picnic was something like a pastoral pause in what could otherwise become a dehumanizing rush, and if the weather cooperated, why shouldn't they? Each picnic ended with the family taking a walk around the park grounds, during which time they might or might not see other families and friends of theirs out on walks of their own.

His mother's slip had occurred on one of those walks. Moving along a fence at the perimeter of the park, they'd come up to a small herd of grazing cattle. Nothing more pastoral. They had paused, and the cattle, to a cow, had ceased to uproot the grass and grind it between their jaws. As if on command, they raised their heads and regarded the Joyner family with a sullen-seeming persistence. They made Frank Joyner laugh. He couldn't remember what they'd made his sisters do, and he remembered his own reaction only because of what his mother had done. She'd stood at the fence and, with a scowling fixity on her face he'd never before seen, stared back at them. It was as if she'd never seen cows before; then it was as if she were saying, whatever they were, they had no business appearing at a Joyner picnic. His father said, "Janie?" but she never took her eyes off the closest cow. His father said, "What's happening, Janie?" and Frank remembered his mother's response: "Look at her. I've never liked them." But who didn't like cows, with their sweet, heavy, udder-swinging ways and their deep-bellied moos, and the plodding pace at which they went about living their lives? Then his mother added, "Ever since I was a little girl," and her husband put his arm around her shoulder and his head against hers and whispered to her it was okay. All of which their son heard.

It was such an uncharacteristic moment for his mother that Frank never forgot it. It only came to mean something later when his parents sat him down and told him about those dark two weeks in the family history. He was a teenager then. He believed fourteen. They wanted him to know in case some malicious person out there sought to hurt him and threw it up in his face. Even as a fourteen-year-old, his first thought was, What if they'd waited too late? Kids a lot younger than he was then could be full of malice when they were trying to get the upper hand. His second thought was, Was this information he was supposed to file safely away, shorn of its ability to shock, or were his parents giving him a cross to carry, and in that case, were they inflicting it on him too soon, at too early an age? His father provided the historical context—the Depression, the loss of one's life work, how sadly common such acts of despair became. There is never any shortage of tragedy, but it always comes back to life. Treasure it, Frank. They did not say this. Rather, they set him this example. They went to church, the Presbyterian, but they did not talk to him about an after-life. This life, Frank. Hasn't it been fine?

His father had known neither man, which his son didn't doubt. His mother said she had been too young, but she seemed to slump when she said it and her eyes to go distant, and because Frank loved her, he looked away. He remembered the time she'd stood bound to that star-ing cow, that dumb, chomping, imperturbable animal life. Her grand-father had cared for cows and measured himself against them all his adult life and had finally hanged himself in their barn. His mother had not liked them even as a little girl. She had not lied to her son. But she was protecting him against a bitter truth, that there was life out there that could care less whether Joyners or Coldwells or any other mem-bers of the human family lived or died, even if one member of that family had spent his whole life taking care of them. The cows contin-ued chomping their hay while above them his mother's grandfather's body swung slowly to a halt.

The two men sitting in their car in front of his house had been there as long as Frank had been leaning back on that rolled bale of hay, perhaps two hundred yards down the road from where his great-grandfather's cow barn had stood. One of the two men had been to his door twice. He was solidly built, of average height, fair-haired, wore an olive-green coat, nothing on his head, and boots. The other man Frank never saw except as a heavyset shadow inside the car, which was a dark se-dan streaked with mud. The license plates Frank couldn't make out. The first man had already walked around the house once, and then more deliberately a second time, pausing at points as though to study the structure and admire the craftsmanship, through snow that hadn't been fresh for more than a week. Then he got back into the car. The two men seemed to be discussing what to do, perhaps consulting pa-pers that would give them options.

Frank's option—the one he liked best—was to wait them out. He was comfortable with his back to the bale of hay; he had the valley to look out over, the day was overcast but the visibility good, the crows, the sailing goshawks, the red-tailed hawks, the surf-sound of traffic passing by on the highway down the road. He could have called the sheriff and asked him to come out and investigate these two persistent, trespassing strangers, who couldn't take a hint. But he couldn't call the sheriff because he made a point of not taking his cell phone with him when he went for his walks. His third option, the one he favored, was to see how Danny handled it when the school bus let him off and he walked down the hill.

The men had been sitting there for a good half an hour. During that time various cars had passed. Having put themselves so publicly on display, they could represent no physical harm to his grandson, or so Frank reasoned. On the contrary, the strongest impression they gave off as they bided their time was that they had the law on their side.

Danny entered the upslope mouth of the drive making knee-flexing, shoulder-turning motions, which Frank assumed bore some relation to skateboard maneuvers. When Danny saw the car parked beyond his grandfather's, and inside it the shadowy outline of the two men, his posture straightened, and in a soldierly way his backpack went to his shoulder. Without breaking stride he walked past the men to the mud-porch door and took his time opening it. It was then that the man in the olive coat stepped out of the car and called to him. It occurred to Frank that Danny had seen his grandfather leaning up against his favorite bale of hay and was putting on a show for him, showing his granddad what, if put to the test, he could do. And that was all right, too.

Danny stood two steps above the man who came up to him, and he didn't step down. Apparently, the man spoke first. He might have been an innocent passer-through asking directions or a neighbor wondering when the weather would turn. Danny wasn't buying it. In a punctuating gesture, he lowered his backpack off his shoulder and squared himself on the top step before saying what he had to say. The man hunched over a little more and appeared to be moving snow around with his boot tip. Danny stood even straighter, if possible, and if he'd swung the backpack at the man's head, his grandfather would not have been surprised. For a boy that age the pull of indignation was hard to resist, and personal safety frequently the least of it. Danny barked something out. The man seemed to maintain his composure. He appeared to be searching for something in his coat pockets. Then he turned, walked back to his car, and visible to Frank, maybe a hundred and fifty yards away, the man inside handed a business card out to his companion, who paused a moment before jotting something down on it. By that time Danny had gone into the mud-porch and then into the house, not bothering to take off his boots. The slamming of the doors Frank did hear, with that instant's delay that made it all a little remote, a little unreal. The man fit the business card into the mud-porch door, stepped back, and looked up at the house again, then turned and got into the car, while the other man backed out of the curving drive cautiously, the last thing he wanted, with that hysterical kid inside, being to back into the ditch.

When Frank entered the house, with the business card in his pocket, his grandson was on the phone to his mother, pleading with an urgent mix of emotions in his voice to find out where his granddad was because they had to act fast.

Jen was at work in the gallery, and the sole customer had gone from thumbing through a bin of prints to inspecting the jewelry inside the glass-enclosed cases. Danny was saying, "If they find him before we do, it could be a bad scene!" and she was saying, "Danny, calm down. If his car's there that means he's out taking his walk and he'll . . ." Then she heard someone in her father's house—a door close, steps—and had to admit her son's overexcited version of events had gotten to her, for, if it wasn't Frank, then who had walked in to do what horrible thing to her son? "That's him now, isn't it?" she said. "What'd I tell you?"

Danny called out to his grandfather, and his grandfather called back, which Jen was able to hear, too. In that moment the browsing woman asked to be shown some necklaces.

Jen showed her three, amethyst necklaces from Brazil, lovely, really, as elegant as anything in the store, elegant and raw, as if there were places beneath the earth's crust—Brazil, apparently, one of them— where nature cut jewels to her own taste. The necklaces were marked up—Luisa had to make some money somewhere—so that they could be, if only slightly, marked down, but the woman wasn't really interested, probably only killing time before a late lunch date. By the time Jen got back to the phone, Danny was off somewhere having a conversation with his grandfather, and she found herself having to shout in an effort to get their attention. Which she didn't want to do. It was her eleven-year-old son who was turning up the volume.

But it was her father who came to the phone. Nothing, he assured his daughter, Danny had handled it all very well.

"So who were those men?"

"Apparently, landmen."

"From Conklin?"

"TransAtlantic. One of them wrote Wilson Michaels's name on his card. Do you remember him, Jen?"

"Brenda's father? I was just a little girl. He terrified me. I remember a high-toned bully."

"Well, it seems these men from TransAtlantic have two employers. Danny sent them packing."

She asked to speak to her son. She saw Michaels's inflamed and bulging eye again, rolled down in its socket to demand from her his kiss, and she did not want Danny to have anything to do with that man, who would be older and less inclined to mercy now, if mercy had ever entered his mind except as one more step in some moneymaking scheme. The scheme would be to get Brenda, then little Cynthia, rich. Little Cynthia with enough money to work her wiles on anyone who came close to her web sent an angry chill through Jen's body. Just how much gas was down there?

She told Danny she'd be out before supper to talk to him. And she told him to be there, as if he could be anywhere else.

Thankfully, before Luisa came in she did sell a lovely Sadanobu print. A geisha looking back over her shoulder to where the hem of her kimono was caught in a thornbush.

Jen's current boyfriend was a boyfriend from years past, her band-following days. He'd played bass, and she'd been attracted to the way he stood beside his instrument, plucking at the strings with eyes closed and a sweet, venturing smile on his face. He built houses now, when there was work. Or painted them. He was not Danny's father, although at times she wished he were, for he was easily the most patient and gentle of all her ex-boyfriends, and that he was currently somebody else's ex, as she was, struck her as providential, in a modest way. His name was Charlie Terwilliger, his nickname was Twig. She was to meet him after work, and the plan had been to ride up the lake, have supper, hear a fusion rockabilly/country band new to the area, then come back to her place and console each other in a time-marking way. Except she was beginning to realize she liked him more than that. So, say, a time-*limited* way. Limits there would have to be. It accomplished nothing to deceive herself about that. She was looking for that other unself-deceived someone. No, she wasn't "looking"—the distinction was important. She was "on alert." She thought of that geisha who'd gone off alert just long enough to get her kimono caught in those thorns. Finally, the world was small.

She told Charlie she'd make it up to him, and he brushed it off so obligingly that she ended up asking him if he would drive out with her when she talked to her son and father, and Charlie, of course, agreed, but not before pointing out what she should have thought of herself—that he would be an outsider in any family conversation with her son and dad, which might make things awkward for the three of them. Of course, he was right.

"Damn it, Twig," she said, and kissed him right there, in the main concourse, running from Luisa's gallery all the way to the end, where guitars hung in a shop window and musical instruments were sold.

Later, they drove out to her father's house. Did her father remember Charlie Terwilliger? He'd have to look back almost fifteen years if he did. A boy bass player, standing lanky and tall beside his instrument. Her father did, although she could see him running back through his daughter's boyfriends in his mind until he came to Twig.

Jen took her son aside. Danny was still jazzed about his standoff with the gas landmen, how he'd held the fort while his granddad had been away, and she wanted him to understand two things, well, maybe, three. First, the landmen were not some kind of marauding raiders or hired guns, they were middlemen doing their job just like most people in the world, so she didn't want him getting in their faces and screaming at them, if that was what he'd done. Understood? The second thing was they might have been sent by his cousin Cynthia's grandfather, and this man, yes, could be one mean hombre who only belonged to the family in the sense that he had a grudge to settle, and she didn't want Danny getting anywhere near him—or his proxies. And, yes, there was a third. The time had come for Danny to think about coming back downtown. She had her eye on a small house down by Kruger Creek. If she could figure out a way to rent it, they might be able to set up his skateboard ramp—

"You mean leave Granddad by himself? Now?" He was incredulous, genuinely perplexed.

She sighed. "Danny, that's what I'm talking about. You're not listening. This isn't a war. I know some kids in your class said some things—"

"No fuckin' way!" he replied, his favorite expression, it seemed, but in a lowered voice so that it was just between the two of them, she'd give him credit for that.

"That's enough."

"Granddad's all alone out here!"

"Because he wants to be. It's what *he* wants. Do you know how long he lived out here by himself before you showed up?"

Danny didn't. He wasn't interested in such information. He went stony in an instant. Hard to argue with a stone.

When she came back into the living room, Charlie Terwilliger, who, it turned out, was well-informed on the antifracking movements, was telling her father about a group in the county who, township by township, was trying to activate certain zoning ordinances that would not allow the drilling to begin. Another group was concentrating on keeping the gasmen out of state parks and forests. A third—allowing for some overlap—was going county by county around the state in an effort to get the governor to extend a drilling moratorium until the environmental impact could be fully determined. Yet a fourth group, of commando activists, was vowing to disrupt the drilling by bodily means. Charlie personally knew one of them—and Jen realized she did, too—a real Luddite, back-to-the-soil type, who could be found at the farmers' market every Saturday, selling honey produced by his own swarm of honeybees, the most catastrophically endangered species on the face of the earth—who had proclaimed he would climb the first drilling derrick erected here and, literally, throw a spanner into the works. A spanner, Jen believed, was a wrench of some sort, and she supposed if you climbed a derrick to the top and inserted the wrench at just the right time, you could catch the drill bit before it made its plunge and stop the whole operation in its tracks. Drilling interruptus. She said, "What do you really think Wilson Michaels has to do with all this?"

Frank sat deep in the sofa, looking up over his knees. "I guess it's his way of letting us know he's still in the game. I'd say he's giving us one more chance to play by the rules everyone else plays by before we have to play by his."

Jen explained to Charlie who Wilson Michaels was, and Charlie, after a moment's pause, pointed out what they'd missed.

"It's Conklin that's leased all the land around here. But this Michaels goes for TransAtlantic, who'd love to drive in a wedge. Trans-Atlantic puts a well right down in Conklin country and takes their gas, too. Michaels has probably convinced them if it goes to court, it's a done deal. You say the man can talk?"

Her father was pondering this new slant on things so it was up to Jen to say that, yes, the man could talk.

"And here's something else," Charlie went on, warming to it in his slow-spoken way. "If TransAtlantic does get drilling rights on this land, they'll drill as many wells as they can. I've heard of as many as twelve per pad, but what they'll probably do is build multiple pads—north, south, east, west. Course, that means you'll be rich, I mean really rich, and your neighbors won't be as rich as they thought they'd be. It's beginning to look like this Michaels fellow is one smart dude."

An agitated Danny stood in the doorway to the entrance hall. He reminded his mother of a dog dying to get outside. He let out a strangled and baffled "Granddad!"

Frank hadn't moved. Perhaps he'd sunk a bit more deeply into the sofa, trying to see where this bass-strumming boyfriend his daughter had taken back up with might be wrong. Jen saw Michaels's eye again, like a bulging, bloodshot planet pushing up close. "Ray Whittaker!" she suddenly said.

"Yes," her father said, "I'll want to talk to Ray."

"But Granddad," Danny expostulated from his doorway, "they can't make us do anything!" Then he boasted, "They can't make me!"

She had to check herself now. Danny was due at least half an apology. If this wasn't war, it was an ominous gathering of forces, a little skirmish that had occurred right out in front of her father's house, something like the first shot fired.

Frank said, in a quiet, marveling tone, "You know what Mickey said?"

Marveling at Mickey? "No, what did Mickey say?" She had no patience with her willful little brother now.

"He advised me to commit the symbolic act."

"Just what the hell is that supposed to mean?"

"To hold out even if it doesn't do any good. The good might come years later when there're bigger issues involved."

"Did he say what those were?" She didn't give her father a chance to answer. "Don't you know how Mickey is? He's my brother and I love him," which was true and worth a curse in itself, "but he can't make up his mind about anything. He's pro and con the world, which includes himself." And that was also true. She remembered what Mickey had said, that he could use a few thousand bucks, couldn't she? Well, who couldn't use a few thousand bucks? Gerald, she thought. Apparently, Gerald had all the money he needed. But Gerald kept his distance, bided his time, then, come summer, paid his respects. Gerald, who made you come to him. Well, everybody went to California once in their lives. It was the one geographical truism in the land.

"Gerald," she said.

"What about him?" her father said.

"If we're looking for sound advice." Then she added, aware she was flailing about and coming back empty each time, "But by the time summer rolls around, there'll be wells up and down this valley, and then what good will he do us?"

"Jen," her father said.

"I know," she said.

"I'll talk to Ray. Even if we have to divide the land, I'll keep the house. It'll be here for your kids and grandkids."

"That wasn't the idea."

"Well, you know"—her long-legged father sat up on the sofa, hands on his knees, feet squarely on the floor—"you have to consider what Mother meant in her will. Whatever it was, Dad would have seconded it in a flash. But they never did anything in a flash. I'm sure they talked it over." At this point her father looked over at Charlie, the outsider, including him. "Jane and Arthur Joyner, who made it their mission in life to keep the peace, maybe to a fault, I don't know, that's for somebody else to decide. It's safe to say they never thought about natural gas. I know they liked the whole idea behind land trusts and nature conservancy, and maybe that's what they'd want me to do. Dad had seen some horrible things during the war, and not just what human beings did to each other. To the land and the forests and the rivers. Absolutely everything was defiled." Frank drew a long breath. He seemed tired. Jen heard a shudder under his voice. "I'll have to talk to Ray."

Jen found herself not looking at her father or at Charlie, whom she'd carelessly involved in all this, but at her son, already halfway to war. He stood in the doorway because he didn't belong in this room, but what went on in this room would determine where he did belong, and it hurt his mother deeply that it had to be this way. In that moment she saw no avenue of escape for her fearless and fatherless little boy.

6

A week before Christmas, when Frank called, Ray Whittaker was out of town. His son, Ray Jr., did not offer to say where his father had gone, and Frank did not insist. In the meantime, Ray Jr. was taking up the slack. He chuckled when he said this, affecting a weary willingness to indulge his father yet again, and Frank wished him a merry Christmas and said he'd wait. The next day a fresh snow fell, always a lift to Frank's spirits, the illusion of a fresh start, an untracked world when he ventured out into it the next afternoon, untracked except for the animals, of course, but they were part of the freshness and their tracks counted as such.

The day after that, when the Assembly was out of session, the governor of the state issued an executive order ending the moratorium against natural gas drilling, specifically horizontal, hydrofracturing gas drilling, and, in effect, invited the gas companies to go to work. The reasons he cited were understood by all and didn't need to be stated again, but, true to his nature, the governor spoke at length about the financial woes of the state, the chronic unemployment, the soaring property taxes, the woefully underfunded schools, the crumbling in-frastructure (the previous year a bridge on the interstate had given way, killing four), the increasingly strapped heath insurance program, and the list went on. Simply the way towns, once the bedrock of the state, were turning into their ghosts, the sadness and the disbelief there to be seen in the townspeople's faces. As opposed to the near future, when a plentiful and clean and beholden-to-nobody fuel would course through the pipelines of the state, and the skies, blackened by so much coal and oil exhaust, would clear.

The following day the governor issued a clarification: yes, within certain yet-to-be-specified bounds, state parks and forests were also open to gas exploration. "Sensitive habitats" (stream banks, wetlands, steep slopes, rare communities, etc.) would have to be redefined. Frank thought of the various parks where he and his family had gone for their picnics. There were sensitive habitats everywhere you looked. He tried to imagine it all with the storage tanks, the trucks, and the derricks in place. He understood when the drilling was done, the tanks, trucks, and derricks would be gone, and in their place no more than a spigot-size wellhead, a minitank or two, and a metering unit would be left.

The next day Frank received a call from a conservationist he knew, who was a member of the group determined to keep drilling out of the state lands, and who remembered Frank's insight in the town paper (he identified it as an "insight," not a quip) about isostatic balance. Would Frank come to an emergency meeting the group was holding that night and talk about that? Frank held him off and asked to be kept posted.

He had forgotten the boy's name—it was Timmy O'Donnell—but the next morning, five days before Christmas, the nation awoke to the news that Timmy O'Donnell had suddenly died from a brain seizure, the possibility of which the doctors had discounted when they had concluded that he had miraculously survived. Little Timmy O'Donnell had been struck down just before Thanksgiving. He had died just be-fore Christmas. Once again the news teams were out, and once again the question, still unanswered, was what price were we willing to pay?

Frank turned the radio off. As he made his grandson's breakfast (down those stairs, into that kitchen), he couldn't help but wonder what if it had been Danny and not Timmy O'Donnell walking down the road. What price? Of course, if you studied history, present-day generations were always being sacrificed so that future generations could survive. He himself had been a baby boomer, and all that meant was that his father, with those fields and forests of corpses fresh in his mind, had done his procreative duty in repopulating the planet, having himself been spared. Timmy O'Donnell died so that Danny's children could drive their cars, heat their homes, go soaring off on their vacations, have their life spans prolonged.

Jen called. How was her father going to break the news to Danny about that poor little boy? She thought she should. That wasn't something her father should have to do. Maybe after he'd eaten his breakfast.

Danny came down and ate breakfast with an enormous appetite. Frank made more pancakes, and because he'd been thinking of soldiers and wars, thought of what soldiers, laden with their arms and ammunition, were famously said to do: carry their rations in their stomachs. He told Danny nothing, but observed him closely, the man's bones in the boy's face and the working of the jaw. Danny's eyes had a way of seizing on something—in this case, his food—until it was consumed. Then the eyes, never idle, looked for something else. Gerald had been steady-eyed, but none of Frank's children had gone quite so avidly after the things of this world.

Frank thought of Mickey. The phone rang again. This was Helen, who apparently had not heard about Timmy O'Donnell, but then, Frank remembered, she had not heard of Timmy earlier when he'd been just a boy with his dog. She was calling to tell him that her daughter, Cindy, had no intention of visiting her mother for Christmas, so Helen was being forced to go up there. Blackmailed, Frank thought, but didn't say it. He said, When? Helen told him the next day, and he asked her to have dinner with him that night.

The statistics he'd heard, it seemed, all his life. There was no way to sort them out and, hence, no way to calculate their significance. Nor would the numbers stay in his head. How many children died from lack of clean water to drink every day? How many from crushing child labor? How many were born with AIDS? How many were conscripted into armies? How many were kidnapped and forced into prostitution? How many had their innocence strangled out of them at birth? He remembered the day Jen had appeared with Danny, a day of shattering midsummer light. It had been Marge who'd picked Danny up and held him before her, eye to eye. And Marge who'd asked in the most forgone way, prepared to hear anything, What do we know about the father?

He thought of Mickey. No family, no parents, as far as Frank knew no girlfriend to keep him company, and if there were neighbors his son could reach out to, his father didn't know about them either. One fewer boy, Timmy O'Donnell, in Mickey's part of the world, and in that boy's absence, news teams with their cameras and cruising news vans to compete with the trucks on those country roads. And under it all, those tunneling drill bits, spewing chemicals, water, and sand into every crack they could find and releasing anything down there to find its way up into your life. You could turn on your faucet and welcome it with a match. He, too, had seen the watery, methane-blue flame and had thought, It may kill them, but at least those people will have had that moment of beauty in their lives. He was reminded of the instant the blood had appeared at his wrist, and he'd known that the cost of such beauty-worship would be his death. His grandson finished his pancakes and began to look around for what was next, but Frank Joyner in that moment ached for his younger son. He had never been in Mickey's town, nor his house, nor the room where he slept. He did not know, when his son woke, what he would see. Frank had spent his whole professional life thinking about the spaces people chose to occupy, and the ways they shaped those spaces, and the evocations those shapes gave rise to, without once having devoted himself to the case of his son, the ways in which Mickey chose to enclose himself. For every well-housed person there were so many transients. There was a ratio. There was a logic.

Mickey was not alone. He now lived on the second floor of what had been a large sandstone mansion, built by a magnate of blue-slate mining before gas drilling had caught on in that part of the world, and his bedroom window looked into the limbs of a beech tree, not so inspirational as the soaring silver maple, but of a sturdier, burlier wood. The woman there beside him in his bed taught Spanish in his school. She'd been raised in the Bronx. He didn't know if her Spanish was flawless, but certainly it was good enough for the school in which they taught, as his command of American history was. They had everything in common—age, civil status, professional frustrations, various students—except that Fina, short for Josefina, had Latin blood. She lived on the third floor of the same house. One evening after school they'd drunk a bottle of red wine together and revealed to themselves how much they shared and concluded they should pool their resources, such as they were. There was no question of their occupying the same apartment, but they would spend the occasional night together, and if the wine they drank didn't make them angry at certain people or twists from their pasts, they would make love. It was lovemaking in the spirit of default, which they both understood, but which, happily, allowed for some tenderness.

When Mickey opened his eyes on the morning of Timmy O'Donnell's death, he saw the ceiling of his high-ceilinged room, with its molded cornice and its medallion out of which a nonfunctioning brass lamp hung, and he made out, past the beech branches, patches of a watery-blue sky that was about to cloud over. That was the room Mickey was housed in, and on this morning Fina was the company he kept. As his father had done, Mickey rose first, went to the kitchen to make coffee and think about breakfast, and, also like his father, turned on the radio there, although at a lower volume, and learned that little Timmy O'Donnell had surprised his doctors and the rest of the country, which had begun to forget about him, and died.

A buzzer sounded to tell him the coffee was made. He took a mug to Fina and gave her the news.

She rolled back over. Then she sat up angrily, swept back her black hair, and accepted the mug. The news media would be here with Christmas bells on this time. She didn't know about Mickey, but she was getting out of there today. A more wishful man might have read that as an invitation to join her, but the light in her dark eyes had a stony cast, and the curses she muttered under her breath were not in his language.

The last number he had called on his phone belonged to his father. Out on one of his walks, his father had not answered. Fina gathered her things, threw on a robe, and found it in her to offer her colleague and co-sufferer a parting kiss and merry Christmas, and Mickey sat down to his desk with the phone in hand. The desk he had carried with him from town to town, living quarters to living quarters. It was the one thing he had. It was unremarkable except for a single broad and deep drawer where he could store anything of significance in his life. He'd bought it out of a barn at an estate sale when he was still a graduate student. His father had never seen it. If Frank Joyner tried to imagine where his son sat as he talked to him on the phone, he would fail.

Mickey told his father he would be coming home for Christmas. To look for him Christmas Eve night. He asked after Danny. Danny, of course, gave them Timmy O'Donnell, and Timmy O'Donnell, in his youth and the passions he aroused, was both a Christ child and a martyred Christ on the cross, although neither mentioned anything as dramatic as that. Yes, Mickey had heard what the governor of his father's state had done, and, no, he couldn't imagine the turmoil that was about to ensue. Although he could.

He hung up the phone, settled his breathing, then opened his desk and, reaching into the back left corner, took out a set of keys. He packed a bag, ate something later on, then waited until dusk and drove the three hours to his father's town, which he acknowledged had also been his, arriving just after nine. There was a back stairway up the Deweese he could use. It was narrow and unheated and had gone without fresh paint for years. He assumed it had once been used by janitorial staff or by teachers and principals hoping to sneak up on misbehaving students. He and his sister had known about it; Gerald had, too, but he did not remember Gerald ever having to sneak up on anyone. As Mickey ascended those four flights, he didn't see a soul. His sister lived on the third floor, his father's friend, Helen, on the second, but he made it unobserved all the way to the fourth, then used the keys he'd had made before returning his sister's set, opened the dead-bolt lock, and entered the apartment, the house, the castle keep, call it what you will, where he'd been raised as a boy. He did not turn on any lights. The streetlights were well down below, and the sky was overcast, so he couldn't rely on the moon, but he found his way into the long hall that had once provided passage to twelfth graders, he'd been told, and at the end of which was his old room. Because Frank had insisted on moving them all into this resurrected school, his younger son had been deprived of the great out-of-doors, but if there was any single space where he'd run as a boy, this was it, down this hall to the sanctuary of his room. He treaded lightly as a ghost now, not wanting to wake anybody who might be sleeping below.

He stayed there for three days and nights, venturing out only late the next night when he could drive to a supermarket open twenty-four hours a day and buy essentials. On the way out to the Coldwell house on Christmas Eve, he realized he'd forgotten to bring gifts, so he drove to the shopping mall and bought a heavy woolen shirt for his father for his walks in the woods, a sweater for his sister, and for Danny a book by the self-proclaimed foremost skateboard authority in the world. On the front cover was a photograph of the author at least ten feet above the release point of a ramp with a skateboard seemingly glued to his feet. The expression on his face was fiercely concentrated and entirely turned in, as if he had been caught in the act of inflicting some triumphant violence on himself. Mickey had left the mall when he remembered his mother and went back in search of a particular jewel he saw in his mind's eye. He'd visualized his mother staring at such a jewel, hypnotized by the light breaking inwardly along its gleaming facets; he imagined her captured and held. He didn't find it, settling for a necklace of rugged amber beads instead.

On Christmas morning the family lit a fire and gathered around the tree, a bushy white pine Frank and his grandson had cut in the woods from an area where the pines needed to be thinned. They exchanged gifts. The skateboard book was an immediate hit, which they all marveled over, unable to believe such gravity-defying acrobatics were real. The astrakhan cap Jen gave her brother she claimed went with his beard. Mickey said, whether she believed it or not, he'd go days without remembering he had one. Frank wore the shirt his son gave him over a faded red-and-green plaid one for the rest of the day. Frank gave various little gifts to Danny, as Jen did, but the one he singled out was a geology book and accompanying video, with a chapter devoted to the last ice age and the glaciers and the formation of the gorges, and even though it was written for young readers, it contained information that Frank had not had available to him when he'd studied geology in college. Plate tectonics, for one thing. To his children, he gave each a hundred-dollar bill, confessing he never knew what to get them they'd want, it wasn't a knack he had, and for just a moment someone was missing, their mother, of course, and Frank's ex-wife, who knew what her children wanted and needed and could sometimes be said to corner them with her gifts.

The phone rang. This was Gerald, up early in Southern California, with the sun breaking over the hills and out over the ocean, heralding a great day. They were to get on Skype. That had been Gerald's gift the previous summer. He had brought his father a laptop computer and taught him how to access that one program, if nothing else. At the time, with Gerald and his family before them in the flesh, it had seemed like an extravagant and superfluous gift. Now it was a necessity. It was Gerald's way of being here and not being here. It was Gerald's nonstrenuous way of straddling a continent.

Frank brought the computer down and the family saw their son and brother and uncle, his wondrously tanned wife, and their two healthy and well-behaved daughters. Then Gerald walked his laptop out to his deck and showed them the ocean in the early-morning light, too radiant for their unaccustomed eyes. He panned over the garden, all the flowers in full bloom. The pool, in a deep sapphire shadow. Butterflies flew by. They heard a jubilant racket of birds. He asked his father to take his computer to the glass deck doors and show them a view that Gerald's wife and kids, at least, only knew in full summer. The sky was overcast, with drifting flakes of snow. The snow on the deck was four days old and looked it. The day was gray; they hadn't realized how gray until they showed it to their branch of the family in Southern California. They each took a turn in front of the camera, Mickey in the cap his sister had given him and his scraggly beard getting the biggest reaction. After they'd exchanged greetings and taken turns at filling the screen, Gerald said how sorry he was to hear that that little boy hadn't made it, and for just a moment no one knew what little boy he meant. Then Frank agreed, it was terribly sad, and added that Gerald and his family were better off out there in a world that hadn't gone drilling mad— except just how much better off could they be, Mickey wondered, a fire, a flood, a landslide, an earthquake away from oblivion?

Jen, Mickey, and Danny left in Jen's car. Something about her brother's driving set Jen on edge. To call Mickey a careless driver didn't come close. It was as if he didn't have a destination in mind, didn't believe in them, in fact. You don't get it, do you? she said. I guess not, Mickey replied. What are we talking about? A presentiment, she said. She was talking about a presentiment, brought on most probably by that little boy's death, which she didn't want to talk about openly, although Danny already knew. I've got this feeling that something is going to happen, and we're not ready for it.

She sat through her brother's silence, ten, fifteen seconds. Then she voiced her disbelief. You really don't know what I'm talking about? You don't feel anything? Like things ganging up, forces at work . . . A deer ran across the road in front of them in that moment, which she managed to avoid. How she forgot what any driver in that part of the country knew to a certainty and her brother somehow remembered was beyond her. There was always a second deer, frequently a third. Mickey shouted, Jen! and she braked just in time to avoid the second. The third turned back around. The afterimage of their leaping bounds was clear to her, very clear. She took deep breaths, both hands squarely on the wheel, then accused her brother of playing dumb.

Meanwhile, her father brought up an armful of wood and went back to sitting in front of the fire. He was still there when Helen called. She wouldn't complain about her daughter's possessiveness and disapproval of the life Helen seemed determined to lead, and didn't, sympathizing instead with Frank and his attempt to hold the broken pieces of a family together, especially his devotion to his grandson. They wished each other a merry Christmas and then, practically in unison, wished that the other were there. Frank remembered, of course, when Helen had appeared like a snow angel out of the night to minister to both of their needs. He said, When you come back, I'll see if I can leave Danny with his mother and you and I can . . . And he paused to see if she would complete his thought. Helen said, Get away for a few days? Now, there's an idea, Frank replied, and laughed, his first quietly joyous—seasonal—laugh of the day.

Then nothing happened. The twenty-sixth, the day of returns in all the stores, the day-after day of bargains, didn't affect him in the least. His grandson came back. He practiced his skateboard and listened to his music and read his sorcery books and began to read the book that Frank had given him about the earth he stood on. The video contained a section on the advance and retreat of the glaciers, the formation of these gently shelving valleys, the gorges, the glacially deep lakes, but mostly computer generated, the glossy fakery of which Frank resisted. One day in that week between Christmas and New Year's, he

drove his grandson to the highest waterfall in the area, not so that
Danny could see the horse's-tail fall itself, but so that he could see, in
concrete actuality, the enormous, rounded-out basin, the plunge pool,
and so that he would know that once enough water had flowed over
those falls to create that great hemispheric shape in the rock. That was
an astonishment beyond the range of computers.

Ray Whittaker called Frank on New Year's Eve, not yet officially
back in his office but back from his vacation in Maui, and Frank was
asked to imagine him tanned and overfed with a head full of balmy
thoughts. Frank said what he had to talk about could wait till Ray came
down to earth. New Year's everything in town was closed except Ray
Whittaker's office. Frank could find him there. Ray was indeed tan, no
more plump than normal, and since he had always been a man of enormous energy, it was hard to tell whether he was rested or not. The boy
Ray Whittaker had been when he and Frank were students in the Deweese was still alive in the bird-quick movements of his eyes, the mobile mouth, the way he brightened to an idea. He'd never lost his smart
kid's strut.

They reasoned it through, and Whittaker said if the county or any
township tried to stop the drilling now, the lawsuits on the part of
both the gas companies and the property owners who had leased their
land would pile up like plowed snowbanks that didn't melt till June.
Townships that tried to pass some zoning ordinances, something to do
with excessive noise, for instance, or all that truck traffic, would have
to make them retroactive to before the leases were signed, and that
wouldn't fly. And why would the county or the towns want to do that,
anyway? Drill a well on your property and your Clean and Green tax
rate goes from 6 percent to 35 percent, and that might well be 35 percent on all the acreage, not just the well site, since those hydrofracking
drill bits seemed to go everywhere. Figure out what that does for the
tax base of the town and county, not to speak of the state. Who's going
to pull the plug? Contamination of the aquifers, wetlands, streams, the
lake? Prove it. Thanks to the Bush administration, the Safe Drinking

Water Act of 2005 exempted the gas drillers, and if they aren't forced to tell you what they're pumping down there, how can they be held accountable if certain contaminating chemicals show up in your well water? Amend the Safe Drinking Water Act? Why, that would mean the U.S. government would be playing right into the hands of those oil-filthy Arabs, and no one is going to get reelected doing that. So you've got Washington, every statehouse in the country, every county seat and town clerk's office in every township lined up against you, and who are you? Just so Frank knew. And Ray Whittaker wasn't even a gas-lease attorney. He was just using a lawyer's common sense.

"So who *are* you, Frank?"

"If anyone in town knows that, you should, Ray."

"And you want my advice?"

"Give me my options, first."

"Just how retired do you want to be?"

"What are you suggesting?"

"You could run for public office."

"And?"

"Make it your cause. See how many votes you get."

"Ray."

"I'm not a cynic, you know."

"You've always had a streak. You used to like to shock people so you could sneak in and get what you wanted before they came to their senses."

"We got the Deweese, didn't we? We teamed up to do that."

"And I never thought we ceased to be a team. That's why I'm sitting here and not—"

"What? Watching football games? You never liked football, Frank. No contact sports."

"Wilson Michaels?"

"I took the liberty of investigating a little. Definitely a contact-sports type. It seems to amuse him. He may be slowing down a step or two, though."

"Conklin's leased the land all around me. It looks like TransAtlantic wants to lease mine, and it looks like Michaels is teaming up with them. Can they do that?"

"Team up?"

"Can TransAtlantic come in and lease what Conklin doesn't get?"

"Are you asking if these gas companies have something like spheres of influence marked out that they will actually honor? My turf's over here, your turf's over there?"

"Do they?"

"I wouldn't think so, Frank."

"Is it worth the fight, Ray? I've got my sisters teamed up against me, not to speak of Marjorie. I'm not even sure of my own children. I've got gas wells set to be drilled up and down the valley, and there I sit. I'm a sitting duck for compulsory integration."

"What's that?"

"You don't know?"

"I told you I'm not a gas-lease attorney, Frank."

"But you were always the smartest kid in the class. Or the one who could outbullshit the teachers."

"They bought it. It's what they graded on back then. Compulsory integration?"

"Something my son told me about."

"Which son?"

"Mickey."

"Frank, you know I love all you Joyners. But if you'd said Gerald . . ."

"What, Ray? I'm going to ask you to complete that thought."

". . . I would have taken the time to look it up."

"Meaning?"

"Your youngest marches to the beat of a different drummer, Frank."

"Who said that, Ray?"

"If I'm not mistaken, Henry David Thoreau. *Walden?* Miss Dickinson? You were there, too."

PART THREE

LEAVES TO THE TREES

7

W HAT KENNY BREWSTER COULD NEVER GET HIS MIND AROUND, NOT entirely, was that a man would give his son his own name and then within two years abandon him—not unless that man had detected in his son something that amounted to a fatal flaw. Kenny didn't know his father's last name—it wasn't Brewster, that was Kenny's mother's—or where he'd gone when he'd run off. He and his mother lived in the Arkansas half of Texarkana, and he supposed his father had gone to Texas since when men wanted to disappear, that was where they did it. The only things Kenny knew about his father were that he hadn't come from thereabouts and that, when he'd left, Kenny was two. And the fact that he'd insisted on giving his son his name, which Kenny understood from the start had been his mother's way of telling him what an irremediable son of a bitch his father was. His mother had worked herself raw when Kenny was growing up, then, when he was abroad in the navy, in Rota, Spain, she married a man from St. Louis and went to live there, so that when Kenny returned home, the only person waiting for him was a girl he barely remembered, a year behind

him in high school, named Gloria, Glorie to her friends. She'd had some
time-marking romances, she admitted, but she assumed that navy men
had their share, too. Was she sure she had the right man? After high
school Kenny had even gone a year and a half to the local community
college, and he had absolutely no memory of her during that time.
Memory was funny, she said. One day, even one minute, could be
clearer and longer lasting than things you did for years and years. He
assumed it was a game, but at least when he came home after that time
abroad, he had somebody to play with.

Growing up, he'd had only one man in his life. That was his grandfather, his mother's father (his father's forebears had, of course, been
wiped off the slate of existence). He lived in the town of Magnolia,
some eighty miles away. He was a distinguished gentleman, honored by
every civic organization in town, who, if Kenny's mother had been less
angry and proud, would have been gracious enough to take her back
in. In which case, Kenny would have seen his grandfather daily and
not three or four times a year. He was fine-featured with elegant gray
hair and small, never-rushed hands that had his grandson hypnotized.
He had a cool, shadowy study, with a large desk and beside the desk a
small, round table, and it was over that table that he and his grandson
conversed. Since they saw each other so infrequently, Kenny seemed to
remember everything his grandfather said, and how the hands sized
up the significance of it all, the final shape they took. On the way back
home he'd tell his mother about these conversations, but his mother
wasn't interested. She knew all about his grandfather's pearls of wisdom. She knew all about those infallible hands.

The last time Kenny sat across that table from his grandfather, he
was a teenager, with all the wildness and doubts and shipwrecked cer-
tainties peculiar to that age alive in his head. In school they'd been
studying the civil rights movement and addressing some of the atrocities attributed to the Ku Klux Klan, and he asked his grandfather if
he'd ever known anyone who'd belonged to that infamous organization. Kenny asked the question as if he were now man enough to har-

bor such information if his grandfather chose to pass it along, and his grandfather looked at him and smiled, his hands at rest—at peace—on the table. In the most even-toned voice his grandson had ever heard come out of his grandfather's mouth, he said, I belonged to the Klan, Kenny. I no longer do because there is no longer as urgent a need. But if the need arose . . . And his voice hung there, unquivering, to put his grandson to the test. Was Kenny man enough, now, to look a thing unquiveringly in the eye?

Kenny bent forward, sure he hadn't heard right. But one look at his grandfather's untroubled hands told him he had. He'd always called his grandfather "Granddad," but this time he said, "Sir, I don't understand." And his grandfather gave him a brief history lesson. The oil boom in the late thirties, the war years, and the years after the war with all the soldiers, both black and white, flooding back into town. After seeing what they'd seen and doing what they'd done in Europe and the Pacific. Order had to be restored in the town, and the only organization capable of doing that was the Klan. "But, sir . . ." And his grandfather told him that without order nothing was possible, all civil discourse failed. In the military they had a term. *Exemplary punishment.* Punishment that set an example and punishment that was carried out in an exemplary, that is, flawless, way. Order was restored. The town survived. As a result, Kenny and his grandfather were sitting there quietly conversing on that very day.

When Kenny joined the navy at the age of twenty, it was to put an ocean between himself and all that he'd been. When he returned, he told Glorie about his mother, his absconding father, he even told her about his distinguished grandfather, who in the name of order had marched with the Klan, and nothing dissuaded her. Yes, he, too, had had "romances" (although they were hardly that), and she said, great, they'd start from scratch.

His mother came down from St. Louis for the wedding, bringing her new husband, a big man who had been a trucker but now owned part of a fleet. He had few words to spare and stood off on the sidelines

like a deeply dissatisfied coach at a high school game. Kenny's grandfather was dead. His new parents-in-law were as perplexed as he was
but used, it seemed, to their daughter's sudden attachments and her
willingness to keep her word. Kenny and Glorie swore their vows.
They had what was left of Kenny's mustering-out pay for a honey-
moon, plus the sum his stepfather had budgeted for his gift. They went
to New Orleans for a week, and each time he made love to his wife he
felt as if he were leaving a debt of gratitude at her feet. She kept prodding him, with a needling voice at his ear, You see? You see? And although he didn't—he would never know how she'd done it—he said
that he did.

They returned to Texarkana, Glorie to her job in the Youth Bu-
reau, where she helped get kids off the street and into programs of
various sorts, and Kenny found work selling cars. They rented a two-
bedroom apartment in a leafy complex on the edge of town. They
considered buying a house. When Glorie began to talk of children as
more than just a future goal, Kenny experienced a muscle-tightening
and a hot-cold freezing sensation. It took him a while, but he came to
understand that none of it meant anything unless they took this step,
too. They tried. They both ended up going to doctors to make sure
they could, and then they tried again. They got informed. They practiced fertility charting. They learned about the right vitamins and de-
toxifying liquids to take. Tired eggs, they heard. Poorly swimming
sperm. In vitro fertilization was mentioned as a distant recourse, then
a not-so-distant one. Kenny took a step back. He wanted a child so
that he could stand by him as his father had not stood by him? Was
that it? As his mother, for all her tireless and thankless effort, had
gone off and left him? As his grandfather, in a voice he could still hear,
its tone as even as if he were reporting the time of day, said, I belonged
to the Klan, Kenny?

At work he had not taken a vow to not do what he did, but it
amounted to that. A friend from high school came in looking for a used
car, came to his old friend Kenny Brewster for some inside advice and a

haggle-free sale. He had his eye on a little Civic out in the lot, and Kenny, employing one trick after another, kept him there at his desk for two hours, well past the time it made any salesman's sense to work a customer. But it was as if the very notion of friendship had become alien to his state of mind, and before it was over, he'd signaled to a fellow salesman to employ the ultimate trick and make what they'd dubbed the tag-team call, pretending to be a prospective buyer who was coming in half an hour later to drive that Civic off the lot. Then fifteen minutes later. Then ten, until this high school friend, who called Kenny, affectionately, Rooster, caved under the pressure and paid the price. For those two hours of phony camaraderie and betrayal, Kenny'd made himself perhaps a hundred bucks. He went home and they talked about it. His wife put it to him that he hated his job, he wasn't making that much anyway, and between the two of them she wasn't getting any more pregnant, was she? She'd heard that over in the Fort Worth area they were hiring all able-bodied men to work on the new natural gas drilling rigs, and paying good money, twenty-two dollars an hour, it was said. That was a lot more than he was making selling cars, and she hadn't married a disabled man, had she? When her husband pulled a long face, Glorie said, Jesus, Kenny, you don't have to go over there and get a gas well pregnant. Just get the stuff out of the ground. I'll be waiting. I was before, wasn't I?

Texas was where men went when they didn't want to come back, when they didn't know what they wanted except to get out of town. But he took his wife's advice and drove to Fort Worth. He had never been that far into Texas before. The land was brown, the patches of scrub-oak forest a dusky green; it rolled on and on under a hazy sky with some cattle grazing around, until he began to see areas of an alkaline white where the ground had been graded level, on which gas tanks and long, rectangular storage tanks and some derricks stood. Connecting these leveled sites were narrow corridors where the earth had been turned and under which pipelines ran. For every six or seven drilling sites, he seemed to drive by a fenced-in area with several identical tanks in a row and a hard, compact curling of pipe, and these, he'd be told, were the compressor stations. He never entered Fort Worth. More than one gas company was hiring, but the one he chose was called TransAtlantic, and he chose it because he had actually been transatlantic, he knew what it was like to cross that ocean, and he considered it a good omen. Twenty-two dollars an hour was, indeed, the starting wage, but there was as much work as there was land, and overtime could take it higher. He knew some Spanish, good, since half the workers came from south of the border. He was a navy man, he'd handled cargo; even better, there was room for advancement. And he was ready to go, that very day, no time to be sitting around. He got outfitted, hard-hatted, and given a pep talk on the run about hydrofracturing for natural gas in the Barnett Shale deposit a mile below their feet. Then he was driven out to a rig a worker short on the drill floor, where he became a member of a drill rig team.

But before the shale was hydrofracked and the gas brought up, he and his team had already moved on to drill another hole. He took it on faith that the gas was brought up and that these holes were not drilled in vain. The plain—the prairie—on which they worked was limitless, and another way to ask the question was how many holes did each man have in him. There were seven of them, one in harness up on the work platform, four on the floor, one, the driller, at the control board, the seventh, the foreman, troubleshooting all around. And, of course, the men on the ground—they were in and out in their water trucks, pipe trucks, sand trucks, trucks containing chemicals whose contents were not disclosed, men in graders and bulldozers and backhoes preparing the ground for additional wells, men working the generator, men mucking in the impoundment ponds, men moving equipment from one part of the pad to another with no apparent purpose in mind, men with pens in their pockets and clipboards in their hands and a checklist of things to accomplish going in and out of trailers, from site to site. But where the hole was being drilled there were only those seven, and when the hole reached down and took its swerving turn toward the bed of shale, they got into their trucks and, traveling light, drove to the next derrick waiting to be manned. Derrickmen, they were called. Roughnecks.

Kenny was not the runt of the litter. There was a shorter, skinnier man than he was, and a couple of men were taller but more loosely limbed. The two Tex-Mex workers were heavyset, and the foreman was big and round, too big for the cramped space on the drilling floor, with a shaved head and goggle-thick glasses. Kenny was the new-comer, the man who had yet to pit himself against thirty-foot lengths of steel pipe and huge wrenching clamps called tongs, which swung loose over the borehole unless they were kept fastened and were used to loosen and tighten the lengths of pipe, as were heavy-duty chains, which the Tex-Mex workers swung as freely as if they were lassos. Combined lengths of pipe were called a drill string. When they needed to change the bit, they had to remove the pipe, flush out the drilling fluid—the mud, they called it—separate the rocky debris, and release what they couldn't reuse into the impoundment pond. All this was known as tripping pipe, and the man in harness up on the work plat-form got the worst of it. He had to rack the rinsed lengths of pipe up the mast of the derrick until they could be sent down again, and he couldn't get behind. Once the pipe had been extracted and racked and the worn bit retrieved, the crew reversed the process. With the tongs, the workers on the floor wrenched the drill strings in tight and kicked the restraining collar at the entrance to the borehole loose with their feet. The pipe began its spinning descent.

The drill bit looked like a small torpedo, its nose a helix of ridges and steeply carved hollows. They kept the pipe hosed and tried to hose the clayey-slick mud off the drilling floor. In the heat of the day they hosed themselves. As the pipe descended, it made a loose, clattering din, which, at first, reminded Kenny of the sound his bike had made when the chain had come loose from its sprocket and begun to clash with the spokes of the wheel. Then the sound went beyond any boyhood association and became the strangely futile clamor of some elemental transgression—except that it worked. When the bit hit rock, the whole derrick began to shake, but the bit continued to bore down. The smells he'd smelled all his life—the smell of the clay, the staleness of steel, the diesel fumes from the generator, the sweat stink of the men. A clean gust of air from the prairie, when it came, was a reminder that all this drilling would eventually end. It was the sound, that shattering-loose pounding into the center of the earth, that was new to him, and, minute by minute, a contest whose outcome was always in doubt. Except they never failed to drill their hole, not once. No rock was that hard. When they reached the shale, the drill pipe made its turn toward the horizontal and ran out for another five thousand feet. The casing in that horizontal hole was perforated, and then, under extremely high pressure, slickwater and sand would be shot into the shale cracks and the gas would be released. But by that point they'd done what they'd had to do and been driven on to the next derrick awaiting its men.

That was vast, open country north of Fort Worth, but the pads on which the derricks were erected could be anywhere. The first pads seemed to have been located along highways, but with the ground so level, connecting roads could quickly be built so that one pad gave way to the next the farther you went back into the prairie. To return to their sleeping quarters at night, they'd have to retrace their steps from pad to pad. They saw wells when they were being fracked, when as many as five million gallons of water and fracking fluid per well had to be trucked in, and they saw the wells when they were finished, the wellheads no more than chest high and looking like spigots you might walk up to in a park and turn on. They called these finished sites Christmas trees, for reasons Kenny never understood, except that the wellheads might be likened to small trees, and their pressure gauges and control valves to ornaments, and if Santa Claus had been there, he'd certainly left riches. Once the final trucks had rolled away, everything was landscaped back green.

He began to take pride in what he did. The before, during, and after became a story that made it all make sense. Being a roughneck did not make him feel more like a man, but all this drilling down into a shale bed that 350 million years earlier had been an ocean floor, until the continent had shifted and buried it, gave him a sort of progenitorial thrill. Bringing the distant past up into the present and giving it fresh life was what it amounted to, and they seemed to be getting it done again and again. As far as he knew, they had drilled no dry wells.

In the late summer, they found themselves drilling in a field behind two rows of homes. The pad they drilled on was tucked into the L-shaped angle the rows formed. He knew enough now to know that when the hydrofracking was done, the drill pipe would pass under some of those homes, and if, as was usually the case, multiple wells were drilled on this pad, drill pipe might pass like the spokes of a wagon wheel under all of them. How much these homeowners would be paid in compensation he didn't know, but something, he assumed. That day would come, sooner, he was sure, than any of these homeowners believed. For a couple of days he took his turn up on the work platform, responsible primarily for shifting the pipes into their vertical racks and then, with the bit changed, for sending them back down in the borehole. Once the drilling resumed, he had time on his hands, nowhere to sit but, strapped in a safety harness, a sort of grilled runway, called the monkeyboard, to move up and down on, as he waited until the moment came to rack another string of pipe. He liked it up there, and he didn't. It wasn't really dangerous, as long as he didn't step out of his harness, as some fellow workers did, and the views could be uplifting, strangely reassuring, but it was lonely, and when the wind began to blow, or, worse yet, when the bit hit rock and the whole derrick began to shake, he found himself holding on to the rail and wondering just how much shaking a hastily erected derrick could take. But he had time to gaze, and time to think, and he was thinking of his wife and gazing out over those nearby homes when he saw a woman sunbathing beside her backyard pool. She had a drink beside her and a book she'd put down. She seemed to spend her time gazing up at the derrick looming over her, the distance too far to make out the expression on her face, but close, less than a hundred yards. He kept waiting for her to take off the top of her bikini and sunbathe bare-breasted, but she didn't oblige him. Her body, what he could see of it, was almost defiantly tanned.

When he was down on the rig floor, he was still high enough up to see through the derrick's struts that the woman continued to spend most of the day out by her pool. He wasn't looking at her when he got hurt—it could have happened to anybody. Workers frequently slipped on that clay-greased floor. The foreman himself had fallen with a thud that had almost brought down the derrick. The fault probably lay with the two Mexican workers, Pedro and Jesus, who were trying to see if they could break the drill team's previous record in adding pipe. There seemed to have been some sort of a bet. They raced, someone left that clamping wrench called the tong unfastened, and as they were feeding in a fresh length, the tong swung free and knocked Kenny a couple of paces to the side. As he tried to right himself, he slipped on the rig floor and fell, landing hard on his left hip. The time it took for him to get back to his feet and on the job was just enough to mean that the old record continued to stand. The clanging of the pipe as it went down drowned out the Mexicans' curses. A lot of *chingar, chingar* was all Kenny heard. The pain didn't hit him till the next morning. He did the hosing for that day and the next, which he could have done with one eye on the mud-smeared pipe and the other on the sunbathing woman, if he'd wanted to. Only she was no longer even pretending to sunbathe. She had cranked her chaise lounge up to a sitting position and was staring directly at the rig, fueling herself, it seemed, with whatever she was drinking.

When she began her charge across her backyard and out onto the field, Kenny was still working the hose, although he felt considerably better. The woman took powerful strides but couldn't hold to a straight line, and he assumed the drink had taken its toll. They had at least ten minutes before they'd have to add more pipe, and Kenny found himself climbing down off the rig, skirting the impoundment pond with its vinyl liner and black-settled scum, passing between two tank trucks with their snarls of pipe, and breaking into the open just before the woman reached the pad. They stood in a field of sun-browned grass, Kenny in his hard hat, sodden T-shirt, muddied jeans and boots, and she in the thinnest of bikinis and sandals with sequined straps. He guessed her age at midthirties. Her eyes were puffed from the drink and squinting in the sun. Marching out here so suddenly, she'd left her sunglasses behind. He smelled the coconut lotion she'd covered herself with, and he smelled, in the waning heat of the day, the heat that she herself gave off, the boiler heat he remembered from the navy when they were steaming full speed ahead. She was about to explode.

He said, "It won't last much longer, two weeks or three. After that the gas will flow underground and you'll never hear it. You can heat your house and cool your house and sleep well."

She said, "Do you know what it sounds like, day after day after day? Do you have any idea? You don't. How could you? Look at yourself! You're just some poor, wet roughneck, trying to make enough to buy your next six-pack. Goddamn it all to hell!"

"What does it sound like?"

Her expression turned suddenly grief-stricken, pleading with him to unstop his ears. "It sounds like animals in pain! It sounds like a whole zoo out here, every hour of the day and night, but the animals are all in mortal pain. You don't hear it? What's the matter with you?"

He stopped. He listened. Past the pounding, under it or out on the edge, he heard pipe scraping pipe, old steel grating against old steel, and with the animal likeness in mind, the pipe sounds became yelps of pain, old, repeated moans and groans. He checked an urge to reach out and touch the woman on the bare upper arm.

"You're right," he said. "It's sad."

"Twenty-four-seven! You try listening twenty-four-seven and see how long you last!" She was screaming at him over the noise. Then he was sure she was about to cry. In a quieter, more bitter tone, as if suddenly admitting defeat, she said, "We didn't move out here for this."

Of course, he understood. Anybody standing out on that derrick, looking out over the land, and giving it a moment's thought would have. She'd moved to a subdevelopment out in the country. The developer had promised streets, neighborhoods, parks, schools, and stores. Then the natural gas boom had hit and he'd stopped development and begun to drill gas wells in all of their backyards.

Kenny told her he understood. With his voice if not his filthy hands he soothed her and stroked her cheeks and the back of her head and the round of her shoulder until she was quiet, even though the pounding continued around them and underground. He shared a vision with her. There had once been life on the floor of an ocean, not very deep, something you could have scuba dived down to and admired for its incredible beauty and abundance. Then a continent had rolled over it, and all that life was lost. An ocean was lost. He had sailed over oceans himself, and nothing was more peaceful, oceans were like long, unending afternoons. That life that had once been down there on the ocean floor was part of that peacefulness, until it had been buried and squashed and turned into rock. But now they'd found a way to retrieve it, did she understand? They were bringing it up now from where it had been hiding in the cracks of the rocks down there, as terrified as those animals she heard when they did their drilling. This was like the spirit of the life that had lived there millions and millions of years ago, and they had to go down and rescue it, that was what this was all about, that was what natural gas really was, the spirit of the life of eons past. She'd see. They called the finished wells Christmas trees because they brought life back to life, that was the gift she'd find waiting for her if she could just put up with this incredible din a little longer.

He finished his spiel, which had come on him from God knew where, only he realized he believed it, he believed in the rescuing of life, he wasn't a salesman trying to sell an old school buddy a used car, and said, "Sorry."

She stared back at him, her eyes, it seemed, trying to hold him in focus. She began to list to one side. He checked his dirty hand. But he'd been manning the hose, and his hand, except for what was caked under his fingernails and deep in the lines, was clean. He reached out with his left hand and steadied her at the right shoulder.

She said, "You're full of shit, you know. Aren't you?"

"No, I don't think so. I think I'm right."

"It's still a helluva lot of noise, isn't it?"

"It's a long way down there. That life down there's been asleep a long time. But we'll wake it up. We'll bring it up," he said, making her that promise. He realized he felt for her. She'd been a lonely sentinel sitting beside her pool, and he would champion her cause.

Then she laughed at him, a kind of incredulous but good-humored guffaw, and turned and started back across the field to her house. He stood there waiting to see if she'd make it, and she did seem to be holding to a better line. And the heat of the day seemed to have let off. Something good might come of this, he thought, even as his foreman began to bellow at him and a sharper note in the clanging of the pipe—what might be considered a yelp of pain—told him they'd have to add pipe soon. But he waited until the woman had made it back to her chaise longue. She picked up her book. Then she put it down and did the nicest thing. She waved at him, and he waved back. After that he felt he'd accomplished what he'd gone out there to do and could go back to work.

The next day one of the men with pens in his pocket, a clipboard in his hand, and a checklist of things to do called Kenny into his trailer. This man wasn't much older than Kenny himself, but was cut from a different mold than the men he worked with, that was clear. His eyes were clear and bright. He looked as if he'd had a good night's sleep and had never taken a drink in his life. He told Kenny he'd seen what he'd done with the woman who'd come charging out to the rig, he'd observed it all. Later, he and an associate had called on the woman—by then, her husband was home—and had had a long talk. This fit and clean-cut man, whose name was Hubbard, had asked the woman if she had any complaints and if there was anything they could do to make this trying time until the drilling was done less an ordeal, and did Kenny know what she had said? She had said, no, she understood it all now, the worker who'd explained it all to her had made it perfectly clear. And then she called him, the worker, you, Kenny, a sweetheart, a real peach. And the company executive, the spokesman, whatever he was, said, We need more men like you, Kenny, making TransAtlantic's case. What would you say to coming off the rig and working for TransAtlantic as a landman? It's where you belong. About that I don't have a doubt in my mind.

But not in Texas. In Texas they were home free. They wanted to send him North where they'd begun to drill in the Marcellus deposit and where men with his patience and compassion and learning—what they thought of as his learning—were in urgent demand. Kenny was thirty-three. Because a woman he'd hoped to see bare-breasted had veered across a field and he'd taken the time to calm her down, he was being handed a career. We need some of your Southern gallantry up North, a second TransAtlantic official had told him, and when he'd relayed that comment to his wife, she'd laughed. Maybe with women about to bare their breasts he'd been gallant, but she kept laughing and ended up joining in TransAtlantic's praise. Damn straight he'd done good, and she agreed he should go, and once he was established and making good money, she'd quit her job and join him. Behind his wife's sense of humor was something like a crazy light, but since he'd known her it had lit his way for him, and Kenny had no reason to doubt her now.

So he went. In the Marcellus the leasing and the drilling were well under way, but he made do with what was available to him. Of course, the vision he'd shared with a drunken woman in a bikini with a whole zoo of distraught animals in her head would not fly with these Northern farmers tucked back in their crabbed hills. The upper reaches of the Appalachians had little in common with the Texas plains, and the couple of times he'd started talking about resurrecting a buried life after 350 million years (380 million, he soon learned, for the Marcellus) earned him him some queer looks and a quickly closed door. He fell back on what had drawn his attention to the sunbathing woman after all, beyond the prospect of seeing her bare breasts. Her need for sympathy. He could do that. He could step down off a drilling rig and go out to console an outraged woman because he could share her plight. There was a before, there was a during, and there was an after, which these Northerners could understand, and once you got them believing in that storied sequence, it wasn't hard to convince them that they had a wondrous future in store.

Because it was true.

They did what they could do with the unleased land left, then hunkered down in their field offices and waited for the governor in an adjoining state to issue the decree that would open the doors. Christmas was coming—Kenny had already booked a flight home—when at his desk in a modular office that could be trucked off to another site in a day, he had a call routed through to him because he was sitting there and his partner had stepped out. He took the call because he didn't have anything else to do.

"Somebody there wanna make some money?" the caller said.

The voice was hard and staccato-quick. It made Kenny accentuate his drawl. He told the caller making money was one of their objectives. They had others.

"Where are you now?"

Where was he? He was in his office talking to a caller who had yet to identify himself.

"No, where are you on the map?"

Kenny named the town. He named the county and the state highway the office was located beside. He gave the date on the calendar and the time on his watch. Outside, he could see, it had begun to snow and a wind to blow.

"I get the idea. All business, which is what I've got in mind. Here's what you do."

The caller then gave Kenny an address outside a town no more than a hundred miles to the north of where the landman sat. He gave him the name of the man he'd find there. That man sat on a hundred-plus acres that were surrounded by land all leased to rival gas companies. If TransAtlantic could lease those hundred acres, it would be like drinking the best Scotch those other companies could offer before the party even began. Did Kenny Brewster like a good Scotch?

And why, Kenny asked, would the landowner in question want to do business with TransAtlantic if the other gas companies had failed?

"Because you're going to give him my name. And you're going to tell him TransAtlantic is the way to go because it's the horse I'm riding."

The horse the caller was riding?

"The horse my money's on."

Wilson Michaels was the caller's name. And Kenny told this Michaels, who seemed to be mounted on a fast horse and drinking good Scotch at the same time, he'd think about it and let him know.

"What do you need to think about? You're all about leasing land for gas drilling. I'm offering you a plum—"

Kenny asked for a number he could call and jotted it down, but once he'd hung up, he wanted nothing more to do with the caller. When his partner came back, a man of few words who could talk business and the limits TransAtlantic was willing to go to in customizing leases, Kenny told him he'd had a high-handed call from some pompous New Yorker—that was clear from both the accent and the area code—and his partner and something of a mentor, Chuck Kohler, who was sometimes afflicted by a sour stomach and this was one of those days, told him to forget it. Unless Kohler missed his guess, there'd be some family dispute at the bottom of this. Unlike in Texas with all that land, the holdings up North were small and rarely free of disputing claims.

But because they had nothing to do and it had begun to snow outside, Kenny spent a few idle hours at his computer. Wilson Michaels was, indeed, a New Yorker, a lawyer with a florid, scruple-free face and

a long list of successfully argued cases, the most notable of which had
been his defense of two famous New York athletes who had a right to
spend an evening unwinding at a New York nightclub, unseduced by
fortune-hunting women. Michaels had his own website, but the man
Michaels had instructed Kenny to call on didn't. Frank Joyner was an
architect. Or had been, since the office he'd run his business out of
seemed to have closed. But houses and buildings Frank Joyner had
designed could be found online, and once Kenny had developed the
knack, one project led him to another. Almost all seemed to have something in common. They were before and after. In most cases there
were photographs. There was a barn with bowed walls and a sunken
look, a battered cupola on top, whose shingles had flown and whose
weather vane looked rusted in place. There was the same barn restored, erect, strong, a match for every season, whose interior retained
the wide-plank floors, the rafter-spanned space, the loft, rather two
lofts, one stepping down from the other, and on the ground floor, in
the way in which the rooms were arranged and counters were placed,
even a suggestion of the stalls. There was a lighthouse abandoned out
on a point of one of the Great Lakes. Restored, it spiraled upward past
three flights of rooms, which let the light in, and arrived at a sitting
room with a wraparound deck and a view that was the Northern equivalent of what could be seen from a Texas derrick. He saw a neighborhood fire station, of a dull, brown, functional brick, squat and square,
with its two bay doors closed, that, when it was restored, somehow
seemed to rise off the ground, but in a not-unneighborly way, so that
he might have been looking at a small church whose peak was the brass
bell, which now shone. It began to fascinate him—on a snowy, gray
afternoon—the stories these buildings told. There were larger ones—
warehouses, industrial buildings, converted into apartment and office
buildings—and there was an enormous brick school, the likes of which
Kenny had never seen in the South, which seemed to have become a
small town unto itself, and which, Kenny surmised, was Joyner's chief
accomplishment. But what caught his imagination and held it until

Chuck Kohler told him his stomach was coming around and he was beginning to feel hungry, was a boathouse built out over one of those cold Northern lakes. Before, that was all it had been, a boathouse with winches to lower speedboats into a deep well, and the gloom and the mildewed rot in the before photographs were palpable. An accompanying text said it had once been owned by some whiskey-running bootleggers who, when Prohibition ended, were either behind bars or out of business and the boathouse was abandoned. Kenny Brewster was used to muggy bass-fishing shacks in the South, and this Northern boathouse made into a two-story home full of mild summer breezes and a blue light made him ache for a life he'd never had.

Chuck Kohler was closing up his desk and putting on his coat when Kenny came across a photograph of the man Wilson Michaels had badgered him to go to see. It had been taken inside someplace, from the waist up, but Frank Joyner had already put on a winter coat, which he had yet to button, so that the flannel shirt he wore was visible and the V at the neck. The neck was weathered, the jawline pronounced. The nose was prominent and not entirely straight. It might have been broken and not set perfectly back in line. Or perhaps age did that to all straight lines. The mouth was open, and it looked as if Frank Joyner had been about to speak, then had thought better of it. The eyes were terribly misleading. They had a sadness about them, overhung by the heavy brows, but this was not a sad face. It was the face of a man who thought, as Kenny did, of the before, the during, and the after, and with a lot on his mind took a true measure of his life. The sadness, then, must have come from the fact that men such as this Frank Joyner, who rescued things from disrepair, were so ill suited to the times.

Kenny Brewster was not a fool. It had been an utterly uneventful day and the days would continue to be so until the governor of that adjoining state got off the fence and said what he had to say. A man named Wilson Michaels had stirred Kenny up, and then a man named Frank Joyner had made him smile. You surfed the Web long enough, he supposed, and you got used to these swings. His partner, a man operating from within a citadel of common sense, was telling him to come on. Kenny put on an olive-green car coat he'd bought when winter had set in and joined his partner for an early supper. Two days later, without ever having returned Wilson Michaels's call, Kenny was sitting in front of Frank Joyner's house. It was not as if Chuck Kohler owed his younger and more suggestible partner a debt of any sort, but he had decided to come, too, and had actually done the driving. Another car was parked in the long, looping drive, but since neither man knew how many people lived in the house, that car could mean anything. One thing it might mean was that they were not welcome. Kohler told Kenny to leave a card in the door, and Kenny told Kohler, with nothing else going on, why didn't they sit for a while and wait. Twice, Kenny got out of the car and walked in the snow around the house. To Kohler, his partner seemed to be inspecting the house, as though he were a potential buyer. Kohler threw down a couple more Tums and waited. Of course, he saw what Kenny had seen, what even Wilson Michaels had: if TransAtlantic could sneak in here and break Conklin's hold, they could steal some of the show. But Kohler also knew what he'd told his partner was true. Courthouses all over that part of the country were opening separate wings just to deal with title searches and the multiple ways a piece of property could be divided before some judge threw it all out of court. No reason to think things would be any different up here—if the state's governor ever made up his mind. Kohler would give it another ten minutes, but if his partner took a third tour around that house, he was out of here.

The screaming kid saved them any further deliberation. Kids like that, home alone, walked into the house and called the police. Ever since that kid had been hit playing with his dog, no landmen, not to speak of truckers, took any chances on that score. The kid screamed. Kenny stood there and, as far as Kohler could tell, didn't say a word. When the kid had gone into the house, Kenny came back to the car. He asked for a card. With his pen removed from his breast pocket, Kenny hesitated, and Chuck Kohler withheld his advice. If he'd decided to give it, he would have told Kenny to forget the whole thing. But instead Kenny played his hole card and wrote down the name. Then it was just a matter of not backing into the ditch as they got out of there before the police could show.

8

It wasn't that she couldn't sleep. She hadn't even tried. She got out of bed, leaving Charlie behind, and stepped into the living room. The apartment was small, with a wall of windows that started at the waist and rose to the ceiling, which was high. Through the windows trees were visible in the park across the street. The trees moved darkly in the wind, and Jen sat at her small, round oak table, which had taken a beating, and called her brother Gerald in California.

"Is the sun still shining out there?" she asked. "Does the sun ever stop shining out there?"

"It's night, Jen."

"So what do you see when you look outside? Can you see the ocean? Do you see boats all lit up? Or some kind of fish that glow in the dark?"

"We could Skype, then you could see for yourself."

"No, I don't want to see it. I'm not even sure I want to see your healthy, handsome face."

"You all right?"

She laughed. She said, in a hushed tone, setting the scene, "I've got a sweet man lying in my bed. Life is good."

"I'm glad."

"What I want you to tell me is what we look like from out there. What you make of us."

Gerald drew a long, patient breath and let it out. That was all Jen heard, no children, no wife, no birds singing, no neighbors contentedly going about their lives.

She added, "We're a strange bunch, aren't we?"

"In what way?"

"We're stay-at-home outcasts. Something like that."

Gerald held a silence.

"Is that how you see us?"

"Not exactly."

"Then what the fuck do you see?"

"What I've always seen."

She had had enough of her brother's evasiveness. "Gerald, you better get back here and take care of this!"

He didn't pretend not to know what his sister was talking about. "Really, what can I add to what you already know?"

"You can cast the deciding vote."

"I don't know how I would vote, Jen."

She laughed, a weary sort of growl. "I *do* want to see your face. Rather, I *wanted* to see the look on your face when you just said that. Too late." She laughed again.

"Why can't you believe me?" Gerald asked quietly.

She watched the dark on dark of the trees in the gusting wind. These walls were thick, the windows double-, maybe triple-paned. The trees swayed silently back and forth. She might have been on the floor of the ocean. Her voice rose. "Because you were the only one in this family with a sound head on your shoulders, and you were the only one to get as far away as you could. What do we look like from out there, Gerald? Is it the human comedy or is it outright farce?"

Charlie appeared in the bedroom door. He wore his briefs and an old gray athletic T-shirt. He was long-legged, thin-shanked, and no one had unbony knees. He was housebuilding the next day in the freezing cold.

Gerald said, "I'm not even sure what you're talking about, Jen."

Now—too late—she lowered her voice. "The gas companies have already started moving in and leveling out their sites. You know what they call them, Gerald? They call them pads. Isn't that a nice, soft, cuddly word? You know what they're really like? They're like the first sores that appear on your body when you've got the bubonic plague." She gave a little fatalistic laugh into the phone.

From the doorway, Charlie said, "Jen, give it a break."

"How does it look from out there, Gerald?" she said.

"If it's the plague," he said, "all you can do is inoculate yourself, and that means risk getting sick yourself. Is that what you want me to say?"

"Yes! That's it!" she cheered him, and turned a sharply ironical face on Charlie, who disappeared from the doorway and went back to bed. "You drill a little well you can live with so that a whole rash of big wells don't kill you off. Problem solved!"

"Jen, it's late there. I'll go on the Internet and see what I can find out, then let's talk tomorrow. How does that sound?"

"It would sound great if my sweet man wasn't mad at me and I didn't have to sleep on the sofa."

She didn't have a sofa. When Danny stayed with her, he slept on an inflatable mattress, which he enjoyed—it was like camping out—and which she kept stored in the disproportionately large closet, large enough to walk around in, or store boxes and tubs of things in, as though this had once been the janitor's quarters. But janitors belonged in the basement, not on the third floor.

She hung up. She returned to the bedroom, and Charlie held back the covers for her to get in. But when she finally drew breath, opened her mouth, and prepared to speak, he repeated her brother's word, "Tomorrow," and it ended there.

The next day her father heard from Ray Whittaker. Whittaker had looked it up. Mickey was both right and wrong, maybe on this occasion more right than wrong. He was right in that if you were a landowner who was compulsorily integrated, you received no leasing payment. That all went to the landowner on whose land the well was vertically drilled. But he was wrong if he thought you, the horizontally drilled under landowner, received nothing. You were due some royalties, too, on the gas extracted from under your land. But he was right if he thought you were probably going to get screwed. Score one for Mickey, this time, just not a full point.

"And there's something else. I gave our favorite Realtor, Jimmy Paulding, a call. I said, 'Hypothetical case. Say there's a guy with a farm who's not really farming it, and say he's surrounded by some other farmers and maybe some absentee landlords who have all leased to the gas companies. What's that going to do to the value of that non-farmer's property?' And Paulding tells me, and Jimmy's no dummy, 'You tell Frank Joyner they've got him by the short hairs. The value of his land's going down, no two ways about it.' Jimmy said if you had a mortgage, the bank would probably have recalled it by now. But the instant you sign a lease, the value of your land goes jumping back up. Then there's this: Wilson Michaels has got another point in his favor now. The land is yours, but, per your mother's wishes, the benefits are to be spread around. If you willfully neglect the value of the land by not signing a lease, you are willfully reducing its benefits, which depend on its value, which, simply because you haven't joined the crowd, has hit rock bottom. Again, it would depend on the judge, but Michaels has a stronger case to argue now, no way around that."

The following morning Frank called TransAtlantic and got a man named Chuck Kohler, who asked him to hold the line, and then he got a younger man, he thought, with a soft, subdued twang in his voice, and an almost boyish eagerness in his tone, who identified himself as Kenny Brewster. This was the man Frank envisioned in an olive-green coat standing at the foot of his stairs while, from above, his grandson screamed at him. The same man who had walked around his house twice, as though sizing up its owner. Then had written Wilson Michaels's name down on his card.

Frank said, "I'd like to talk to you about leasing my land. I assume you represent the TransAtlantic gas company and not someone named Wilson Michaels."

Kenny had finally called Wilson Michaels back. He'd told him he'd seen the property and left his card, with Michaels's name written across it, in the door. If any more came of this, he'd let him know. Michaels had given him an aggressive pep talk, and Kenny had heard him out, holding in his mind's eye the face of the man Michaels berated for his backwardness and the work he'd accomplished. Who Frank Joyner was to Wilson Michaels was the secret Michaels was baiting Kenny with, and he didn't bite.

Kenny said, "We've made no commitment to Wilson Michaels whatsoever, sir. I can assure you of that."

When Kenny and Chuck Kohler arrived at Frank's door, Danny was safely in school. Which was as it should be. Frank didn't need his grandson standing hostilely off to the side or venting his opposition in the basement on his skateboard ramp. Frank admitted that he'd put his grandson into an untenable position. By his comment to the local paper he'd made Danny the target of jeering classmates, and now Frank was about to sit down with the very people Danny had taken such grief for. This was no time to be eleven years old or to be the grandfather of such a true believer.

Frank led the two landmen down the mud-porch and into the kitchen. He had a pot of coffee brewed and there was hot water for tea. He'd set out a plate of bite-size cinnamon rolls and cookies. The heavyset man declined, asking only for a glass of water. He sat at the end of the counter, seeming to cast himself in the role of consultant or arbiter of complicated contractual points, leaving his partner and Frank to sit across the counter from each other. Frank said he wanted to apologize for the way his grandson had screamed at them that day they had called at his door. Whether he had actually witnessed the scene he left it for them to decide, but he wanted them to know that that wasn't the way his grandson had been raised. In the boy's defense, he would only add that these were controversial times and tempers were running high, and if Frank and TransAtlantic came to common cause, he wondered if they, the company's landmen, could tell him what he should say to his grandson to win him to their side. He addressed the question to both of them, but he was looking at Kenny, as an older man singles out a younger and sets him an instructional task.

Kenny said, "Tell him, sir, we all have to sacrifice until better times come. One day there'll be a way to do it without drilling into the earth, but until that day we have to make do with what we've got."

"Sacrifice? And all those people who plan to get rich? That's not going to sound like sacrifice to him."

"No, it's not, sir. I agree. But say you make enough money to go around the world. Sooner or later you've got to come back, and when you do and things haven't changed, then you realize you've only made it worse. There was a story we read in school called 'A Man Without a Country.' It's about an army officer who cursed his country, and all he could do was sail around the world because he had no country to come back to. That's the punishment they gave him. If I had a boy that age, I'd tell him that."

"So they're still reading that story. . . ."

"Well, they are down where I come from."

At his end of the counter Chuck Kohler bit back on a laugh, amused and a little put off by his partner's unconventional antics, but Frank discovered he had a certain degree of sympathy for this displaced young man. That Southerner's twang, subdued as it was, was like the soft flutter of a flag. Frank recalled his walking around the house. Frank had been too far away to read anything on the young landman's face, but the way he'd paused and lingered over the elevation and roof pitch, the size and spacing of the windows, did not inspire thoughts of a housebreaker looking for a way in. Rather, of an outsider patiently seeking to understand why he had been excluded.

Frank said, "My grandfather built this house back in the 1920s. He built it on land his father had sold him from his farm. There was a bill of sale. It was not a gift. My grandfather paid the going price, but the end result was after business was done, it all stayed within the family. I'll ask the question now from my point of view. Money matters aside— remember, you just told me after you made enough to sail around the world, you still had to have some place to come back to—why should I want to invite TransAtlantic to be part of our family?"

Kenny knew the answer at once. It wasn't a trick question. It was simple, elemental, and could be talked around just so long. There was a sort of surface sternness in Frank Joyner's face. The eyes were a sun-browned army-green. The answer to the question was because we're homeless, a grand multinational operation like ours. Because I am.

But he said, "Because we could be a good team. We'll get the gas up without doing damage to your property, and we'll put things back the way they've always been. Just a little area, not even half an acre, fenced off."

Frank said, "About the size of a family cemetery."

Kenny looked him in the eye. "Cleaner, better kept, and nothing falling over. But no larger than that." Then he took a liberty, which didn't feel like a liberty. It had, astonishingly, the feel of an intimacy earned. "Who is Wilson Michaels, sir?"

"The man whose name you wrote on your card."

"He called the office. By chance he got put through to me. He acted like he was giving me a tip. He talked about horse racing, and that's what it felt like—an inside tip. He said to go see you and just mention his name. He said it like . . ."

Frank waited, curious to see how far this young man would go. Chuck Kohler made an admonishing, throat-clearing sound.

". . . like it would make all the difference in the world. Like as soon as you heard it, you would jump."

"He's the first husband of my older sister, and the father of my niece. He's a lawyer in the City. There are legal issues involved."

Kohler, who had told his young partner so, didn't really make a sound, just settled himself on his stool.

Frank said, "What did you think of him?"

Kenny turned to Kohler and, this time, made no attempt to disguise the look he gave his partner. He was seeking advice. Kohler returned a clipped cock of the head to indicate, quickly, Kenny had reached a critical point and was on his own.

"I thought he was a braggart and a bully," Kenny said.

"Yet you did what he told you to. Why?"

"Because . . ." Kenny hesitated because the fascination he'd felt when he'd gone online and seen those buildings Frank Joyner had rescued from the ruin of daily life had had such a humbling effect on him that he feared if he tried to express it now, he would lose any businessman's advantage he might possess. But he wasn't a businessman, not really, the two men sitting at this counter surely knew that. ". . . I went online and saw some of the buildings you'd restored and wanted to meet you to tell you in person how much I liked them. It's probably as simple as that."

Frank glanced down the counter at the older man, who returned his glance with an expression—perhaps practiced, perhaps not—of bemused indulgence toward his younger partner, which might or might not have amounted to a routine they had worked out between them. Except Frank saw the young man again, in his olive-green coat, standing before his house, and was struck by his stillness, by the almost solemn way he'd stood and looked up until Danny had come along and shouted things back into their proper place. They were landmen out to violate the earth, poison the wells, and make a killing.

"I'm pleased," Frank said.

"I looked at your buildings and they made me wonder why we're so quick to build new ones if it means tearing the old ones down. Down in Texas—"

"Is that where you're from?"

"On the state line. Texarkana. But I worked in Texas on the rigs."

"You did the drilling?"

"Yes, sir."

"And you'll explain it all to me, the drilling, the fracking, how it all works."

"Chuck and I, sir—"

"First you, Kenny," Frank said, calling the young man with the curly, fair hair, the large ears, the flesh in the cheeks and the cleft chin, and the blue eyes misted over with some vague sort of yearning, by his first name for the first time, "you explain what it's like to drill that far down into the earth, and then Chuck and I will talk money, which, if we end up doing business, I intend to get a lot of, I warn you in advance."

Later, Frank called Ray Whittaker, and continuing to plead ignorance until pushed, and then pushing back, Ray said, All right, you asked for it—A, B, C, D. A/leasing payment: There's no ceiling, bargain to your heart's content. B/Royalties: So far, 18 percent seems to be as high as anyone's gone, but do not invest money of your own in exchange for some big uptick in royalties. It's got scam written all over it. C/Storage rights: Don't do it. The tanks will be there till kingdom come. D/Pipeline right-of-way: Can't avoid this, but make it a separate contract, twenty dollars a rod, if you know what that is, seems to be the standard price. If the pipeline goes through your woods, you're entitled to the trees they cut down, and the habitat has to be restored for all animals, from bears all the way to mice. Don't leave an animal out.

X, Y, and Z? Hire yourself a real lawyer, Frank.

And, before going to work, Gerald, from just south of L.A., called Jen back, who was already down in Luisa's gallery, after having gotten up and made a peace-offering breakfast for Charlie, before he went out into the freezing cold.

"Conklin, Chesapeake, TransAtlantic, GeoVest, you look at the hydrofracking chat sites and there's not much difference. The gas

companies are rushed and arrogant and careless, and then they are
called on it and they are as good as they can be. That seems to be the
pattern. They sit down with you as if they were the local preacher welcoming you into the neighborhood. You sign the lease. Then nothing—
not a word. Months and months go by. The day you're least expecting
it, a hundred trucks block your road and you can't even get in to work.
Is this the kind of stuff you want to hear, Jen?"

Jen said yes, no, she didn't know. Luisa was showing a customer
some prints, and Jen could afford this moment of uncertainty.

"You want to know if anything can stop it, then. I spent an hour
listening to a panel discussion of scientists and college professors and
got the sense that with something this big, a few casualties are to be
expected. A few wells poisoned is a small price to pay. Everybody is
downstream of some place where something disreputable is going on.
One geologist said that the great thing about rivers was that they re-
new themselves every minute on the minute. The old quote: You can't
step into the same river twice. He started talking about this slug
of carbon tetrachloride that years ago leaked from some chemical-
processing plant on the Kanawha and got into the Ohio. But you give
it a day and it's gone. Brand-new river again—"

"Gerald."

"You want to know the chemicals the gas companies are using? I
can't tell you. They won't say. But all the online speculation points
to benzene, toluene, naphthalene, xylene, at least those are the four I
wrote down. They can contribute to nervous-system depression, ane-
mia, liver damage, and, of course, cancer. The radioactive elements
released from the earth, radium, barium, strontium—"

"Gerald, I'm sorry I called you last night. But since you called back,
how do we look this morning?"

"All I can say is I don't see the sense in being a martyr."

"No, you wouldn't."

"What is that supposed to mean?"

"In the whole history of martyrdom there's not one with a level head, that's all. Some beheaded, but those with a head still on their shoulders—"

"Jen, I've got to go to work."

"You know, Daddy is going to do this, and I have no idea why."

"Tell him I'm behind him, whatever he decides."

"You tell him." She hit her off button, slipping the phone into her jeans pocket, where she would feel its buzz when Gerald called back, even though she didn't expect him to. But others might call—starting with her mother. When people wanted to get to her father, they had to go through Jen. When had she taken on that role?

"Jen, what is Frank going to do?"

"I'm sorry?"

"If you're going to have an out-loud discussion on your cell phone, remember there are people around. And Frank is an old, old friend."

The customer had gone, and Jen and Luisa were alone in the gallery. Luisa was a small, trim woman with a flinty-angled face and dark eyes, who liked soft things, such as Peruvian alpaca shawls, around her shoulders, and large, rounded jewels—amber, citrine, rose-colored quartz, anything opalescent—around her neck. She had come from New York long ago and had always claimed she had been the first of the Deweese's tenants and, therefore, the first to give her Big City stamp of approval to Frank's cause. Back when she thought incessantly on such things, Jen had wondered if Luisa and her father had been lovers, but Luisa had never said or dropped a conclusive clue, and her father, utterly unlike his unabashed daughter, would take such secrets to the grave.

"Don't ask, Luisa," Jen said.

"But I just did."

"Then, between the two of us, I think Daddy is about to lease his land to a gas company."

"And you say you have no idea why."

"Well, yes, I do. Because he doesn't want a fight. He moved out there and the fight went out of him. He'd rather philosophize than fight. Danny does the fighting now for the family."

"And not you?"

Jen sighed heavily, overdid it as if the weight of a thousand battles had fallen on her shoulders.

Luisa said, "Frank has always been a philosopher. If you hadn't been so man-crazy, you would have seen that years ago."

"I thought you liked me, Luisa."

"I do, a lot."

"Did you and my father—"

"No."

"You're sure you know what I was going to ask?"

"Positive."

"And the answer is still no?"

"And if I said yes, would that make you any happier?"

Jen paused. "I'd be pleased."

"Sorry." Luisa touched Jen on the cheek. "I'll be back mid-afternoon."

Before then, Jen's phone had buzzed in her pocket and it was not her mother but Charlie, calling from the building site, where he said he'd spent a cold morning packing insulation into walls. He was catching his first clean breath now. She all right? Yes. She apologized again for last night, for waking him up, thoughtless of her, and he didn't disagree. He said no one was getting much sleep now, then described what was going on where they were building this house. From the breakfast nook, you looked out across the way to where a gas-drilling pad was being built, with trucks rumbling in and out, and there was nothing you could do. Except enjoy the view. The owner was pissed. Of course, he'd taken the chance, he knew the risk. Charlie had found himself packing in as much insulation as he humanly could.

When her mother didn't call it could only mean one thing, but she still caught Jen by surprise. She was only thankful no customers were around and Luisa was still gone while she got a sense of her mother's mood. Marjorie Joyner came in looking like an Eskimo, with her fur-lined hood still up and her face almost as flat as one's, claiming before she took her hood down that Jen was keeping her in the dark and threatening, without saying as much, to confront her daughter face-to-face like this every time she failed to call.

"So he still doesn't know what he's going to do?"

"If he does, he's not telling me."

"Then he doesn't because you'd be the first he'd tell. He trusts you."

"And not the rest of you? You're dead wrong about that, Mother."

Marjorie Joyner took her hood down, unzipped her coat, shook out her gray curls. "Dead wrong I'm not about anything, sweetie. It was a game he played: 'Don't tell your mother, but I'm doing this, I'm buying that.' Remember the tropical fish, three aquariums' worth? One day they appear in the house and there's nothing I can do. Except feed them. And separate the mother from the babies once she's given birth. 'Cause she'd eat them, ten, twenty, at a gulp. That was a little secret you shared."

"Don't be silly, Mother. He knew I liked them, that was all."

"You were like his spy, his go-between. That year you went off with the band, he was like a lost soul. We didn't know what you were doing, and he went around with this squinting frown on his face like he was trying to see a hundred miles away. But you were a lot farther away than that."

"I'm sorry about that time. I've told you. But I wrote. You pretty much knew where I was."

"What kind of man lives through his daughter and not his sons? Let me ask you that."

Jen tried to laugh it off. "If that's what he's doing, he's having a piss-poor time."

"He's got Danny, and he's got you in a nice little setup here in the Deweese."

"Mother, I don't like the way you're making this sound."

"He's sweet on you."

"Well, I'm glad."

"So what's he going to do? Is he going to make you a wealthy woman? Isn't that what they always promise in the end?"

"Mother, stop it!" Jen closed her eyes. Drew a long, calming breath. She prayed for a customer to come in, but no one did.

"You're my daughter," Marjorie Joyner declared flatly, as though asserting a legal claim. "I want you to have what you deserve. I don't want to see anyone take advantage of you, not for anything. I want this for all my children and grandchildren, but you're not just his sweetie pie, you're mine, too."

Jen studied her mother, whose emotions were always slow to show on that tightly fissured face.

"It's a done deal now," Marjorie Joyner went on, "and since Frank is not an utter fool, he knows it, too. If he's still holding out, it's because of some game he's playing with himself. I'm not interested in his games. I'm interested in you getting what's yours, and Mickey, although there's no telling what he might do with it. Gerald could buy more house insurance, I guess. I've got all I want. Just so my motives are clear."

"I've never doubted you, Mother."

"I want what any mother wants."

"I'm one, too. I understand."

"Of course, you do, sweetie."

"I can't tell you what Daddy is going to do."

Her mother squinted her eyes skeptically, with just a trace of a knowing grin. Sometimes a forgiving grin, sometimes an accusing one, but it was the expression Jen had engraved on her memory when she thought, Mother, close quarters, no escape.

Marjorie Joyner said, "The *only* thing I want for myself is a smoke."

She deliberately went into her purse and brought out her Marlboros and, just as deliberately, but not in slow motion, removed one cigarette from the pack and put it into her mouth. Then the lighter she had had forever and which she could snap shut with a pistol-hammer report. She held the lighter cigarette-high and waited for her daughter to deny her this small pleasure, too.

That was when a customer did come in, two of them, fresh off lunch and there strictly to browse while their food digested. With the same deliberation, Jen's mother returned the cigarette to the pack and the pack and the lighter to her purse. She conceded a small tactical victory to her daughter, who had allies, such as these two browsing nonshoppers, everywhere Marjorie looked. But she'd raised her hood and come out in some bitter weather and made her point. Frank had his confidante and she was sure as hell going to have hers, and that they would turn out to be the same person made her daughter a sort of double agent, in fact.

9

THEY STEPPED OUT ONTO THE ICE, WHICH WAS ROUGH-SURFACED, NOT slick. She was unlikely to slip and fall. Still, she held on to his arm. They could see to the end of this lake, and as far as they could tell, it was frozen all the way. Shallow, she'd been told. The lake they lived on was forty miles long and four hundred feet deep in spots, but this was a puddle in comparison and, in years past, had been harvested for its ice. That ice had ended up in drinks in Park Avenue penthouses a hundred, a hundred and fifty years ago. This she'd read in a brief history in the lodge, accompanied by photographs of wagons and teams of dray horses and men with two-man saws all out on the ice. Still, she held on tightly to Frank's arm and listened for the sound of cracks. But it was like walking on the hardest stone, as if the water were frozen to the last drop, and the fish, which there must have been, were encased in ice, like those woolly mammoths you heard about in Siberian glaciers. In unseasonably warm summers, Siberian farmers and their dogs sometimes dug those mammoths out. Helen's husband, Paul, had known a professor in the geology department who, as a graduate student doing field research, had claimed to have witnessed such an un-icing and then to have joined the townspeople in eating meat ten thousand years old. He'd said tough, but with enough vodka . . . When Paul had told the story, his listeners had laughed and gagged at the same time. Ten thousand years old. Cryonics was what they called the scientific equivalent. Paul had joked about that: wake up ten thousand years later and you're so outdated and odd your fellow humans decide to eat you. What Walt Disney had in store. The gallows humor seized Helen's stomach. She held tightly to Frank's arm, as if any gap, ten thousand years or two years, three months, could ever be bridged.

Out at what seemed the very center of the lake, they stopped and turned around. So much ice was like some elemental barrier between the two of them and their life as they'd known it, and it was probably for that reason she couldn't stop thinking about her dead husband, as if only now was she about to abandon him, betray him at her core.

He'd been a professor of English Romantic poetry. He'd quote a line from one of John Keats's letters: "If poetry comes not as naturally as the leaves to a tree, it had better not come at all." That's what Paul's book on Keats had been called, *Leaves to the Trees*. Not just poetry, but all that came naturally, all that blossomed into life of its own accord, had been sacred to Paul, which included his disease. Death, too, came as naturally as leaves to a tree; life hung on, but eventually, over the months, one by one the leaves fell off. It was as if she'd collected them all and pressed them between the pages of his beloved books, and when it was over, she realized he'd become something of a hero for her, who had left these beautiful memories, like pressed leaves, behind. He'd been a happy man, with full, ruddy cheeks and bold, unbullying eyes, and not once had she heard him complain that his lot had been unfair. When he made love to her, it was always with a fresh sense of joy. He didn't whisper poetry in her ear, but when his hands moved out onto her body, she sensed he was on a quest of some sort, and she waited for him to arrive so that she could crown him her champion. Practically with his last words he'd pleaded with her to be happy, for he swore that he'd been. With the little strength he had left he'd squeezed her hand. Don't let me down, he'd said.

The clear-but-clouded-over weather held. No snow, no shattering light. They walked the town's streets. Surely, there was a modern subdivision of some sort, but they never saw it. The town was a marvel of preservation, like a town behind glass. Yet you could walk up and touch it. On Main Street no neon, apparently no bright lights of any sort, were permitted. The old hotel still stood, four stories of unadorned brick. The old church had a towering, brittle-looking steeple. The town offices were located in an elaborate Gothic cottage with a dimly recessed front porch. There was an opera house, a few modest mansions. But the streets they walked up and down were lined with small homes of differing styles—Federal, Greek Revival, neo-Gothic— all neatly kept and in daily use and each with a small sign attached unobtrusively on the front facade giving its year of construction and the name of the original owner. A college was close by, a quad of responsibly maintained Georgian brick buildings, but it was to the rows of small, wood-frame houses they returned, with their doorsteps, their curtained windows, their scaled-down size, their dates and names. They were smaller people back then, Frank said. A biological fact. 1798. 1801. 1809. They lived apart, and they lived cheek by jowl. Through facing side windows they could have reached out and touched. He read the names off: Susan Parkinson. Richard Ewing. Frank Collingsworth. The names as he pronounced them seemed stark. He might have been reading them off tombstones, except that these had been living quarters, and that, she knew, was his point. They lived discrete, close-but-not-touching lives. If you gave those smaller but sturdier people back then the houses they wanted, these were the houses you designed.

They ate their meals in the lodge, which had been built by an associate of J. P. Morgan's and was a huge, brown-shingled pile of no discernible style. Through a heavy-limbed spruce their room looked out onto the lake. The fireplace downstairs was big enough to stand inside, J. P. Morgan and his robber-baron associates having been, of course, larger-than-life. Frank and Helen sat there, after dinner, gazing into a downsize fire, thanking each other for giving themselves this four-day reprieve. She had told her daughter, Cindy, she would be out of reach for a few days and left her to surmise what she would. Cindy would surmise just this. Perhaps something more decadent but with the same result. She was not likely to imagine her mother walking out to the center of a frozen lake and standing there as an isolated point while all past life remained onshore, but she would imagine Helen forsaking the memory of her husband, Paul, for the arms of her lover, Frank, and would fill in the details as they suited her. Sitting before a fire in a lodge before they went up to their room to make love was well within Cindy's range, but probably not the kindness and companionship with which they would do it, and that pained Helen, to think that her daughter had no relief from the deep-seated bitterness of her life.

Frank had given his daughter, Jen, the choice of taking Danny down to the Deweese to stay with her for a few days or of coming out to the house and staying there, in which case her boyfriend, Charlie, could come, too. They would be headboard to headboard with her son, in a room with a radiator slow to heat up, but that was what they'd decided to do. Quietly, so as not to wake Danny, they lay in bed talking about Frank, who deserved this four-day vacation from his life, with the decision he had to make and the animosity he was bound to incur the second he made it. Probably even from her own son, Jen said, until it could be explained to him, but until Danny was old enough to weigh everything in the balance, how could she even start? Charlie said the tough part would be the kids who'd been ragging him. Danny'd taken the high road getting away from them, and now he might have to eat some shit to get back in their good graces. She'd be damned! Jen said. Little money-grubbing mouthpieces for their get-rich parents! Anyway, she said, her father might decide to stick it out. Yeah, well, then he's got his sisters breathing down his neck, Charlie reminded her, and that loose cannon of a big-city lawyer. What was his name? Jen had forgotten his name.

She only remembered his gloating, salivating red eye. Charlie, she'd said, say something sweet, but quietly. Sweet and quiet and low so we don't wake Danny up. Charlie whispered to her that if anybody deserved to get off the warpath, she did, and he'd like to be around that day because she'd be some kind of woman. She murmured her thanks and snuggled in close. Later, she did remember and turned to Charlie's ear, but he had to work the next day and had gone to sleep, so that what she whispered to him she was really whispering to herself, back on the warpath again. Wilson Michaels, that son of a bitch!

Helen slept late but Frank woke early as he always did, had breakfast, and prepared a tray from the buffet table to take up to Helen. She couldn't eat half of what he brought her, even if she woke famished, but he gave her the choice and he wanted the choices to go on. All sorts of eggs, rolls, sausages, cereals, juices, sliced fruit, coffees and teas—a little of everything, the illusion of no limits. He felt a great yearning to tell Helen things he'd never told anyone, to claim a bit of her allegiance if not her love. She had large, watery blue eyes, which seemed too heavy for their sockets, and partially lowered lids. She smiled with her full mouth, which was large, the lips parted, her teeth exposed and her breath seemingly held. The next breath, she seemed to be telling him, could change everything, the next blink of the eyes.

He persuaded her to come out again with him onto the ice. This was during their third day, and the weather had sharpened, bringing a gusting wind and blowing snow. The lake was less than two miles long, but with the snow blowing in squalls, reducing their vision, at moments they might have been arctic explorers a continent away from the rest of humankind. The ice under their feet felt as solid as concrete. Ducks and geese that remained in the area the year-round flew over them, but the houses that lined the shore with their docks and swimming floats were closed for the season. They were unobserved. They were alone. Frank had walked the woods and the fields almost every day these last few years and, although alone, had never felt less lonely in his life. This was different from that. He'd had the company of animals in the woods and the fields, and so attentive had he been to their ways he could almost convince himself he was one of them, or at least a creature to their liking. This was more fundamental. He had at his side a fellow sufferer, a survivor, a mate. They held on to each other so they wouldn't slip on the ice or be blown over by a gust of wind.

When they turned around and started back, the tracks they'd left in the thin covering of snow were not theirs. They seemed cluttered and clumsy, utterly unfaithful to the deliberate steps they'd taken, and they found themselves giving them a wide berth. Their feet were cold, and the effort to keep their footing and measure their steps had begun to tell in their backs and thighs. In the lodge they sat before the fire in the waning afternoon, the only ones there. They exchanged idle congratulations for having weathered the ordeal and for having made it back to where they'd begun. They listened to the quiet, consuming burn of the fire. The day darkened, and a part of Frank wished they were out there still, their way lit only by the treacherous phosphorescence of the snow. He felt his age, every day of it, and he felt a curious closeness to the boy he'd been, as though only now could he speak for that boy, bear witness, and he told Helen that as a boy, a very young man, he had been prepared to kill himself to make sure he wanted to live, and he placed his arm on the broad wooden armrest that separated them, pulled back his sweater sleeve, slid his expandable watchband up his forearm, and asked her if she could see the scar. The firelight was inconstant, with a cathedral-like gloom in this raftered hall. She looked at his left wrist, saw nothing, and then at his long, weathered face, the exact opposite of her husband's full-bodied one, while Frank rotated his wrist in the firelight until he, if not she, detected that pale, thin, cartilaginous line.

"I was just a kid, but it's something I've thought about over the years, and I almost wonder if I hadn't done it then, I'd have to do it now." He continued to look at his wrist, still rotating it to catch the light, even though he could feel she kept her eyes on his face. "It was nothing, something an overdramatizing kid might do. But, then, it was everything. I have a hard time now putting myself in that state of mind, but out there on that ice . . ."

"Frank."

"It didn't bleed much. I think I only nicked the veins. And it was easy to stop."

He studied his wrist in the watery firelight, then something shifted in him, he might have blinked, suddenly the world was bereft of color and it was as if he were back out on that snow-whitened ice. He saw the blood fill the cut from one end to another, then he saw it, almost cautiously, spill out. Nothing in his life had been more deeply and powerfully colored, he realized then. He might have been witnessing a birth. The red, the purple, of plums. It was the richness. Yes, he'd realized in that moment he was incalculably rich. But, then, he was only twenty years old.

She reached out and took his hand on the armrest and, slowly, as if she'd expected resistance, turned the inside of the wrist down. Then she held it there.

"Helen."

"I can't keep you alive, Frank. I'm no good at that. But promise me you will."

"As I said, I was only a kid."

"Promise me, Frank."

It scared him. For an instant he went cold because he wasn't sure it was a promise he could keep. But she sighed noisily, as though angry with herself, and he thought she was fighting off tears. So he made the promise, which sounded to his ears like a solemn vow.

Only then did she release her hold on his wrist.

It dawned on him: he had just vowed to live for her. He had plighted his troth.

He had brought her to this town as a surprise. He would only tell her they were going someplace quiet, pretty, and apart. On the way they'd cut across a corner of an adjoining state, where they had seen gas drilling rigs set up on their plateaus, or pads, where the drilling had been completed and everything was small, orderly, and sanitized—smallish tanks, shoulder-high wellheads, and an economical running of pipe. When they finally found a site where drilling was in progress and trucks were lined up along the road and where the pounding of pipe made unshouted conversation almost impossible, what seemed to interest him the most was the house across the road. He had actually pulled off in a bare area just above the house and sat waiting, it seemed, for somebody to appear. Helen was about to suggest that he simply knock on the door and ask whoever answered the question he had in his mind when a woman appeared at the door with a child maybe two years old in her arms. A little boy, it seemed, whom she lifted up to her eye level so that together they could see what was happening across the road in what had probably been a pasture for their cows. They saw a good part of the derrick and a fresh string of pipe leaving the rack to go boring down. They watched this for maybe ten minutes with looks of mounting wonder on their faces, as Frank watched them. He didn't pull away until they'd gone back inside.

He and Helen passed the local high school, and she said she remembered that his son Mickey taught somewhere down here, and she asked him what so far had been her only question of the day: Where was Mickey's town?

Frank shook his head, avoiding her question. Then because of something she saw at the corner of his eye and the downturned set of his mouth, she wondered if he even knew. His son did not hold jobs long. They talked on the phone. Frank would have known an area code, but an actual address?

He said, That last well was being dug by TransAtlantic. Did you notice the sign?

Those were the landmen who had come to see him. Apparently, one of them had made a not-unfavorable impression, a young man, she gathered, around Mickey's age. That's right, she said. I did.

Well, let's put all that out of our minds, at least for four days. We're getting away. I have a surprise.

She reached over and patted him just above the knee, and he took his right hand off the wheel to cover hers. He held her there for a moment, as though welding her to his will. Accomplices, they *would* get away, although Mickey, in that moment, was not far from them. In their twisting Appalachian valleys these towns were close, coal-mining or steel-mill towns most had been, and some quite prosperous, until the world had become small and Asia or the Near East had moved closer than the current town in which Mickey taught school. He actually had a student now he liked, with the risible name of Jimmy Flesh, except that no one laughed at him. He wasn't an athlete, nor was he handsome enough for the girls to compete for his attention. He was thin, as thin as Mickey although not quite as tall, with sharply faceted gray-blue eyes set close over the ridge of his nose. When he moved, he seemed to have unerring balance, as though he'd been brought up on a farm, making his way down clodded corn rows or across the ruts of a cow pasture, and if anyone during the eight years Mickey had been on the job had had a true read on the human comedy, he decided it had to be this boy. Jimmy Flesh. Mickey, of course, was part of that comedy—perhaps, in this small world, one of its stars—and maybe for that reason Jimmy was happy to listen to what he said.

Mickey said, Take Cotton Mather. If everything those card-carrying Puritans saw testified to either their election or their damnation, sans appeal, then imagine what a stock market of the soul they had to wake up to each morning. If you were the least prone to doubt, and one morning you're out riding, say, in your election-mobile, also known as a one-horse shay, and your horse pulls up lame, is that a sign? It is if the shay had been taken as one. If a man out in a shay like that was a sign of God's approval, then if the horse pulling it suddenly pulls up lame . . . well, even the Puritans were subject to the laws of logic. But imagine it: in a world where anything could be read as a sign, the Dow had to be going wild.

Jimmy's expression, as Mickey would say things like this, was wise, discriminating, and, to an impressive degree, won. Those remaining, unwon degrees intrigued Mickey. He didn't want all of Jimmy Flesh's approval. He could get that from any number of students if he broadened the farce. He wanted to know how Jimmy was constituted. If he could match it, he wanted to know if he could be so constituted himself.

Then Mickey had to laugh. Teachers did this. At some point in their careers, they found themselves a student neither this nor that they could picture themselves as, if they could be relieved of the person they'd become. Mickey had reached that point when his father and that lady friend of his, who had cooked them such a fine Thanksgiving meal, had passed through a corner of his adopted state in their effort to get away. It wasn't as if Mickey had had an intuition. Every so often, toward the end of an evening, he'd call his father, and he did so again, thinking of Jimmy Flesh and wondering if his father, who hadn't had students, per se, but apprentices of a sort, had ever had anything like that happen to him.

He got his sister instead. She said their father was getting away, he was out of reach for four days, and unless it was a matter of utmost urgency . . . and Mickey told her nothing was, everything could wait, which clearly disappointed her. No crisis? No crossroads? She'd begun to tease him, play him, confident that at the other end of the line the hook was well set. In effect, Mickey set his own hooks, then passed the fishing rod on to his sister so that she could have her sport. He said, Well, as a matter of fact there was this student, wait till she heard his name. Jimmy Flesh. As in "the sins of"? his sister said. And a whole fleshed-out family of them, besides, her brother said. There was Bitsy Flesh and Bonnie Flesh, not to speak of Randy Flesh, and he ran off a string, until Jen stopped him and said, Mickey, I get the idea. What have you done? And he told her, Nothing, absolutely nothing, sorry to disappoint you, I really did want to speak to Dad. Nothing? C'mon, Mickey, you can tell me, you always have, and the cajoling tone to her voice was so apparent, so naked to his ears, that he almost did, almost told her, Well, the fact is, I can't take my eyes off him, this Jimmy

Flesh, this student of mine, he's a natural, everything comes natural to him, smartest kid in the class but no show-off, he sees things, he discriminates, he might have been raised on a farm; in a world where everything is awesome he knows what truly is, more than the flesh made spirit it's the beauty of intelligence, but intelligence as old as the land, what's been down there for millions of years, you following me, Jen?

But she wouldn't have been following him, she would have been waiting for the foolish misstep to come, and in the end he didn't tell her a thing. It wasn't even true, what he might have told her about Jimmy Flesh, not in so many words, and her impatience with him had become palpable on the phone. So, instead, he said, What's Dad getting away from, anyway? She released an incredulous breath and said, This leasing stuff! You know, Mickey, they're drilling up here. He and Helen—and Mickey broke in, He and Helen? Good for him, good for her, they make a beautiful couple! It's time for Dad to move on. His sister held a pause, and in the background Mickey heard somebody else in the house, he heard the sort of music playing Danny would never listen to, a throbbing, warbling, country female vocalist, and when Jen resumed speaking, the last trace of humor, of playfulness, had gone out of her voice. That's really the problem, isn't it, Mickey? He can't move on. It's like there's a hundred times more gravity in these hundred acres of ours than anywhere else. He might make it for four days, but maybe the only way he'll ever really get away is if he leases this land. They can drill down and siphon some of that gravity off. He might make it then. Are you ready for that?

Mickey almost responded the way they always did when faced with a dilemma of this sort: What does Gerald say? But the question had been directed at him. Was he, Mickey, ready for that? Was he, tucked away in a remote valley, ready for the family estate to be converted into a cash cow? Down and out. Down and out. Plumb your depths and, then, swing wide. Compulsory integration.

He hung up, and after having passed through that corner of his son's state, his father and his lady friend began their four-day escape.

Not long before that, TransAtlantic had dismantled their field offices and moved the whole operation a hundred miles north. Kenny Brewster called his wife, Glorie, on the Texas-Arkansas line and told her they were here for the long haul now and the time had come for her to quit her job and make the move North. It was a hard decision. Glorie, it turned out, liked her job a lot. Getting kids off the streets and into programs that worked was a little like marriage. Whether those kids knew it or not, that adventure-filled life she was taking them away from was nearing the edge of a cliff. They were going over unless they pulled back. An element of hypocrisy was involved, but once she had them settled into sports or nature study or the tutoring of smaller kids or any number of other sanctioned activities, she could forget some of the near-lies she'd told and pat herself on the back. Give that up and go North?

All he could tell her was that he felt closer to fatherhood up here than he did down there, where a father had deserted him and a grandfather with his conscience-clean hands had opted for order before everything else. But he couldn't tell her that—not in those words. He felt on the verge of something, he felt large with whatever it was. Or tell her that. She'd laugh at him. He missed her laughter, her sense of humor had carried her through a lot. But people were different up here. They didn't tear down, they didn't run off. They rebuilt, they stayed. Without getting carried away—he wanted the playfulness of her laughter, not its dismissive disbelief—he felt he was about to become a new man, all that she might have bargained for when as a sort of wonderful prank she'd waited for him to come home those many years ago. So without begging—he was not about to do that—he told her to come.

PART FOUR

PEACEKEEPING

10

I⊤ DIDN'T TAKE MUCH, THREE STRAIGHT DAYS OF LATE-APRIL SUN, THE
birds singing, the forsythia blazing, lilacs on the way, and cresting the
last hill before descending into the town, they looked out over the
lake, a body of water that zigged and zagged its way north for forty
miles, today as blue as the sky, bluer, in fact. Frank identified the exact
shade as robin's-egg blue, but that might have been because the remains of robin's eggs that had already hatched lay scattered on the
ground. His maples were in leaf, the blossoms of his apple and pear
trees had already given way to a speckling of green. For a moment in
the morning, the sun caught the trunk of a towering cherry tree up the
slope, giving it a burnished garnet glow. It couldn't last. Four, five, six
straight days of this kind of weather in April were not the norm. Aware
of that, a number of sailboats had already found their way onto the
water. Frank counted eight sails bobbing and tacking, each at its own
particular angle, before he descended into the town and lost them to
view. Up the lake, before it took its first jag to the west, the slopes of
vineyards were too distant to make out anything more than a fine,

veiled, orderly wash of spring green, but at the limit of sight, that was just right, it was enough.

At his side, Kenny Brewster said, "She needs to see that! You'd have to know her. Something like that and she'd be here in five minutes!"

"So she hasn't come."

Kenny shook his head. "Still making up her mind."

Frank made a sympathizing sound down in his throat, then motioned to the glove compartment, where he always kept a camera. "Send her a photograph."

But Kenny had his eyes before him or on some other distant place. "In the navy, we spent months out on the ocean and all you saw was water. Maybe some other ships, maybe not, but finally, it just gets to be a lot of nothing out there. This is like the opposite of that. You see the land, you see what happened, how the glacier withdrew. There's a real story there, isn't there? It's like you're opening a history book."

"So you're still a student, Kenny."

He gave a brief, self-deprecating laugh. "I like to learn." Then he narrowed his eyes and in another tone, a quiet proclamation, stated, "I like looking at beautiful things."

They drove through the town. For a moment, at a distance of a block, the rampartlike tower of the Deweese was visible. They crossed the train tracks. They crossed one of the four creeks flowing through the town into the lake, started up the west shore, entered a forest, and then emerged with a closer view of the water, blinding in its light if you stared at it for long, a bodying-out, no-quarter-given resurgence of spring, the end of ice. Still, at the depth at which the glaciers had gouged out the trough, very, very cold.

"I don't know who owns the place now," Frank said. "You understand we probably won't be able to get inside. We might not even get to look in the windows."

But they did look in the windows because Kenny wanted it so badly and Frank couldn't bring himself to deny him. The boathouse was closed. The stone mansion up the slope that the boathouse had once

belonged to also looked closed and as massively out of place as a fortress from some period past when this lake had been a shipping artery
and a means of moving troops. Three days of heady April sun were not
enough to throw open the doors, yet Frank had called Kenny Brewster
and told him, today, tomorrow, might be the day to drive up the lake if
he was still so anxious to see that boathouse, and the young landman,
up to his neck in contracts, had made time and come. Since Frank had
seen it, the boathouse had gone from white to some café-au-lait shading of beige. The trim remained white, the cupola, the railing of the
three-sided deck. Pilings driven deep into the lake bottom held the
boathouse in place, yet there was always the illusion of movement, just
enough to let you know you had strayed out onto a foreign element.
Curtains were drawn across the windows, yet the light off the lake was
strong enough that Kenny was able to get a shadowy sense of the living
room and its loftlike space. A companionway took you down into the
bedrooms, built over the stir of the water where speedboats had once
been moored. The architectural effect was of a truce, a reconciliation
of water and land.

Hands on the railing, Kenny Brewster stood looking out over the
surface of the lake. He said that he'd read that bootleggers had once
owned all this, and that made him sick. That a bunch of common crim-
inals could ever have set foot in this boathouse and run their whiskey
up and down this beautiful lake. He shook his head and sighed and said
if his wife could see this, she wouldn't hesitate a minute. Then he said
what it seemed he'd come to say, but differently from what Frank had
expected. Not, How do you do this, sir?—full of admiration for the
conversion of a damp and drafty boathouse into a home. But why?

He said, "Where I come from, everybody is tearing down whatever's in the way and building buildings of glass and steel in all sorts of
crazy shapes. They say the average life span of a shopping mall is
twenty years. Drive-through banks and Burger Kings, McDonald's,
they're all the same. They're gone even faster. When I was in the navy,
I was stationed in Spain, and over there it's just the opposite. They

never tear anything down, but they don't always fix things up either. Why do you do it, sir?"

Frank had been asked the question many times before. Architecture students had interviewed him and gotten him talking about the importance of preserving the vernacular, of incorporating certain humble but time-honored structures into newly created designs, of not cutting our umbilical cord to the past. Barns, silos, grain elevators, railroad stations, lighthouses, carriage houses, dogtrot houses from the South, Shaker meeting halls—he could talk about this at length, and although it would be nothing students hadn't heard before, they would take notes. Eventually, they'd get around to asking if he thought of himself as an architect who restored, renovated, or, perhaps, rescued buildings? When he received a question like this, he tended to fall back on ready-made phrases: it was better to preserve than repair, better to repair than to restore, better to restore than reconstruct. In truth there was an art to keeping things alive, to holding off collapse; instead of creating something out of nothing, to arresting the fall of something into nothing, of inverting the hourglass, as it were, when the last grains of sand were about to trickle through. But to describe this deeply personal art of his, he had never quite found the words.

He said, "I guess I just hate to see anything torn down before it's run its natural course. Say what you've heard is true—that bootleggers had this boathouse built. Bootleggers have notoriously short lives. That doesn't mean their buildings have to die with them. That would be the same as saying that when certain self-proclaimed divine rulers died, they had the right to have their dogs or horses or sometimes even their favorite wives buried with them. Buildings are better than that. I guess if you put me to the test, Kenny, that is what I'd have to say, that most buildings deserve to outlive their owners."

Frank laughed. Of course, he didn't believe that, so stated it was a misanthropic point of view, but he knew when he took his long walks in the woods and came upon the remains of a shack or the stone foundations of a cabin, that was as much as he was prepared to accept, that was it, and if he imagined those remains rebuilt, he imagined them unpeopled.

Kenny Brewster gazed out over the water, then with a strong sense of resolution and no amusement in his face turned back. He was summoning his conviction, that was obvious. His blue eyes took on a storm-gathered intensity. "I think you sell yourself short."

"You do?"

"I do. I don't think you realize how important it is to stay here and do the work you do. I don't mean to be presumptuous, but I've been around and seen some things, and mostly what I've seen is people turning their backs and moving on. You don't know how many stinking, falling-apart boathouses there are down South, and I've never seen anyone take the time to make something beautiful out of something that's falling apart like this." Kenny paused, as though winded, or shocked by his own boldness, but in a lower, more intimate tone, added, "I told you I like looking at beautiful things. Although you might not believe it, I've seen some beautiful things in my life."

"Well, I'm glad you like it, Kenny. After all, that's why we came out here."

"No, sir. It's more than that. I've seen cathedrals and Moorish palaces in Spain. But they're museums now. I mean people go in them and go to church and all that, but it's not like this. Someone lives in this!" With a sudden rush of emotion Kenny moved to the nearest window and, fixing his eyes, tried to ride the light through the curtain and into the room. He turned back to Frank and seemed to be urging the older man to step forward and add his testimony, too. Didn't he understand? What was a skyscraper with thousands of offices to get lost in compared to this? Kenny said grandly, but with a trace of a sheepish smile, "It's like when a war is over and everyone looks around and says, 'Let's see what we can save from this mess we've made. Hey, here's a boathouse. Why not start here?'"

"Now you're flattering me," Frank said, realizing he'd just been called, if not a peacemaker, one of the architects in restoring the peace.

"Not if I mean it, sir."

The contract had been signed on the Ides of March, which Ray Whittaker pointed out to Frank Joyner, and which Frank, no Caesar but like him, chose to ignore. It was signed on the third of three meetings with TransAtlantic. Chuck Kohler and Kenny Brewster were present, and when Danny came home from school, Frank asked Kenny to take him aside and explain what they were going to do, which Kenny did. Essentially, he told Danny what he'd told the woman who'd once charged a derrick down in Texas because the drilling had sounded to her like animals in pain. The pain would pass. The gas, which in the form of plants and shell life that had once lain tranquilly on the bottom of a sea until eons of rock had rolled over it, would be released. People would continue to cook their food, heat their houses, take warm showers, and life would go on. In something like this it helped to see the human race as a team, and teammates, as Danny would know, had to get along. Later, Frank would talk to him, but Kenny's had been the decisive word.

The money was good. Ray Whittaker, who had for his friend's sake educated himself on land-leasing contracts, had shown surprise that TransAtlantic would accede to all of Frank's demands and pay as much as it did ($4,200 per leased acre, $27 per rod of leased pipeline land, and a high 18 percent royalty on all extracted gas), which could only be explained by Frank's having enabled TransAtlantic to break Conklin's stranglehold in the region. In exchange, TransAtlantic agreed to make every effort to drill in the fields, not the forests. Frank had shown Kohler and Kenny where he wanted the pad constructed, where the access road was to enter, and how the pipeline would run away. He showed them on the map and then walked them to the spot, down to the right from where he leaned against one of those uncollected bales

of hay and gazed over the valley. Chuck Kohler said it would depend
on the tests, but he drove a stake with a fluorescent red flag in just past
the point of Frank's boot tip to mark the spot, which was the first public indication that common cause had been made. Frank said if it was
to be done, let it be done quickly, and within two weeks TransAtlantic
had run their tests, which consisted of two thumper trucks sending
down vibrations to provide a seismic map of what they already knew
was there, the gas-rich shale. The stakes had gone up to mark off the
pad site Frank had chosen and the access route in. Up on the main
road TransAtlantic erected its sign, the same sign Frank and Helen
had seen before the house in Pennsylvania, where a woman had come
to her door and held her child up in wondrous astonishment that right
on their property, just over the brow of that pretty plateau, a pipe was
being drilled to the center of the earth, and that sign was all it took for
the town to realize that Frank Joyner had been playing possum and
had suddenly charged to the front of the drilling scene.

There was no commando activism, no sabotage, nothing like an
uprising on any sort of scale. The one newsworthy act, instead of spark-
ing outrage, caused head shakes of chuckling disbelief. During the
night in the southeastern corner of the county, where drilling had already begun, someone had climbed a derrick fully lit and in full operation, and instead of throwing a spanner into the works had removed
the American flag and hoisted a Jolly Roger in its place. Since a rig
worker was usually stationed partway up there to help in the handling
of pipe, it did not seem possible a second person could have scaled the
derrick, changed the flags, and gotten away undetected. Suspicion was
directed at the worker himself, a young drill-team member who had
just signed on and offered to fight anyone who questioned his loyalty
to the company or his country. The skull on the Jolly Roger had a
cockeyed look—one eye was enlarged and set out of line with the
other—and it quickly became a joke. Instead of removing it, the Conklin authorities granted the drill team's wishes and allowed it to fly
alongside the quickly restored Stars and Stripes. It was regarded as the

drill team's emblem, and when the team went off to drill another well, they took it with them, playing the role of pirates to the hilt. They began to wear eye patches and gaudy earrings, and that was when Conklin said enough. Its workers needed two eyes and nothing dangling at such length from their ears. This was serious work to which the Jolly Roger had provided some comic relief. The governor himself was said to have laughed. The prankster who had risked a beating and all sorts of bodily harm to climb that derrick never came forth, perhaps embarrassed at how quickly his actions had been co-opted and made to serve the enemy's cause. There was an enemy, a few lone voices kept insisting. When all the drilling was done, desolation was in store.

When her father and his companion, whom Jen identified at once as the landman from Texas or Arkansas, wherever it was, walked in to Luisa's gallery, Jen was alone and reading a book. Charlie had left behind the book, about an abortion-clinic bomber who had taken his survival skills to the Smokies but had been caught when, like any other stray, he'd come down into the towns to raid the trash, and the truth was, she wasn't sure if and when Charlie was coming back. He'd mentioned something about a job out of town, nothing certain, something about banks and building loans and the guys who poured the foundation turning out to be unreliable bastards, something about someone possibly absconding with funds, a bunch of guys strung out waiting to hear, and then she was strung out, waiting to hear, and it had been a week Charlie'd been gone. The landman at her father's side was blond, neat featured, healthy looking without a sag or wrinkle or wasted line anywhere to be seen, and with unabashed, beaming blue eyes. He wore clean khaki pants and a light blue dress shirt with the sleeves rolled up. In his breast pocket he carried an assortment of pens. The way Kenny Brewster paired off with her father and then stepped forth to claim his due (shaking her hand as she shook his) she took exception to, that and his twang, which in the company of her father sounded like some poor practical joke of a sound effect. From things she'd heard before, she judged that she and the landman were about the same age, but the baby fat in Kenny Brewster's face and the flesh Jen knew she carried in hers had nothing in common. Baby fat had a lifetime before it, while her flesh, in spite of all it might have owed to her mother, was like the slag left over from a life that had consumed itself too quickly and at too hot a heat. But Jen wasn't being fair—she knew it and in recompense directed a smile at the landman. The upswing in her fortunes had been his doing. He'd laid a sort of courtly siege to her father and carried the day, while Charlie, in spite of his protestations to the contrary, had cooled off. There might really have been some bad bank folk and some actual bastards among the men who failed to pour the foundation for a house, and someone might have absconded with some funds, and Charlie, worried about where his next paycheck was coming from, might have lost contact with his fingers as they moved out over her body, which would, naturally, have felt older, lumpier, and less alive as a result. And how could that have been the fault of a baby-faced landman from the state of Texas, if it wasn't Arkansas, two states against which she realized she bore an unreasonable grudge? She smiled and said, "I need to thank you. Emotions are running high in this county, and landmen aren't always everybody's favorite people. You've been very patient." She added to her smile an insider's wink. "My father can be a pretty tough sell."

Kenny Brewster said, "You need anything, you have any questions, just call me. I mean, your dad doesn't have to be the one. He has my number. You can call me, too."

She looked at her father, who had brought the landman by the Deweese for some reason. Her father came to see Helen, and he came sometimes to meet people for lunch, but to come just to show somebody around, that didn't happen often. Or showing up at Luisa Bowen's gallery just to say hello to her. Or to Luisa, an old friend. Frank said, "Kenny's worked on the drilling rig. He knows the whole process from beginning to end. Vertical, horizontal, how far down they go, how far out. When they come in with the trucks. You can ask him things like that."

Frank sounded as if he wanted her to test the landman, to see if he could live up to her father's boast. Instead, she turned to Kenny Brewster, and this time her wink was real. "It sounds like you've got a real fan."

He ignored the wink. Or he used it to rise to a higher purpose. "Your father has meant a lot to me," he declared.

"Already?"

Kenny held his tone. "Yes. His work is very important. It's very important *to me*. It's a whole view of life."

She couldn't get the condescension out of her voice and didn't really want to. This boy-man, who was married—that she could see from the ring—and who had attached himself to her father with what had begun to sound like hero worship, needed to take on a broader view, broader than whatever town it was he came from down there. "Kenny, I grew up in this old school building." She performed a sweeping gesture, too large for the room. "I think the lockers were down here, and some more out there in that hall. High ceilings, a lot of windows, drafty stairwells, and hell to heat. There were times I could still smell the chalk. Lunch boxes, lunches in sacks. Soggy sandwiches, that sort of thing. People have been coming through here, oohing and aahing for years. Right, Dad?" She didn't often call her father Dad or Daddy unless she was dating him, locating him in her past. He'd been her old, ineffectual sweetheart of a Daddy when she'd been out on the road. He'd been her father since then. She realized she didn't appreciate the landman's striking that tone of reverence toward a man she'd felt a whole gamut of emotions for. Landmen were encyclopedia salesmen, for Christ's sake, just with a lot more money on the line! And where was Charlie, her interim guy? Her eyes fell on the book he'd left behind, a man gone to the mountains, raiding the garbage pails of the workaday world. Goddamn it! She said, "Well, you know what I mean. You grow up with it, you get used to it. You come on it the way you did and it's a whole different scene. Congratulations."

She hadn't meant that sarcastically. She hoped he understood. Something in the way he studied her, with that smile still showing in his eyes, made her think that he did. She wanted to ask him something to put them both back on solid ground. When was the drilling going to start? How long would it take? How much gas was down there? When the gas was gone, would he go back home? Did he miss it? Did he miss his wife? Would she come to join him? Until she did, did he want to come up and see Jen's apartment, which might once have been a counselor's office or a janitor's room, and one-half of whose bed was now empty? Did he want to match his baby fat against her quickly aging flesh and see what came of that? But she didn't get the chance. Her father, it appeared, had brought his landman to see the Deweese. They'd started in the basement and would work their way up, and before Jen could make any amends or advances, her father had taken him away.

They might have had lunch at either of the two restaurants in the first floor—it was the hour—but Frank knew that Kenny's time was short, and if they'd sat down, they would surely have been greeted by well-wishers, who if they learned that Kenny was a TransAtlantic man would have been curious to learn more. Frank steered Kenny down the basement hall, past the bookstore, a toy store, a store whose contents came mostly from estate sales, which might mean anything (Frank had once thumbed through a stack of *Life* magazines there of World War II vintage, looking yet again for news on the Battle of the Bulge), to a music store with guitars hanging from the ceiling. The little mall's illumination came from windows set at head height so that even on the gloomiest days there was the illusion of light-filled skies. Frank offered no commentary. After the still-closed boathouse, his intention was to give Kenny a look at a building in daily, multipurposed use. There was an eagerness about the landman he liked, but there was a groundedness and an unwillingness to be won by a phony bill of goods he liked even more.

Frank guided him up to the next floor, the mezzanine, where commerce gave way to administrative offices, another art gallery, and a small atrium or assembly hall, which had once been part of the school gymnasium and retained a horseshoe portion of its balcony rail. Lectures and poetry readings were held there; a small theater group put on its plays. The offices were mostly rented by legal-service people, civic or grant organizations. If you discounted the offices of two psychotherapists, an acupuncturist, and a masseur, the two following floors were taken up entirely by apartments, and with natural light available only at the end of each hall, you had to enter one of the apartments to get any real idea of what had been done. Frank hesitated, debating whether it made sense to continue, but he could hardly wave two floors away, either, so he walked Kenny up to the second floor, mentioning that the apartments, once classrooms, began here. When redesigning the space, his rule of thumb had been an apartment per classroom, and for that reason the classrooms remained undivided, intact. If you had fond memories of your Latin class, say, and wanted to relive those days, you now had the means. You could even drink water from the same little ceramic fountains set into the walls. He'd kept some of the lettering on the doors (GYMNASIUM—GIRLS' ENTRANCE; FACULTY MEN) and an ornately scripted quote from an Emily Dickinson poem ("There is no Frigate like a Book . . .") over what had once been the entrance to the library. The floor was laid with quarried, earth-reddened tiles, impossible to find nowadays and more durable than concrete.

As he and Kenny proceeded down the second-floor hall, Frank considered knocking on Helen's door—he knew she was in town—but for reasons he didn't linger on, resisted the temptation. As they passed by her door he even found himself dropping an arm around the younger man's shoulders in an effort to move them along. He left his arm there long enough to guide Kenny into the staircase at the end of the hall, and then, when going down would have been the sensible thing to do, to direct him upstairs to yet another long, dark hall. Only here they quickly came to the door to Jen's apartment, which allowed him to say that if he'd thought of it he could have asked her for the key, and knowing her—the implication being that she was not finicky about such matters—she wouldn't have minded his showing Kenny around. Should he go back down and get the key? Would Kenny like to look around inside? No, no, and Frank knew that Kenny's native courtesy would make such a request unthinkable and was embarrassed for even having suggested it, so much so that he willingly walked Kenny down this next long hall, commenting that he could still remember this hall, when the bell rang, trooping with students when the bell rang. Yes, he had been a student in the Deweese, and what had always stuck in his mind was the way a school, as quiet as a church during class-room hours—so quiet that what a student sent to the principal's office heard, from one room to the next, was the tapping of chalk on the blackboards—would suddenly erupt, then five minutes later go quiet again. That tapping of chalk had been as faithful as the ticking of a clock. Now, with everything computerized, he supposed that was a sound from the past.

Kenny began to assure him that, no, he remembered it, too, the tapping, the trooping, and then the quiet tapping again, when a door opened toward the end of the hall and one of Frank's tenants stepped out, a woman who kept a calendar of complaints, one for each day, un-til she had recycled them all and could turn the page on a new month. Today, Constance Lauder had leaped ahead. With this unusual late-April heat she had turned on her air conditioner just to make sure, and, of course, it hadn't worked. She was a tall, pale woman, who dressed in long, flowing robes and scarves and skirts, and who had once told Frank he could call her Connie, if that made matters easier. She never looked at Kenny. Frank Joyner's walking down the hall with her com-plaint of the day fresh on her lips was positively providential. Frank told her he would see to it, and as he and Kenny reached the staircase at the end of the hall, the younger man told the older that the woman had been a dead ringer for a grade-school teacher of his, and, as he remembered, there'd been no way to satisfy her either.

They went up the final flight of sandstone stairs. A rarely used service staircase would take them up on the roof, which suddenly seemed like a good idea. From there Kenny could look out on the town and up the lake, which would be a fitting end to their outing, with Constance Lauder, Connie to her friends, to chuckle about and wonderfully warm, late April light to spare.

But that was not what he did. He wasn't sure why. On the fourth floor he walked Kenny to the door of his own apartment, which he hadn't entered for months. The "why" would be that if what interested this young landman from Arkansas or Texas was ultimately a home created from something that had once served another purpose, then they stood before the door. The "why" would be that if a school become a small city didn't ultimately become a place to live, then none of it made sense. Or maybe Frank just thought he owed Kenny this, the living space in that boathouse having been obscured behind its scrimlike curtains. Whatever the reason, he opened the door, telling Kenny that here was where he and his family had once lived, and, of course, it was like walking into a mausoleum, a tomb. It needed to be aired, curtains needed to be opened, and light let in. It needed flowers, it needed the smell of food and clothing and daily usage and human warmth. They entered the living room, and Frank went immediately to the tall, twin windows across the way, built in a sort of embrasure, threw back the curtains, and opened the available panes. Beyond these windows was a small balcony and, extending past that, what had once been the school flagpole. Every Fourth of July, Veterans and Memorial Day, Frank had flown the flag, and there'd been a flagless period when a red-tailed hawk had perched on the pole long enough for the family to consider him a pet, but Frank stopped short of telling the landman any of that. The ceiling in the living room was high and remained, in spite of the inrush of light, shadowy. The plants had all been removed, and the

coffee tables and sofa and wing chairs and end tables had a barrenness
about them that seemed irreversible. Directly across the living room
from the tall, twin windows, a spiral staircase led up to a loft that for a
time had been Frank and Marjorie's bedroom, and there'd been mornings, April mornings like this, when they'd lain late in bed and light
had filled the living room and the bedroom with an opulent glow. He
found himself apologizing to Kenny. Here was where they'd lived, but
before he showed this apartment to anybody, he should have thought
to make it habitable again. And just how was he going to do that? The
landman said he understood and said it didn't matter, he could imagine
it all.

Frank led him down what had once been an intersecting hall to the
dining room, with the rich wood of its long teak table dusty and bare.
The kitchen, with its terra-cotta tiles and its butcher-block counter,
came next. It was faced with a wall of windows, whose light, when
Frank pulled the curtains, was harsh. A sunroom/breakfast room followed, full of heavily padded wicker furniture, where in the morning
the light was mild and where plants had thrived. The philodendron,
the rubber plants, those broomlike palmetto plants, some flowering
cactus, were gone, of course, but a trace of their earth-mold remained
in the air. An L-shaped jog gave way to the children's bedrooms,
where Frank had installed skylights so that his children could lie in
their beds and study the stars. They'd been gone so long that little of
his children's presence remained. Their photographs and posters had
long ago come down, and whatever had once counted as their mascots
or totem animals no longer sat on their shelves. The closets were bare.
The rugs lay flat. The spreads on their beds were stretched as clean
and blank as a canvas on a frame. Gerald's room and then Jen's, where
the pile of pillows had lost its improvised freshness and begun to
resemble some hardened natural growth.

Frank and Kenny might have stopped there. They couldn't see it
all. There were bathrooms and closets and storage areas and a utility
room that the landman would simply have to imagine. He might have

imagined Mickey's room, too, the last of the three. The exterior walls of the Deweese did a cutback there, limiting the space but providing an alcoved extension to the room that Frank had always liked and would want to show any visitor as the final touch. Still, they might have stopped short. Kenny had work to do; they were in the apartment's far reaches and it was time to go back. But Frank opened the door to where his younger son, as a boy, had lived, and a ghost might have gathered before him, filling the room, for the bed had been slept in and only half-made, a glass with an inch of some dark liquid stood on the bedside table, two dirty socks lay on the floor, a paperback book thrown down beside them, the closet door stood open, and there was the trace of a smell, alien, intrusive, until Frank realized he had been smelling it much of his life. It was the smell of any human habitation gone stale, but, more particularly, it was the smell of his son trapped inside his various needs.

In that alcoved space, where Mickey had positioned his desk so that sitting behind it he could control the room, Frank saw his son. He had an angry, wounded look, as though he might weep or break into a rage; his mouth was open and he was mouthing words that nobody could hear. Instinctively, Frank realized his obligation was to shield Mickey from Kenny, Kenny from Mickey, so with the sad and certain awareness of how little any father could do, Frank closed the door on Mickey's ghost. Instinctively, Kenny Brewster realized that one room in every house must remain off-limits and did not take it personally.

11

H E'D LOST A CASE HE'D HAD NO BUSINESS TAKING. BUT HE'D TAKEN IT
because he'd developed a reputation for defending wealthy clients with
high-spending habits, so he'd defended a state detective instead, accused of planting evidence at a crime scene to promote his career. The
ADA had called the woman the detective was accused of incriminating
to testify, and all the papers agreed Wilson Michaels had lost the case
when he'd savaged the woman, a poor black mother hoping to shield
her son, on the witness stand. To right the ship, he'd agreed to defend,
pro bono, a woman accused of concealing a weapon allegedly used by
her boyfriend in a robbery attempt, only to have the ADA convince a
jury that the woman had been in on the robbery all along, a possibility
Wilson Michaels, in search of a poor, falsely accused woman to defend,
had discounted from the start. Pro bono had, in fact, been pro Wilson
Michaels, which the press was quick to point out and ride hard. His
career never really recovered after that.

When he could no longer afford his Upper East Side apartment,
his second wife's mother had conveniently died and left her only

daughter her apartment in the Garden District of Sunnyside, Queens. Looking from Skillman Avenue down Forty-seventh Street, he could see the skyline of Manhattan at midtown, and if he was willing to use public transportation, could get to his office there in half an hour. There came a time, of course, when he could no longer afford that midtown office either, and since their Sunnyside apartment was really a three-story row house (if you included the basement), he set up an office at home. He was sixty-one. His second wife, Melanie, was twenty years younger and looked every day of it. When she left him to go off with a man younger still she'd met at her fitness center, she told Michaels he could stay put if he wanted to, just as long as he knew he was living on borrowed time. The day he came home to find the locks changed was the day he'd know his time had run out. They had had no children. He'd had a daughter by an earlier marriage, who'd given him a grand-daughter, and maybe daughter and granddaughter would come see how Dad and Granddad were getting along. And maybe not. His problem. Melanie was gone, to the great Southwest, if he took her at her word.

Behind the house in which Wilson Michaels now lived was a patio, which gave way to a slate walkway connecting his patio to others up and down the row, and that walkway led to a communal backyard, large enough for kids to play football games in. There was a kind of garden haven back there, with flowering bushes and arching trees, and the smell of cut grass could still evoke something of that lighthearted, light-limbed time when Wilson Michaels had earned money as a lawn-boy. On a post at an intersection of lanes, he'd hung out his shingle, a plastic plate you'd mistake for marble unless you tapped it with your fingernail: WILSON MICHAELS, ATTORNEY AT LAW. He couldn't imagine its generating much business, but it seemed like the right thing to do. There were days—those first ones—when rather than feeling hum-bled, he believed he might finally have found a home.

He'd taken the time to talk to a few neighbors, and the old lady who lived next door, a Mrs. Hoffman, who twice a day took her cairn ter-rier out for a walk, he'd been especially attentive to. Later, when he got a glimpse into her house—or, rather, a thwarted glimpse because Mrs. Hoffman lived behind a wall of trash—his mood took a turn. The Garden District of Sunnyside, Queens, began to seem like the place where your life piled up behind you, and its heralded timelessness closer to stagnation than to the distillation of all things healthy and true. He began to smell the mildew and the rot and the foul dankness of pipes. For years he'd been fighting a losing battle against his increasing weight, and he began to feel oppressed in the low-ceilinged, undersize rooms. The few cases he had amounted to little more than the filing of motions, which he could write from home, and on his few trips into Manhattan he took the crowded trains. If he dreamed of cases he'd tried, the following mornings what remained of those dreams were not the details of the cases themselves, or even the outcomes, but the palatial size of the courtrooms, the grandness of the scene.

The case that occupied him now had not made it to court, although Wilson Michaels did not discount that possibility. What it came down to was that his ex-brother-in-law Frank Joyner had gotten such a good deal from the TransAtlantic Gas Company because he, Wilson Michaels, had done all the heavy work. The pittance of a percentage his daughter, Brenda, had been assigned failed to take into account the difference her father's intercession had made. What you had to do was take the average a company such as Conklin was paying those farmers thereabouts—a grand an acre on the leasing, no more than 12 percent on the royalties, and no more than twenty bucks a rod on the pipeline route—and calculate how much more Joyner had gotten from Trans-Atlantic and recognize that that difference had been Wilson Michaels's doing. It was a finder's fee. Michaels had found TransAtlantic, and he'd found Frank Joyner sitting on the fence, and he'd put the two of them into bed together. His first wife, Carol, could call him a finder and a go-between. She could call him a pimp. But somebody had to do it, or a small-town guy like Joyner would be sitting there still wondering why the gravy train had passed him by.

Michaels called Carol that night. From the start she had gotten him all wrong. Wilson Michaels had never had a taste for luxury, had never been greedy for the things of the world. He'd had a reputation to uphold and he'd had to dress and act the part, but all he'd really ever wanted money for was to buy himself some peace. To buy real peace took real money—she, with her small-town mentality, might not be equipped to understand that. Once she'd gotten caller ID on her phone, most of the time she wouldn't pick up when Michaels called, so he sat in his small, crowded office, looking over the little patio gone to seed, and called her from his computer.

Speaking into a blue screen crowded with rows of files, something like the cemetery of his career, he said, "I need a couple of minutes is all, Carol, and I need you to listen before you hang up."

She surprised him, the sound of her voice did, its mildness broadcast into the room. "I wouldn't hang up on you, Wilson. I don't think I've ever done that."

He could think of a hundred times, which, of course, he couldn't. "I'll come to the point—I don't want to take up your time. You're all right, aren't you?"

"I'm fine."

"It's about Brenda's share of the gas money."

"I assumed that it was."

"I need you to consider something, then I need you to tell me what you think is fair."

He recited his figures, what he knew the Conklin mean to be, information she could get off the Web herself if she had any idea, and the deal her brother had gotten from TransAtlantic. He asked her to consider the difference, how it had come about.

He recognized her tone of voice from the years they had spent together: it was the calm after one of their storms had passed. It was the infuriatingly imperturbable calm of someone who'd put herself out of reason's reach. She said, "I suppose Frank can be a hard bargainer. That's a side of him I never really knew."

He tried to match her tone, as if they were reminiscing about matters long laid to rest. "Actually, I suspect I had more to do with it than your brother did. I had to call that fellow from TransAtlantic, I don't know, three or four times before I could get him to see what he had right under his nose. All that land leased to Conklin and there your brother sat on the real prize, a driller's delight. I don't suppose he told you that."

"What, Wilson?"

"That I was the one who told TransAtlantic to make the call."

"I believe he did mention it. He mentioned something about your name on a card the TransAtlantic man had left in the door."

"He did, did he? Well, that was . . . up front of him." Michaels struggled to control his tone.

She had no trouble with hers. "Frank has always been honest. A sweet and honest man."

"Carol, some of that extra money I made for your family should go to Brenda. I mean, she deserves a higher percentage, a higher share. And let's be as honest as you say your brother is: some should come to me. If it hadn't been for me, you'd be picking up the peanuts Conklin left scattered around."

He thought he heard a sadness, a sadness and a sweetness, come breathing into the close confines of his undersize office. "But, Wilson, dear, you no longer belong to the family. Brenda seems content with her share. You're right, it's more than any of us expected. We should thank you. I *do* want to thank you. I'm sure Frank would thank you, too. But you belong to another family now."

Half moan, half rage, he pleaded with the first of his wives. "Carol, this isn't like you!"

"No, I suppose not."

"You might not listen to reason but you've never been . . . cruel."

"Thank you, Wilson."

"I need a little help here, sweetheart."

"I wish I could but there comes a time . . ."

"A time for what?"

"A time for . . . Is it just money you're calling about?"

No, it was fairness, it was age and loneliness and grief everywhere he looked, but he set his jaw. "Yes, just money, just enough, just what's mine."

"Then the person you want to talk to isn't Frank. It's Ray Whittaker, an old, old friend we all grew up with. He's a lawyer, just like you. His office is handling the distribution of the money. I'll even give you his number, if you'll hold on."

One of the many attractions of the Garden District in Sunnyside was the availability of parking nearby on the streets. Once a week for a couple of hours you had to move your car when the garbage trucks came through, and all you had to remember was what street you'd moved it to in any given week. When he emerged from his house carrying an overnight case, Wilson Michaels realized before it could even begin to show on his face that he was about to draw a blank. Mrs. Hoffman, a little plastic sack in hand, was out there with her cairn terrier, who was sniffing around the base of a tree until he found his spot. The dog raised his leg and peed, and Michaels stood there, as though in appreciation, as he scrolled back the weeks. In his mind's eye he was trying to see a burgundy Buick Riviera, long enough to take up the space for two compact cars, and too long not to occasionally encroach on the exaggerated space the city required around its fire hydrants. Since he had been living in the Garden District, he was not aware of a single fire truck's having been called out, not one, and that observation, which had become a pet peeve, gave him a clue. Wherever he was parked, he was suddenly sure he was in violation. He visualized himself with his luggage in hand walking up and down the streets until he found his car. If it had too flagrantly encroached on fire-hydrant space, his car might have been towed, in which case he would be walking with his luggage until he dropped or was willing to admit the obvious. The intelligent thing would be to leave the overnight case inside his door until he found his car and then drive back and pick the case up. As embarrassing as that might be, he was about to do it when Mrs. Hoffman asked if he was going on a trip. As soon as he said that he was, he knew what her next question would be, he could see it forming in the cataracted squint of her eyes. Would he be joining his wife and where would that be and how was she? His only defense was to answer her as he was striding off, as if he knew exactly where he was going. Yes, he said, a trip, and he set off so abruptly that her dog began to bark, a series of rapid-fire yaps that accompanied him up the street. And where would that be? And how was she, that lovely young woman, who had so improbably become his wife?

He found his car, and it was properly parked, and three days remained before he'd have to move it again. He knew people in this city for whom that would have been reason enough to postpone a trip.

Sometime later, he found himself driving up a broad valley beside a rushing stream in which fishermen stood in hip boots casting into the current. The hills were blanketed in two shades of green: a dark, stony green for the pines and spruces, thicker at the higher reaches, and a light wash of spring green for whatever the deciduous trees might have been. Deer had emerged from the forest to graze on grassed-over banks of the expressway, and in little time he passed the carcasses of three who had strayed down too far. Buzzards circled overhead. He had not been on a road trip in some time, and the traffic was sparser than he thought it would be. With such weather, such views, and so many reasons that not just he but other people would have for getting out of the city, he'd expected the roads to be clogged. The valley made leisurely bends this way and that, and the stream, in a braiding effect, passed back and forth under the road. He watched the fishermen, the birds, the deer, and the always-available sparkle off the water, without having to lower his speed. Eventually, it dawned on him that he was going to run out of valley and road before he'd gotten his fill, so he lowered his speed and hugged the right lane until even that, he realized, wasn't going to work.

A state park allowed him to pull off. He didn't make the mistake of sitting in his car, questioning his next move, but got out and walked across the moist park grounds to the river, where he found a toppled tree trunk to sit on with a clear view of the current rushing down on him. The smell was fresh, rank, ironlike. The water was the color of burnished steel. He saw no fish, but upstream, before the river bent out of sight to his left, he did see another fisherman, working his line in lengthening loops, a filament that either caught the sunlight or didn't and that finally Wilson Michaels had to take on faith. There was a line, there was bait, and there were fish, and if one stood there in the middle of a river and cast long enough, something good would come of it. He had caught fish as a boy. He could remember that electric tug on his line when a fish struck, and that darting muscle-force under the water, and his boy's realization that he was engaged in a struggle of life and death. He'd survived and a few fish hadn't. In summer camp he'd been taught how to gut and clean a fish, and he remembered the multicolored, neatly packaged guts until he'd touched them and made a mess. It wasn't hard to get caught up in these boyhood memories. What helped bring him back was the sun, the rushing, rank water, and the imprint of that toppled tree on his backside. Finally, he left it up to the fisherman. He began a countdown. Catch a fish by the tenth cast and I'll do one thing, without hesitation, and not another. The fisherman failed him, or Wilson Michaels simply lost interest in his count. He went back to his car, stopping on the way to use the bathroom. His mildly malfunctioning prostate had taught him to take advantage of bathrooms when they were at hand; the times he'd had to request a ten-minute recess from a judge had not been to his advantage. Those times seemed almost as remote to him now as his boyhood. He peed, he washed his hands, he looked in the lavatory mirror and reminded himself he had nothing to go back to, nothing and nobody, did he understand?

. . .

Off the expressway and onto two-lane roads, the streams were narrower than the one he'd stopped beside, as were the valleys when they
were pinched into shadowed defiles and the road ran along a slope. But
the towns were where it all opened up; the valleys widened or formed a
sort of sheltering bowl, and he drove into them with essentially the
same question on his mind. For a truly good-natured man, no longer
blinded by big-city lights or scheming big-city ways, why not here?
Why not have a town hall, a town square, a town school, a town library,
one tolerable town restaurant, and call it quits? He saw a number of
towns like that, with their requisite streams running quietly alongside
and a few of their citizens quietly going about their affairs. If he didn't
see a town hospital, that might have been because nobody ever got sick.

He enjoyed himself. He saw no reason not to. It was not as if he
were going off guard.

Still, he was taken by surprise when he found himself boxed in by
trucks that made a tremendous racket and left a stench of exhaust behind so that he could no longer drive with his window rolled down. He
began to see the gas-drilling pads and the occasional derrick when the
drilling was actually under way. Even with the windows up, the drilling noise as he drove through it was a prolonged, unwearied, and clattering din. He could feel in his accelerator and passing up his leg the
vibration of the drill bit as it bore into rock. Going from one county to
the next, he must have entered prime drilling ground, and the vibration was a reminder that he had business to take care of. Still, he had to
admit that when he left that drilling county and returned to cows on
their pastures or sprouts of green corn or some sort of beans in rows,
he was pleased and relieved.

On the last leg of his trip, he turned north. He drove in and out of
another drilling county, tank trucks and dump trucks and pipe trucks
and drilling rigs and graders and earthmovers of various sorts. CONK-
LIN NATURAL GAS COMPANY almost all the signs now read. Along with
everyone else he'd heard reports about the gas companies playing loose
and easy with the nation's wells, aquifers, lakes, rivers, and estuaries,

and he didn't doubt that certain chemicals had a shelf life that would put our mortal span to shame, but he also knew that time was a personal matter and that over time things washed clean. It didn't help to get squeamish now. Since the Industrial Revolution, Luddites there had always been, but show him a single one who went around dressed in hides that he'd cured himself from animals he'd shot with his own homemade bow and arrow.

This last leg was over land he recognized, a valley he'd driven down before. He had been a happy man then, when Brenda was just a little girl and he was married to Carol and they'd driven off to pay a visit to her hometown, her parents, who'd always struck him as two aging, well-behaved children, looking enough alike they could have been twins, and his brother-in-law, the architect, who took old barns, like the smartly painted yellow one he'd just driven by, and turned them into homes, as if humans and animals were peas in a pod and could be bedded down in the same stalls. There'd been nephews, too, and a niece who had been Brenda's little playmate, whose name he couldn't remember but whose wanton little look he could. A family to which, by legal consent, he'd once belonged.

He took a room in the first motel he came to that wasn't a relic. A small restaurant was attached, and there, sitting in a booth and having a cup of black coffee, he took out his cell phone and began to make his calls. He called his daughter, Brenda, to ask her if she could guess where he was and what he was about to do. But Brenda was in no mood. The breakup in her marriage had been followed by another false start, during which time her daughter, Cynthia, had gone off the rails, and Brenda didn't need her father to be playing guessing games with her. Sorry, Daddy. Bad day. He told her if he played his cards right, he was going to get her some more of that gas money, and that might brighten her day a little. Before they hung up, he asked her if she could remember the name of that cousin of hers she used to play with, but she couldn't, or was rushed, or wasn't sure what cousin he was referring to, but then just before she hung up she said, You don't mean Jen, do you? and apparently he did.

He called Kenny Brewster, both at his office and, when he didn't reach him there, on his cell phone. Brewster was out somewhere where pipe was clanging and trucks were pulling hard in first gear, and Michaels, realizing this was no time for small talk, courteously put the landman on notice that he might be called on to testify about how instrumental Michaels had been in getting the whole Joyner-TransAtlantic deal done. Then Michaels called the lawyer Ray Whittaker. When Whittaker answered, Michaels identified himself and told Frank Joyner's lawyer the name of the motel he'd just checked into, and Whittaker, in a deferential tone with a smile attached, as if he were a welcoming committee of one to the town, said he knew who Wilson Michaels was and told him if he could hang on just a few minutes longer, Whittaker would be there in person to greet him.

Wilson Michaels ordered a second cup of coffee, used the bathroom so he wouldn't have to later, and in that same booth he and Ray Whittaker met. A small man with thick glasses, a beak of a nose, a shock of graying-brown hair, and eyes that made jittery, precise movements like a bird's. He was dressed in some kind of Hawaiian shirt. The man sitting across from him was seemingly twice his size, heavy-shouldered, shaggy-haired, with slumberous movements and an affable, sleepy-eyed grin, except the eyes were wide-awake. Dressed in a tieless shirt and his third or fourth best suit.

To what did their small town owe the honor?

When Michaels explained it to him, Ray Whittaker responded that they could have dealt with this on the phone, that Wilson Michaels hadn't had to drive all the way up here, for which Michaels had no explanation, except to say that it had been a nice day, he had nothing else on the calendar, it had seemed like years since he'd been out of the City, and he'd gotten a little education, driving in and out of gas-drilling land, in among all those trucks.

Ray Whittaker said, "It's not just the noise and the exhaust; they can be deadly, you know."

"So I've heard."

"That little boy and his dog."

"If the media didn't make the whole thing up."

"They saw the angle and they jumped on it. A day in the country. Every boy's got his dog. Mine was named Smokey. Actually, he was one of four, but he liked to chase cars. Stands to reason he'd have been the one."

"Restitution?"

"For the dog, or the dog and the boy? Timmy was his name, Timmy O'Donnell. Cute kid."

"It was Conklin, right?"

"Conklin it was, and the parents had leased their land and were waiting for the drilling to start. They probably got a big spike in their royalties. I wouldn't be surprised if they got their whole contract rewritten."

"But not as good a one as Frank Joyner got."

"Ever since I've known him—and we go all the way back—Frank has been snookering people into getting deals. I guess you'd say he 'disarms' them and then asks me to come in and clean up the details. Frank doesn't like a fight. If he didn't come from a family of Quakers, they were the next best thing."

"Ray—you're all right with Ray, aren't you?"

"If you're all right with Wilson."

"Ray, we've got a problem."

"Not yet, Wilson."

"That's good to hear."

"Because if it's just a matter of money—"

"Whoa!"

"Whoa?"

"Something my ex-wife said."

"Whoa?"

"'If it were just a matter of money,' as if that were a minor matter, a mere nuisance."

"Because if that's all it is, we've got no problem at all. I've been hired to handle the distribution of the gas income, both the leasing payment and the royalties when they start to come in, to the members of the family. And since you no longer belong to the family—"

"Whoa again!"

"Again?"

"Something else my ex-wife said."

"I hate to keep taking words out of Carol's mouth."

"She said you went back."

"As far back as I go with Frank."

"A lovely lady, fine mother, I'm the first one to admit it. Class act. Not a mean bone in her body, but I guess you'd agree, with none of the persuasive powers of her brother. No deal-maker."

"Both quiet types—that whole family was. Not like us, Wilson, used to our days in court."

"Ray, Frank got the better of the deal."

"Don't see how you see that, Wilson."

"Because Frank didn't account for where the deal came from in the first place, and Carol, being the soft touch she is, didn't have the heart to remind her big brother."

"And we're back to the part you played in contacting TransAtlantic to start off with?"

"We're back."

"Well, I'm still stuck on the numbers, Wilson, because once it's in my hands, that's all it is. You start dividing it up, proportional shares down through the generations. If I'm not mistaken, there'll be some for your granddaughter when she comes of age."

"It's not all numbers, Ray."

"Wish you were right because number crunching has never been my thing."

"What *is* your thing?"

"How to put it? 'One could do worse than to be a swinger of birches' would be one way."

"What's that, Ray?"

"A little something Robert Frost dreamed up. 'The Road Not Taken?' guy? 'Stopping by Woods on a Snowy Evening?'"

"You know what my thing is?"

"Defending Donald Trump against an abusive shoeshine boy? Sorry, bad joke. Tell me, Wilson."

"Some peace of mind."

"I'm with you there."

"Call it what you like. Call it a finder's fee. I found TransAtlantic and I found Frank and I kept at them until I made it happen. Call it a broker's fee. Just make it happen, Ray. I don't know about you, but I've had enough days in court. Do we really need another one? That would eat up time and a lot of Frank Joyner's money. Just find me a number."

Ray Whittaker sat shaking his head, such sad news he had to convey, no way to sugarcoat it now. But some of the sadness appeared to be real. He raised his head and the bird-quick eyes went still. In a "there but for fortune" tone he said, "I'm sorry. I truly am. Numbers are for family members, Wilson."

"Then find a way, Ray, to make me one of them."

12

You heard stories. One story Jen had heard she told Helen, who could sympathize. A mother has a little girl. The little girl has a birthday. The morning of the birthday party the mother wakes up to find the road to their house clogged with trucks, no way to get around unless you're willing to drive with two wheels in a ditch. And absolutely no advance warning the trucks were coming, not a hint. The mother pleads, she ties balloons to the mailbox and begs anybody she can get to listen to see how crazy that looks, those trucks and those gay, lighter-than-air balloons, and no one disagrees that balloons and tank trucks carrying water and fracking fluid and chemicals too dangerous to be named belong in different worlds, but once the decision has been made and it's all been set in motion, there is nothing anybody can do. The birthday party is called off. The most you can get these gas companies to say when you ask them when the hydrofracking will start is, Could be anytime.

It was late May. There wasn't a flower that hadn't bloomed. That was part of it, too. The earth went on about its business as if cataclysms occurred only on other planets. The fear now was that so much deep drilling, accompanied by underground explosions, could provoke earthquakes; some forces you just didn't tamper with until you knew what those forces were. But Jen was reminded of something Charlie had told her. Poppies, with their crepe-thin, bloodred petals, grew right up to the lip of the trenches over which soldiers stumbled to their deaths in the fields of Flanders during World War I, and, of course, somebody had written that song. In the midst of that slaughter, the world went on blooming.

Charlie was off again to build a house on week-by-week funding, which, as plausibly as he could explain it, she wasn't sure she believed. She'd broken down and called Kenny Brewster, as he'd invited her to do. TransAtlantic was drilling two counties away. Her idea was that TransAtlantic wouldn't move into their part of their county until Conklin did, at which point TransAtlantic would want to beat Conklin to the punch, but that was probably just her melodramatic and unscientific intuition telling her that something had to happen soon. Kenny Brewster said he didn't have any idea, and she believed him. He didn't know where those decisions were made. If there existed a calendar of drilling dates and sites, he'd never seen it. He'd call her the instant he knew anything for sure, and he insisted she and her father could count on him, but his wife continued to put him off and Kenny continued to not get the idea, and his was almost too pathetic a case to contemplate.

Helen surprised Jen, asking where Frank's peacekeeping efforts had gotten him if he was continually at war inside? Jen said that was not an expression she would use to describe her father, and Helen said Jen would have to take her word for it, that since Helen had known him, Frank had not been of one mind. Did Jen mind Helen making her her confidante? Talking to her in this way? They were having lunch on a terrace that the vegetarian restaurant in the Deweese opened on fine days. Helen wore a muslin blouse with a tasseled cord, and Jen a sleeveless blouse with the top two buttons undone, the flesh in her upper arms and a portion of her chest bare. When Jen didn't mind, Helen took one of Jen's hands in both of hers and told her she had been married to a man of an undivided mind, so fully in accord with the terms of his life and death it had pained her terribly at times, so she knew a divided mind when she saw one. And Jen surprised herself by asking Helen which she preferred. Which she preferred? Yes, a man with a divided mind, which at least left an opening, a crack in the defense, or a man with an undivided one, which you could only stand back from and admire.

"It all comes down to what's down there, doesn't it?" Jen said.

"Down there?"

"Down there, a mile, two miles away. Say *gas* to a man of my father's generation and before he's had time to think he's thinking Auschwitz and Treblinka. I'm thinking of something like a spirit, a genie in a bottle. Or something to get high on. Danny'll probably be thinking of rocket fuel, some supersonic speed. Some of all of that and a lot of dollars, Helen. A lot of dollars. Oil is different. Oil just gets you filthy and rich. But you wash it off and you shine like gold. Oil is the good ole days. Texas roughnecks and there she blows! . . . Wait, that was a whaling expression, wasn't it? An even better time! Light up your life with whale oil. Back when there were more whales than you could throw a harpoon at . . ."

They had salads, then shared a brownie with whipped cream. Acquaintances walked by, whom they greeted, if no close friends. Did Jen even have close friends left here? What if she took her share of the gas money and went back on the road? On the road she made friends—it was amazing what a change of scenery could do. On the road she made friends immediately, it was electric, with a great, gleeful appetite she made them, and the next day they were gone.

She was forgetting her son. A foundling of the road she had brought back to civilization, the way Old World explorers had brought back New World natives and displayed them at the courts of Europe as magnificent freaks of nature.

· · ·

During this period while they waited for the gas companies to make
up their minds, Jen saw Danny frequently. Since Charlie had been away,
Danny had come down twice to sleep on his air mattress, but mostly she
saw him out there, where she and her father would make simple suppers
or they'd cook out on the fieldstone grill that had been there perhaps
as long as the house had and every spring her father would rebuild.
After supper they'd take walks up the road. Occasionally Helen would
be with them, but then they paired off differently, paced differently,
and it all felt a bit like a procession.

One evening, instead of walking up the hill, Danny said to her,
"Wanna see where the pad's gonna be?"

The proprietary tone to his voice surprised her. His granddad
wasn't asked to come along, and Frank made no attempt to join them.
They left him on the deck where the family had gathered on that unseasonably warm Thanksgiving Day, and started up the road, only to
turn left onto another road that cut the long, sloping Joyner pasture in
two. There was the great rolled loaf of hay her father might lean back
on after his walk in the woods. It was shaggy and weather-grayed and
large enough so that both she and her son could lean back on it, the
most curious sense of weight at their backs, a softness packed hard that
if you leaned against long enough would take you in, mix you into its
mass. Her son led her down to an area of the pasture where Trans-
Atlantic had planted their sign and rows of fluttering red flags marked
out the entrance to where the access road would be graded and, farther
down, to where the pad would be built.

Danny told her, "They're drilling right here, they can't go outside
these stakes. There's plenty of room, but if they go outside them,
they're breaking the contract and then they have to leave. Kenny—
you know Kenny, don't you?—said they would never do that, that he'd
guarantee it, and when they did leave, this would look the same as it
does right now. He said we should come down here and look at it and

take pictures if we couldn't remember. And then the gas pipe would go underground, you'd never see it, it would go right down there. From there it could go anywhere in the world."

Danny pointed down another length of fluttering flags to where the pipeline would run. He talked about it as if it were a lifeline, and she supposed she could thank Kenny for that, that the gas line had made her son feel less lonely, less abandoned, more in contact with the world, for that was what she heard in his voice and saw in his eyes as they followed the line of flags downhill. He might have been a soldier out on patrol. He could have been a lonely and fiercely proud sentry patrolling this communal link, yes, that was her son, a lonely boy, fiercely proud, patrolling his link to the world, and she had Kenny Brewster to thank. Although it was her aunt Carol she thought of in that moment, something Carol had said at Thanksgiving dinner, that had made them all laugh—at Carol's sweetness and her fond, transparent way of promoting a cause. Wisconsin has its cheese, Maine its lobsters, and we have our gas. We're all pitching in.

They moved into June. You kept hearing the word *imminent*, just one more word that failed to make sense. Post-eleventh-hour defense lines had been thrown up, and now the talk among the antifracking movement was that all the damage could be contained in that southeastern corner of the county, and that the town itself would be spared the bulk of the truck traffic, at least, and much of the contamination. Members of the board of the town in which the Joyner property lay had proposed one ordinance to keep the trucks off their roads unless an expensive road-reconstruction agreement had been reached in advance, and another to set strict limits to the amount of noise drillers could make. Either ordinance might lead the companies to conclude that that little township was more trouble than it was worth, and with gas plentiful everywhere they looked, why bother? Of course, landowners who had already cashed their leasing checks and had an eye on their royalties would be left scanning the horizon. Other board members pointed out that the lawsuits brought by the gas companies or the affected landowners could be staggering, and two members of the board who had leased their land said the board could count on it and that the town would be broke within a week.

Kenny Brewster called Jen once, just to tell her that he still didn't know when the Joyner property would be drilled, but he sensed that his not-knowing was coming to an end. He had a new partner now. Chuck Kohler had decided to go back to Texas, and Kenny's new partner, who was from the area, claimed that the Joyner property was in a sweet spot. You don't go off and leave it undrilled and then have to come back after everybody else has drilled all around it. That would be like coming back to fish in a pond after the water'd been stirred up. Jen asked Kenny to go back to something he'd just said.

Chuck Kohler had decided to return to Texas. Did that mean the decision was theirs, the landmen's, to make, and if that was so, why hadn't he—she was already thinking "their landman," "her landman"—gone back, too, since she assumed, without speaking the words, that Texas had not come to him.

Kenny dodged the question, and not long after that, she saw him having lunch at a table by himself in the hall just outside Luisa Bowen's gallery. She immediately assumed his presence in their town meant that TransAtlantic was about to come their way and he was an advance man, sent to prepare the ground. But gas companies were famous—*infamous* was the word—for showing up unannounced, and if he wasn't here to do TransAtlantic's bidding, why hadn't he come into the gallery, because she had something she wanted to say? And why now, as she stood before him, didn't he invite her to lunch? Where were his manners? So, with those unanswered questions on her mind, she sat down anyway.

She said, "I never got a chance to thank you for taking the time to explain the drilling to Danny. I'm sure my father did, but that was something I needed to say."

"He's a great kid. He thinks things through. You better know what you're talking about with him."

"And you do?"

"Well, who ever *knows*? You think you do. But you make mistakes."

"You told him that the gas line that starts with our well ends up going everywhere else in the world."

"I did? Well, it kinda does, doesn't it?"

"And that as lonely as you might feel, you're always in contact with everybody else. Kids are always lonely. The most popular kid in his class is lonely, he just doesn't know it." Then: "You didn't come in to the gallery to say hello."

He said what made perfectly good sense to him. "I figured if I sat here, I'd see you if you came out, and if you didn't, that meant you were busy."

She laughed at him. "It wasn't because you didn't have my father with you?"

He cocked his head at her and frowned.

"Or was it because you didn't want me to ask you if your wife was still down there in Texas because that was something you didn't want to get into again?"

He gathered himself. "You come to the point, don't you?"

She laughed at herself and lowered her eyes. "You know what it is? It's all this sitting around waiting. Putting things off. Making plans and unmaking them. To stay sane you finally have to spit things out. It's really your guys' fault. She's not coming, is she?"

"Not yet." He drew a breath. "I don't know what she is going to do."

They had lunch together. Kenny had the day off. Jen didn't, but she'd behaved so well all the way back since Robert's time, when she'd driven down to his town week after week in the vain hope of running some steel up his spine, Luisa would probably give her the rest of the afternoon off if she asked for it. Did she want the afternoon off? It depended what Kenny said when she asked him, if TransAtlantic wasn't set to move in—*imminently* was again the word—what had brought

him to their little town on his day off? And he'd said the town had.
He'd been living in and out of motels for weeks now, and this town of
hers, in his mind at least, had begun to feel like home.

Did her father know he was coming? Did her father know he was
here?

He said no, he didn't intend to bother her father, not today, and the
humble conviction she heard in his voice was such that she understood
that for Kenny Brewster her father had become a resource he had to
portion out. She excused herself and stepped back into the gallery to
ask Luisa for the afternoon off. Luisa narrowed her eyes skeptically,
but Jen didn't blink.

She showed him the town in her little car. Other than the Deweese
and a street or two of storefronts left standing long enough to make it
onto the historic register, there wasn't much man-made worth pointing out. Leafy neighborhoods with buckled sidewalks, some still made
of slate, one of the town's four creeks, and some old houses, one of
which, with a widow's walk and a wraparound porch and a lot of dark
woodwork inside, she'd lived in as a child. Her mother had come close
to being happy in that house, but, even so, when the Deweese had happened and a chance to live on top of that world, she hadn't said no. Jen
at that age had been in search of novelty, and the Deweese was certainly
that. Gerald had understood it as a step up, but Mickey had treated
their old house on that leafy downtown street like a test of personal
loyalty and, hence, the upcoming move as a personal affront. It was as
if he'd resented being bound to an old house like that, but he didn't like
his personal attachments to be taken lightly, either, so he resented that,
too. If she took the time, she felt she could understand her younger
brother; it was usually a case of one thing in his life canceling another
out and thus providing a strange sort of motive force.

The day they'd moved to the Deweese, they'd had to look for him
in that house. Her mother had told her, Go find your brother, tell him
it's time to go, and her mother might have saved her breath. Jen knew
exactly where Mickey was. In the attic they had their little private spaces

marked out; Gerald had his, too, although that was simply a matter of fair-mindedness on their part because Gerald almost never went up there. Mickey'd had a big throw pillow tucked into the slant of the roof. He'd hung up an old blanket, setting off his space from hers. The heat was something they took personally, a way to earn their apartness and a way to hold off the casual intruder, who wouldn't be up to the test.

When she'd gone up to get him this last time, she remembered exactly what he'd said. He said, I'm coming, but one day I won't. She'd said, What if you don't get another chance? What if this is the last time anybody comes looking for you? Did you ever think of that? And her little brother overdid it, rising wearily from his pillow and shaking his head. That's all they ever do is come looking for you. That's gonna go on as long as the world does. And she laughed at him, she barked her contempt, that dusty, distilled heat now something her brother was inflicting on her and she could hold against him. I'll tell them you went on a hunger strike, you fucking little creep, she flung back as she started down the ladder stairs.

She told Kenny Brewster, paused before the house in her car, it had been a good house, like a lot of other old ones here downtown. But they'd known, even then, it wasn't where they'd end up.

Her mother lived up on the hill, looking down into the basin the town was built in, but Jen didn't take him up there. She took him to the park at the end of the lake with its old stucco and wood-shingled pavilions that went back a hundred years. It wasn't a matter of getting out of the car, not yet. She drove them down to the far end of the park, up along another of the four creeks that flowed into the lake. She asked him to take note of it. The trees were tall, enormous old cottonwoods whose airborne seeds caught the sun in a silky sheen.

Once out of the park, she drove up along the base of a hill back in the direction of downtown, until they reached a point where she told him to shut his eyes. When he was told to open them, they were stopped on a bridge passing over that creek that they'd driven along down where it entered the lake. She asked him to look upstream, where, right in the middle of their small to middling town, a wall of white water a hundred feet wide and a hundred feet tall flowed over huge shoulders and protrusions of shale, and to tell her if he had seen anything quite like that in his life. She heard the catch in his breath, and she laughed.

A rocky path along the stream led to the base of the falls. There came a moment—not because the footing was treacherous and not because he'd failed to catch up—when she took his hand. The footing did become slippery the closer they got to the falls, and a mist now covered their faces, but she led him to a ledge that provided the last available vantage point before the footing ran out. They were about fifteen feet above the plunge pool. A couple of couples and a couple of kids were down by the water. Two teenagers had waded out up to their knees. Jen had swum there before. It had been like swimming in an enormous Jacuzzi of frothy river water. Back then, she hadn't much thrilled to the flow of the water over the jutting rock, or the way the rock bodied the water out into thick, foaming green sheets or into something as shimmering as lace when the creek was low. But whether the creek was high or low, the pounding was always there, and water never ceased to pass with a green translucence over the lip of the falls, and there was always a great, thunderous supply of something you only needed a little of, just a little.

She looked over at Kenny, who had been in the navy, so that an endless abundance of water was nothing new. Kenny was also into energy, but perhaps nothing quite as fundamental and firsthand as this. When they were back at the car and Jen had pulled out a towel so that they could dry their faces, Kenny asked her who Danny's father was. On any other occasion, he would have taken her by surprise with a question like that, but the falls, the abrupt way they had come on them, the powerful way the water pushed everything else aside, made small talk impossible, even as it threw up its shimmering veils of spume. She looked him in the eye and said she didn't know. She couldn't be sure.

He was not completely dry yet when she returned the question; she asked him who his father was, and he shook his head. Someone named Kenny, he said, his mother had despised.

Jen and Kenny got into the car, and following the street that led up beyond the falls, they came to a second bridge, one that looked down into the gorge. They got out of the car and stood on the bridge. Off to their left they could see the brilliant blue of the lake as it made its first jag north. It was crowded with sails. A hundred and fifty feet below them ran the water that ten thousand years earlier had carved out its course in this stone. It flowed in a strong center current, with little lagging eddies off by the shores. A few trees had toppled in. It would soon reach the falls, and everything in it—all its frothy turbulence, all its trash—would be converted into that clean, translucent green as it flowed over the lip. Jen told Kenny that although no one talked about it, everybody in the family knew that her great-grandfather had thrown himself from this bridge, two weeks before his own father had hanged himself in his cow barn. That land that TransAtlantic had leased to drill the gas out of had belonged to those two men. Just in case Kenny wanted to know the family he was doing business with, that is, if he wanted to back out now.

She meant if he wanted to go home to Texas—or was it Arkansas?—where she pictured everything as flat and dry and the only way to do away with yourself was to stand in the path of a tornado and wait till it gave you a ride.

The smell of the creek water rising up to their nostrils was refreshing and rank. She didn't wait until they were back in the car and out of public view. She kissed him there, his lips like the rest of him, cautious and alert, but eager in their way. He was not surprised, not in the least. Which surprised her. He looked as if he was settling something in his mind.

Before he could settle whatever it was, she kissed him again. He was not your typical Texan, whatever that might have been. He was not long-boned, narrow-eyed, and weather-cured in complexion, given

to abrupt exclamations and nothing else. Not a trace of a washed-out
hollow was in his face or neck. As a boy he would have been a study in
boyish symmetry, and as he aged, he would tend toward knobbiness in
the cheeks and chin. The hair might dull to a sandy gray, but the eyes
would only get bluer and the teeth looked too tightly fitted in to decay.
Hers, of course, was the larger mouth.

She said, "Where are you staying?"

"Nowhere, yet."

He'd come to the Deweese and she took him back there. Her apartment might have been a janitorial space, or it might have been a counselor's office, or even a little detention center stuck off by itself. Her
father knew. Grateful to be given a place to live, she had never asked
him point-blank, but when she brought Kenny Brewster back here, she
couldn't shake the thought that her father had had this in mind, too,
that this fatherless young man, who'd positioned himself in an orbit
not unlike hers, had to be treated with the utmost courtesy, and, as her
father must have known, courtesy for his daughter was never a formal
affair. It had an appetite of its own.

She said, Kenny, we've got to clear our minds. She took him inside,
sat him on her bed, and said, It's just you and me, okay? We're in an
in-between time. It doesn't matter what came before or what happens
tomorrow, let's just make this little time ours. Okay, Kenny? He said, I
don't talk, Jen. Other guys might, but I don't do that, and she was
forced to admit that that wasn't what she'd meant. But before she could
say so, he kissed her. He unbuttoned her blouse and unfastened her bra
and swept past her precautions in his own step-by-step way, if precautions were what they had been. All she'd meant to say was that as members of the same team waiting for the drilling to begin, they enjoyed a
camaraderie and a special license that only teammates could understand. All she'd really meant to say was that she'd find the words for it
if he gave her the time. They lay down together, and Kenny, far from
being a rangy, sun-browned Texan, was pale, just a little chubby, and
basically her size. Her father had said he'd been a roughneck and had

worked on the rigs, but his hands as they moved over her were chamois-soft—too soft, his touch tending too much toward the reverential for her taste. She pulled at him, caught his cock and balls in one full-spanning grip, and pulled him down on top of her, feeling the rush of something like creek water in her blood, the way it had no choice but to mix life and death, fairness and foulness, in its flow. Water was like that as it came crashing down. Maybe it all got sorted out later as it flowed into something as peaceful and universally admired as a lake, but the pounding came first. She could close her eyes and lift them up to that green translucence high above her, but down where she lived, the creek was roiling and the pounding never stopped. For an instant her appetite amazed her. She laughed, and Kenny paused long enough to say, Jen? and then added with a sweetness that caught her entirely by surprise, Jenny, a name no one, except maybe her father, called her. She laughed again, a kind of chuckling moan of approval, and bound now by an intimacy of a more familiar sort pleaded with him not to stop. When she came, it was not as if that thudding fall of water had stopped. Rather, it was as if she'd caught a current and allowed it to take her away, and the pounding of her passion was back there in her past. Kenny was back there, too. She'd wait for him if she could, but really couldn't, and then she experienced an extraordinary relief and tenderness—new to her, pretty much unprecedented in her life—when she found him floating beside her, sharing her current, and when he called her Jenny again and, in his gratitude or wonder, sounded as if he were about to cry.

While Wilson Michaels waited to see if the lock on his door would welcome the key he held in his hand, or not. He knew he had a right to his things, and he knew he had a number of other rights as well, but a small part of him, anxious for a confrontation of any sort, hoped the key would not fit. He had only been gone four days. He'd made his position clear: unless Ray Whittaker wanted to fight it out in court, he was to find some way to write him into the Joyner family, if that was what it took, but it was as if he'd been gone much longer, as if he'd crossed some divide, and in returning to the Garden District of Sunnyside, Queens, with its octogenarians at one end of the spectrum and its privileged little kids at the other, and with some neighbors-or-else in between, he was approaching his own jail cell and opening the door. The key fit, of course, and the door opened.

He closed the door, and the house was suddenly full of the amplified sound of his laboring breath. He didn't even check his answering machine or e-mail messages, but grabbed a beer from the fridge and crashed through to the patio beneath his office window, where the smell was of rain-soaked patio pillows he'd forgotten to bring in. Children played in that commons area whose cut grass had such an evocative appeal, but they were fighting about something and screaming at a decibel level their parents seemed unwilling to do anything about. He listened for birds and finally heard a few. Jays, cawing back and forth.

None of this was out of the ordinary. He told himself to draw deep breaths, and then he told himself not to despair.

Despair was the word he used, as he might have in defense of a falsely accused client in court. Despair as black as the darkest dungeon in Sunnyside, Queens, New York.

He took those breaths and reminded himself that his little trip might have had a legal objective, but what he'd really wanted to do was get out of town for a while, take a few days off. That he'd done. He'd crossed the GW, cruised out over the land, paid his respects to rural America, taken a breather out where the air was fit to breathe—if he hadn't been caught behind one of those hydrofracking trucks, that is. He hadn't seen Frank Joyner himself, that was true, only that wily, small-town representative of his, but a meeting with Joyner would come later, after this preliminary round, a round that, from every angle he knew to examine it, he considered he'd won.

Business and pleasure, objective accomplished, and tax deductible, every mile and minute of it.

He rose and went back into the house, where he remained for fifteen minutes, during which time he unpacked his small suitcase and, with a reluctance that came close to anger, returned his various bathroom items to the medicine cabinet and the pills he took—for the prostate, for cholesterol—to their allotted spots in the kitchen cabinet downstairs. The valise containing the papers on which he'd worked out the figures on how much he had made the Joyner family with his various intercessions with TransAtlantic he returned to his office, where no light flashed on his phone to tell him he had messages waiting, and where, when he finally decided to turn it on, his e-mail box was empty of anything except the usual exotic-vacation ads, or erectile-dysfunction ads, or urgent last calls to pick up the millions he had waiting for him in various banks, or the pleas of Russian ladies to believe them when they said that they dispensed soul and sex like nobody else in the world. He didn't even bother to trash these messages. After all, they were the only ones he'd received.

He walked out his front door and into an evening that was even milder than the one he'd sampled out on his patio. Two blocks away, he'd parked his car. He knew exactly where it was, fire-hydrant free, a lucky find and perhaps from some perspective a good omen, but when he walked there, he saw what he'd forgotten in so short a span, that he had five days remaining of untroubled parking if he left well enough alone. The Italian restaurant he had in mind was twelve, thirteen blocks away. He ended up walking there, which he assumed would improve his appetite and do him some good. Instead, the physical exertion brought a queasiness to his stomach and a sourness to his mouth, and all he could do was bring the bulk of the veal scaloppine he'd ordered back in a doggie bag as he slowly made his way home. By the time he got to his kitchen he was sick of its oily smell and threw it all in the trash. He turned on the television but was not in the mood for sitcom jokes, had no patience for issue-filled documentaries, could take car crashes or howling sex scenes just so long, and the Yankees, with their outrageously overpaid players, were getting trounced, which would normally have pleased him but tonight just seemed like a waste.

He turned his computer on and called Carol, and either she'd discovered some way to identify his computer phone on her caller ID or she really wasn't at home. He got her recording, her kind, quiet, ever-so-obliging voice expressing how sorry she was to have missed his call, and without waiting for the message to end or the little recording signal to sound, he began to assure her that he'd seen Ray Whittaker and it wasn't anything like what she might have feared, in fact, it was good, very good, really, and pleasant because, of course, Whittaker had understood, as any reasonable man would, that he, Wilson Michaels, had gotten the ball rolling and kept it rolling when it threatened to stop and that without his friendly assistance—and it had been friendly, whether she knew it or not, she still had a friend—nothing would have gotten done, a real opportunity would have passed them by, and they were eternally in debt to him, which was really all he'd wanted to hear, that he wasn't some kind of mercenary opportunist looking to prey on some innocent family who just couldn't get off the fence, that in some ways—well, the ways were clear, weren't they, and they even had names, Brenda and little Cynthia—he was part of the family, too, even though she and he had for reasons he still couldn't understand, after all these years, parted ways. Why had that been, Carol? he wanted to know. You come to a certain age when you can't help but look back and you realize . . .

His recording time ran out. It was as if a gavel had come down, and the man prepared to rule in his favor had without legal precedent walked off the bench.

He pushed away from his computer screen, but the room was small, he couldn't go far, and he sat there trying to catch his breath and trying not to break down. He tasted bile in his mouth—the little veal scaloppine he'd eaten was working its way back up—and he didn't like the thudding of his heart, which went back and forth from fortissimo to pianissimo so quickly it was like listening to an isolated alarm in the midst of a swelling and subsiding storm.

When the storm passed, he called his daughter, Brenda, and got her, and seemingly, this time, in a receptive mood.

He said, "I was up there, talking to the family lawyer, this guy Whittaker, and one way or another I'm going to get you more money, sweetheart, so just hang on."

"Whittaker, the one who signs the checks?"

"That's him. I don't know how he's done it, but he seems to have insinuated his way right into Frank Joyner's hip pocket. Or maybe he just idolizes the man, but you'll see some more money coming your way."

"Get some for yourself, too, Daddy. Uncle Frank always acts like he's got all the virtue on his side. What's so virtuous about letting all that land go to waste? What's so virtuous about not letting old buildings, which are pretty much eyesores, fall down?"

"Not any I can see."

"So get some for yourself, Daddy. Get a lot."

"I mentioned that, sweetheart. He's seen the figures. Whittaker knows the part I played in all this. What I'm more interested in is you and Cynthia getting your fair share. And how is she, by the way?"

"Cynthia?"

"My granddaughter."

"Starting her period and going full bore."

"Really?"

"She's demanding I put her on the pill. She calls it—you'll like this—her 'legal right.'"

"Did she bother to cite a law?"

"Good question."

"So what are you going to do?"

"I don't know. I'm thinking about it, asking some of my friends. It'd be just like her to come home pregnant to spite me."

"Like her?"

"You all right, Daddy? Like Cynthia, your granddaughter, the young lady we're talking about. Who'd you think I meant? My cousin Jen? Did you see her while you were up there?"

"Jen? Little Jenny? No."

"You said you'd forgotten her name. It sounded like you wanted to talk to her. If you do see her, ask her what I should do. By the time she was Cynthia's age she was pretty much sleeping with every boy in sight."

"Frank Joyner's daughter? When she was twelve years old?"

"Daddy, Cynthia's fourteen now. We're talking about fourteen years old. Where have you been? You really all right?"

"Well . . . more or less."

"Daddy, you're not gonna come apart on me, are you?"

"Don't plan on it."

"If you don't think you have many allies left, well, how about me?"

"You're in the family, Brenda. As far as you're concerned, there's no shortage of allies out there."

"Like Uncle Frank, you mean?"

"Like Uncle Frank."

"And like Cousin Jen."

"Like Cousin Jen."

"Why'd you want to know her name, anyway, if you weren't going to see her?"

"No, nothing. Something I remembered from when you had your sleepovers, a little look she had . . ."

"*That's* the look! Whadda you think I've been talking about? Same look Cynthia's got when she sees anything vaguely male. Like a little scared, Daddy? Like if you come any closer I might scream—or I might not? You'll just have to come closer to find out. That look, Daddy?"

. . .

And when Jen called Mickey after Kenny had gone back to work, it wasn't because she had anything pressing she'd intended to say. It was because they hadn't talked for some time, and because it was nearly summer and school was nearly out, and because they'd gotten into the habit and she needed the illusion of something nearly forbidden to share, whether anything actually forbidden got said or not. He sounded tired, distracted. She might have caught him correcting a stack of exams. He could joke and charm and bullshit his way through an entire school year, but finally he'd have to deal with those exams. She tried to take his mind off it for a while. That student he'd liked so much with the funny name, she'd forgotten it, something as common as dirt? That would be Flesh, Mickey said, then added, Jimmy. Yeah, Jimmy Flesh, she said. How was he? All right, she was told, but the flattening out in his tone meant his erstwhile prize student lay somewhere down in that stack of exams. And that teacher he'd been seeing, the one who taught Spanish with a Bronx accent? She meant Fina, and Fina was still there. If Jen would be quiet a minute and he held up the phone, they might be able to hear Fina moving around upstairs. She indulged him, and Mickey held the phone up. D'you hear her, the nice lady upstairs? Jen didn't even bother to answer him. And nothing else is going on? She prodded him a little. With that gas-lease money you haven't found some way to misbehave? He said he hadn't touched it. It lay in his bank account, drawing its fraction of a fraction of interest. And? she said because she knew something else was coming, they hadn't been sharing intimacies, titillating each other all these years, for her not to know that. Until what? Until when? Until the city gates were about to fall, he declared. What's that mean, Mickey? It meant they were close. The town was under siege. They were moving their battering rams in, their catapults, their flame-shooting archers. They? The gas companies, of course. They were the only army left in the field.

This was stale stuff by Mickey's standards, and she chalked it up to just how tired he must feel with a stack of demoralizing exams still unread. But she couldn't quite let it pass. She'd thought his town had decided to hold the gas companies off. And did those gas companies include TransAtlantic?

That brought a burst of bitter, hard, raucous laughter, which she knew could lead anywhere, well, almost anywhere. She told herself to tell him to get some sleep, wake up tomorrow, and see if the day didn't improve. And then hang up. Only they'd never hung up on each other. They'd never failed to let each other's fantasies run their course. But he could be a real pain in the ass. He could ball himself up on that pillow of his, stuffed back into the slant of that roof, and never grow up. What had he said? I'm coming but one day I won't? That all they ever do is come looking for you? Well, one day, Mickey, *they* won't.

She said, TransAtlantic may be a cut above the rest, Mickey.

Because one of their trucks had the good fortune not to leave a little boy and his dog for dead in a ditch?

That was an accident. It could have happened to any of those trucks.

It's blood money, Jen.

Then here's what I think you should do. You should go take a hundred dollars out of that bank account of yours and take your lady friend upstairs or that prize student of yours or both of them out to dinner.

Incriminate myself, you mean.

Reenter real life, Mickey, just a little at a time.

He laughed at her again, exhausted laughter, almost unforgiving, it seemed. She should have let it pass. She should have hung up. But she said she had a confession to make. She had a new boyfriend. And guess what? He was a landman. Of course, she could have stopped there. Landmen were in town. Mickey knew all about his sister's appetites and her conquests and the ease she seemed to feel in slipping free from one to the next. A landman. It had a ring. A man of the land. And guess what? she said. He was a decent guy, probably misinformed like most of the rest of us, making a buck, intending no one any harm. Or stopped there. She waited for her brother to respond, his interest to kindle.

Mickey? she said. You still there?

Here, Jen. You fucked a landman, a man of the land. What took you so long?

It wasn't like that. It was just between the two of us. Private. An in-between-times thing.

In between what times? One fuck and the next? C'mon, Jen.

Good night, Mickey.

But she didn't hang up.

Mickey, I'm telling you this so you'll know. It can be nice. Everything has to be right. Maybe things have to be like they are now, I mean with everything uncertain, with so much at stake, so that if you can get away from it, just for a day, with someone else, get close to someone else . . . You see what I'm saying, don't you, Mickey? Everything has to be just right.

Your stars and planets all in order? Something ascending, something in retrograde? I never went for all that astrological crap. Which landman, Jen?

Ours, she said, as quietly as if she were curled up beside him on his pillow in their attic hideaway.

If I'm not mistaken, we had two. Which one, Jen?

But that she wouldn't share, not the name, not Kenny, it was all she had left from the vow of secrecy she'd sworn.

Nevertheless, Mickey's spirits seemed improved. He laughed, a sort of yippie-ing, roundup laugh, as if he were welcoming her back to the fold.

The Imp of the Perverse strikes again! You know who the Imp of the Perverse is, don't you, Jen? But of course you do. An irresistible little fellow. Welcome to the club!

Still, she didn't hang up on him, and neither did he. Later, it seemed he had. She spoke his name once more and got nothing in return. She might have been holding a stone to her ear. And what if this really is the last time anyone comes looking for you, Mickey? she whispered into that cold thing in her hand. Then she put it down.

PART FIVE

BEYOND THE MARCELLUS

13

T HE GAS COMPANIES *WERE* AT THE CITY GATES, HIS SOMETIMES GIRL-friend Fina from the Bronx *was* moving restlessly around upstairs, his special student and his back-to-the-earth family *had been* the first to lease and drill their land, and, no, he didn't have a stack of exams to grade. He had already graded them and half his students had failed. The next morning, Fina was still moving around, and he was waiting for a call not from his principal but from the school-system superintendent herself, Judith Ballinger, who pulled the principal's strings. Half your students, Mr. Joyner? Obviously, something has gone terribly wrong. Judith Ballinger had a pleasant oval of a face, eyes of flint, and a cool, laid-in-place smile. The wave in her graying hair she wore over her forehead in a positively girlish way. In the late fifties, perhaps the early sixties, she had been a girl. Even Jimmy Flesh had failed. Imagine someone writing an essay tracing a line of descent from Benjamin Franklin to J. P. Morgan, identifying them as raiders of the Old World and champions of the New, one loved and one mostly hated but essentially the same man. Imagine, Ms. Ballinger. Benjamin Franklin, homespun Ben, *Poor Richard's Almanack*, a penny saved is a penny earned, but also avuncular Ben, who advised his nephew to marry an older woman because she would be eternally grateful, and if she was ugly, you could always put a sack over her head, a fount of popular wisdom, our Ben, and to put Ben and J. P. Morgan, a robber's robber baron, a megaconsumer, a whale of a man, in the same bed together? Can you see it, Ms. Ballinger? I can't. And if I can't see it, I consider F the only suitable grade. F for failure, F for it freaks me out. And Fina continued to move around upstairs, only at a faster pace, nearing the end. He showered, brushed his teeth, and shaved around his mustache and goatee, all that was left of his beard. Then, in the spirit of hiding nothing, including his weak chin, he shaved the mustache and goatee off. In the same up-front spirit, all defenses down, he reached into his desk's drawer and brought out his savings account book, which he slipped into his jeans' hip pocket. He wore his New York Yankees T-shirt, in a nod toward her Bronx. Measuring his steps, in contrast to Fina's back-and-forth bursts, he went upstairs.

The walls in her apartment were bare, her luggage was collected by the door, and she had begun to clean. He stood before her, arms at his side, hands open and empty, and asked her to stop and give him five minutes. She took one look at his T-shirt, another at his goatee-less chin, and gave him a long, rueful smile. She seemed to be counting her breaths. Finally, her eyes performed a longer-than-usual blink, a last breath ended in a sigh, and she sat on the couch, indicating he could do the same. But before he could begin to plead his case—replead, although there would be things she hadn't heard before—she said, "This time they're going to fire you. You know that, don't you?"

"Not rehire me, you mean."

"No, fire you. *Fuera, despedido, echado,* once and for all. And they should. You fail that many students, it's the same as firing yourself. Couldn't you do any better than that?"

"Not without lowering my standards."

She barked a contemptuous laugh and rose to continue her cleaning, to be followed by her leave-taking. He closed his eyes and sent her a strong, silent appeal to sit back down. They had been comrades in their opposition to almost everything around them, and in that spirit she gave in.

"You know what I hate?" she said. "I hate to see you give that bitch Ballinger the satisfaction."

"Well, at least we agree on that."

She lowered her head, snorted, and swore, "What the fuck, Mickey!"

"What difference does it make? You're not coming back. Can you see me here by myself?"

"What difference does it make? The students, Mickey! They deserve better than that!" Then she paused and allowed some of the tenderness that had passed between them these last few months into her voice. "And you do, too, you stupid shit."

"Thanks for that."

"*Mierda*," she muttered, then looked around her, at the cleaning she still had left to do, before sinking into the sofa, as if she'd just lost the will.

He said what he'd come to say, while her defenses were down. "Don't marry that guy, what's his name—Carlos, I know his name. If you have to marry somebody, marry me."

It took a moment to sink in, then the incredulity gathered on her face to a scowling point. She cocked her head, inviting him to repeat what he'd just said. More than an invitation, it was a taunt, and it reminded him of what he had first liked about Fina, back before he'd really known her, when they'd coincided in the teachers' lounge or across a conference table from dumbfounded parents and their nonachieving child: her resistance to the easy avowal, the fulsome word.

"I mean it," he said.

"No, you don't."

"Try me."

"Who said I was getting married anyway? I said I'd had enough of teaching here and I was going back home, and there was a guy there who had proposed so many times it was like the refrain of an old song. I didn't say I was going to marry him. I might have said that marrying him would be better than hanging on here. *Might have.*"

"Carlos."

"I might have said Carlos was his name."

"Fina . . ."

"Jesus, Mickey! *Qué te pasa?*" The scowl on her face seemed to soften, although not the disbelief. She made a confused movement on the couch, neither rising nor settling back nor moving toward him, a movement to no immediate purpose. Her broom and dust cloth were too far away to reach. Finally she leaned in. "You didn't mean that, did you?"

"Don't go."

"About marrying you if I had to marry somebody? *If I had to marry somebody!* Do I look like the kind of girl who has to marry somebody?"

"We get along, Fina."

"As long as we're each other's only option—sure we do."

"We get along better than that."

"Yeah? When's my birthday, Mickey?"

He shook his head. He was about to say ask him a less conventional question when she did.

"My saint's day, then?"

He closed his eyes and bowed his head in mock-contrition.

"Josefina. Same as San José. March nineteenth. It came and went. My birthday did, too."

He drew a breath, raised his head, and held her bold, unwavering gaze. What had his sister said? That in these uncertain times it could be nice. With so much at stake, if you could get away, just for a day, everything could be all right. But it would take the female equivalent of a landman—if not a landwoman, an earth mother, he supposed. Thinking mostly of his sister, and the little, overwrought secrets they shared, he laughed.

"Glad you see the humor in it," Fina said, "but in my world we still celebrate things like that."

"Marry me."

"And live on what? Tomorrow or the day after you won't have a job."

"I've got money." He reached into his hip pocket and pulled out his bankbook, which he laid between them on the sofa, like his ace in the hole.

She shook her head and tried to keep from laughing at him.

"Open it." He nudged it farther along.

She did him the courtesy, her eyes recorded what to him seemed an impressive sum, then she laid the bankbook back on the couch. In a worldly-wise tone, the tone of bankbooks and investment portfolios and IRAs, she said, "Mickey. Carlos is a pharmacist. Do you have any idea how much a pharmacist makes, guaranteed, no way to lose, down through the years? Do you really want to know? You don't, I'll tell you right now."

He thought of the corner pharmacist—any corner pharmacist—behind his counter, in his white smock, counting out the pills. Carlos, meaning there would be a Saint Carlos, so Carlos would have his day, too. Mickey thought of the pharmacist's wife as a wholesome adjunct to her husband's pill counting, perhaps measuring powder out into neat, little packets. Patience and precision and a pharmaceutical faith, which would be rewarded with a steady influx of dollars, while he . . . he had to go maybe a mile down and maybe another mile out, blast into rock to coax, just maybe, the gas back up the pipe, bringing perhaps all that was foul and hidden (for the last 380 million years or so) along with it. Down and out. Down and out. Compulsory integration.

"What you don't seem to understand, Fina, is that that's old money, it goes millions of years back, and there's plenty more of it. Inherited wealth, Fina."

"It's goddamn gas money, Mickey!"

"With a certain aristocratic lineage behind it. What girl doesn't want to marry into nobility?"

"I thought you were never going to touch that money."

"Not until the right emergency came along."

"Why do I think with you it's going to be one emergency after another? Why do I think that?"

Because, he was about to say, those are the times we live in. If we can hold out for better times, somewhere else, a world away . . . and his brother, Gerald, suddenly appeared in his mind. Gerald, with his house and family behind him and a handsomely paid job he drove off to every day, and the Pacific Ocean spread out before him, bathed in an evening sun that refused to set. Out there was a place called the Golden Triangle, where it was not uncommon to see movie stars clad only in terry-cloth bathrobes stroll out to get their morning papers and to greet passersby. Movie stars' houses ran on natural gas, too, and as long as the gas kept flowing in their bed of shale back home, who was to say that he wouldn't be able to offer her a house of theirs?

"I never told you about my brother, Gerald, did I?"

"The one who lives out in L.A. with the wife and the kids in some kind of Republican stronghold?"

"San Geraldo? There must have been a San Geraldo, or something like that."

"Mickey, what is it?"

"Just to let you know I've got a brother in my family who is as solid as rock, has never had an emergency of any sort, and will never be a martyr for anybody's cause, but can still be named after a saint and can still have his day."

She laughed at him then, and it was what went into her laugh that he wanted, its sympathy and its disbelief and its scorn, because the scorn was just lighthearted enough, and its willingness to play up to a point, the point at which she would force him to fight for her or fight for his own life, but until that moment came there was enough good humor there to last them for a while. . . .

She said, "Every little brother's got a big brother like that."

"I've also got a sister you would like, but she's no role model, which is what makes her likable."

"Jen, the one who calls you late at night?"

"Who's taken up with a landman although it's not what you think."

"What do I think?"

"That the gas companies have lured her over, but it's not like that. You'd have to know Jen. And then I've got a father whose whole shtick is finding old buildings and bringing them back to life. Not everyone's got a father like that. But that's the way he is, just when something is about to topple over into its grave, he reaches out—"

"Mickey, I'm leaving."

"This is a family you don't want to miss out on, Fina. My mother's a real piece of work. She sits off on the sidelines, it's all the human comedy as far as she's concerned. You could sit off on the sidelines, too."

"Don't make me hate you for doing this to you, Mickey."

"You and your fucking Carlos."

She shook her head. "Carlos is a sweet guy, *un tesoro*, if you know what I mean."

"And your Bronx, and your Bronx Bombers. I didn't think there were any Yankee fans left."

He puffed out his Yankee-clad chest, he raised his goatee-less chin, he was going to lose this fight, he knew, and short of begging on his knees he didn't know what else he could do. Onto his knees he would not go, so he stood. He shook his head. She was making the mistake of her life, which he knew was rank nonsense. She was giving him up to Superintendent Judith Ballinger, and he'd be damned if he'd give her that satisfaction. Now, she, too, had stood and come up to him and had the effrontery, characteristic of her, to kiss him once flush on the mouth, as her hand went to his ass. But she was only slipping the bankbook he'd brought to impress her with back into his hip pocket. In his ear, she half-whispered she was honored by his proposal and in another life might have believed it and leaped at the chance, but this was the life she was stuck with, worse luck, and she'd miss him, and, of course, Carlos could never measure up, and without caving in to the bitch Ballinger he should really find some way to rescue those students he'd failed, at least the four or five they shared, not that he should stay on here, because if he couldn't picture himself a day longer in this town and county about to be drilled to death, then neither could she, so why not wipe the slate clean? She said all this with her mouth to his ear so that he could not see her face, but he responded to the mix of things he heard in her voice anyway, the provocation, the regret, some notes of kindness scattered around, and the mockery that was close to his—of course, they'd made a good match—except that hers was more weighted with loss and, in that way, more open to alternatives than his had ever been, which made it harder still to give her up.

But he walked to the door without looking at her again, and only when he was downstairs and could hear her hurrying about upstairs did he know he was in a race. He would not wait to be summoned by Judith Ballinger, and the students he and Fina shared would have to fend for themselves. Even Jimmy Flesh, with that farmboy insouciance of his, would have to find someone else to champion his cause. Mickey was in a race. He was way behind, but by refusing to clean and by taking only what he absolutely had to have, he would beat Fina out of town. They parked their cars side by side in a paved area out back, and the last thing he intended to do was to sit there and listen to Fina drive down the drive and out of his life. He went through the bathroom, kitchen, and bedroom on a packing blitz. Only when he sat before the desk he'd carried with him all these years, fondling a cigarette lighter he'd taken from its drawer, did the heart go out of him. Fina pulled out of the drive, slowly he thought, dragging out the crunch time under each wheel. She was giving him the chance to get up and go to his bedroom window, where he'd be able to catch her taillights blinking farewell to him down the street.

He didn't move, and there came a moment when it was only the birds he heard and the trucks rumbling through town, trucks transporting racks of pipe or portable generators or pressure-building compressors or earthmoving equipment, but mostly tank trucks taking water or lubricating chemicals to the frack sites, or taking befouled fracked water and, perhaps, a salty radioactive residue away. There'd be citizens who removed their hats and held them over their hearts as these trucks passed, as though they were welcoming a liberating army. Through their contributions to the police department, the fire department, the highway department, the parks department, the schools, the library, and the community center, the gas companies had won over the town supervisors, who had granted them a permitted-use ordinance, a one-case-fits-all permission to drill right up to the town line, and open access for their trucks anywhere they needed to go.

He sat at his desk continuing to turn the worn, nickel-plated lighter over and over in his palm. He struck it once, just to see, and was surprised to discover it still gave him flame. Eventually, he stuck it into his side jeans' pocket. The other contents of his desk drawer he would leave behind. Other than the lighter and the bankbook in his hip pocket, he was the clothes on his back, nothing more.

Still, he sat there. The birds and no end to the trucks, with so much backed-up drilling to do. Then he heard the noon whistle, a harkening sound, whether signaling a catastrophe or a cause for celebration, there was no way to tell. But the morning was over, a long afternoon had begun, and he reached for his cell phone and turned it off. The time was now his. Superintendent Judith Ballinger would have to look for him on time of her own.

A truck awaited him at a downtown light. There was no way to pretty these tank trucks up, and the gas companies hadn't even tried. They rode heavy into the town's asphalt and fouled its air and ran through their gears with their outsize growls, and the elaborate networks of pipes and gauges and spigots and levers they carried at the rear and

down their sides spoke of some operation too complex for the average
man's comprehension.

The one Mickey had pulled up behind contained hazardous chemicals—it was honest enough to say so—and he followed it through
town. His intention had been to follow it to its site, so that when the
right pipes were attached and the right levers pulled, he would be
there when those unnamed chemicals were spewed into the bowels of
the earth, but as they passed over the creek that looped around the far
side of the town, he changed his mind. Unless it was in flood, this was
not a big creek, and the bridge of old iron girders was not a bridge you
would look at twice, but Mickey stopped on the highway's shoulder
perhaps a hundred feet farther on and began to walk back. By the
time he got there another truck, this one containing sand, had passed,
the bridge giving under its enormous weight. A close examination of
the girders and their bolts led him to believe the bridge dated back to
the WPA days. It had been painted and repainted many times since
then, but the navy gray was heavily discolored now. The creek itself he
barely looked at. In the absence of trucks and normal car traffic, it
made an idle creek murmur, no more. Never discount the value of a
symbolic act, he'd once advised his father, encouraging him to commit
one for posterity's sake. There was a reason many years ago when, as a
harried grad student, smoking a couple of packs a day, he'd hung on to
his cigarette lighter—and a reason the lighter still worked. Mickey
struck it and held the flame under the girder closest at hand. He held
the flame there until, in spite of the breeze that blew along the creek,
he'd begun to smell the paint burn. A thin, industrial taint was in the
air when a town cop passed over the bridge, stopped, and walked back
to stand at Mickey's side.

They knew each other, from minor infractions in the past. The
cop's name was Roy Shelton, and this was another infraction, destruction of town property, although the bridge was clearly indestructi-
ble—by the likes of Mickey Joyner—and the paint, arguably, not a
property at all but something as evanescent as a cloud shadow or a fine

coating of ice. So what was it this time? Officer Shelton wanted to know. Mickey was surprised Shelton couldn't see for himself. Mickey was burning this bridge, a last one, behind him—see, he was parked up there—as he got out of town. Shelton repeated it. Mickey Joyner was burning his last bridge behind him as he got out of town? For a moment, Officer Shelton stood there, regarding the tiny blowtorch of a flame. Making any progress? he asked. Almost done, Mickey said. Shelton laughed then, that cop laugh that any violator of a town's statutes knows before it all turns serious and the hammer comes down. With a hammerlike flourish of his own, Mickey clicked his lighter shut and announced the job was done. The bridge was down. And what were they standing on? The illusion of a bridge, or the memory of a bridge, the bridge that had always been there until somebody really, really wanted to get out of town. Mickey weighed the lighter one last time in his palm, seemed to be on the point of offering it to Officer Shelton, before tossing it into the creek. And Shelton informed him that even if he wasn't drunk or drugged, he could now be arrested for littering, for the creek belonged to the town. But he'd burned this bridge, Mickey pointed out, so there was no crossing back over.

Officer Shelton let him go, probably reasoning that if Mickey Joyner was only making a shred of sense, there was still a chance that when he'd burned his bridge, the town could be rid of him once and for all. What was certain was that Superintendent Judith Ballinger had yet to put out an all-points bulletin for his detention for Shelton would certainly have hauled him in then. If he didn't consider the trucks a curb to his mobility or some form of countywide arrest, Mickey was free. He drove until he came to the well pad where the trucks were pulling off, set at a considerable distance back from the highway so that, so far, the trucks waiting to unload had room to park on the access road. He saw the derrick flying the Stars and Stripes, and he believed he could make out a section of pipe rising then spinning down. He was surer about the sound—at that distance, a dull grinding and a clattering din. But he could also hear human voices, raised in a cheer.

He was on the outskirts of a small county town, and on a field adjacent
to where a gas well was being drilled, a Little League baseball game
was in progress, and he had a choice to make.

He had played in Little League for a season himself. He'd been terrible. When he swung at a ball he'd blinked, and when one was hit in
his direction, he'd mostly tried to get out of the way. His father came
and sat in the stands faithfully that summer, as if to say, there's a lesson
to be learned. Learn it and we'll make something of you yet. But his
father didn't speak. Or only a little, a few words of encouragement—
Next time, That was a good swing you had at that foul ball—but he
kept his son company in his suffering, and by the end of summer the
lesson seemed to have been that for every act of public humiliation you
endure, you're entitled to a rich compensation within, and such a compensation a son and his father could share. The fathers Mickey had
seated around him now were all loud, and the ones coaching down on
the field even louder. They screamed at each other, at their players, at
their sons; and the umpires, it seemed, were particularly perverse em-
bodiments of wrongheadedness visited on the scene, while the next
field over the pounding of the drill bit continued within a loose-bolted
clattering that sooner or later would have to bring the derrick down.

He thought he knew something about the drilling for shale gas
known as horizontal hydrofracturing and believed that if the water,
chemical, and sand trucks were arriving at the rate they were now, the
hydrofracking had either begun or was on the point. But he also knew
that before the hydrofracking began, the derrick-mounted drilling
would have ended, the derrick would have been removed, and the
drilling crew driven to a new well pad. Since the drilling had clearly
not ended and the trucks were beginning to line up, he concluded,
one, that the drilling was well into its horizontal stage and, two, that
for some reason the rig team had decided to drill farther out still. The
chances they would be drilling under some portion of this Little League
ball field were fifty-fifty, Mickey calculated, and those were odds
he liked. The season as a ten-year-old he'd played they'd stuck him out

in right field, where the fewest balls were hit. The chances that the drilling was passing a mile beneath the right fielder's feet were down to, maybe, 25 percent, which were still odds he could live with. Of course, there were two right fielders, depending which side was up to bat, but a Little League right fielder was, by consensus, a misfit, a stumblebum, a klutz, so it hardly mattered which of the two little boys was out there.

Still, he asked. The two women sitting directly in front of him were screaming just as loudly as the men, only they seemed to be having more fun. They groaned and cheered and laughed a lot, and Mickey had no idea if their children were on the winning or losing sides or what positions they played. What were the chances one of the two right fielders would be a son of theirs? On paper, one in nine, two in eighteen, but these women had a fun-loving manner about them, along with a savvy when it came to the points of the game, and he had to raise the odds. They would not be the mothers of right fielders. But they would know, so he asked. Hey, that ball took a bad bounce. Tough break. Who's that kid out in right field? And an inning or two later: The coach should have had him playing closer to the line. That's the coach's fault. What's that poor kid's name?

He wandered out there. Right field when it ended gave way to a cow pasture, and he wandered among cow pies turned a scabby and odorless brown in the sun. The cows were somewhere else, but he walked up a fence line, visible he knew from the stands, but so far up to no harm. He stopped and leaned on a weathered post. The right fielder was within easy hailing distance, the one named Tommy Blankenship, if he'd heard the last name correctly. The gas-drilling derrick was also closer, and on the elevated rig floor he could clearly see three men in mud-stained clothes, plus a fourth in a clean shirt and a hard hat with a clipboard in his hand. They were all gathered around what must have been the borehole, and instead of a grinding, what Mickey now heard at the heart of all the motor noise was the close-compassed clatter and scrape of a pipe being extracted from deep within the earth. What were the chances that pipe was being extracted from a mile beneath his feet? From Tommy Blankenship's feet? The chances were good.

An inning ended, and the right fielder now was a skinny kid, all elbows and knees, whose name was Kevin something, something like Gainer or Gaiter, and who seemed to be as interested in the gas drilling as Mickey was, for that was where he was looking most of the time. The fathers back in the stands shouted at him to get his head in the game, and he tried, he went into a fielder's crouch, his eyes, under the enormous bill of his cap, directed back to the infield, but in the long stretches of downtime when a Little League pitcher couldn't get the ball over the plate, he kept coming back to the world of the derrick and the trucks and the rig workers gathered around their hole, where pipe was being extracted from under his feet, too. He felt it, little Kevin Gaiter or Gainer did. A long way down, but he felt it, and Mickey from the other side of the fence began to cheer him, Attaboy, Kevin, attaboy, to welcome him to the team.

A ball was hit into right-center field, raising a cheer and a chorus of crazed pleas and instructions from the stands, and Kevin, in the pull of that pipe, barely moved, forcing the center fielder to run the ball down. Returning to his position, the center fielder had an ugly word to say to Kevin, who did suffer a moment's embarrassment with his shoulders slumped and his head bowed, but, then, he must have felt that pipe again returning from its long outward journey, for he straightened up and defiantly, it seemed, turned his attention there. Attaboy, Kevin! Now you're playing like a right fielder should! Kevin looked over at the man dressed in a New York Yankees T-shirt leaning on his fence post and smiled. Mickey smiled back, and then, in an act of spontaneous solidarity, he climbed over the fence and onto the field of play.

If this had been Yankee Stadium, they would have stopped play and run the attention-seeker down, but this was a Little League game in Nowheresville, and Mickey had chosen to wander out into right field, and out there with little Kevin Gainer or Gaiter playing the position things couldn't get much worse anyway, so in spite of protests from

some of the fathers, the game continued. Mickey stood beside little
Kevin, and together, in their fielder's crouch, they watched a series of
misplayed balls back on the infield while behind them trucks continued to pull in, motors chugged on, and the scrape sound of a pipe being extracted from beneath their feet seemed to sharpen to the ear.
The time had come to give Kevin a pep talk, but the only tip Mickey
remembered about baseball was to keep your eye on the ball, and if the
ball made a fool of you again and again, why would you want to do
that? About the game at their backs, where one pipe was about to be
extracted and two others, one packed with explosives, followed by a
second loaded with water, chemicals, and sand, were about to go down,
well, if Kevin Gainer or Gaiter couldn't get worked up about that on
his own, what could Mickey Joyner say? Finally, the only piece of advice he could think to give the little Little Leaguer was to find some
way not to spend his life out in right field, where you barely belonged
to a team and could only cover yourself with shame.

As the inning ended and the other right fielder wandered out to
take his lonely turn, Mickey was advising Kevin to get back where he
belonged, to the family that loved him, even though they might love
him to death. Even when two of those fathers had had enough and
came out to bodily remove Mickey from the field of play, that was the
gist of the pep talk he continued to give. Even when those fathers
made a swaggering spectacle of themselves, one a little twelve-year-old
would never forget, he kept it up. Until he couldn't anymore. The fathers were full of righteous indignation and anxious to steal the show
from their sons, and how in good conscience could Mickey ever advise
a little boy to return to one of them?

He got over the fence before they could get their hands on him
and, instead of going back by the stands to reach his car, skirted the
margin of the drill site, where the clattering had ceased, and he could
actually hear the flapping of the American flag. Apparently, the pipe
was up. Between trailers and fracking vans assembled in ranks, some
still wrapped in their plastic sheeting, he could see workers milling

around, and he was tempted to walk up and see how far he could get.
Below the derrick he caught a black glint from the vinyl-lined impoundment pond, and still he was tempted. Diesel fumes fouled the air, but if
you were willing to smell past them, it was not impossible to detect the
tempting odor of wet clay extracted from deep within the earth. But
he left the site, and with open country on his left and a row of trucks
on his right, he continued to circle back to his car. Now that he had
been run off, cheers had risen at the ball game again, and the fathers
had resumed their upstaging ways. He was also tempted to go back
and retake his seat in the stands, but nothing tempted him quite
enough. The only thing he knew for sure was that a burned bridge was
behind him. Before him, as he pulled out onto the highway, was the
open road in a lovely time of the day, late afternoon, early evening, late
spring, early summer, very, very near the longest day of the year. If no
one came to get him, as his sister had warned one day no one would,
that did not mean that he was stranded. Fina was most likely in the
Bronx by now, was certainly in the Bronx by now, and Carlos would
have resumed his pharmacist's wooing, pills and pill-dollars for life,
and that did not mean that he, Mickey Joyner, was without resources,
homeless on the face of the earth. The day was long. At each intersection one road handed him on to another, as vaguely he headed north.

14

In less than two days they'd graded a road in, running down along the forest for about a hundred yards, and then they'd gone to work on the well pad, and Frank leaned against his bale of hay and marveled at how efficient they were, how practiced, a team of earthmovers as skillfully meshed as any sports team he'd seen play, and how irreversible it all seemed. Kenny had shown him numerous photographs of sites that had been "reclaimed." How slopes to pastures like his had been restored, to the exact degree, the bumps and gullies ridden out, the topsoil returned and re-grassed with some fast-germinating seed, and yet he couldn't help but feel that the transformation taking place before his eyes was once and for all.

They brought in a bulldozer-size roller studded with deeply notched teeth to compress the earth so that derricks and generators and pipe racks and frac vans could rest flat on their pad. Frank didn't hear Helen drive up and was only aware of her presence when she took two folding chairs out of her trunk and positioned them in front of his bale of hay. She had also brought lunch and a cooler of drinks.

Since he couldn't take his eyes off the earthmoving going on, she
would join him.

He sat in Helen's chair. There she had the access road, with a bed
of light stone over a heavier base, and there she had the four-acre pad,
so level to the eye you could have drilled a company of soldiers on it.
Just beyond the cut in the bank, an excavator had been called in to dig
out the pit for the drilling fluids, which would, he'd been assured, be
lined with the heaviest-grade vinyl available. Kenny had advised him
to take photos, just to see how faithfully restored it would all be. Frank
said there was no need.

Helen said that she trusted Kenny. She'd seen the way he looked at
Frank.

How was that?

"Like you're an idol for him. He'd lie down in front of one of those
machines if that was what it took."

They sat into the afternoon, the heat holding off, the sun behind
a succession of thick, white clouds, the valley quilted in cloud-shaped
zones of light and shade. Danny came running up, outrunning his
mother, who drove. Yes, as long as he stayed out of the way, he could
go down and watch the men work, although it looked to his grandfather as if they were almost done. Danny ran down to the cut in the
bank and sat with his feet hanging over the edge, watching the excavator gouge out ten to twelve feet. Jen, when she came, accepted a can of
cold iced tea and leaned up against the bale of hay. So it was happening, she said. So he'd been right.

Yes. She meant Kenny.

"So how's it look?" she asked her father.

To Jen, Frank said what he wouldn't say directly to Helen. "I hope
I've done the right thing."

Jen said, "The Deweese runs on natural gas, every apartment, office, and store in it, but it's gas coming from somewhere else, maybe
somewhere not as scenic as we are here. But that's 'eye of the beholder'
stuff, the scenic part, I mean. The fact is we burn somebody else's

natural gas because it's a lot cleaner than burning somebody else's coal. Now it's our turn to supply the gas. As long as we're talking about the right thing to do, I've never heard the antidrilling crowd give a satisfactory answer to that question."

Frank didn't try to answer it. Neither did Helen.

Jen said, "Of course, it's the money part that's the problem. Somebody might be getting rich and somebody else might not, but that's all history's ever been about anyway, isn't it? The spoils-of-war stuff. The good part is we're not taking it from our neighbors at gunpoint, or swordpoint, just from the land, our little part of it."

She looked out over the pasture. All the earthmoving equipment had now been pulled off to the side, near to the tree line, where two Porta Potties stood. Her blond-haired son was walking the pad's perimeter, she was almost sure counting his paces, which he would then report back to his grandfather so that an even more faithful record could be kept and the gas company, TransAtlantic, held to their word. Before he got back, Kenny Brewster had unexpectedly pulled up in his car, gotten out, and come to stand with them. He wore sunglasses, but once he joined them, he took them off, and she saw the light, trusting blue of his eyes.

He said to Frank, "Well, that didn't take long. How's it look to you, sir? Anything you'd like them to do?"

Frank shook his head. "I don't think this slope gave them much trouble."

"That road look all right?"

"They're pros, Kenny. You heard anything about a drilling date?"

He shook his head, looking at Frank, looking at the field. Then Kenny looked at Jen and said, "Hi, how've you been?"

She smiled and, affecting an offhandedness and hoping it would pass, said, "Good to see you again."

Danny, when he returned, came running. "They're just sitting down there!" he reported more to Kenny than to Frank.

"Probably waiting for a call to see where to go next," Kenny said.

Then Kenny made a promise: when the drilling began, he'd make some free time and come show Danny how it all worked. It could be really cool for a kid like Danny to see. Kenny had worked on the rig floor and wouldn't mind seeing it all again himself, but that had been down in Texas, and it was another world down there, it almost seemed like another life.

He looked from Jen's son to her when he said that about Texas's being another life, and Jen was looking at him. Their smiles were identical, as if both were holding their breath. Then Kenny said he had things to do, he'd just been checking in to make sure everything was all right, and he was back in his car, and soon after that, Jen, who also had things, was back in hers. Danny returned to the pad, marching out to the red-flagged spot where the well would be drilled, where he stopped and waved at Frank and Helen, still seated in the chairs Helen had brought.

"You saw that?" Frank said.

"I did," Helen said.

"What do you think it means?"

"What it's always meant, I suppose."

"How long do you think it's been going on?"

"Are you asking if I knew?"

"No, but did you?"

"Not until he said that about Texas being another life and looked at Jen as if his real life was right here."

"He's married, you know."

"And not until I saw the way Jen looked at him."

"He's been trying to persuade his wife to come up here. For a while that was all he seemed to have on his mind."

"Frank . . ." She reached out for him and placed her hand on his arm.

"I don't like it, Helen."

"Jen leads with her heart. She's an adventurer. And she's generous. I imagine for a father that might lead to some anxious moments, but I have to admit it's one of the things about her I like. I wish Cindy had some of that. I know that's easy for me to say."

"And if the wife shows up?"

"Then somebody'll have to decide. Jen's been through this before, you know. But, of course, you do. Last summer and fall, you remember those trips she took."

"Helen, were you ever like this?"

"No, never."

Ray Whittaker called him. Wilson Michaels had gone from being a curious case, almost sad when you looked at it over the course of a career, to the sort of pest who didn't know when to stop e-mailing or making mildly threatening, vaguely abject calls. He'd begin to plead one day, threaten the next, and Ray Whittaker was no longer sure which Wilson Michaels he was going to get. Frank called his sister Carol. Carol could tell him that she was also getting phone calls and e-mails that for the sake of her own family she could no longer afford to answer. She was afraid Wilson was coming apart. His wife had left him. From one day to the next he was living in her little town house in a Queens neighborhood where the neighbors valued civility above all else. Civility had never been Wilson's strong suit. Brenda still tolerated him, but love him as a faithful daughter should, take the time, sacrifice a little of each week . . . ? Frank heard his sister's voice go soft. What could he do? Money set aside for Michaels would have to come out of all of their shares, but Carol now thought it was more personal than that. Would Frank believe that her ex-husband from his big-city perspective had always admired Frank in some strange way? Strange, because all the time she was married to Michaels he never ceased to talk about her brother as a victim of his small-town mentality and his hang-up about old buildings and barns and the family homestead and the like, when she'd actually begun to see Michaels must have admired Frank in ways he couldn't talk about, so he talked in the only way he knew how.

Back in town, Charlie Terwilliger called and then came by. He almost didn't and he almost didn't want to say anything, not because he and Jen had split—what he and Jen had had going could never have led to something as settled sounding as a *split* anyway—but because guys were always shooting off their mouths and almost nothing ever came of it. It wasn't the money that someone might make and someone else might not—the counterculture that Charlie came out of was used to that, needed, in fact, fat-cat millionaires living in overlarge, overheated and -cooled, view-hogging houses for something to be counter to. It was the takeover of their town, the truckers and drill riggers and landmen who would be piling in for whom the word *community* meant nothing.

Frank walked Charlie out to the pad, where they stood looking out over the valley. The job had been cleanly done. Charlie, a craftsman, in addition to being a good bluegrass bass player, admired the earthmoving workmanship. The truth was Charlie Terwilliger was the sort of pro tem boyfriend any father would wish on a daughter slow to settle down. "But mainly it's you, Frank," Charlie said. "It's the fact that it's you and not some fat cat who's going to be opening the floodgates and letting all the shit flow through town. That's what's got some guys talking about something needing to be done."

Down in the southeastern corner of the county, where the first wells were being drilled, somebody had climbed up on a derrick and hoisted the Jolly Roger. But those wells had taken their water from another county, and the town had been spared the bulk of the truck traffic, and the flowback fluid had been dumped somewhere else.

Charlie wasn't talking about another Jolly Roger, was he?

"It was probably nothing, Frank."

"A spanner in the works?"

"I'm not naming names, but one of the guys worked road construction a few years back and knows something about dynamiting cliffs."

"Dynamite? The gas-drilling derricks I've seen you could probably throw a rope around and pull over."

"Set an example, Frank. Make a statement."

"Why don't they come after *me*, then?"

"Oh, they wouldn't do that. Even if they think you fucked up big-time with this gas-well business, you're still one of us. It's crazy. Like I told you, there's not one chance in a hundred anybody's going to do anything."

"Yet you drove out here to tell me."

"Well, the truth is, everybody's a little on the fence on this one. If those guys drinking that beer had any property to lease, they might not be saying a thing. And . . ."

"And?"

"And you're Jen's dad."

And Mickey's. The next call was from a woman named Judith Ball-inger, who identified herself as the superintendent of the school system where Mickey Joyner was employed. She needed to talk to Mickey about school business, but he didn't answer any calls, and when she'd sent someone by his apartment, it became clear that he had left town, and now she wondered if his father could tell her where his son was. How did he know Judith Ballinger wasn't some bill collector or credit-card solicitor or someone masterminding an Internet scam, or anything like that? Her voice was level, courteous, warmly inflected enough not to be thought cold, with a multitasker's pacing and poise, and if she wasn't a school superintendent, she should have been.

He said, "I hope it's nothing urgent. As long as it's not a matter of someone's health, I mean."

"It's a matter of grades."

"Too easy or too hard?"

Judith Ballinger wouldn't say. She asked Frank to take down a number and ask Mickey to call when he spoke to his son, and Frank did write the number down, but he wanted something in exchange for this position she was putting him in, party to whatever her design might have been, so he asked her to tell him what kind of teacher his son had been, and by that he meant how persuasively he'd presented the history both of them shared, and by *both of them* he meant Judith Ballinger and himself. And she wouldn't bite. She repeated that this was a matter of grades, and Frank heard himself going on that sometimes it was the little things and the little people, not the Washingtons and Jeffersons and Lincolns, who made the real difference—for instance, how something Henry David Thoreau did and then wrote about had saved them all from World War III, something a little person such as his son had taught another little person, namely himself . . . and then he stopped when he realized Judith Ballinger had switched into her tolerance mode while almost certainly attending to other tasks at hand. Was it some form of civil disobedience his son was engaged in? He didn't ask.

He put off thinking about it, making a conscious effort. For the next three mornings he awoke expecting their country road to be clogged with trucks bringing in drilling equipment, generators, fuel, personnel trailers, tanks of various sorts. When on the fourth morning it hadn't happened and a raucous medley of birdsong woke him, he lay in bed until the birdsong was replaced by the perfectly impersonal sound of Superintendent Ballinger's voice in his ear. It was as if he'd made a recording of a voice that already sounded like one and had no idea now how to turn the damn thing off. He left a note to Danny about getting his own breakfast. The voice least like Ballinger's he knew belonged to his ex-wife, which came in rasping bursts and, when he'd been a young man, seemed to have gathered a whole wealth of experience behind it, experience he lacked. He drove to Marjorie's house, on the other side of town, a good half an hour away. It was on a street of other small, prefabricated houses, only hers had a big sycamore out back and a little wisteria arbor over a concrete-slab patio, and that was where he found her. With no desire to enter her house, he walked around back first and surprised her having a cup of coffee and a cigarette, dressed in a washed-out, lime-green house robe he remembered from many years back.

"Christ, Frank! Whistle or do something, crack your knuckles, creak a joint, don't just come sneaking up on me like that."

He agreed, "I should have called."

"There's an idea. A courtesy phone call."

"How are you, Marjorie?"

"Out of the line of fire. What's going on out there?"

"They've put in their well pad. They could start drilling anytime, if that's what you mean."

"That's what I mean."

"You've got your lease money?"

"Straight from Ray Whittaker's hand." She took a long drag on her cigarette. "You'll remember I didn't ask for it."

They'd been married for over twenty-five years, and at times since then he'd looked at her and concluded it had all been a case of mistaken identity. He simply couldn't see himself at her side. The dailiness of their lives together was converting into a blank. But he had a clear memory of her as a girl he'd paid court to in her father's bar. That was a vibrant memory for him, and the impact of her presence at his side while others were calling for her attention he could still feel—it had felt electric, it had lit him up. She'd said, "How's my long-faced friend? You do have a long face, Frank. But it suits you. You have things on your mind. This town is full of a lot of baby-faced boys pretending to be men. There's a few sitting right down there." Her words. He'd pursued her and she'd seduced him, the oldest story in the world.

He said, "That's all right, Marjorie. You deserve it."

"Are you saying I paid my dues, served my time?"

"No, you are."

"So why'd you stop by, Frank, so early in the morning?"

"I wanted to hear the sound of your voice."

She guffawed, hacking out cigarette smoke. "I bet you did!"

With her congested voice fresh in his ears he could no longer hear the studied and mechanically clear tones of Superintendent Judith Ballinger's, so he told Marjorie about the phone call and Mickey's disappearance and asked if he'd been in contact with her, and Marjorie laughed again, this time a sort of knowing growl down in her chest. It was summer, she said. In the summer Mickey disappeared, and in the fall Mickey popped up, if not teaching in Judith Ballinger's school system, teaching somewhere else. Wasn't Frank used to this by now? Both their children—she excluded Gerald and didn't bother to correct her mistake—went off the rails pretty much every year.

Except with the lease in place and royalties on the way, they had a safety net now.

And if the gas didn't want to come up? If the well was a bust?

"Jesus, Frank! You signed the damn thing, didn't you? And now you're wishing a bust on your own kids?"

"This Ballinger woman led me to believe it was serious this time. Something to do with grades."

"Grades! Someone copied a test, someone got caught, someone's parents came to bitch, and this Ballinger is looking around for some poor jerk she can make a scapegoat of. Something like that."

Frank nodded, hummed in his throat. At least one nest of birds was in the wisteria vine above their heads. He could hear a chorus of squeaks from babies waiting to be fed.

"Ever cheat on a test, Frank?"

The fact was he never had, not that he could remember, but he wasn't about to boast of such a virtuous record to his ex-wife. Nor that his grades for deportment had all been A's.

"So you haven't been in touch with Mickey?"

"Not since he was here last."

And that had been . . . Christmas? Had it been that long?

Again, Frank had that debilitating sense that his life was slipping away, that stretches of it were converting into blanks. He remembered standing with his son beneath the branches of their silver-maple tree, and he remembered that those upwardly flaring branches, like a chalice held to the sky, had been bare.

Commit the symbolic act.

He got up.

"That was quick. Now that you're out here, have a cup of coffee, Frank. There're other things we can talk about. It doesn't have to be our misbehaving children and gas wells. You still seeing . . . I believe her name was Helen Gobright? If you are, I think that's fine. At least she'll pay her rent on time . . ."

She left it hanging, inviting him to respond. When he didn't, she completed her thought. ". . . that is, if you're charging her any. A gentleman wouldn't. But, then, a gentleman who played by the book, a real stand-up sort of guy, probably would."

Which was he? She laughed again, clearing the air as she filled it with cigarette smoke. As her laugh died out, he heard the squeaking of the baby birds.

"You've got a nest of babies right above your head, Marjorie."

"That's the second hatch in that nest this spring. They must like it up there."

She smiled at him, her eyes drawn so thin he could only detect a slate-colored line. What was the real color of his ex-wife's eyes? She nodded at the chair he'd just risen out of, and he had the knee-weakening sense that if he didn't sit back down, he was about to say good-bye to twenty-five years of his life. He understood that any divorce, no matter how bitter or eagerly sought, should include an agreement on memories shared, positive memories, however few, whose sole purpose would be to keep twenty-five years from being converted into an absolute waste.

Another day, he said, when he had time to spare and less on his mind.

Only when he'd gone back around front and was getting into his car did he remember, and once in the car he had no doubt. The question then became did he get out of the car and go back around the house—making some whistling or throat-clearing sound to alert Marjorie he was coming—and inform her that she needn't worry about the youngest of her nestlings, for that was exactly where he was? And where would that be, Frank? Back in the nest, back in his room in the house they had all once shared. What house, Frank? *This* is a house. If you're talking about the Deweese, that was some schoolboy's monument to himself. Something knee-jerk about it, Frank, if the truth be told. Mickey, who couldn't stand the place, would not be there. But Frank remembered—with Kenny Brewster at his back—opening the door on his son's old room, and it was like looking into the barrenness of a monk's cell, or a prisoner's cell, and Marjorie was right, not their son's room at all. Nevertheless, Mickey had been there—the socks on the floor, the paperback book, the inch of dark liquid on the bedside table—and with equal measures of shame and relief, Frank was sure he was there again.

Every time she took a trip like this there was always the chance she wasn't coming back, which was the same as saying there was always the chance of a fresh start. Even though she was not alone and had to come back, the potential for a life-renewing freshness was there. They drove north, between the two biggest of the lakes, on a day of soft light, rolling, green land, long pastured or forested slopes, until the blue of a lake showed, bluer than any of them, driving in their cars, cultivating their comforts, had a right to expect. They fouled the air and the air washed clean. They did all they could to make themselves undeserving of such a beautiful world, and they were forgiven. Someone kept the towns, the very small towns, from falling into decay. A church, a court-house, a library, a boardwalk, and at its corner what had once been the town hotel. The town creek was clear. You kept your car windows down and sounds and smells of close habitation gave way to the up-raised spaciousness of a land without blemish, nothing tightfisted out here, a plenitude of ponds reflecting the sky, livestock grazing at their leisure, fly-free, no flies, no misery, no undue usurpation of any sort, the crops with room to breathe, breathing beans, breathing tomatoes, squash, and beets, orchards of apple and cherry trees, fields of corn, breathing and exhaling that musky sex-smell, like the smell of a vast procreation, and the vineyards stepping down the slopes of the lakes in long, orderly rows, vines in full leaf with bunches of small green grapes hanging off the ground, the earth there between rows worked to a rich reddish brown. She wanted Kenny to see. She was driving so that Kenny would be free to look. On a day such as today, not an abnormal day toward the end of June, when people asked themselves, What do we stand to lose if we go drilling a mile down into the earth without knowing exactly what is going to come up? they meant this. They stood to lose this. Nothing like Texas, she knew, with its endless vistas and towns when you came on them rising straight off the plains like hapless bulwarks against the forces of nature, targets for tornadoes and dust storms and other shows of meteorological might. Nothing like that.

She'd done her homework. Before he'd even announced he had two days free, she'd taken out her maps, one of the region, down to the smallest town, and one a geological map of the Marcellus deposit. The Marcellus, which extended as far south as West Virginia, perhaps even farther than that, reached its northern point here. Then stopped. On the first of the maps she'd determined the last possible town past which the Marcellus simply didn't exist. The town after that was called Sydney Point, and there they turned down toward the lake, came out onto the point itself where a Victorian house stood, with an assortment of turrets and gables and gingerbread facing, once a hotel for the lake-crossing ferry that had docked here, as she'd learned on the Internet, and now a bed-and-breakfast. It wasn't as if she were leading a suspicious man up to the check-in desk, just a surprised one, where a sweet-natured woman confirmed the reservation Jen had made and assigned them their room overlooking the lake with a turret of its own. And in that room Jen announced they had two days and nights here, and guess what? There was nothing down there, Kenny, nothing. Approximately ten miles farther south the Marcellus had petered out, and for two days, at least, he could be his own man. She was out of her jeans and blouse and lying on what had been advertised to be, and actually was, a big brass bed while Kenny was still trying to add it all up. C'mon, Kenny. It is what it seems. The clock is ticking and so am I, so are you. This is our time now. Nothing down there, Kenny. Nothing!

No Marcellus, no Texas, no wife who can never make up her mind. Nobody hating your guts and nobody kissing your ass. How long's it take you to understand?

She willed him out of his clothes and she willed him into the bed, and once she had him in hand, she willed the biggest erection out of him she was sure he'd ever had. Then she simply let it all go, with nothing down there and only the blue space of a lake out beyond them and with no way to trace them here. Never the clinging sort, she wrapped her powerful legs around him and clung to him until he was fighting for his life and that brass bed was sounding its advertised alarm.

He had a naturally muscled body, if a little fleshy, that was true, white with a farmer's tan, but with the still-taut buttocks of a boy. He put on his swimming trunks. From her window, from her lonely damsel's turret, she would watch her lover swim out to sea. He waved at her; piningly, she waved back. And from the bed-and-breakfast dock, beside which a couple of canoes floated for guests to rent, he dove into the lake and swam out, with a compact stroke and no deviation in his course, perhaps fifty yards, right up what she imagined the wake of the last ferry to have crossed this lake to have been. Then she did something she didn't much do. She took out her hairbrush, sat in her window, and brushed out her hair, hardly tresses long enough to hang out the turret window, but maybe Kenny would get the idea. He stopped, treaded water, and looked around. No one at that moment was out there with him. No boats, no one. The water was a blue table, Kenny a blond head bobbing on it like a piece of fruit in a still life, a Cézanne apple or orange with the motion still on it. It could roll off the table. Kenny could go under. She barely knew him, after all. When she thought about it, he was mostly made up. More her father's creation than anybody else's. She leaned out her window and she brushed out her hair, and if Kenny was going to get it—damsel in her tower, knight on his watery plain, surely one of the oldest and most beloved love stories around—he'd get it now and laugh and wave and come swimming back on his amorous quest. Which was what he did.

They had supper at a restaurant just down the lake, then walked back along the shore. Deep-slanted armchairs were set out on the lawn before the dock, and by the time they reached them, the twilight out over the water had deepened from a soothing lavender to a vibrant purple. They were not alone out there. Another couple were sitting in chairs like theirs, younger, perhaps quite a bit, she Asian—Chinese, Korean, Jen couldn't be sure. The boy had a solid, squared-away face with small eyes, a farmboy, she decided, from the American heartland. The lake was quiet, and everything was quietly compassed—even in this last light, the tree line on the opposite shore was still visible. A lone speedboat made its way home, throwing up a phosphorescent wake. Jen wondered about the girl especially; boys were frequently struck mute, they had a habit of projecting the mystery of a woman, or simply a girl, onto the world around them so that everything, the most common of things, seemed strange; but a woman wouldn't do that, not even a girl. So what was this Asian girl doing?

She and Kenny sat there in the aftermath of their meal, savoring the coolness the lake gave off, and the clarity of the night in which only the very first stars had appeared with as yet no trace of a moon. They heard sounds from across the water—a motorcycle, a child, a dog—and they heard the amplified lapping of tiny waves against the piles of their dock. They did not hear the Asian girl and the American farmboy get up and leave, so that when Jen finally did go over to introduce herself and plumb their mystery a bit, the young couple were gone. It was not a total loss. She and Kenny would have them for company tonight in perhaps their own turreted room, their own brass bed, although the wording on the website had made it seem as if the old ferry-stop hotel at Sydney Point had only one brass bed to offer, and Jen and Kenny had gotten it.

Kenny was gone. He had pulled a canoe down off the lawn, and she found him sitting in it, holding on to the dock until she could get in, too. They had paddles but no life-preserving cushions—they must have been taken in—so that as they pushed off and stroked their way out into the darkness of the lake, the aluminum hardness of the seats began to tell on their backsides, the only discordant note in a night where everything else was clean and cool to the touch, their glide across the water silky, silky the breeze they raised against their faces, the sky still mostly starless, moonless, their own faces at opposite ends of the canoe watery reflections of whom they knew themselves to be. When Kenny sculled them around sideways, they saw the old ferry hotel. One turret was lit, the other, theirs, was dark. They could make out the small front porch because the light was on, but the gables and the silhouette of the steeply pitched roof were indistinct in the darkness, on the point of vanishing. She thought of her father, her father being called on to save this old ferry hotel—and just how many of these could be left?—to pull it out of the darkness and hammer it into the upright being of contemporary day. A ferry hotel, it made a fundamental sort of sense. You miss the last boat of the day and there was no other way across. You couldn't walk. You couldn't ride a horse. You bedded down. You had breakfast the next morning as fuel for the crossing. You crossed a body of water that thanks to the abrading glaciers ran three to four hundred feet deep. The American continent, a natural phenomenon, was never not a crossing for those who measured themselves against it, and what could be more in the American vernacular than that? She would tell her father to come out of retirement and find a ferry hotel to restore. She looked down the canoe to tell Kenny, too, and found him nearly naked as he got out of his clothes for a late-night swim. She almost started—his flesh had the glimmering paleness of a corpse—and he said, C'mon, Jenny, you, too.

She did not frighten easily, and she was not frightened now, and a strong swimmer she had always been, but slipping into this black water that from her waist down was sharply cold with a man she knew and loved, but had not known and loved long, and with no way to anchor the canoe, caused her to wonder just how far she was prepared to go. Kenny swam out first and she followed him, as the canoe began slowly to drift away. There were loons on the lake, she knew, because she'd heard them before, but she hadn't heard their ghostly wail that night.

She heard Kenny with his strong stroke swimming into the darkness, where he stopped and gave her time to catch up. When she was within perhaps five feet of him, he swam off again, but this time circling back toward the drift of the canoe, and she cut the angle and, letting her legs do most of the work, again came close, almost within reach, when he sprinted off again. She heard his laughter between catches of breath— not loon-crazy, shrewder and cockier than that—and the steady paddling of his feet, and she remembered he'd been a sailor and assumed that sailors had been taught how to swim for their lives, so she gave up her pursuit and at a pace that pleased her swam back to the canoe, which in the darkness cast its own aluminum light. She reached it before he did. With her arms draped along the gunwale, she extended her legs, and when he got there, he swam right into her trap. She clamped him between her legs. Bastard! she hissed at him. Where'd you think you were going? He held on to her shoulders and she squeezed harder until she'd raised a watery yelp. Swimming back to Texas, eh? Didn't get very far, did you, Kenny? Jesus, Jen, you've got a linebacker's strength in those legs! Let up, you're gonna crush me! What a thing to say to a girl! she upbraided him. What a Texas thing to say! And she worked him closer in, worked him and worked him, until she felt his erection moving blindly against her in this glacial water and moonless night and she worked him all the way in.

She'd made love in Jacuzzis and made love in swimming pools and ponds and had once, inspired by an old movie she'd seen, tried to make love in an onrush of surf, but this was different because she was holding on to the gunwale of the canoe for her life, and the heat they generated between them was only good enough for a standoff with the cold rising three or four hundred feet up from below. Kenny clung to her, she clung to the canoe, they faced the elements together, and with her head thrown back she saw that they'd even brought the stars out. And this—she wanted to tell him—was a real marriage, the only kind she'd be prepared to accept. Survive this and you'd accomplished something. Make a child out here in the night and the glacial cold and water

as dark as the world's preexistence and what more could you ask of two
unrenowned people out on the stage of their lives? The canoe had now
turned broadside to the old ferry hotel. Past his head she picked out
the turret belonging to, she'd decided, the young couple. The light was
still on. She saw two shadowy figures framed in the turret window,
looking out. Then the light went off. She and Kenny were being observed, she was sure of it, and instead of feeling shyness or shame felt a
surge of pride, a genuine heroic daring. Not everyone had to bed
down. Not everyone had to wait for the morning ferry to return.
There were those, after all, who crossed at night, and there were those
who, midcrossing, dared to make love. Such lovers still existed in the
world.

Should she tell Kenny, to excite him to more remarkable heights?
She said, Kenny, Kenny, you're a landman out on this lake, I'm your
piece of land, Kenny, she laughed at him, with him, in time to his thrusts,
maybe, yes, a little loon-crazy now herself, a nondiving loon who held
to the canoe and gave her lover a purchase on solid earth, drill, baby,
drill, she went on laughing, but did not tell him that that young,
speechless couple had them in their sights and were surely asking
themselves if they'd gone too far to back out, if this was where it all
ended up, black freezing water, no rescue in sight, holding on to each
other until a ferry carrying everyday folk either did or did not pick
them up the next morning, that is, if they managed to survive this
long, terrifying night. In the end she did not tell Kenny, who was, after
all, a modest man she'd somehow managed to inflame, but this was
exactly the kind of thing she could tell Mickey, and this time, in spite
of their whole history of exaggeration, make him believe. It happens,
Mickey. Not just in the movies. You look on the Internet, a quaint
bed-and-breakfast on the point of a lake, a sweet woman to check you
in, the brass bed she'd promised, a little two-day escape. A nice meal,
and what more natural, what more scripted, than a canoe ride on a
windless night out on a silky-smooth lake? Skinny-dipping, it's been
going on since time immemorial, and a little race around the canoe to

see who gets back first. Of course, you're not entirely alone, there are always onlookers, there have to be onlookers, voyeurs, a shy couple, perhaps, in their own room, getting a glimmering eyeful, taking notes. Then they go fuck in their own bed, even though it's not brass and even though they have to fall short. But, Mickey, if you're really setting an example, not just playing at it, it can be a matter of life and death out there, you've got to imagine a black and bottomless lake, in a water so cold it goes back to the last ice age, and when I say you're fucking for your life, Mickey, that's exactly what you're doing. You don't want to let your eavesdropping couple down, there *is* such a thing as a performer's code to uphold, but when I say it's the forces of life against the forces of darkness and death, I'm not exaggerating, Mickey, not a bit, not this time, and I'm not sure how it's going to turn out. I may never live to tell the tale. This is real-time storytelling, Mickey. I've got a pretty good landman holding on to me and working his sweet little buttocks off—*our* landman, Mickey—and it's getting wild out here. I'm getting ready to come, and this may be the last you hear of me. I don't know where I'll end up, or where our landman will either. I've never told you about this, Mickey. But I come and, just so you have an idea, it's like you're diving off a stage into the great orgasmic mosh pit of your life, you fly out and they catch you and throw you farther out and farther out, one swelling heave after another, and you don't know where you'll end up. You've got to picture something, Mickey, because it's all cold and dark out here except for a few stars, and the very best possibility is that I'll go star-hopping, and then, of course, there's the unplumbed bottom of this lake and whatever's down there from an ice age ago. But no shale, Mickey, no shale, that's the nice part, we're out beyond the Marcellus, shaleless sex, Mickey, imagine such a thing, there's an end to all that, a point where it all ends, Sydney Point if you want the name, an old ferry hotel turned into a bed-and-breakfast if you want to try this all out, and you really should, you know. Before you give up sex for good, come out here on a moonless night and I'll be your eavesdropper—my landman and I—the source of all our good fortune, a really great guy our father rescued like some pedigreed stray, a Texan, Mickey, with maybe one foot in Arkansas and the rest of him in me, Mickey, it's a manner of speaking, the best part of him in me, Mickey, and it's over now, I'm going, no more storytelling tonight, that young couple have moved away from the window, I'm sure of it, she's Asian, he's a square-boned American, no way they belong together unless they mate those differences down, which is what they're doing, they've learned all they can and they've taken it to heart, and, Mickey . . . Oh, my God, Mickey, I think it's the stars, it's cold and dark but I'm up with the stars, it's the mosh pit of the heavens, Mickey, no way you're gonna believe this, but it's one constellation after another handing me on, I'm sliding down the Big Dipper, I'm riding the Centaur, the twins . . . what're their names? the Gemini . . . are tossing me back and forth, I'm all over the heavens, Mickey, and I have no idea where my landman is, ours, yours and mine, but I'll find him, we'll live to tell this tale, another installment coming up soon, but just so you'll know and won't worry about your sister anymore, it's not age-old ice at the center of the earth, it's the stars, Mickey . . . I'm up in the stars . . .

They had put their clothes back on in an effort to get warm, although not their shoes, and in the darkness Kenny had misbuttoned his shirt. Without cushions there was nowhere to lounge, nowhere to lie back and speak your thoughts to the woman at the other end of the canoe, although that was what Kenny was trying to do.

He told her about the father that never was, who when he'd either been kicked out or had run off on his own had left only his name behind. He told her about his grandfather, one of the most honored men in a not-unprosperous town, out to set an example under his white sheet. He told her about his navy days and about a couple of Spanish girls whose names he'd forgotten. He didn't tell her his wife's name because if it was glory she was offering him, he should have known better, but he told her about coming back to his hometown and no one was there, no one, his mother remarried and moved away, his grandfather dead and laid to rest by his white-robed friends, no one, he tried to describe how empty the town seemed, how strange, like something he'd turned his back on and could never get back, more foreign than the foreign lands he'd just returned from, when this unnamed girl appeared and announced she'd been waiting for him all this time, and even though he barely remembered her, what she was saying was if he'd go to the trouble of believing her, she could make it real for him again, something like that. But it had never been real, that was what he'd finally figured out. They'd tried to have a baby, like another way, biologically speaking, to make it real, and that hadn't worked either. He was trying to figure this out, speak his thoughts along a line he'd believed he'd seen clear, but, and he knew this was going to sound strange, when he met Jen's father and saw the work he did, how he wouldn't let what had once been real disappear, not if it had any reality left, he believed that was like a sign. There were a lot of crazies down where he came from, but he wasn't a born-again anything, and not an easy sell, definitely not an easy sell, but when this Michaels man kept calling and calling and finally led him to her father, he had to admit it had been a sign. But in making this all clear to Jen, it finally went as dark for him as that old ferry hotel, whose doorway was lit but whose rooms and turrets weren't, so that you might enter by the right route but eventually get lost along the way. It was hard to say. All he wanted was something real. That was easy to say, but that didn't say it all. Because a lot of things were half-real, or some fraction maybe less than that. Fractions of reality, degrees of it. Maybe that was why he didn't mind drilling into the earth. He could make himself believe the farther down you went, the realer it had to be. You might not know what it was until you got down there and gave it a name, but at least it was a start.

He reached up the length of the canoe and grasped Jen by the big toe.

"Jenny," he said.

"You're one strange dude, Kenny Brewster. We're out here half-naked in a canoe in the middle of a lake in the dark of the night and it's all becoming 'real' for you? I thought my brother Mickey was strange, but you may have him beat."

He squeezed her toe. "Jenny," he said. "You're real."

"Well, after hearing how you've got it all figured out, I guess a girl should feel flattered. That's one big big toe."

They spent another day and a half in the old ferry hotel at Sydney Point, eating, drinking, swimming, canoeing, making love. Then they drove south, out over the northern reaches of the Marcellus, and went back to work.

15

He'd heard the trucks before dawn, but he'd rolled over and gone back to sleep, and when his grandson woke him—"Granddad, they're here! They're all over the place!"—it wasn't tiredness that kept him in bed, it was inertia of another sort, and he told Danny he could go out there but to stay up on the other side of the road. It was still early. He heard his grandson tear through the house, out the front door, and up the gravel of the drive. The noise was of trucks, trucks coming up the road in front of their house at a steady, growling pace, and trucks backing up, turning, unloading, in powerful revving bursts out in what had once been the family field, but he'd awoken thinking of his son, the younger of his sons, who, he remained certain, would lie sleeping in a room and a bed his father knew well, and that was part of Frank's inertia, too. He'd told no one. A complex sense of shame had held him back. Judith Ballinger had called again and named a student by the peculiar name of Jimmy Flesh and asked Frank to mention that student to his son if and when he talked to him, as, Frank was sure, a way of shaming Mickey into making good on whatever obligations the school superintendent was accusing him of shirking. In failing to offer his son consolation, Frank was incurring shame of his own. But in opening the door on his son and exposing Mickey in what anybody would say was a case of a man's breaking down before the demands of the adult world, Frank would have been adding to his son's shame, and he couldn't do that either. Of course, he needed to remind himself, as he did each morning, that he could be wrong and Mickey might not have been there at all.

Frank stayed in bed.

It was Danny who leaned up against his grandfather's bale of hay and watched the trucks hauling in long, blue rectangular vans, the length, it seemed of train cars, and lining them up. Other trucks carried huge pieces of machinery, with a lot of pipes and gauges, colored a battleship gray. Others brought in tanks, squat, cylindrical, two to a truck bed, and still others trailers where maybe offices were supposed to be or little laboratories. There was a rack of concrete pipes, or some sort of casings. The racks of long steel pipes, when they arrived, were unloaded by cranes and stacked off to the side. In one of those racks the pipes had bulletlike heads, with high ridges and deep grooves, and Danny concluded these had to be the drill bits he'd heard so much about and was on the point of racing back to the house to tell his granddad since drill bits had to mean the drilling was about to begin. Except, he immediately realized, there was no derrick to drill with. There was an awful lot of noise, and a self-renewing stench of diesel exhaust, and a massive amount of weight being moved around, but it was like the stockpiling of a lot of ammunition before a big battle was about to begin but with nothing to aim at and, as of yet, no enemy in sight.

At lunchtime he went back down to the house and found his grandfather out on the deck, with another view of the valley where well pads had yet to appear. Back there, the sound of the trucks held off just enough so that they could talk. Danny asked his grandfather if he wanted a report on all that was going on out there, and his grandfather said, Not yet. Danny then asked him if he was coming up to take a look for himself, and his grandfather said, Maybe after lunch.

Danny decided to call his mother, where she worked at the art gallery. When he told her that they'd started and were loading the well pad up as though for a big battle, all his mother said was, Does Kenny know? Danny told her he hadn't seen Kenny and that his grandfather was out of it, and since neither of them was on the scene, it was a good thing that Danny was, otherwise TransAtlantic could do what they wanted out there. She said when she got off work, she'd drive up and take a look with him. Then, as she was getting off the phone, she told him to tell Kenny, if he did show up, to hang on because she was coming, too. Then she was all the way off the phone but suddenly came back on, calling out his name as if she were shouting it across a field. Danny, be careful! Those trucks! She said she could hear them on the phone. She said they sounded like they were going far too fast. He reminded her they had to slow down to turn into the field. Still, she begged him not to go out in the road. She made him promise.

If he hadn't wanted to go right back out there after lunch—he'd thought about skating since the basement was cool—strangely, all his mother's precautions took away his choice. Now he had to go back out there, walking along the road's narrow shoulder, just beside the ditch. And he was glad he did. Not at first. At first it was more of the same, those blue vans without windows or doors that could contain anything, lined up in rows. But he was out there when the extralong load came by, which he would otherwise have missed. It was preceded by a company car with a flashing yellow light, and followed by another, and it was so long Danny didn't see how it would make the turn down into the field. On first try it didn't and left deep-gouged tire prints in the dirt. On the second try the driver managed to swing his long load up onto that gravel road they'd built, and what he carried, Danny was sure of it, as sure as he'd been of anything in his life, was the already-assembled girders and rods and zigzagging struts of a derrick, or at least half of it, because that extralong load was followed by another, with a second, slightly tapered structure topped by a small platform. The platform and its railings were painted a bright yellow. The two parts of the derrick were painted white. While he'd been at lunch, or perhaps with so much truck traffic he'd missed it earlier on, a drilling-rig platform had been erected over the spot where that stake with the red flag had been driven into the earth, and he watched attentively as the parts of what he'd identified as the derrick were lifted off those extralong truck beds by a powerful crane and linked end to end. The small yellow platform rested just beyond a rhomboid-shaped support maybe ten feet off the ground. The larger end rested on that drilling-rig platform. On the other side of the platform was a machine with pulleys the size of bike wheels and cables thicker than his arms, and these cables were being fastened to the derrick about halfway up. The derrick had a side platform, too, he'd somehow missed, or maybe it had just been added while he was giving his attention to the pulleys and cables. And there was a ladder; there had to be a ladder going from platform to platform, all the way up. He experienced the frustration of not being able to keep an eye on everything at once but, if his conjec-tures held up, was about to know the satisfaction of seeing how it all came together to yield the desired result.

But before anything more happened—except the endless arrival and departure of trucks—his grandfather finally made an appearance, and that seemed to start something, for then his mother drove up. It took a while before Kenny did. Until then Danny's mother and grand-father stood mostly gazing out at what was taking place before them and shaking their heads. His grandfather said, "If you believe Kenny, except for a wellhead about the size of a fire hydrant, and a couple of minitanks, and some sort of metering unit, none of that will be here in a few months," and his mother said, "I do." His grandfather said, "They call the wellhead a Christmas tree," and his mother said, "I know." His mother continued gazing out over the field, emotions gath-ering on her face that even Danny could see did not belong together, an eagerness of some sort overhung by a host of doubts, like the sun shining out under loaded black clouds. His grandfather said, "Be careful, Jen," and his mother said, "I'm always careful," and his grandfather said, "No, you're not," and his mother said, "You just don't know," and finally Danny had to break in: "You guys! We've got to pay attention here! If we don't, they might never raise that derrick off the ground!"

Kenny almost didn't come. It was late. Neighbors, all slowing as they passed, were driving up the hill on the way home from work when he arrived, with some head-shaking exclamations of his own. "Boy, are they fast! They did all that in one day?"

"And part of last night," Frank said.

"What does it mean, Kenny?" Jen said.

"Means the gas is down there ready to come up. Means they wanna drill and don't wanna wait."

"Too late to turn back now?" Jen asked, but it was only a make-believe question.

"Too late, Jen," Kenny answered with his doubt-allaying smile. Danny's mother looked at Kenny and smiled back with a gleam in her eyes and those overhanging doubts practically gone.

Danny said, "When're they gonna raise that derrick, Kenny? Tomorrow?"

"Won't be long. Could be anytime. Could be tonight."

"Tonight?" Danny repeated, trying not to sound alarmed.

"From here on out, it's twenty-four-seven. They'll have some big lights out there to work by. You ready?"

Kenny drove down to see what he could find out, and while he was gone, the only thing his mother and grandfather talked about, Danny believed, was his uncle Mickey, although he couldn't be sure. His grandfather asked his mother if they still phoned late at night, and his mother said they did, but it had been a while. Then she returned the question, and his grandfather said it had probably been a lot longer. They were sitting in the fold-up chairs his mother had brought, and Danny was leaning up against his grandfather's shaggy and scratchy bale of hay. If it was Uncle Mickey they were talking about, they were talking around him as if they lacked the right title to give him, the right words, *son, brother, uncle*, or what?

Kenny returned to say they were planning to raise the derrick the next morning. The man who did the winching was on another job, but would be there early to bring the derrick up and get the drilling started. How early was early? Probably while you're still asleep, Kenny said. The break of dawn.

Danny didn't sleep, not all the way, he was afraid to, and in the predawn light he was back at his grandfather's bale of hay. Not as many trucks were coming in as the day before, but he was there when a pickup did arrive, driven, he'd have been willing to bet, by the winch operator himself, and when he heard the powerful grind of a motor he hadn't heard before and the cables lying slack halfway up the derrick began to go taut, he knew he'd been right to remain vigilant, to stay awake. No one else was going to witness what he did; they would awake to a Texas-size derrick out in what had after all been an average-size field and wonder how it had happened, when such a thing had occurred. Other, weaker motors were making noise, too, and men were shouting things back and forth, and even though the pad had been finished long ago, there was always the snorting sound of a bulldozer moving dirt around somewhere, but the white derrick with its yellow nest at the top began to rise slowly off the earth as if it existed in a world of its own. It could have been on the moon.

Seeing it laid out flat like that, Danny had decided it might not be that tall after all. He remembered it had only taken two trucks to bring it in. In his impatience for it to pick up speed, he prepared himself for a disappointment. It could be stubby, he realized, not Texas-size at all. What looked like a couple of hoses were hanging off it, slackly, like something somebody had forgotten to remove. And no one on the ground was paying any attention. Danny looked away himself, counted to twenty, then added ten more, and when he looked back, he couldn't be sure the derrick was any farther along in its ninety-degree arc, although he could see it continued to move and could hear the winch motor grinding away. It occurred to him he'd been deceived. If his real reward in switching positions on the gas-drilling debate had been to see an honest-to-God derrick rising out of his field, then who was to blame if they owned a field the derrick refused to rise in, the way some crops just wouldn't grow in some soils? Who had sold him a bill of goods? His grandfather? His mother? The answer was Kenny, of course, who on a snowy winter's day had come knocking on their door.

Then the sun rose, directly behind him, out over the field, and he felt its fresh warmth on the back of his neck. He looked up and saw that he'd been wrong. The derrick had risen. It was well into the second half of its ninety-degree arc and was glistening white in the sunlight. The bird's nest on top was as bright as a buttercup or daffodil. That side platform was three-quarters enclosed in metal sheets. A worker stood in it, riding the derrick up. The American flag had already been attached to a pole in the bird's nest and now began to flutter in the breeze.

Danny had been really wrong, which meant that Kenny had been right. The derrick was not stubby, it was going to be tall. Maybe lying along the ground it hadn't looked that way, but as it rose through the last degrees of its arc, it seemed to grow out of itself, so slender and straight in the sun that nothing in the whole valley quite compared to it, certainly no tree, telephone pole, or weather vane on a barn. Down below, with a sound of heavy gears meshing and a locking sound, workers on the drill platform, towered over now, did what they had to do to keep the derrick there. Guylines had been attached on graceful diagonals from a point just below the top platform to the ground. Otherwise, the derrick might have walked off. It clearly didn't belong. It changed everything, the field, the valley, their lives, too, Danny thought. Leaning back on the bale of hay, the lone spectator, if he'd had heavier hands, larger arms, he might have applauded. He shouted instead. Way to go! Don't stop now! Twenty-four-seven! Twenty-four-seven!

· · ·

Then nothing happened. Kenny Brewster explained that this was not out of the ordinary. There were simply more drill rigs than drill-rig teams. TransAtlantic was active in counties to the east. The wells there had been drilled and capped and were now each producing up to a million cubic feet of gas a day, and things were beginning to return to normal, except that landowners in an area where the land had not yielded much else were beginning to see considerable profits. Frank said he understood. Kenny put his hand on the older man's shoulder and asked him to remember that before too long he'd only see a little fenced-in area out there with a Christmas tree, and Frank said the size of a family cemetery, he knew.

In the meantime, Conklin Natural Gas Company had built three new pads, one of which was visible from the Joyner deck, and the truck traffic was now concentrated on the main highway. The trucks moved by in convoys that reminded Frank of when as a boy he'd watched seemingly interminable freight trains pass, and with nothing else to do as he waited at a crossing on his bike, he'd counted the cars. He remembered losing count. He remembered some of the names on the boxcars as if a whole country of jumbled couplings were passing before his eyes. The Penn Central, the New York Central, the Baltimore and Ohio, the Reading, the Lehigh Valley, the Delaware Lackawanna, the Wheeling and Lake Erie, the Wabash. Helen came out and sat with him and stayed the occasional night. Her point of view was simple, clear, unarguable: what wasn't a mess, what wasn't ungainly, at the start? But, in fact, Helen agreed with Danny. That derrick they'd put up had a certain elegance about it she hadn't expected. She'd expected something odd-angled and utilitarian, and it had turned out to be almost lovely to look at.

Neighbors stopped to look. Some walked down the road and some of them ventured onto the pad. Finding it unoccupied, some took the liberty of leaning up against Frank's bale of hay. People drove up from downtown. Frank himself remembered stopping with Helen to watch a well being dug those days they'd gotten away, and he remembered the woman who'd come to her door with a child in her arms and a gasp of joyous astonishment on her face. He remembered the woman communicating that astonishment to her child, holding the baby up to a better line of sight. Imagine, sweetheart, a pipe being driven to the center of the earth right up on our hill! Just imagine that!

He received no visitors from any of the groups opposed to the gas drilling. Of course, it was too late for that. That pretty reporter did not return from the local paper. Ray Whittaker called, but left to himself, Ray would not go around the corner to see a gas-drilling derrick. Frank had not forgotten what Charlie Terwilliger had told him, that among certain erstwhile admirers of Frank Joyner disappointment in him was running deep, but beer drinkers' thoughts often turned dark. Beer drinkers blew hot and blew cold faster than any other species on earth. Like Danny, like Kenny, and Jen, and probably Marjorie, too, he waited for that tower out there to do what it was built to do, drill into the earth, bring up the gas, disassemble itself, and leave behind a fire-hydrant-size memento where next Christmas the whole family could gather and exchange gifts.

Until then, he sat out on the deck with Helen and the convoy of trucks rumbling past down on the highway. They were surrounded by trees, and the trees brought the breeze. If the trucks kept their distance, they could talk.

They talked about raising children, and they agreed there were cycles all parents went through, but there came a time when your children outgrew you, and you ended up deferring to their differences, to the ways they'd escaped you, that is. That was the most curious part. You knew your parenting was done when, in a manner of speaking, your children became strangers in your midst.

"Which may be just another way of saying," Helen said, "that they are no longer children but have become adults, if we're lucky even our friends."

"Except there are things I could never tell them, things I could tell you."

He had told her that when he was twenty years old he had slit his wrist to see if he wanted to live or not. For example.

She nodded. He had told her that. But why couldn't he tell them?

"Because I wouldn't want to put that doubt into their minds, that I had come that close."

"There's another way to look at it, you know."

That he had done it so that his children wouldn't have to do it to themselves. They could learn from him. He'd set them an example, run the risk, and had chosen life. He'd been thinking at least one generation ahead.

And generations back? He was never sure if Helen knew the sad history of his family. That history was known in town, and it wasn't unlikely she would have heard it, except that caring for a dying husband those last years might have provided her with a protective shield. In the measuredness of her movements and the quietness of her gaze, something of that shield remained. Frank extended his arm, rolled back his watch, and shifted his wrist to the light. The trucks filled the sound vacuum around them, along with a few birds. Then, on a sigh, he lowered his arm.

"I only meant I'm sure my children have never even seen this little scar on my wrist. I've never shown it to them. You've seen it."

But she hadn't, not really. She'd looked and looked away. "Scars heal, Frank. The reason people don't see them is that they're no longer there. Are you sure you're not imagining something that's already disappeared?"

He told Helen about Mickey back in his boyhood room, and about Mickey's apparent derelictions in his adult world, and Frank now asked himself why he felt this paralyzing sense of shame when he pictured himself knocking on his son's door and confronting the man who would answer it.

"If anyone answers it, Frank. I don't know about the shame. I understand what you're saying, but if Mickey were a son of mine and I thought he was in pain, I wouldn't hesitate to knock on his door. I'd bring him milk and cookies, if that was what it took. But that would be a mother speaking."

"I took Kenny Brewster to show him the building. He was interested in what I did. The apartment was dusty, unaired. No one's lived there for six years. It was like walking into a warehouse. I opened the door to Mickey's room, and there were socks on the floor, a paperback book, and a glass on the bedside table with something dark in it he hadn't finished drinking. I thought I saw him sitting in that alcove he liked, which he told me once made him feel like a judge."

"If Mickey's *still* there, Frank."

"It was the loneliness, Helen. I thought, if my son's here, he's the loneliest man in the world."

"And what if it was pleasant for him? A nostalgia trip? Perfectly normal people do that sort of thing."

"It's as if he were haunting it."

Helen rose and looked off at where the trucks rumbled by. Tank trucks, dump trucks, flatbed trucks, trucks hauling long, semi-size vans. Some turned in at the pad visible from the deck, others continued on. They were going fast. The wind had changed, blowing in from the southwest, and she could smell the diesel exhaust. It took a crow now to make itself heard above the repeated roar of their motors.

"This isn't like you, Frank. 'Haunting' isn't like you."

"I want to knock on that door and take him in my arms, but I'm not sure I can stand the look I'll see in his eyes. It would be horrible, Helen. 'You don't mind if I hide out here awhile, do you, Dad? Something out there didn't quite work with me. Would you mind closing that door?' Can't you understand the shame a son feels in that moment, being confronted by his father, and that a father feels knowing he's failed with his son?"

"Not so much that I wouldn't take him in my arms." She paused. "Promise me one thing, Frank. Promise me you won't hate yourself later. Do whatever you have to do, but think about later, after it's done, if you can live with yourself or not. Or will it leave a scar you won't be able to take your eyes off of? I'm not going to stay with a man who can't take his eyes off of his own scar."

This didn't help, although he promised her. For her he would not turn himself into a self-hating man. But she really didn't understand. He couldn't do that to his son. He couldn't confront him with his failures as a man until Mickey stood knee-high again. No milk and cookies would do him any good then. And Frank's own failures, as they stood reflected in his son's eyes? He was too old for that, such shame was not for old men, although he promised her he would not hate himself. Before he'd allow that to happen, he would come out of retirement, tear himself down to the foundations, and build himself up again.

The drilling began while they were still asleep, and it wasn't like an artillery barrage that signaled the beginning of a war. It was loose and rattly, like a huge bag of seashells being given a tremendous shake, but amplified maybe one hundred times. The pounding itself was a dull, muffled, anticlimactic thud. That went on for two full days. Then the drill bit hit rock, and the pounding became close and deadly and loud, like two gigantic warriors locked in mortal combat. Everything shook, their house, the valley, the derrick; the birds fell silent, you couldn't hear dogs, you couldn't hear cars, if Danny went into the basement to perform tailslides on his ramp, you couldn't hear them; conversations took place at the top of voices, and sound became the annihilation of sound.

Frank called Kenny on his cell phone, but Kenny had the bad luck to be counties away. The landman assured his client that the first layer of rock was the loudest; the motor noise on the derrick you would always hear, but the pounding would go farther and farther underground. Limestone, sandstone, they'd have to be very unlucky to hit granite, and finally that bed of shale, too delicate to make much noise.

The perforating explosions the hydrofrackers would make—you wouldn't hear those. The diesel engines generating the hydrofracking pressure you would hear, but that was engine noise, pretty much daily fare. The sound of gas entering the pipe, rising to the wellhead, being piped off across the valley, would be inaudible to human ears. Maybe two more weeks of vertical drilling, Frank. Then the turn. Kenny would come when he could. He hadn't forgotten his promise to put a hard hat on Danny and show him the drill-rig floor.

Frank might have asked Helen to go out of town with him for those two weeks, but he felt like a commander who refused to flee to safer ground once the battle had begun, and he hunkered down. He didn't go downtown. With competing obligations, he postponed knocking on his son's bedroom door. Helen came out and shared the din with him until he insisted that she leave. He made calls to all interested parties so that they would know the drilling had begun. He called Carol, who sympathized with him, and who reproached herself for not being at his side when he described the noise. He did not go back to his favorite vantage point, his bale of hay, but observed the drilling from his bedroom window or standing out in his front yard. Once in use, the derrick no longer appeared as an alien or sinister object. In fact, he was struck by how common it all seemed, the smoking diesel engines, the rise and fall of pipe, the purposeless milling of men.

People stopped to take it all in, but because of the noise didn't stay long. Once he thought he saw Charlie Terwilliger up there with another man, but unless he wanted to put his binoculars on them, he had no way to read their expressions or even their body language as they leaned up against their car. He wouldn't do that. He wouldn't spy on people as they came out to spy on him. And they weren't spying on him, anyway. They were bearing witness. This was Frank Joyner. After all that he had done to carve out his little civic and architectural niche, this was the man he'd now clamorously become.

No one leaned up against his bale of hay except Danny, who might have been deaf to the noise he made on his skateboard but not to this drilling into rock, and he took it for only three days. The truck traffic had dwindled. Mainly, all Danny could do was catch distant glimpses of the workers on the drill floor as they pulled up and added pipe. One had a chain he threw around the pipe in its borehole like a bullwhip; another seemed to operate some huge, swinging overhead clamp. Early on they'd drilled through the water table, and by jumping around a bit and catching a slightly different angle, Danny could see that raised pipe gush dirty water, into, he assumed, that plastic-lined pond. The man up in that side platform that Kenny called the monkeyboard mainly just stood around. Eventually, he picked Danny out and waved, but for some reason Danny didn't wave back. He thought of himself now as conducting surveillance. The derrick as it had stood mysterious and tall in the early-morning light was one thing. This sledgehammering, corkscrewing device was suspiciously another.

No one leaned up against that bale of hay until one cool, gray afternoon, with on-and-off rain, Frank saw a man there in a long overcoat, and it wasn't that cool. He didn't see the man's car, which made him wonder if he was a neighbor Frank had never met, who had walked there in that out-of-season coat. He didn't know how long the man had been there, but something about the way he slumped against the hay and the way the coat hung off his shoulders made Frank believe it had been some time. An hour later he checked again, and the man was still there. A third time, and it became clear to Frank he was going to have to walk up that hill to see. It was Wilson Michaels, whom, for all the changes he had undergone, Frank recognized at once.

They had to raise their voices to talk, but everything Frank had to say to Wilson Michaels was quiet. How long had he been there? Where was his car? Why had he just appeared? Why had he chosen this particular bale of hay to lean against? Was he as lonely as he looked? Why hadn't he come down to the house?

Frank shook Michaels's hand. The smirking grin that had been the once-famous lawyer's characteristic expression was almost entirely gone. His eyes were tired, large, and exposed. Nowhere about him was there a sense of a man knit to a purpose, not in the knees, not the mouth, certainly not in the clothes, which were so fundamentally out of place a farmer driving by, or a worker from the vantage point of that rig, might have mistaken him for a clown. Men in suits and vests and big-city topcoats did not lean up against bales of hay unless they wanted to provoke laughter.

Frank moved up beside him and, in his khakis and windbreaker and all-season boots, leaned back. Frank wore a baseball cap with a farm-machinery insignia on front. Michaels's head was bare and his thinning black and gray curls lay wet on his scalp. Perhaps Michaels was used to raising his voice as a sort of oratorical weapon in court. Frank was not, but he raised it and said, "What do you think?"

"A lot of noise," Michaels shouted back. "How far down have they gone?"

"I don't know. Maybe halfway. Half a mile."

"TransAtlantic, right?"

Frank confirmed it was TransAtlantic. The sign said as much.

"That kid Kenny Brewster down there?"

Frank said Kenny was off elsewhere signing farmers up to leases.

"And how's your friend Ray Whittaker?"

Busy. Frank kept it short.

"A bright guy. Smart. Friendly. A poker player. Right?"

Frank had never played poker with Ray in his life. Not that Ray didn't think everything a move or two ahead, as good poker players did. Frank nodded.

"That Brewster kid took some prodding, didn't he?"

This Frank didn't answer. He said, "I'm going down to have something warm to drink. Why don't you get your car and come down to the house? You've been there before. It hasn't changed much since then."

For whatever reason, Michaels had parked out of sight. Frank watched him as in his heavy overcoat he walked in a light rain up the road alone. Michaels knew he was being watched. He tried to put some vigor into his step, but when he disappeared from sight, he was favoring a limp. Frank went back to his kitchen and made coffee and boiled water in case Michaels wanted tea. He set out a bottle of brandy on his counter and waited.

Michaels preferred coffee. Frank hung his visitor's wet coat up for him on a peg outside the door. They had the luxury of relative silence now. Michaels had a shot of brandy with the coffee to warm up, and Frank joined him. At first, they had little to say. The family reunions that Michaels had attended in this house went way back, twenty-five years at least, but then he was just putting in obligatory time until he could return to his practice in the city. Frank added a little more brandy to Wilson Michaels's coffee, and to his own. It was as if they were hunkered down in this kitchen, with all that relentless pounding outside, when, in fact, between the two of them, they had initiated the pounding, and it was wealth the drilling would give way to, not the devastation of war.

Frank waited no longer. "I never thanked you for getting in contact with Kenny Brewster and TransAtlantic. I finally understood it was the right thing to do—for the family."

They were sitting across the counter from each other, but had already shaken hands up at the bale of hay where Wilson Michaels had stood in wait for Frank until Frank had finally gone up to see. So they didn't shake hands now. Wilson Michaels had been an arrogant son of a bitch, whose bonhomie had come down on everybody hard, but Carol had suffered the most. Until the day she'd gotten another lawyer and cast him out of the family.

"You're sure?" Michaels said.

"Sure? No."

"Reasonably?"

"Those chemicals they're using, those radioactive elements that have been peacefully asleep for millions of years. If any of that gets into the aquifers and wells, that coffee you're drinking could kill you."

"What are the chances?"

"I don't know. But it's what we'll have on our consciences."

At one time Wilson Michaels might have laughed that possibility off. A big man, he'd once been nimble-footed around matters of conscience. He didn't ask Frank Joyner for his own private piece of the pie, or for a larger share for Brenda. He supposed he would do that later when this mood they were in lifted. But before then Frank, like Wilson Michaels another mostly retired man abandoned by his wife, had made supper for both of them, and for a boy who'd appeared out of nowhere and whom Frank introduced as his grandson. He was thin, fair-headed, and intense. He looked at Wilson Michaels with an unflinching attention, as if he were cleaving to the bone, or as if he awaited an unequivocal declaration of some sort, and Michaels obliged him by declaring that the drilling out there was getting serious, coming close to the point of no return, and what did the boy, whose name was Danny, think of that? Danny studied Wilson Michaels, who could be an impostor, or worse yet, an infiltrator from an enemy organization of some sort—who wore suits and vests and topcoats out in the country?— and only when Danny's grandfather added to his introduction that Michaels was Cynthia's grandfather, and, hence, a member of the family at a certain remove, did it all come together for Danny. Wilson Michaels was the persona non grata everyone had talked around during last Thanksgiving's dinner, when Danny had taken his cousin Cynthia down in the basement and performed at least one heroic tailslide for her, and she, with her big-city ways, had had her mind somewhere else. Danny finished his pork chop, string beans, and candied yams and asked to be excused.

When the boy had gone back upstairs, Wilson Michaels asked, "You said grandson. Whose . . ."

"Jen's."

"Ah, sweet little Jenny. She always liked to cuddle up. So she married . . ."

Frank shook his head.

The heavy grinding and the loose clattering of machine parts and the exhaust-choked chugging of motors and the occasionally cheerless voices of men. Finally, it all bore Wilson Michaels down, and when the time came, he yielded to Frank's insistence that he spend the night in the guest room, a bed he believed he'd stretched out in before when after a big meal he'd rested before getting his wife, Carol, and his daughter, Brenda, and driving back to the City, where he belonged. But he'd only stretched out in that bed—he'd not gone to sleep there a minute of his life. Tonight, in the company of Frank Joyner and his grandson, and in spite of the drilling noise and all the grievances it brought to mind, he did.

PART SIX

THE NATCHEZ TRACE

16

Hᴇ ᴄᴀᴍᴇ ᴏᴜᴛ ᴀᴛ ɴɪɢʜᴛ, ᴛʜʀᴇᴇ ᴀ.ᴍ. ʜɪs ᴘʀᴇғᴇʀʀᴇᴅ ʜᴏᴜʀ. Bʏ ᴛʜᴀᴛ time partygoers had gone home, the bars were all closed, few cops were about, and on his way to a meter-free area where he parked his car, he saw no one and heard only distant sounds. He drove around town, as if he'd just arrived, never seen the place before, and was taking the time to discover what made this particular burg work. Who would live here, and why, and what about him? Sometimes he drove down to the lake, got out, and sat on a bench and looked up a forty-mile stretch of zigzagging water. Three ᴀ.ᴍ., plus a few minutes now, was a fine time for moonlight, if a moon happened to be out, and he considered a future of silver on black in a valley a glacier had just—a few thousand years ago—dug out. When the Iroquois were driven out by Major General John Sullivan, with Colonels Butler and Dearborn sweeping down the shores of the lake, the intrepid soldiers who'd torched the villages and cut the stragglers down got this land for their private use, and he had no trouble imagining himself as one of them. He sometimes stood before a waterfall, a phosphorescent white, with enough power stored up there to live his life many times over. To go from that waterfall to a neighborhood of frame houses built beneath leafy trees on mindful lots was like going from the source of all dreams to the dreamers themselves in their numbered blocks on streets named after modest heroes of theirs. Who wouldn't want to live here? If he saw anyone on these residential streets at that hour, it was some poor soul who couldn't sleep, or some fraternal spirit who did his sleeping in full daylight and walked abroad at night. In the company of his dog. Or alone.

He saw a woman more than once if he drove through a certain neighborhood. It was hard to tell her age. She wore a dark sweater with a hood, but the hood was always down. Her hair was short. He seemed to see her only in profile, once his headlights had passed her by. She never looked his way and never, by the most insignificant hitch, broke her lovely stride. Only someone who had no destination in mind, he decided, could walk with such effortless ease.

Once he drove up into the hills looking down on the town, but there was too much tree cover up there and the streets wound. He discovered he preferred the flatland grid. He preferred quiet, windless nights, but who didn't? Storms taxed his de-dramatizing powers, his ability to maintain the illusion of a blank slate. He wanted the neighborly night air to pass through his car and pass through him. A walker or two or three on the streets was all right because clearly they responded to needs similar to his. To move to a town such as this you'd need to begin with a kindred base, however small. No man was an island, entire of itself, and so on.

Only when he'd supped his night's fill from those residential neighborhoods did he run his car windows up and drive down to the town's bypass, which in its string of franchise eateries and lodgings and emporiums was no different from any other town's, and where he joined truck traffic and those a.m. motorists passing through on their way elsewhere and who sped up to make the lights. Eventually, his practice became to ride the bypass almost to the end, then to slip off with hardly a ripple into a parking lot of an all-night supermarket where he could have coffee and, combining soup and a sandwich, more or less eat his day's principal meal. When he shopped—for cereal, for instance, or fruit, or whatever juice was on sale—he did so for only a couple of days ahead. The smallest box of cornflakes, one banana, one peach, a quart of juice, or maybe only a pint; he took to buying the little mini-tubes of toothpaste or canisters of shaving cream or bottles of shampoo that air travelers used. It was quiet. The light was a flat fluorescent glare. In it the fruit and vegetables, even the oranges, even the eggplants, lost their luster. The freshest of the smells were all a day old.

He spent time watching the checkout girls manning the two lanes that were open. This was fast-lane, count-your-purchases-on-the-fingers-of-one-hand stuff, except for the occasional shopper who, un-able to sleep, said to herself, why not get something accomplished, why not get the week's shopping done instead of staring at the ceiling all night, and that shopper came through with a cart loaded to the brim.

He never talked to the girls. He shopped, sat, and ate; he drank his coffee and watched the girls do their job. However, he never left until one happened to look his way so that he could wave before walking out. He always did that, and almost always the girl smiled.

When he got back into his car, at approximately 4:45, less than an hour was left before it got light. He knew his way around this anony-mous little town, and by a back route up and over a valley spur, within fifteen minutes he could be sitting in what would have been the dark of a country road if a derrick, lit from top to bottom, hadn't been drilling for gas some seventy, eighty yards away. Twenty-four-seven. For the last stop on his nightly outing, he took to going there with all four of his windows run down so that he could hear and smell the drilling to its full extent and, inevitably, cast back to how quiet things had been when he'd first ventured out and, if this had been one of those fortu-nate nights, reflect on how effortlessly that woman walker had moved through the night compared to how laboriously this derrick with its drill bit bore into rock.

He spent time looking at the house the field had belonged to before
it had been leased. The porch light was on. Beside the house a huge
silver maple soared into the night. The maple might have soared even
higher than the drill derrick itself, who could tell so late at night with
the moon now down and all the light in the world employed in the illumination of that tower? Except for the porch light itself, which cast
just enough glow for him to picture the long, ashen face of the man
lying in his bed, asleep if there was any sleep left to be had in this tu-
multuous night.

At the first hint of dawn, he drove back downtown. He parked in
the spot he'd left vacant, returned to the building that had once been a
school, and, by a back staircase, climbed to the top floor again. If he
carried milk or juice or butter or anything of the sort, he placed it in
the otherwise empty refrigerator. He used the bathroom, washed his
face, brushed his teeth, quickly in and out. He had not outgrown his
boyhood bedroom. It was bare, not bare like a prisoner's cell, for pris-
oners might have photographs of naked women or crude erotic draw-
ings on the walls, and not bare like a monk's cell, either, where one
might expect to find crucifixes or devotional portraits of enraptured
virgins, but bare as a man in transit could make it. There were signs of
his presence but none of his residence, and none that anyone, were
someone to actually come looking for him, could be sure would be
there the next day.

Quickly, Conklin erected derricks on two of the three pads they'd
built in the valley, and the race was on. Except the only valley land
TransAtlantic had leased was the Joyner property, and one man, although the frontrunner, didn't stand much chance if a whole team of
trained runners wore him down. The Joyner contract stipulated that
multiple wells could be drilled on the same pad if TransAtlantic
thought it feasible. An executive from the company contacted Frank to
inform him that a second vertical well would be drilled as soon as the

horizontal drilling on the first well was completed. Two Christmas trees instead of one. The trajectory of the first horizontal would pass under the highway and into the valley; the second, almost certainly, somewhere east of the Joyner house and diagonally up the hill. Neither TransAtlantic horizontal well would encroach on land already leased to Conklin, although both would affect the direction Conklin could drill off of that land. A third, when needed, could pass to the west of the Joyner house and block Conklin horizontal drilling down there. And so on. One pad could accommodate up to ten wells, fanned out like spokes. Frank asked for Kenny Brewster, and perhaps something in his tone of voice led the TransAtlantic executive to understand that the older man was asking for the younger man's progress in the company, and the executive was happy to report that Kenny Brewster was experiencing a great deal of success and that Frank Joyner could be proud. Frank let the misunderstanding stand.

And Helen debated the issue for days before making a lunch date with Jen at the vegetarian restaurant down on the ground floor of the Deweese. They sat outside, under an awning, but in the heavy July heat, while most of the customers opted for the air-conditioning inside. There was a breeze, but also exhaust coming off the cars, and when the first of the trucks rumbled through, it was not only heat and noise they gave off but an almost dislocating sense of incongruity. Helen sought the right moral balance on the tightrope of what she felt her obligation to be.

She said, "Frank thinks your brother is living upstairs in his old room. Something happened down where he teaches, and Frank seems sure he's hiding up there. But he can't bring himself to knock on the door. Of course, he may not be there at all."

Her brother? She had two. But Jen didn't hesitate. She reached into her purse, called Mickey's number, and was told that it was no longer in service. Just that quickly, she felt the loss of a confidant, never more remote than her purse or pocket or bedside table.

Helen reached across and covered the hand that held the phone. "I may be betraying Frank in telling you this. I don't understand fathers and sons. Sisters and brothers I understand better, although I've never had one. I was an only child and I raised an only child. Paul came from a large family, but he's no help since he got along with everybody. It was effortless with Paul."

"Helen," Jen said quietly.

"It's all right," Helen tried to reassure her friend.

A truck passed by with an outsize roar, and they were left looking at each other.

"Get out of all this, Helen. Take a trip. Buy about five tanks of gas and drive till your car runs dry. It's not just Mickey. If it weren't Mickey, it'd be somebody else. Me, probably. Dysfunctional families go on and on. Since no sane person will get near them, they breed out of themselves. It's like a closed-circuit carnival ride. A big incestuous loop-the-loop."

"I have very deep feelings for your father, Jen," Helen confessed, clearly with more resignation than celebration in her voice, and that roused Jen again.

"Goddamn that Mickey! What does he think? That no one gives a shit about him? That he can go on being a ghost up there and no one will care? Do you really think he's up there, Helen? Does Dad? What's he done anyway? He's never done anything really bad, you know that, don't you? Well, you should. He makes it all up, well, most of it, then calls me and tries to make me believe it's real. I should have taped those calls, then you'd see. He's full of—"

The trucks saved Jen. When they'd passed, she said, "It's ironic. It's almost sweet. Mickey never liked the Deweese. Kids never like being kept after school, and here Mickey had to live in one. So where's he come back to when he gets bent out of shape? Almost sweet and very ironic."

"What are you going to do?"

"Do? As in 'Go get your brother, it's time to go?' As in 'Tell your little brother to quit sulking, no one's buying it?' I'm not going to do anything."

But she did do something. She told Kenny, who had to drive two and a half hours to spend one night with her, and the next morning two and a half hours back to be on the job, five hours of driving with no time even to see Frank or make good on his promise to show Danny around the drill-rig floor, all that driving so that he and Jen could make love with no questions raised as to whether it was worth it, and that's when she chose to tell him that her not-so-much-crazy-as-ill-suited-for-all-things brother might be lying one floor up in his childhood bed, or maybe not, but she had to tell somebody because ever since Helen had alerted her to the possibility he'd been like a ghost hovering there, that was how spooky it could get. Of course, she had two brothers, but Kenny would know the one she meant, the one she had a habit of recounting her most lurid and secretive fantasies to, some of which had turned out to be real. As real as clinging to a canoe over a bottomless lake in a night when all the stars came out in a grand orgasmic display. And here they'd just made love moaning quietly into each other's ears.

Kenny said, "I saw his room."

"You saw Mickey's room?"

"When your father showed me the apartment upstairs."

"The penthouse?"

"Where you lived. The last room he showed me he said was your brother's."

"And what did you see?"

"A sock on the floor, and a book, then your father shut the door."

"A child's book? A little boy's sock?"

"Jen, what difference does it make?"

"If he's up there?"

"He must have a key."

"He has a key because I gave it to him, although he did give it back."

"So he had one made." He raised up over her. Her legs opened and he lowered himself until they were face-to-face. "So we go up and knock on the door."

She threw him off and then, of two minds, pulled him back on. "No, Kenny, we don't."

He rolled off her and lay at her side. His ardor was cooling, as was hers. She could kick herself after all that gallant driving he'd done. "He wants to do everything, and basically, he's never done anything except offend some small-town types. That's my brother. I don't know whether women scare him or baffle him or bore him or what. Only when they're ready to walk out the door does he realize they might have been there in the first place. Or maybe not. Maybe they were never there and he made them up. For a while I thought he might be gay, but the only man I've ever seen him look at so that something in him hurt, so that something in him was pulling the wrong way, has been Dad. Not Gerald. So far, Gerald hasn't made any wrong moves, and I don't think Mickey understands people like that. Course, I don't either. Who am I to talk? That's when you begin to feel for people, right, Kenny? When they make the first wrong move?"

All Kenny had known were people who'd made wrong moves, beginning with his father. But when he thought of Frank, he thought of no wrong moves. He thought of a man moving to shore up the world, to hold off collapse, which was wrong, Kenny knew, because eventually the world would overwhelm anybody who tried to do that, but which was right on any human scale he could think of.

"Jen, it'll be all right."

She tried to laugh, and laughing, she tried to shift his weight onto her. "Know what an incubus is, Kenny?" He'd heard the word, which had some obscure religious sense, he believed. "Or a succubus?" He'd heard that word, too. "They're creatures that descend from above to have their way with innocent girls and boys. The only way to stop them is to get a flesh-and-blood human in between. That's you," she whispered huskily in his ear.

. . .

There was enough light to see him by, but not enough so that Mickey, returning from his a.m. outing, could be seen. He'd stepped into the small city park, whose treetops reached his sister's windows, and watched the landman walk out of one of the Deweese's side doors. How did Mickey know he was a landman when he didn't look like one? Neither rugged nor harried nor poorly nourished and overweight nor ambitiously lean. The landman stepped out onto the sidewalk and walked a block down to his car, and he had a look about him of setting out on an errand that was no idle matter but not terribly urgent, either; a man walking into a day that promised some fulfillment to add to the fulfillment he already felt. He was smaller than Mickey had imagined; he had a boyish head of hair and, when he held his face up to test the air, the features of a boy not nursing some boyish grievance but a set of reasonable prospects, backed up by a prowess about which he wouldn't brag. His car was parked close by, in a metered area, which could only mean that he'd arrived after the metering time had passed and knew he would be leaving before it began again. Mickey arrived in time to make out what could have been a TransAtlantic decal on the back left passenger window, the *T* and the *A* figured disproportionately large. A landman, roughly his age. Walking out of a building where Mickey had spent his youth. Driving off to a job with a future. His immediate past having transpired in the bed of a person Mickey, too, had shared certain by-proxy intimacies with, many the long, lonely night.

Carrying a single plastic supermarket sack—containing another day's banana, peach, and quart of milk—he climbed by their own private back stairway to the third floor and stood in front of his sister's door. He stood there until he heard noises coming from inside, first the sound of running water, then the tiny, deadened report of silverware and plates striking the metal of a sink. She had made breakfast for her landman, something that required a skillet, for he heard the duller, heavier report of cast iron. At the very limit of his hearing his sister poured herself a cup of coffee, and he knew then, even before he

heard her weight settle into the cushions of the one easy chair she possessed, and the chair's frame give, that she was not going back to bed
but had decided to sit there, sip her coffee, and relive every moment
she and her landman had just spent. He knew his sister to be too rest-
less a person to savor past experiences at the expense of the present, at
least for long, but why, then, had she poured herself that cup of coffee
and settled into that chair, and why was she humming a down-tempo
version of that song she liked so much, "Rollin' in My Sweet Baby's
Arms"? He didn't come close to knocking on her door, but he stood
there before it, straining his ears, until he began to hear sounds from
apartments around hers and light passed down the hall and over the
dark, gleaming tiles of the floor, reaching where he stood. Then he
went back upstairs, left his milk and peach in the refrigerator, his banana in a bowl, used the bathroom, and entered his own room, where,
if anything, that song was more distinct—"Gonna lay around that shack
till the mail train comes back, rollin' in my sweet baby's arms"—and
for hours he couldn't get it out of his head.

Ray Whittaker said, "You're sure?"

"It looks now like TransAtlantic wants to drill at least a couple
more wells, which means more royalties when the gas comes in. Give
him a full share. It's not charity, Ray."

"Even though it looks like that."

"I told you he was out here. He stood up there in the rain watching
them drilling. He had a topcoat on, and a suit and vest, and you know
what he reminded me of? A snake trying to slough off a skin he
couldn't carry anymore, it was too heavy, too old, and he'd just forgotten how to wriggle out of it."

"You've been living in the country too long."

"He may still be in town, I don't know. He spent the night here. He
didn't say where he was going when he left, but I don't think he's got
much of a practice left."

"He doesn't. Zero. Nil."

"I don't particularly want him back, Ray. I can't forget how he treated Carol when he was riding high."

"So we buy him off?"

"Weren't you the one who said we didn't want him to take us to court?"

"That was before I saw the state he was in."

"I still don't want him to. Danny came in when he was here, and the only way I could think to introduce Michaels to him was to say he was Cynthia's grandfather. You start talking like that, it's not easy to wipe the slate clean."

The thing about drilling for natural gas, Frank had come to understand, was if you harbored any doubts at all, you paid a terrible price because the drilling never stopped. The derrick clanged and shook and sounded as if at any moment it might come apart, and trucks arrived with more and more pipe and more and more fuel for diesel engines, which operated full throttle, twenty-four-seven, and a bed of shale that was supposed to be a mile down might be two or farther, and at that depth, who really knew? Even Danny, who had waited for Kenny to come give him that insider's glimpse, which could have made all the difference, seemed beaten into submission. He no longer went to the basement to fire off a countering barrage on his ramp. He stayed in his room. When his grandfather called him for his meals, they stared at each other over the countertop, neither accusing the other but both victims of some cruel hoax they had played on themselves. And the pounding went on.

Then it simply stopped. It had stopped temporarily many times before, when the rig workers were adding pipe or changing the bits, Frank supposed, or flushing things out. But during those times, the motors never fully stopped, they idled with a rough burn until they revved up again and the drill bit began to bore down. But this time it all came to an end. It was midafternoon. Danny gave it five minutes, then opened his door and appeared at the top of the stairs. Frank stood at the bottom, and the two of them remained like that for perhaps five minutes more. They heard trucks passing, not a lot, and between trucks some clashing, wrenching sounds of heavy metal on metal surely from the rig itself, but these sporadic sounds obeyed no rhythm, were the finishing touches on something that was clearly done. Frank took Danny by the hand and they walked up to the crossroad, past the bale of hay, and down the gravel road TransAtlantic had built. Neither had been here since the pad had been a broad, four-acre stage, looking out on the valley. The stage was still level, but the surface was rutted and rough, and they had to watch their footing. Pieces of machinery were scattered about, pumps, generators, Frank supposed, plus units he had no idea about, before he and his grandson came to the ordered area of the pad where those doorless and windowless vans were lined up and a trailer was parked, with metal stairs leading up to a side door. The man who answered Frank's knock filled the door. He had small eyes, a burly face, and a white line high on his forehead where the band of his hard hat had bitten into the flesh. Whoever Frank and his grandson were, they were unauthorized, until Frank identified himself as the owner of the land on which all this drilling had taken place. The man then relinquished a minute of his time. Frank was not mistaken. They had reached what they called the kickoff point, where they were ready to make the turn. They had drilled to within approximately five hundred feet of the shale and would now be making a long, curving turn toward the horizontal. Danny asked how far down were they, a mile? And the man said that would be a good round number. Frank asked how much time they had. Time they had? Of drilling-free bliss, Frank didn't say. Not even, Of time to collect our thoughts. Before the horizontal drilling begins, he said. The man returned a smile, which meant that Frank and his grandson were no different from other landowners who had come to his trailer, with or without grandchildren, and he wished he could tell them what he didn't know. Could be tomorrow, or next week. Could be next year. But all these frack vans were lined up here for a reason, so sooner than later would be the safest bet. But when he knew, would he let them know? The man's smile took a turn toward the philosophical. He leaned down. He'd like to know where he was going to be tomorrow himself. Wouldn't we all, Frank? Then he told the landowner and his grandson what neither of them doubted. One morning you'll wake up and they'll be hard at work. You won't even have to ask.

They went back home and Frank ended up doing something he hadn't done in he didn't know how long. He took his sketchpad out into the yard and, in the shadow of the maples lining the road, sketched the derrick as faithfully as he could. He left the two men still on the rig floor out of it and devoted a pointillist's attention to the Stars and Stripes. He froze it all before a backdrop of a midsummer tree line and a vacant sky. He was reminded of what the earliest humans did when they painted animals on the walls of their caves before they went out on the hunt. They killed the animals they'd depicted there with such loving fidelity and used their blood to produce more paint to paint more animals, which they then went out and killed. With his sketch complete, he thought of his son and felt an immediate impulse to show the results to him. Frank could imagine knocking on his door, and before either could register the shame of such a long-postponed encounter, Frank would say, Look, it's done, it no longer belongs to them, they can't bring it down and carry it off to another field because it's ours. Yes, he could do that. Yet, he was still seated there when his daughter drove up and his grandson ran out and they began to cook burgers on the grill. He went back inside without having shown the sketch he'd drawn to anybody. When he came back out, it was as if he'd hidden the sketchbook from himself.

The letter (delivered by a postal employee he almost didn't open the door for, suspecting a ruse Melanie had cooked up) was signed by Ray Whittaker and said, in effect, that with the likelihood of additional gas wells being drilled on the Joyner property, the family to which he,

Wilson Michaels, had once belonged had decided to grant him a full
share in any future royalties. Since the leasing money had already been
disbursed, the dollar amount that Michaels would receive would depend entirely on how much gas was down there and could be made to
flow through the Joyner line. There was reason to hope. Little reason
to despair. And since Michaels lived in a part of the country free from
truck traffic, drilling noise, and almost certain air, water, and soil contamination, there was reason to rejoice. To enjoy these ancillary benefits to their full extent, Michaels was to stay where he was. When Ray
Whittaker had further information on the dollars-and-cents front, he
would be in contact. Receipt of this letter, for which Michaels would
have signed, constituted a contractual acceptance of terms. Whittaker
concluded in a personal aside, "Congratulations, Wilson, you got what
you wanted. You're back in the family again. But from one lawyer to
another, you might want to think of this as a sort of probation, with all
the usual provisos about good and bad behavior that entails."

The letter produced in Wilson Michaels conflicting effects. It
aroused an immediate resentment toward Ray Whittaker, who would
take his sport in such a difficult moment, no different from kicking a
man when he was down, and it caused Michaels to reach out for the
nearest chair as, with the suddenness of a nosebleed, his tears began to
flow. He'd gone misty-eyed before—during certain movies and
songs—and when his beloved Mets had won the Series in '86, he'd let
fall an actual tear. But cry-cry, bend over and shed tears into his
cupped hands—that he'd never done. The tears brought with them a
number of truths. As a lawyer, he'd mismanaged his career into an
early retirement. As a husband, he'd driven off the one good woman
he'd known. His daughter he'd mis-raised into an embittered man-
hater, and, apparently, his granddaughter had gone on something of a
self-gratification warpath. His second wife had been on a warpath as
long as he'd known her, which was all right when they'd both been well
armed and had made common cause, but that kind of thing lasted only
till someone got the upper hand. The ultimate truth Wilson Michaels

was being asked to acknowledge was that once he'd torn his life down to the foundation, the only person left standing was Frank Joyner, whose decency Michaels had always equated with his capacity to be duped, and whose attachment to old things with his inability to live in the here and now. Turns out Michaels had been wrong. Frank Joyner might have been the only true friend he had left in the world.

He left his suits and topcoats for Melanie to find and throw out and packed a suitcase from the lower rungs of his life. He found boots, work pants, an old pea jacket he'd never managed to throw away, and two flannel shirts. His papers and files and books he'd leave to her, too. She could cull through it all and build an airtight case against him in divorce court. She'd have to find him, though, to serve a summons, and since where he was going would be the last place she'd look, they might be married for all eternity. He didn't care. He had the sense that he was about to step outside the law, just a little, just enough, to qualify for another life. Being honest with himself, he admitted he'd had this sense before—he was, after all, a quickly aroused man—but never after having bathed himself in tears, never after a cleansing of that sort, and the Garden District of Sunnyside, Queens, began a slow but irreversible dissolve.

The fact was his mother had left his father and gone to California in the company of another man. His mother had always insisted—but to his sister, never to him—that she had simply caught a ride and there was nothing more to it, and all that Mickey knew for certain was that his mother had stayed a month with Gerald and his family, before rethinking her position and coming back. He imagined his mother was capable of taking a lover for the duration of a cross-country trip, to make good on a bet or a boast, say, but what he couldn't imagine was her stay, even for a month, in California. He couldn't imagine her sitting before the ocean in a long, declining afternoon, or strolling at the surf line with her shoes in hand. Or shopping in a mall the size of an airport. Or cruising down a street tunneled over with palm trees in a neighborhood where the rich and famous lived. She was a cold-weather person who preferred small rooms, and her mothering of him had had the effect of starving all his superfluities out until his life could fit into such a room as well, heated by something like her vigilant good humor and scorn.

He thought of her sparingly, and always with caution, but as he drove through the low-lying neighborhoods of the town at night, his thoughts came back to her as the one hurdle he had yet to clear. To turn his thoughts elsewhere, he looked for the woman walker, so light on her feet as to seem disembodied, although he knew she was no ghost. When the time had passed for him to turn off onto the bypass and spend his hour with the checkout girls in the supermarket, he turned up into the hills instead and allowed himself to be led to his mother's house, which sat at the end of a small, circular cul-de-sac, her house no different from those of her neighbors, all built small and low, under tall trees. He sat there in his car until it was time for him to be climbing the back stairs at the Deweese and entering his boyhood room. When the day still failed to dawn, he got out of his car and walked around his mother's house, and by the time he'd reached her patio in back, he'd brought a dingy gray light up out of the ground.

The patio was quite small, but it was out of doors. He lay back on a chaise lounge, which was damp with dew. Above him, beyond a vine growing thickly on an arbor there, he heard a sound of wingbeats, successively, as if one by one a family of fledglings was abandoning the nest. That brought a smile to his lips, as if the world still thought it had to stage for him these childish shows. He and the world needed to treat each other like adults, negotiate a new contract, strike a nonhumbling middle ground. For instance, the world should take the fledglings back, but leave him the walking woman. He'd give up the checkout girls at the supermarket if the world would allow him to keep such bracing natural phenomena as a glacial lake and waterfall. His sister and her landman lover? What would he have to give up to keep them? He'd already given up his girlfriend. With such goodwill on both their parts, why shouldn't he and the world come to terms? To keep his father and his outdoor life, he'd give up his mother and her indoor one? Is that what the world was proposing?

He awoke, chilled, to a woman offering him a cup of hot coffee, which he accepted.

She said, You gotta make a noise. You can't just sneak up on a person like that.

He agreed.

She said, I knew you were coming once, and that was a bloody mess.

He said he didn't remember but didn't doubt it.

She said, After you, I closed up shop.

She invited him to laugh. She lit a cigarette and blew it out, more and more smoke, until it was almost certain she was blowing out the smoke of cigarettes past. Her laughter ended.

For a moment there was no sound, rather the sound of the last-bird-gone, empty nest, which the world had seen fit to remove.

She said, Let's go inside, I'll make us some breakfast.

He had a tradition of pleasing her, although she wouldn't believe it. He said he couldn't do that.

She said, You wanna go hungry then?

Mother bird, worm, empty nest, all flown. He joined her in a laugh. He said, I'll feed myself.

She said, How are you going to do that?

He realized he'd missed a night on his shopping. His refrigerator was empty. He'd come to see his mother instead. Here was the first of his choices in this new deal he'd struck with the world. He said, Maybe I'll fast for a day, see how I like it.

Are you counting the days, Mickey? I did, you know. You hit your due date on the button. A textbook birth. I told myself then, keep an eye on this one. What's your count now, Mickey?

Day one, Mother.

Have you really burned your bridges?

I've tried.

If they catch you, what are they going to do?

Nothing. Nobody's going to do anything. It's as if I didn't exist.

That bad, eh?

Clean slate.

She laughed again. More smoke.

I've made a deal, Mother. I've had to give some things up.

And I'm one of them?

What difference would it make?

She stubbed her cigarette, got up, went back inside, and closed the door. But that was only what he imagined her doing. She had actually moved in closer and was staring him down. She wore an old lime-green house robe, so old it might have gone back to before his time. His mother had a rough-barked timelessness about her, yet she was a devoted habitué of those small rooms.

I would grieve, Mickey. But I would figure the odds. Two out of three is not a bad result if you can get it and keep it. One husband for twenty-five years is also better than average. You give me up and I fall back on the law of averages, Mickey, and I win.

He smiled at her, his first smile of the day—or the night. Certainly his first smile since dawn. He reached out for her hand, squeezed and released it. He said, I want you to win. You deserve to win, married to a dreamer and raising children like us. Now I'm going to close my eyes, he said, not having to add, so that you can go back inside. Not having to doubt it, either. No pussycat lingering over spilt milk, his mother. He closed his eyes, and he was back where he'd begun, square with the world unless he opened his eyes again, when the battle would resume. So for a longer time than normal, actually, an inordinate time, he kept his eyes closed.

17

F OR SOMEONE WHO KNEW THE JOYNER FAMILY, WHICH REACHED MATRI-lineally back to the dairy farmer Alvin Coldwell and could now be said to include Kenny Brewster, none of what happened came as a complete surprise. Mickey Joyner, during his summer break from teaching, had been living incommunicado in the Joyner family apartment on the top floor of the Deweese building. Late at night, early in the morning, he appeared on the streets and, after driving through town, spent time in a local supermarket, making a few, minimal purchases and having a bite to eat. From there, he would drive up Willis Springs Road to where, a valley away, the Joyner homestead was located. He had gotten into the habit of sitting in his car and watching the TransAtlantic Natural Gas Company drill for gas. The derrick was well lit, but at that distance all he could see was a faceless team of roughnecks on the drilling-rig floor and an all-but-invisible string of pipe fitted with a drill bit as it bore into the earth. By dawn he was back in the Deweese, and until his next a.m. outing presumably stayed there.

On this last night, he arrived at the Joyner homestead and parked his car on a side road only to find the drilling derrick, except for a single light burning in the bird's nest, dark and abandoned. The night was clear, with a near-to-full moon and a light-to-moderate breeze. The breeze rippled the flag, which had been left flying over the derrick, and in the moonlight and that single light's glow, he saw the flag's animation and the derrick's silhouette, a pale, underwater white. He sat there for a while, perhaps until he could resist no longer, then got out of the car.

In the moonlight, Mickey Joyner made his way down the access road TransAtlantic had built and onto the well pad. He did not understand why the drilling was not continuing. By his calculations, it was far too soon to call a halt. He knew about vertical drilling and horizontal drilling and knew there came a point where the turn would have to be made, but he never thought there would be a rift in activities, amounting to a rift in time he could step into. He came to the derrick stairs leading up to the drilling floor. Two lengths of steel pipe were propped there, perhaps eight inches in diameter and thirty feet in length. Pipes held in the ready but pipes never employed, at least in the vertical phase of the drilling, which momentarily gave to the site the feel of a Pompeii, frozen in its dailiness but stripped of its human life. He walked up the stairs and onto the drill-rig floor.

Around him he sensed the presence of heavy machinery, suspended, chained back, within a web of wires and tubes and hoses, and directly overhead a vacated shaft erect as a mast. When he moved to the borehole and put his nose to the pipe, a breath of mineral-fresh air caused him to start. He put his nose back and beneath the freshness detected a staleness at least a million years old. In the moonlight he saw another staircase of four steps leading to the rungs of a ladder mounted on the outside of the derrick. On the second of those rungs a worker had left folded over a pair of thick canvas gloves. He interpreted the gloves as a propitiatory sign, a pair of welcoming hands extended, and he stuffed them into his hip pockets and started up the ladder.

Physically, he was not a strong man, being far too sedentary for that. What he had was a certain wiriness—of sinews, of nerves, and, it could be said, a wiriness of purpose—and, for short spans and if his mind didn't wander, that was enough. One rung at a time, with the sound of the American flag flapping overhead and the wind weaving its way through girders and struts, he climbed more than halfway up a derrick that measured ninety-five feet from bird's nest to drilling floor, although he wouldn't necessarily have known that. The moon had yet to set, the day to dawn, and he reached the platform that jutted off to the side of the derrick, perhaps two-thirds of the way up.

This platform was ample and walled in on three sides with metal sheeting to above his waist. On the fourth side it looked directly down to the derrick's drill floor and borehole, and standing there a man would be perfectly positioned to help center lengths of pipes, should such assistance be called for. A hose, thick and black, hung to just below this platform, perhaps to facilitate the discharge of contaminated water from raised pipes into the impoundment pond. When that rig worker had completed his duties with the pipes and hose, he could then turn around and observe the goings-on at the Joyner house, for by chance the platform looked off in that direction. The view of the house was still obscured by the thick foliage of the Norway maples that lined the road, but there was a better view if you continued all the way to the bird's nest, perched squarely on top of the derrick.

Like any other rig worker taking his turn, Mickey Joyner climbed the derrick ladder to the top. The bird's nest had no protective sheeting, only a single rail that barely came to the waist. A pulley was mounted to one corner of the platform, whose purpose escaped him. Perhaps it was to help raise pipe up the derrick's shaft or to send supplies up to a worker stationed here for a prolonged time. At another corner a pole was bolted, at the end of which burned a metal-shaded light. The flag was attached at a third corner, and buckled to the rail directly across from him was what appeared to be a safety harness. What a man might accomplish here escaped him entirely. He thought of crow's nests in ships, he thought of lookouts in various sorts of dramatic situations, most of them military, and none of those had to do with what was being extracted a mile or two from beneath the earth. It was as if to gain the favor of the gods for exploits at that depth, someone had to be sent aloft, some scapegoat, some lone, unintegrated soul.

He did not put on the safety harness. He lowered the flag, presumably to spare himself its flapping, which he folded before placing it in its corner. Making use of the gloves he'd found waiting for him down on the ladder's second rung, he unscrewed the light that burned above him. The moon was about to set, and in the last light it provided he took firm hold of the rail and, high above tree level now, at least the tops of those maples, he peered into the Joyner house. Unlike his father and nephew, he had never lived there, it had never been an official residence of his, but he knew the house, knew what it had and had not contributed to the life of his family, and he studied it at length, perhaps, from this unique vantage point, looking for a secret door that had never been opened to him. For however long it took, he stood there, hands gripped to the railing, and rode out what must be assumed was his failure to find what he sought. In a front bedroom, his father slept. At some point, Mickey Joyner granted his father his rest and took a seat on the hard metal floor of the bird's nest, directly above the drilling floor's borehole, should a pipe ever be launched from deep in the earth and, like a rocket, find him there.

Kenny Brewster, the TransAtlantic landman from Texarkana, Texas or, perhaps, Arkansas, had what he imagined to be various debts outstanding with the Joyner family. These debts *were* imaginary, yet they weighed on him. His debt to Frank Joyner was a debt of gratitude, and of an admiration bordering on reverence, in payment of which Kenny felt he should be at Frank Joyner's side, step by step, as the drilling progressed. To Frank's grandson, Danny, like his grandfather, an erstwhile opponent of the whole hydrofracking scene, Kenny had failed to keep a promise: he was to have taken Danny up onto the rig floor and shown him the stages by which the drilling took place until contact was made with the fossil life of what had once been a continent-covering sea and Danny could feel good about himself, something like a pioneer going back in time. In his defense Kenny Brewster could say he had been hard at work, leasing more and more land so that other wells could be dug, but he couldn't quite convince himself. This was because the times he had managed to get away from his job in an eastern part of the state he had devoted to Jen Joyner, with whom he was in love, and to his pleasure, the likes of which he had not experienced before. In addition, there was Jen's brother. She had two, but she had expressed her concerns to Kenny about her younger brother, Mickey, with whom she'd had a close and, it seemed, confessional relationship since they were children, and had implicitly asked Kenny for help—at least to him the implication had been clear. Yet he had done nothing, nothing on any of the Joyner fronts. Put simply, it was as if he had yet to pay his dues. For that reason, which were many reasons in one, when he'd taken his pleasure with Jen that night, instead of sleeping through to the predawn light, he had left her bed and reentered the night, but this time had driven to the Joyner house and that rig out in their field, where he sensed all his obligations converged.

He did not see Mickey Joyner's Corolla. Except for the porch light, the Joyner house was dark, and he parked his car beside the ditch, under that row of maples, and, instead of proceeding down the access road TransAtlantic had built, simply walked through grass that came to his knees across the field. The moon was about to set over the ridge to his west, and it would be an hour at least before the first glimmer of dawn broke over the corresponding ridge to the east, but he could see well enough. It was as if the grass shone with a watery light of its own. The derrick gave off its own lunar-pale glow, but it surprised him that no light burned at the bird's nest. He heard nothing, a light wind in the derrick, wind parting the long grasses, rustling the distant trees. The cool, early-morning smell of grass began to give way to whatever chemicals had been disgorged into that impoundment pond, which should have been trucked away by now, and to the smell of wet clay dried to a light mud on steel pipes retrieved from the inner earth. He remembered walking across a field of grass like this—only the grass had been seared, that had been Texas, and the irate woman he'd walked to meet was an oiled mahogany-brown—and he registered the fact—and it *was* a fact—that if he had not taken it on himself to comfort that poor woman in her distress, he would not be here now. The next day he'd been singled out for praise by TransAtlantic executives, and he was on the way to this field, this derrick, not to a woman sunbathing to a lustrous brown but to a full-fleshed woman, pale and strong, with whom he'd fallen in love.

For whatever reason, but perhaps in commemoration of that moment in Texas that had brought him here, he climbed the stairs to the drill floor, and then, rung by rung, testing his way, continued up the ladder on the derrick's side. He heard nothing, nothing above him, that is. From down in the valley floor came the sparse sound of early-morning traffic, a quiet, breaking-of-surf sound, nothing more since Conklin's trucks would be approaching their pads from the south and had yet to head north to the wastewater-treatment plant to have their flowback neutralized and released into streams. With the moon down, the lights from the farms on the slope across the way came out, little man-made constellations, equitably distributed and part of the quiet. With few minutes left before day dawned and the hustle of commerce began, Kenny Brewster breathed it all in. He'd just come from the bed of the woman he loved and who seemed with a willingness far exceeding any he had known before to love him. Of course, two-thirds of the way up a tower like this, it would have been hard for him not to project his private state of being onto the world. But why shouldn't he? Rather than hear, he seemed to feel a vast chiming sound, and why shouldn't he dedicate himself to keeping that chiming alive? There would always be moments in the day when the world's strenuous give-and-take relented, took a breather, and in those moments why shouldn't he share that vast chiming well-being he felt with the world?

He was on a work platform two-thirds of the way up a drilling derrick, but he might have been in a pulpit, so called upon and so full of a generous truth did he feel. He did not say, I hear you, Lord, I will do

your bidding, but he did say something, he made an avowal of some
sort, for it was then that Mickey Joyner, perhaps thirty-five feet higher
up, became aware that he was not alone. Somebody was following his
steps, somebody was looking to supplant him in the bird's nest, and at
first he went on guard. But given the quiet of the night in which no one
seemed to seek the upper hand, he took another tack and considered
the possibility that someone was coming to relieve him, that he was
about to be offered relief. A third interpretation, which he also entertained, was that during this lull in drilling activity a shadow crew was
forming, to what end he couldn't imagine except that it would not include setting off a series of subterranean explosions and hydrofracturing the inner earth. He sat there, legs crossed in a lotus position,
except that he slouched, more like a bird folded over on the nest than a
Buddha, while below him Kenny Brewster stood at the rail looking out
on the world. The next sound they made in unison. Before dawn, in a
murky half-light, a light came on in the Joyner kitchen, which meant
that Frank Joyner had risen at his customary early hour to make his
breakfast, and both men on the drilling tower made a quiet guttural
sound of going on alert. But it was enough. Kenny heard it and now
knew he had company above him, and Mickey knew by the way his co-
occupant of the derrick had harkened to his father's light just who was
below him. They kept this knowledge to themselves for an indetermi-
nate period, perhaps time enough for Frank Joyner to fry his egg, before Mickey—it would be Mickey—broke the silence in a voice so
quiet he might have been whispering down a pipe left suspended for
just that purpose in the derrick's vertebral shaft.

You're a landman, aren't you?

Yes.

Our landman?

Yes.

Does my sister know you're here?

No.

Are you going to tell her?

I don't know. Are you going to tell her you're sleeping in the room above her?

Am I?

I saw a sock on the floor, and a book, and something in a glass on a table before your father shut the door.

Our landman? Mine, too?

Yes, the family . . .

The family?

Yes. You're Mickey, the youngest.

Definitely the youngest. The one slowest to catch up.

My name's Kenny.

And you're ours?

Yes.

Not an in-between-times thing?

In-between-times?

The times my sister . . . between certain romantic interests of hers . . . no way to put this delicately . . .

I know all that.

There's a lot to know.

It doesn't matter.

Sometimes in-between-times is all there is.

If your father believed that, he would never have built a thing. Everything would have fallen apart before its time was done.

And your father?

I don't have one.

You want to marry my sister and don't have a father?

Marry your sister?

You do, don't you?

That depends on her.

But you're ours, our landman.

Yes.

Who was conceived . . . parthenogenetically.

Partheno . . . ?

Without the benefit of a father, holy or otherwise.

He gave me his name and left before I was two. How do you name a child after yourself and then abandon him? Would you name a child Mickey and then abandon him?

I don't have any children. I'm not a landman.

I don't have any children, either.

But there's a father over there, having his breakfast, wondering if he has any sons. You see his light in the kitchen window?

Yes.

My father gets up early. Usually, when you think of an early riser in the kitchen, you think of a woman, maybe a grandmother, but when I see that kitchen light go on, I think of my father. You ever been in that kitchen, Kenny?

Yes.

Nothing extraordinary about it. A stove, a sink, there's a mud-porch door. When were you in that kitchen, Kenny?

Your father signed the leasing contract on the counter there.

That's good. That means he meant it. His hero *is* his grandmother. Every day, down those stairs and into that kitchen. He's always saying that. It's like the family refrain. You must have heard it.

Come on down and we'll go over together and knock on the kitchen door.

Like brothers?

Just friends.

Tell me something first—from one friend to another. Why'd you talk him into it, Kenny? And how? My father can be a very stubborn man.

He did it for you. It's a big responsibility he has. But he means it. He faces it. . . .

He doesn't run away, you mean.

No.

I have a mother, too, you know.

Yes.

I bet he doesn't talk about her much.

No.

Jen more?

Not a lot. Not yet.

There's still time. In-between-times can go on for a while.

Mickey, you could make your sister feel a lot better if you'd just come down and knock on her door.

I had an in-between-times girlfriend, too, once. Name of Fina. *Fina* means "fine" in Spanish. It can also mean "refined." Also "delicate." Also "exact." But also "subtle" and a little bit "cunning." She was all of that. You'll never guess what she did.

Tell me.

She got religion. A form of religion. She went home to marry the corner pharmacist, the most dependable guy on the block. Home was the Bronx, by the way.

I'm sorry.

Me, too. I didn't think anybody ever went *back* to the Bronx. You'd have to be awfully desperate to do that. I bet you think she was desperate to get away from me.

Go see your sister, Mickey. Tell her all this.

But you really want to know why Fina went back to the Bronx? From one family member to another, because you're in the family now, too, Kenny. Maybe off in the wings, but still a member.

Why, Mickey? Tell me if you think it'll do any good.

Any good? Not for me. She's already married by now. But you know why she was in such a rush? Because she couldn't stand one second more of that whole hydrofracking scene. And you're thinking, he's blaming it on the gas drilling because he can't face the loser's truth about himself. But you don't know how many times she was run over by a truck, Kenny. Or how much of that slickwater poison she drank. Or how that drilling hammers at you until anybody would think they'd made a fool of their lives. So tell me one thing, Kenny, and don't give me any of that landman lingo. Straight English, at the dawn of day, up here on our own Tower of Babel. Why'd you do it? I know it was your job, I know all that, but when it was just the two of you sitting over that kitchen counter, why did you talk our father into letting this happen? He had responsibilities and he had to keep the peace, all that's true, that paterfamilias stuff, but you said something to him, Kenny, and he signed. What was it?

He'd convinced himself. It was nothing I said. I don't think you'll believe that, though.

Why not?

I don't know. Maybe because of the things you haven't said to him.

I've talked to him a lot. The only time we talked about leasing the land I told him not to. That big maple over there beside the house, we stood under it and I told him he could hold off World War Three if he just stood firm.

World War Three?

Then you came along and advised him to do something else and he did it.

No, I didn't, he'd already made up his mind. After he signed the contracts, he took me up the lake to see a boathouse that had been falling apart. He saved it. I told him, to take something that was falling apart like that and make it into a home was more important than anything I could think of. I told him it was like getting started again after a war. I did tell him that. But that was later. Then he showed me the Deweese and all he'd created out of an old school they were going to tear down. That was when I met your sister for the first time. And when I saw where you'd lived . . .

The sock, the book, the glass half-full?

I didn't advise him to do anything, Mickey. I just told him what an important man he was.

Why do you think he closed the door, Kenny?

The door?

After he showed you my room.

He didn't show me your room. I never got inside it.

Because he closed the door so quickly. I know. But why?

I don't know. He didn't say.

Was it because ever since I was a little boy I never kept my room clean, and he was thinking, will you look at that, when is that boy ever going to grow up?

I'm the same way. There's always something laying around.

You? I don't believe it. Landmen have to be neat, exact, *muy fina*. You can't throw any inexact terms around. Vertical drilling, kickoff point, horizontal drilling, so many pounds of pressure per hydro-fracked explosion, so many million cubic feet a day once the gas starts flowing. Compulsory integration for those unreconstructed land-owners who don't get on board. In fact, the only piece of sloppy phrase-making is *hydrofracking* itself. But, come to think of it, that's *fina*, too, the most *fina* of all. In the cunning sense, I mean. You slip those un-identified chemicals in and still call it water.

For lubrication purposes.

And what penetration doesn't require lubrication? More good *fina* phrasemaking. I wonder, does my sister keep a neat room?

Your sister?

If that's not too intimate a question. If that's not betraying intima-cies.

I don't know if it is or not, but you should come down and knock on her door yourself.

Or is it full of junk, things lying around, hard to get into unless you kick some stuff aside?

I know what you're saying, and I'm not going to answer that.

I'm sorry, Kenny. We were talking about my room, but I just want you to know that Jen may have led a cluttered-up life, romantically speaking, I mean, but she really is a fine woman, no *muy fina*, no, but if you keep looking and are willing to overlook a lot of stuff, you'll find whatever it is you want.

Mickey, c'mon, it's getting light. It's time to come down.

Hard to tell if my father is in his kitchen or not.

C'mon.

You don't want to come up? Better view. Up here with the birds. A bird's nest, right, Kenny?

That's what they call it.

The vertical drilling is done, but now comes the horizontal. The down and the out. Could start today, could start tomorrow, after so many million years. Right, Kenny?

You know as much about it as I do, Mickey.

What I don't know is why my father shut that door.

You probably had it right. Because he'd been telling you to pick up your stuff—

From the beginning of time? Geologically speaking?

From way back.

Whereas if he'd invited you in, you'd have felt right at home. A sock, a book, a glass half-full—that could have been your room, too. In an old school brought back to life. Never too late to go back to school, Kenny.

Let's go, Mickey. Let's go see Jen.

Not my father? He's kind of like your father, too, isn't he? Until Kenny Senior shows up.

You're right. Let's go see Frank first.

Because I need to remind him of something. It has to do with symbolic acts, and the great thing about them is they're never out-of-date. They're kind of timeless in that way.

What symbolic acts? What do you mean?

It's really something else, Kenny. Really. Commit a symbolic act right now and a hundred years later, say, it can take effect. When everybody's dead in their graves, whoever commits a symbolic act comes back to life. He rolls up time behind him, he makes the past present, the future past. But you've got to do it. You can't wait for some tank truck to come run you down, the way they did poor Timmy O'Donnell. You can't go out walking your dog beside the road every day and expect a tank truck to knock you into a ditch. One might, but that's leaving things up to chance. A symbolic act all has to do with timing, choosing the right time to escape time so that you can command it later on. Are you following me, Kenny? I ask because I recently found out that most of my students didn't understand a word I said. So half of them failed. That's no better than flipping a coin. Doesn't speak well for a teacher. But I've made up my mind, I'm leaving the profession. You may be the last student I have.

Let's talk about this down on the ground.

But you understand, don't you, Kenny? Every teacher likes to think his last student's his best.

I understand you're going through a tough time. And you're Jen's brother and Frank's son. And you want to make a difference. I understand that, Mickey. C'mon down.

TransAtlantic can't be all bad if they gave you a job. I wonder if they'd give me one, too? A landman. Finally have your feet on the ground. Does that sound like something I could do, too, Kenny?

We could ask. Sure, I'd put in a good word.

But then half the people I know would hate me. Fina wouldn't talk to me again. But what am I saying? Fina's not going to talk to me again, anyway. Fina works in the corner pharmacy now. She might give me some medicine, count out a few pills, but that's about it. I've got a better idea, Kenny.

Mickey . . .

You do my talking for me. You tell TransAtlantic if they know what's good for them, they'll respect the symbolic act right now, and not wait a hundred years. Tell them the Joyner field was never meant to be drilled in. Tell them a derrick like this in a field like this is an abomination. Tell them they can get ahead of the curve and get out of this valley right now before the whole world comes down on them because of what they drove one poor, out-of-joint Joyner to do. They'll listen to you, Kenny. Convince them where their real interest lies.

Mickey, I'm coming up.

To the bird's nest? Before you do, here's the thing about birds' nests. They're small, tiny some of them. Baby birds get too big and they fly away. But there's always one that doesn't. You know that's true. Just look on the ground under any nest and tell me what you see. An egg that never hatched or a slimy little worm of a thing with tiny sticky feathers and a big membrane of a head—there's always one, Kenny, so that the others can get big and fly away. It looks like they'd have thought about that when they decided to call this a bird's nest. Wouldn't you, Kenny? Have thought about the one who got crowded out of the nest? . . . Kenny? . . . Where'd you go, Kenny? Don't you know not to listen to a word I say? Didn't Jen tell you? What do you think Dad meant when he closed that door? There's nobody in there worth bothering about, that's what he was saying, let's just close the door and move on. And it's true, Kenny. . . . Kenny, wait a minute. Stay there, I'm coming down. . . .

But Kenny Brewster had already started up. He'd gone halfway. The sky was a paling pearl gray, nascent, brightening by the instant. The car surf was breaking at shorter intervals now, early risers going to work. He heard the first tank truck, unmistakable, combustive, followed by a second. A crow cawing on the wing. He looked up. The crow had passed out of sight but he saw two gloves—the kind workers wore when fastening and unfastening the wrench called the tong around upcoming and downgoing lengths of pipe—holding to the bird's-nest rail, and for just an instant he was back on the plains of North Texas, with a wife across the state line waiting to get pregnant and a worker above him waiting to be relieved. Then the gloves above him left the rail, there was a sound, a sort of dull, almost indifferent groan, as if something that had long been postponed now had to be borne, and an equally dull and clumsy tumbling of a body past him, except that one of those gloved hands reached out, or in its tumbling just happened to pass Kenny Brewster's way, so that his hand, either in an effort to fend off the tumbling weight or, perhaps, to seize hold and arrest the fall, made contact. Barely a brush, as casual-seeming as any hundred brushes passersby might achieve on a city street. The sound of the body hitting the ground below was a clumsy, not very resonant thud, as if the legs had gotten in the way, or perhaps the shoulders and head, before the trunk, where the body's resonance resided— where any body's resonance resides, even the wiriest—could hit flush. Then silence, which was the same as the morning's sounds, minus the drilling, of course, and Kenny Brewster did a peculiar thing. He completed the climb up to the bird's nest, stepped over the rail, and stood in the daybreak and closed his eyes. The plains of North Texas, with their scrub oak and seared grass and hazy hemispheric sky, came back to him, not as a refuge but as a site of dailiness and a workweek grind, and as long as he stood there with his eyes closed, he knew that work awaited him down on the rig floor. Maybe thirty, forty years of work until they'd drilled North Texas dry. Then he opened his eyes, looked directly before him at the Joyner house, behind its row of maples under which he'd parked his car, and Texas was as lost to him as if he'd dully turned a page in a book he'd only half-read. Mickey Joyner's body lay sprawled on the ground at the base of the derrick. It could have been something the drilling crew had gone off and left in this interlude in the drilling, as a worker had gone off and left those gloves. The only thing that made Mickey Joyner Mickey Joyner in that first look Kenny Brewster had at him from above was how much he resembled a baby bird forced out of its nest before its sad, gaping, and life-hungry beak could be fed its first worm. That was how the body lay sprawled, as if those legs and arms had never managed the first coordinated act. As if that head had never stood up on that broken stalk of a neck. Kenny climbed down the ladder, went around the rig, and had his first look at Mickey Joyner, a man he'd never seen before. He didn't look like Frank, he didn't look like Jen, or anyone else Kenny had known. Perhaps he had once, but nature was performing one of its conversion feats before Kenny's eyes, which meant that Kenny had waited too late to make the acquaintance of this man.

. . .

No one stepped forward to challenge Kenny Brewster's testimony, and since there was no sign of foul play and no reason to believe otherwise, what Kenny stated to the police stood: that Mickey Joyner had climbed the inoperative derrick all the way to the top, Kenny had come at the break of day to check on things and seen Mickey up there in what they called the bird's nest, a dangerous place to be and for that reason equipped with a safety harness, but that Mickey was unharnessed and before Kenny could climb the ladder and reach him, he had panicked and fallen to the ground. What had Mickey Joyner been doing up there in the first place? That Kenny couldn't say, but, perhaps, since the drilling had been suspended, Mickey had come out at first light to take advantage of this once-only opportunity for a bird's-eye view of the family field.

And why had Kenny come to check on things? He'd been in town and, since the Joyners had treated him so well, before he left had wanted to see with his own eyes that nothing was amiss and, sadly, had seen what he'd seen. And why had Kenny Brewster been in town? A personal matter. How personal? As personal as an affair of the heart?

But then, before he saw Frank, he told Jen the truth. His first impulse had been to protect the family and the memory of her brother, but Mickey had seemed determined to commit what he'd called "a symbolic act," which meant he hadn't suffered an accidental fall from a derrick but had sacrificed himself so that future wells would not be drilled and the gas would remain where it had been for the past 380 million years. Those had been almost his last words.

And his very last words?

That little birds had to fall out of nests so that brother and sister birds could grow big and strong and fly away.

In her grief Jen had entered, for perhaps the first time in her life, what appeared to be a perfectly becalmed state. But she wasn't calm, she was numb. Since she hadn't been sure if her brother had been in town, she couldn't be sure if he was dead, and as one uncertainty gave way to the other, her mind went blank, which amounted to a numbing, but whose immediate effect was to usher in a state of calm. She looked at Kenny Brewster and felt neither the urge to embrace him nor to drive him away. He was someone from her past, between which and this singular present moment a gulf had opened. He held her, and she allowed herself to be held, but that was in the nature of a formality and in no way a gulf-spanning act. When the numbness wore off, it was as if all the emotions that had been suppressed were suddenly brought to life in her eyes. She was alarmed, she was suspicious, she was solicitous of her landman, she was nearly repelled. Above all, she was urgently called to command. She told Kenny he had done the right thing. Her brother had spent his whole life talking—she had to say it, talking big. It was how he'd earned his living—talking big to impressionable minds. Late at night, he talked big to her. And up on that drilling derrick he had talked big to Kenny. The problem was that Kenny hadn't known him the way she had, so that when Mickey began to talk about committing a symbolic act, Kenny had had no way to know that was what Mickey was doing, talking big. Without knowing that he knew, Jen maintained that Kenny had gotten it right: Mickey was a man in hiding, who came out at night and, when all the workers were gone, wanted to take one last look at a field he'd known as a boy. That was all. He'd gone up too high, discovered he had an audience, said some last big things, and then fallen before someone could get him down. She knew Kenny had tried to save her brother and she loved him for it, but, whether he'd known it or not, he had told the police the truth, and in no way could he take it back now.

But Kenny also understood that Mickey Joyner's death, however unlike Mickey Joyner it might have been, had in that last instant become the meaning of his life, which he, Kenny Brewster, was being asked to forswear. Mickey had asked Kenny to speak for him. Instead, he would speak for Mickey's sister. He said, "Jen, you'll have to stick by me in this. You'll have to promise."

She was with him when he talked to Frank. Helen was there, too. At the last minute Jen changed her mind and brought Danny down-

stairs. Helen sat beside Frank on one of the matching living-room sofas. Facing them, Kenny and Jen sat on the other, with Danny in
between. Kenny kept his word. He told her father what he had told the
police, but he added things and she knew they were true. The interlude in the drilling had given Mickey and him both a chance to come
out and watch dawn break over the Joyner homestead. It was as if, un-
beknownst to one another, they had decided to take possession of the
derrick to stage their own private celebrations, really to pay a sort of
tribute, with the only difference being that Mickey had never climbed
a drilling derrick in his life and Kenny had, many of them. They'd
discovered each other's presence when the light had come on in the
Joyner kitchen. That had raised a quiet little cheer, and they'd introduced themselves and begun to talk. Mickey had assured Kenny that
that light meant that his father had come down to make an early
breakfast, as he had been doing all his life, and that of all his ancestors
it had been his grandmother that his father had admired the most.
Every morning, down those stairs and into that kitchen—Mickey had
told him that.

Helen stifled a sob then, and Frank released what had been a long-
held breath and sank more deeply into the sofa. Kenny said they had
heard the wind—it was not blowing hard—and they had heard the
early-morning traffic just starting up, which included a tank truck or
two from the Conklin pads, but that it was all peaceful, and that he
and Mickey had been able to talk quietly about where they'd both
come from to reach this point and how they would go on from here.
Kenny had told Mickey about his life in Texas, and Mickey had told
Kenny about a girlfriend he'd had, with whom he'd broken up, but that
was all right because he'd come home and gotten over it and was now
stronger and ready to reenter the world. Although Kenny'd never had
one, it felt as if he and Mickey were talking like brothers, for it was as
one brother to another that Mickey had said he was coming down, it
was time to go see his father. That was when Kenny had started up the
ladder. To help Mickey down, because of the impatience he'd heard in

his voice, now that the day had dawned. Kenny simply hadn't gotten there in time. Mickey had missed a rung coming down and tumbled out of the bird's nest. Mickey'd reached out, and Kenny had, too. There'd been an instant's touch but no way to take hold.

Kenny stopped speaking. Frank was looking at him with large, inconsolable eyes. Jen didn't know whether her father had believed Kenny or not, but what she sensed to a certainty was that Kenny was all that her father now had. To get to Mickey he would have to go through Kenny, and if Kenny remembered more later on, or simply chose to add a detail or two, her father would be there to receive it. Which meant that not she but Kenny had Mickey now—he was truly a brother's keeper. With one hand she reached across her son to hold the landman's hand. With the other, she tried to take possession of Danny, too.

Frank said, "It's too easy to blame it all on the gas drilling. And cowardly. It's not even true. I won't do that."

"No, sir," Kenny said.

"If that derrick hadn't been there . . . it's too easy to say."

Kenny shook his head.

Helen took Frank's hand, which he surrendered at once, and said, "But don't make it harder on yourself than it has to be."

"I could have gone to him, Helen."

"But not before he came to you. That was the way he wanted it. Listen to what Kenny just said. It was what Mickey was doing, Frank, when he fell."

Kenny said, "He'd gotten stronger. He had to make up for lost time, sir. He just didn't know how to climb a drilling derrick. I mean, he didn't know how to come down. It takes patience. It's not like climbing down a building."

Frank had restored buildings as high as that derrick. He'd made a boarded-up lighthouse into somebody's home. The Deweese, itself, rose above all the trees. "Why isn't it, Kenny?" he said.

"I don't know. It's different. The ladder may be just as high, but it's not the same."

But Frank seemed determined to pull it out of him. "But why? What's the difference?"

Jen squeezed Kenny's hand, which she still held. He was to get through this, to give her father whatever it was he wanted.

Kenny said, "It's like a derrick is not really real. I mean it's so slim, so skinny. It looks like a pencil sometimes, sticking up in a field. But even a pencil is solid; a gas-drilling derrick is mostly air. The wind blows through it. And when the bit gets into rock, it shakes a lot. There're times when it can make you feel . . . I don't know . . . weird . . ."

"No," Frank said. "Not *weird*, Kenny. How?"

"It depends on the mood you're in, but going up there sometimes is like going up inside yourself, maybe just to take a better look around, and then, when you're ready to come down, you can forget where you are, just for an instant, and think you can float down, or settle down like a bird."

Kenny looked at Jen then, but what he saw was Mickey's broken body on the ground, wingless, all overgrown head. And Kenny was almost ready to believe what he'd just told Frank, that Mickey hadn't thrown himself to the ground, that tumbling out of the bird's nest he'd fully intended to take flight, assuming that finally his time had come.

Jen was squeezing Kenny's hand now, hard. Danny, who knew his mother's strength, saw it and looked to her first, then to Kenny to see how much he could take. Helen looked at Jen, the sadness in her eyes and the mothering wisdom and the oldest of pleas, for sanity, as a last defense, all there to be seen. Helen had just heard Kenny describe Mickey's last state of mind as momentarily deranged. All Jen could hear was that Kenny was about to tell her father that Mickey had jumped. Before their lives together had really begun, she had stood beside the landman on the very bridge from which her great-grandfather had jumped to his death and asked him if hers was the sort of family he wanted to do business with. Her father tried to sit up straight on the sofa, but he was a bowed man, and those eyes in his face were like hanging pools.

They were at an impasse, which, suddenly, Danny tried to break through. "We'll get 'em to take that derrick down and leave us alone! Won't we, Granddad?"

"I don't know, Danny," Frank said.

"But that's what the trouble was—the derrick! That's what Kenny said!"

"Kenny said you don't want to climb up one unless you know how to come down."

"But, Granddad!"

Jen said, "That's enough, Danny," but no one knew how to explain any of this to him, and if his presence was permitted at this gathering— even requested, his mother had done that—it was so that he'd understand how limited their understanding was.

Frank said, "Thank you, Kenny."

Kenny said, "No, sir . . ."

Jen said, "Mickey was coming to see you, Daddy. Whatever else was going through his mind. Just remember that."

Frank thought of something, an annoying side thought that somehow seemed to bolster his resolve. "I'll have to call Judith Ballinger."

"Who's she, Daddy?"

"The school superintendent where Mickey worked. There was some problem about grades. Now she can settle it as she sees fit."

Helen caught the edge of bitterness in his voice. "I'll take care of that, Frank. There's no reason you should have to deal with her."

Kenny said, "And there was that ex-girlfriend he told me about. Fina, I think was her name. The one who went back to the Bronx."

Before Jen could check herself, she said, "Do you really think that's what she was?" When no one answered her or offered to correct her misimpression, she added, "I mean, that they were that serious, that there was anything more to it than . . . you know . . ."

"He called her his girlfriend," Kenny said, remembering Mickey had called her his "in-between-times" girlfriend, which only then did he realize might have been Jen's brother's way of establishing another brotherly bond between the two of them, in-between-times being a status they might have shared. Kenny felt a sob rising from deep in his throat, something entirely new to him. He swallowed hard.

Frank said, "I do want to thank you, Kenny."

The formality in Frank's voice brought Kenny around. He might have been back in the military. He might have been snapping to. He choked his sob all the way down and said, "Sir?"

"For bringing me the sad details of my son's death."

But Frank had two, two sons, and that was what they were all in need of in that moment, the presence of the senior son to impose some perspective, some reasonable coping outlook, on it all. But Gerald, who should have been back East by now, had decided that this year the girls were old enough to profit from a cross-country trip by car, and they were presently in Colorado somewhere, and whether he would be able to attend the funeral, scheduled for the following afternoon, was uncertain. Not only had Gerald and his family decided to make the cross-country trip by car, but with a minimum of modern devices, which meant that the girls had had to leave their electronic toys behind, and only in case of direst emergencies had they carried a single cell phone, which turned out to be Sue Ann's. Jen had had to call her sister-in-law's parents in Ohio to get the number. She'd left the sad news on the answering machine. Gerald had had his family up a trail somewhere in Rocky Mountain National Park and had returned the call to say that if it could be done, he would do it, fly alone from Denver, if he could get to the airport in time and catch a flight. He'd sounded tired, as if he'd just climbed to some exhilarating peak and what had he seen? He'd seen this, the family he'd thought he'd held at a continent's remove now but a peak away and under this mortal cloud.

Jen had gone to the kitchen to make coffee when she heard the knock on the door. Her impulse was to run back and answer it, assuming it was some neighbor still friendly to her father come to offer condolences. Except that the knock was not subdued and in keeping with grief, but was close to being the opposite. Jen hesitated. She did put another coffee cup on the tray and allowed Helen to go to the door. The voice of the man who had knocked she recognized at once, even though she had never heard it speak in such a humble and unaggrandizing tone. She left the coffee on the kitchen counter and hurried to the front door. Would Helen bring the coffee in while she saw to the caller, who was indeed dressed like a neighbor, someone who'd just come in from the forests or fields?

Wilson Michaels said, "Jenny, is that you? Of course, it is. I'd recognize you anywhere even though you were just a girl—"

She took him by the arm and led him back out to the front porch. She closed the door. "You don't know, do you?"

"I don't know? What don't I know?"

"You don't know what's happened here." She admitted to a small, mean-spirited thrill, withholding information from this man who had always assumed such a lordly bearing with her. His face had fallen, and his shoulders; when his smile vanished, his mouth trembled. His eyes, which had once had that roving red gleam, were ashes now, but she, too, would recognize him anywhere.

"I just got in town."

"So you don't know."

"Is Frank all right?" She heard his alarm like a wave welling up in that old barrel voice. Alarm for the well-being of a man he had never ceased to look down his big-city nose at?

"Yes, he's all right. He's inside." But she didn't move to open the door.

Michaels shook his head. He was missing something. "Frank wrote to me . . . well, his lawyer did . . . he wanted me to have a share in the gas royalties, like the rest of the family, for the little things I'd done. I just came to express my gratitude, Jenny, and to tell him if there was anything else I could do . . ."

He smiled weakly, a pale facsimile of his old one-upman's grin. He made what may have been a gesture to the work clothes he wore, as if to indicate his willingness to pitch in. All he could do would be to attend the funeral with the other family members who would be flying in, and how could he go dressed like that and being the man he was?

She touched him on the upper arm and turned him around, facing out past the line of maples and onto the field. She could feel how diminished and unsure he was just by the way his weight turned under her hand, but she couldn't give in to him yet. She said, "You see that derrick out there? That belongs to TransAtlantic Natural Gas Company. I believe you were in contact with one of their landmen. A few days ago TransAtlantic completed their vertical drilling, and yesterday morning, just about dawn, my brother Mickey climbed up to the top of that derrick, but lost his footing and fell. I know you'll remember Mickey, mostly as a pest back then. By a strange coincidence the same TransAtlantic landman you talked to found the body. The funeral's tomorrow. Family are coming in. My father's holding up so far but . . ."

She stopped when she no longer had Wilson Michaels's attention. He had turned back to the door and she knew why. She knew who was standing there behind the oblong panes, panes that had always had a wavy distortion in them and that had survived the three weeks of drilling and were probably original to the house. Her father would be standing there, the wavy distortions passed on to him. She said, "I'm sorry," to Wilson Michaels, and with her strong hand back on his upper arm steered him toward the door, which she opened. Michaels bowed his head and reached out to his ex-brother-in-law. Soon, Kenny came out, and for a moment the two men responsible for that derrick being erected in the Joyner field in the first place stood side by side, although neither knew who the other man was. Helen had brought the coffee into the living room. Frank led Wilson Michaels, dressed for the out-of-doors, to a seat on the sofas, and Jen took Kenny aside and told him they now had to go to her mother's house, where he would be asked to repeat the same sad story, not changing a word, and where Danny, himself with one foot in this family and the other God knew where, would be forced to hear it all again.

18

THEY WERE CAMPED IN THE GLACIER BASIN CAMPGROUND—LOOP B, site 51—of Rocky Mountain National Park, and he'd been building a fire from a bundle of firewood they'd bought at campground head-quarters when his wife brought him her cell phone and told him he should listen to this. He almost didn't, so determined had he been that they manage a three-week, cross-country camping trip beyond the reach of any of the instruments of the telecommunications world in which he made his living. He had not grown opposed to that world, or to the life it had allowed him to live, but the older he got and the further along in his fathering, the more he felt the presence of his own father rising up in him, and perhaps this year's road trip back East was in some measure a tribute to him. He had said it was for the girls' sake. Death Valley, the Grand Canyon, Bryce Canyon, and the Rockies. They were on their way to Frontier Days in Cheyenne, and then the Badlands and Mt. Rushmore. Depending on how the girls took to it, on their way back they could swing farther north and, in addition to the Tetons and Yellowstone, stop and camp in the Lewis and Clark National Forest, so that they would know where the hinge of all this westward exploration was located. They had their lives in California because those two explorers had traveled the Missouri to that very point, Great Falls, Montana, where they'd been forced to pack their canoes around the falls and over the mountains all the way to the Columbia River if any of it was going to make sense.

If the message on his wife's phone had been from his father and not his sister, he wouldn't have hesitated. His father loved his woods and fields, and as Gerald had led his daughters up canyon or mountain trails, or alongside clear, rushing rivers, he'd sometimes felt his father matching him, stride for appreciative stride. But his wife told him he should listen to what his sister had had to say, and he did. Afterward, it was his brother Mickey he had striding beside him, only Mickey could never maintain a pace, he stopped and started and turned half circles and made a mockery of any forward movement.

His wife put her arm around his shoulder, and he said it was all right, that he was all right, it was the smoke from this fire he was building that refused to catch.

They poured water on their nonburning fire and folded up their family tent. As rushed as they were, they still left the campsite neat. Denver was maybe a hundred miles southeast, but they had to get out of the park and out of the mountains first. They passed scenic overviews, looking down on valleys with snowmelt pastures as lush and green as anything from any rain forest he could imagine. Herds of what had to be elk grazed there, and for the girls' sake he forced himself to stop. Regardless of their rush, they couldn't be swept past all this as if it weren't there, as if the smog-filled freeways of Los Angeles did not have this pristine world as their counterpart. In rhapsodic national-park prose, the park signs told them what vegetation and wildflowers and wildlife they were likely to see. The Rockies were young and raw and still growing, perhaps the geological equivalent of his daughters in age, and the signs went on about that. The elk were there. They put the binoculars on them, and some had magnificent racks of antlers. Were they real? They weren't, like, zoo elk, were they? If they wanted to, they could, like, get up and run away, couldn't they?

His wife did the driving to Denver. He turned in his seat and tried to explain to his daughters in back what had happened to their uncle and why their father would have to fly back East. His youngest, Jo- anna, age seven, had Mickey confused with one of Sue Ann's broth- ers, which surprised Gerald at first since his brother-in-law, Andrew, was quiet and contained and never without an approving if undemon- strative smile, but on second thought he realized this might have been the sort of behavior Mickey had aspired to if he could only get over some last hurdle on his lonely trip back from nowhere. Katherine, go- ing on ten, remembered Mickey well. She remembered him strug- gling out of the ocean with strands of kelp on his shoulders and in his hair and said she thought to herself then, as her younger sister couldn't possibly have, that her uncle was like some amphibious creature that didn't really belong in either world, on land or at sea. Their father tried to explain. It had been an accident. Back East, a lot of drilling for natu- ral gas was going on. Some in the West, too. Their uncle had climbed up to the top of one of those derricks, but it wasn't like those scenic overviews they'd passed with their fences and signs telling you what you could and couldn't do, and Uncle Mickey had fallen down and died. We don't know why he had gone up there, maybe just to get a better look around, and Katherine interrupted to say she knew why. Joanna had begun to cry, but Katherine shook her head. Her uncle didn't belong in the ocean or on dry land either, so it made sense he'd tried to climb up to the sky. It was as simple as that. No, it was not that simple, their father said, but with a lack of conviction in his voice that his older daughter wouldn't fail to pick up on as he cupped his hand around his younger daughter's head and held it there until she'd finished her crying.

Gerald was in luck. A red-eye special and a connecting flight would bring him close enough to his hometown so that he could rent a car and arrive in time for the funeral. If Sue Ann and the girls didn't want to continue the camping trip, they at least had plenty of the country to see before they reached Ohio. They had the Great Plains; they had the Missouri and the Mississippi Rivers to cross. Under that cloud of Mickey's death, Gerald experienced a moment of genuine disorientation. It was as if he were sending his family off on some pioneering quest. They were to leave, to forge their way in the world—when it was not like that at all. They were going back East, as he was. But they were free to tack this way and that, like Lewis and Clark on their return trip, revisiting wonders only slightly less wondrous now, while he was the tethered one, responding to a yank he'd received from a wafer-thin instrument that fit easily in the palm of his hand. No, they could not sit in the airport with him until his flight was called. They were to leave, take advantage of the little daylight left. This country hadn't been settled by people sitting in airports, they had to get out there and feel what it felt like under their feet, or, at least, under their wheels.

His wife only said she hadn't seen him like this. Should she be worried?

The grown-up Katherine, sensing their parents needed this moment alone, took her little sister aside. They were standing just beyond the roped-off corridors that had travelers lapping back and forth until they reached the point where they emptied their pockets and took off their shoes.

His wife told him that accidents were bound to happen. Most families, nowadays, had someone like Mickey, neither in nor out, too smart to stay home but not smart enough to stay away for good. In fact, her brother, Andrew, was something like that.

His wife made clear judgments. The lines in her forehead came from the Southern California weather, not inconclusive thought. And she was right. He kissed her. He kissed his daughters. They always had the return trip west, he said, when he would make it up to all of them.

But, alone, waiting for the flight to be called, sitting among travelers bent over their computer screens or thick paperback books, he began thinking of his mother and father and saw quite clearly how any family's well-being was determined by its weakest member. The family as a whole had decided to drill for gas, but once the derrick was up and the drilling under way, it was as if somebody had to go up there to test himself against it to make sure it could go on, and that someone would always be the person least equipped, the weakest link. With Mickey everything began with a violation of some sort, a transgression, so you lived on borrowed time until the crime was discovered, and only if you borrowed enough time could you live anything resembling a normal life. Except that someone had to pay for all that borrowing. You belong to a family and you inherit debts; if you're not careful, you spend the rest of your life paying them off, and his wife must have been right: in every family there had to be someone who piled up debts like that. Which only meant that every family had to locate its weakest link fast and protect him with all of its might, and they, the Joyners, hadn't done that. So they had to pay.

He flew the red-eye back, and then a twin-propeller commuter plane to within forty miles of his hometown, where he rented a car. Soon, he saw the drilling derricks, and once off the expressway and on state roads, he had to deal with their trucks. Trucks of all shapes and sizes, hauling sand, water, pipes, hazardous chemicals, portable tanks, portable generators, Porta Potties, industrial units he couldn't identify, and parts of the derricks themselves. All this massing of machinery, all this weight to coax something out of the ground as light as air, or perhaps lighter, he wasn't sure. But something combustible, as air wasn't. But not breathable, as air was. The well pads built into the hillsides looked like emplacements for artillery. Families in these valleys were squaring off. The flags on the derricks were the same Stars and Stripes, meaning the war was civil, to see whose country it was. He pulled off to let a convoy of trucks pass. All advances in civilization, he knew, had messy beginnings, some of them barbaric. Lewis and Clark themselves had left a trail of blood and butchered carcasses behind them. Of course, they'd had manifest destiny on their side, while the gas drillers had energy independence and a network of pipelines in handsomely cleared corridors across the land. At every turn a wise man took the long view. He was going to a brother's funeral, a casualty if not of this war then of some other. And he reminded himself, wars required casualties if they were ever going to end.

Approaching his hometown from the south, he had a decision to make. The funeral home where the service was to be held was on the far side of town. If he rushed, he might still have time to make it, but if he didn't, he could go straight to the cemetery, four miles farther on, and wait for his family to come to him. He was tired. He wanted those forty, forty-five minutes to lean back his head. He drove to the cemetery, saw where the canopy stood, identified the fresh gravesite, then drove on to a knoll at the far end of the cemetery and parked his car under a tree. He closed his eyes and woke to the sound of a hearse and mourners' cars crunching gravel, various gravesites away.

He waited until the casket had been removed and most of the mourners had gotten out of their cars. He saw his father, who, on this occasion, was with his mother. His sister was with the woman he recognized as his father's friend, Helen. On the other side of Jen stood his nephew Danny, and beside him a man he didn't know of fair hair, average height, and a stocky build. Chairs had been set out under the canopy for the family, but no one occupied them. He saw his aunts Carol and Sharon, with their husbands. These, he understood, were the beneficiaries, equal sharers all, in whatever future royalties the gas drilling would bring, and he saw the man his father had asked to administer it all, Ray Whittaker. Behind this family grouping another small group had formed, made up, he supposed, of the few friends Mickey still had left in town. The only one he recognized was a tall bass player his sister had once dated, but Gerald had been gone a long time now.

He got out of the car and began to walk down the gravel road to Mickey's grave. He saw yet one more mourner he thought he recognized, he couldn't be sure. He wore an ill-fitting suit of clothes, too tight in the shoulders and waist and too long in the sleeves, a suit that might have fit his father but not this man. Gerald looked away. He himself was tall, he was fit. In spite of the camping trip he'd been on, he had brought a good suit of clothes, which he'd managed to change into. No one called out to him as they saw him walk up—this was not the moment for that—but he was aware that in appearing to them like that he was presenting himself as an alternative of some sort. He embraced his father, his mother, his sister and her son, and stopped there. The minister presiding over the ceremony was from the Presbyterian Church, which, as long as his grandparents had been alive, Gerald had attended as a boy. The minister had little more to say. He prayed that Mickey would find the peace he deserved, the peace, it was understood, that had eluded him in this vale of tears. The casket had strong brass handles but was otherwise plain. It wouldn't be lowered and the grave wouldn't be filled until the mourners had driven away. Gerald's arrival, from under a tree, slightly up the hill, had seemed providential. He was the picture of health, always had been, and the funeral had taken on a whole new perspective as he'd passed from shade to sunlight on his way to his brother's grave.

As Helen had once seen to a Thanksgiving dinner, she now saw to the reception at the Joyner house. She'd had a roast turkey brought in, and a Virginia ham, and although the young woman from the catering service stayed to help, Helen spent most of her time in the kitchen. Until she had Frank alone, she had nothing to say, and even then nothing she hadn't said, it seemed, countless times before. Her mantra—"as naturally as the leaves to the trees"—meant you don't force a life-generating act to go on. She understood when John Keats had written those words, he was talking about poetry, the spirit by which the words found their way onto the page, but she also understood when her husband took them from the word-rich but tubercular poet he meant we had to obey the bright, rich flow of our being as long as it lasted.

From the kitchen she saw Frank talking to his ex-wife, his sisters, his remaining children, his friends, his dear friend Ray Whittaker, and this shabby, out-of-place man wearing one of his ex-brother-in-law's suits, who looked as if he might just have been released from prison dressed in one of the odd-size suits they gave you there. Did Helen know the dark history of Frank's family? She did. She even knew the names. Alvin and Jonathan Coldwell. She knew what the son had done and what the father had not resisted doing, and she knew in families as closely bound as Frank's that history could repeat itself unless you found a way to inoculate yourself against it. Is that what the twenty-year-old boy had done by spilling his blood? Built up an immunity? Twenty years old and soon to be father to a man who would climb to a forbidden height and, as though in history's tow, fall to his death. Calling out as he fell, Follow me, Father?

Helen stayed in Frank's grandmother's kitchen, and Frank came to her there.

He said, "You know you don't have to do this, Helen."

"I'm not doing it because I have to."

"Step out the door. It's a summer's day out there. I hate to see you stuck in this kitchen."

"It's a nice kitchen, Frank. You can stand at the sink and look out over the valley."

"When this is over . . ."

She touched his lips. She shook her head. "Gerald seems like a fine man. Decent and very strong. Lean on him if you have to. He wants to help you."

"When this is over, you and I will go away. A lot farther this time."

"We'll see."

"Helen . . ."

"I do love you, Frank. That means I'll do all I can. I just don't know how much that is. Have you tried the ham? The turkey's dry but the ham is moist. There's a nice mustard, too."

She sent him back out to the food on the dining-room table. Jen was there. Jen had introduced Gerald to Kenny, but Gerald had learned from Danny that Kenny had been with Mickey when he'd died. This wasn't the time to interrogate Kenny again, but it was the time to thank him for being at his brother's side, for offsetting the terrible loneliness Mickey must have felt up on that derrick by a single human presence, if nothing else. This was especially not the time to ask about the future of gas drilling in the Joyner field—and, anyway, Ray Whittaker would take care of that—but it did seem like the time to make some allusion to what Jen had already made clear: that she and Kenny had become a couple, more of a couple than she had been with any of her boyfriends before. So Gerald told Kenny that although he didn't see his sister as often as he liked, he wanted him to know that he loved her very much and wanted, as much as he did for his own daughters, for her to find the happiness she deserved.

To his own ears, he sounded more like a father than an older brother. His father now stood close by, and Gerald was tempted to reach out to him, to include him as a witness to what Kenny was about to say. But Gerald didn't, and Kenny said to Gerald that he felt the same way, in respect to Jen's happiness. He'd never known women like Jen existed, so honest and open to experience, so unafraid, so he assumed she was one of a kind. Gerald nodded, and although flattery and a Southern accent went hand in hand, he believed this landman from Texas, if it wasn't Arkansas, meant what he said.

Gerald's mother stood nearby. He moved to her. She was listening to Ray Whittaker, a man she had known all her life, it seemed. Whittaker had the end of the fingers of her right hand in his hand as he talked to her, punctuating what he had to say with little tugs, but she wasn't responding, she didn't seem to hear a word he said. Her face was an emotion-clogged mask. Gerald heard Ray Whittaker tell her that all she had to do was pick up the phone, or come by, or just go out on any corner and shout his name, and he tugged, and tugged again, but she disengaged her fingers, whispering in a barely audible voice that she knew, she knew, even as she turned to Gerald, now her only son, and asked him to step outside. He assumed she wanted to smoke a cigarette, which she did, and as she exhaled her first lungful of smoke, she got her old, gravelly voice back and asked him if he'd follow her home. He said he would, could she give him ten minutes, while he told certain people he wouldn't see again good-bye, and she said the problem with this house, the Joyner family house and the fields and the woods, was that all her memories of it were of them, the children, when they'd come out here for days in the country. And of the children, Mickey was the one she remembered the best.

She pointed to the frayed and weather-grayed ends of a rope hanging from a limb of the white pine. There they'd hung that swing that swung out over the terrace, and who had been swinging in it when the old rope had broken and who had fallen into that little basin down there? The lightest and slightest and hardest to please of her three children had, and would he, Gerald, please get in his car and follow her home? He repeated he would. While she finished her cigarette, he would go inside and quickly tell certain people good-bye, but his mother had no patience, and when he returned to the deck, he saw the butt of her cigarette where she'd ground it underfoot, the way some cowboy might grind his under the heel of his boot. Gerald stood on the deck, looking up at the frayed rope ends hanging from the limb of the pine. A homey touch, quaint, a little scrap of family history left there to weather and rot. His eyes misted over again and he waited for them to dry.

Later, he went to his aunts and uncles, conveying his message of stability, of reinforcement, of ongoingness in the midst of grief. His aunt Carol was the most affected, she kept going back to the last time she'd seen Mickey during Thanksgiving, bearded and almost new to her eyes, how he'd arrived late and how gallantly he'd made up for lost time, and if she and her family hadn't brought up the whole matter of gas drilling on that fateful day, there would have been no derrick for Mickey to fall from. And Gerald stopped his aunt right there. It was the kind of thing he could do best. Guilt was too easy to accept or assign. For as long as he'd known him, Mickey had been a latecomer trying to catch up. He'd gone to school longer than any of the rest of them, but that only seemed to have put him further behind, so he'd rushed, tried out the shortcuts he knew, crossed the country to see if he could catch a ride on whatever it was that had propelled people out there, and finally come home to regain his strength, and that derrick would let him look out over it all. He had to climb it. It offered a fresh outlook at the break of dawn. So the fault, Gerald worked hard to convince his aunt, was all Mickey's own.

With his father he didn't talk about Mickey. He waited until most of the mourners and well-wishers had gone, and then embraced his father as if he'd just walked in the door and told him about what he and his wife and his daughters had seen in Death Valley, the Grand Canyon, Bryce Canyon, and then, as they'd begun to race to the Denver airport, about the herd of elk in that lush river valley seen from on high. His girls had loved it and couldn't believe the elk hadn't escaped from a zoo, but Gerald had thought of his father then and had taken the elk sighting as a good omen, that the natural world, in spite of the personal cloud we might be viewing it from under, continued to shine.

Frank said, "Thank you, Gerald, thank you for the elk. I've never seen one."

"At least twice, maybe three times the size of the whitetails around here. More broad-chested, more muscular—and not deer-colored. More a bright golden brown. The racks on the bucks look like strong limbs rather than twigs."

"Of course, those are the Rockies."

"I want you to come out West and spend some time with us."

"Yes, that's something I should do."

"Come soon. Bring your friend, bring Helen, if you want to. We'd love to have you both."

"That *would* be a way to get away. About as far as you can go."

Gerald paused, closed his eyes, and for just a moment the erect and broad-shouldered strength seemed to go out of him. A continent away, an only son. "Father . . ."

"I didn't mean that the way it sounded. It was because of something I'd said to Helen. We want to get away, go on a trip."

"You're very close to her, aren't you?"

"She won't marry again, I don't think."

"Have you asked her?"

Frank made a quiet chuckle down in his throat, being interrogated on his intentions by his son. Only Frank was open to advice. He was willing for the right person to put words into his mouth.

Gerald said, "Just come. Get on a plane, both of you, and come."

"I don't know how it is out there, but in this state anybody can get a license and marry anybody else. You don't have to be a minister in an evangelical church or anything like that, you can even have a criminal record as far as that goes. Just pay your fee and tell your first customers to step up to the altar. Keep it all in the family if you want to. Doesn't that strike you as strange, Gerald?"

"For instance, if a son were to marry his father? Yes, I'd call that strange."

Just then Wilson Michaels walked up and caught both Frank and Gerald with sheepish grins on their faces. Not only did Wilson Michaels not belong in Frank's suit of clothes, he didn't belong in the house, either, which was large, but in walking through it in his flat-footed prowl, Michaels made it seem smaller and unkempt. All he really wanted to know was if there was anything he could do. Gerald moved away. He wanted to talk to Helen, he wasn't sure why, perhaps to extend the same invitation to her, but Jen came up to him. He knew who that man talking to their father was, didn't he? Gerald did and he didn't. Wilson Michaels was like a shadow of somebody, swollen then somehow collapsed, a darkened figure whose features were no longer distinct enough to bring to mind a name. So Jen gave him the name and Gerald said, No, then, Yes, of course, as they turned to face their father and this shadow man standing by the fireplace, exchanging, it seemed, deep thoughts. The way that Wilson Michaels's shadow fell on her father caused Jen to go up to them both.

She felt for Michaels, with his ex-wife there but not there for him, while his daughter, Brenda, had stayed away, perhaps feeling she had enough misery on her plate, as had his granddaughter, Cynthia, a recent inductee into her teenage world where funerals were taboo. Jen hugged her father and told him in his ear that it was almost over, that soon they would pick up the pieces. Then she turned to Michaels, the shadow man who had once eaten her alive with his gleaming red eye. He had not terrified her so much as represented a terror she would have to fight off for years to come, and until this moment she'd hated him for it. Looking into his eyes, she realized she no longer did. Her father's eyes also hung, but with wisdom and, perhaps, too much kindness. Wilson Michaels's once terrible eyes now hung with defeat. She stepped into his shadow and gave him a fierce embrace, knowing her strength and knowing his weakness and knowing the right instant to step away. She said, This family has a big hole in it now, you understand. She didn't mean that he could fill it, but she might have meant that what was left of him, when he stepped out of his shadow, could make a contribution of some sort, she wasn't sure.

Michaels said, Jenny . . . and she found herself placing her right palm against the fall of his left cheek. She didn't leave it there long, perhaps just long enough to certify the presence of a flesh-and-blood man, before taking it away.

Later, when everybody had left, Gerald stood with his nephew Danny out in the yard looking out from under the maples at the derrick across the way. Nothing had changed, except the light in the bird's nest had been screwed back in and the flag once again flew. It did not fly at half-mast since there was no mast for it to fly from. There'd been no word on if and when TransAtlantic would resume drilling. When Gerald stood there with Danny, the well pad was quiet and the derrick rose like an ethereal wand against the clouded blue of the sky, and you had to look hard to make sure it was there. It did not look as if it could support the weight of one man, much less two.

Would they continue to drill? Gerald asked Danny, and if it was up to him, what would he do? Danny was twelve years old, only two years older than Gerald's older daughter, but he looked like a boy who had reached adulthood, achieved a certain leanness of attitude, of attention, a wolfishness if you were being unkind, and had then returned to serve out his years as a boy. Danny said they were already down as deep as they would go—Kenny had told him this. What was left was the horizontal part, and Danny didn't know if you needed a derrick that stood straight up like that if what you were going to do was go out flat. Danny mimed the progress of the drill bit with his hand as it bore down and then made the turn and crawled horizontally through a bed of shale that crumbled at his fingertips. They should ask Kenny that. And if Kenny said you needed a derrick to do the hydrofracking part, you needed *that* derrick, what would Danny say then? Danny understood the question. He also understood Gerald had been Mickey's only brother, as his mother had been Mickey's only sister, but brothers took a tighter hold than a brother and sister ever could do. One brother might take another brother's place—a sister could never do that. Danny told his uncle, whom he saw only a week or so each summer, barely at all, that they should finish what they'd started, that if it took a derrick to do that, *that* derrick, they should leave it up. What did Gerald say?

Gerald owed his nephew an answer. Later, he would have to give it to his father and sister, to the family at large, and he didn't know. He didn't know the right and he didn't know the wrong. That derrick had been the instrument of his brother's death. Mickey had climbed it as though to take a look at his life from the vantage point of his death, for how else could anyone ever see his life clear and whole? Reentering his life, Mickey had fallen. Shouldn't he have known that at that point reentry was forbidden? Leave the derrick up as a monument to what he had seen? Take it down as a monument to his heedless folly? There was another possibility, of course, Gerald didn't even entertain. It took him back into family history and past violations of the sane and sacred order of things. Violations had held a special attraction for Mickey, but

Gerald wouldn't go there. The country had been settled not because
Lewis and Clark had clawed their bloody way west, but because they'd
gone and come back and sewn up the wounds so that they didn't show.
They'd gone *and* come back. Then Gerald remembered Meriwether
Lewis hadn't come back, not really. Wilderness was wilderness, regardless of which side of the Mississippi you found it on. In Lewis's
case, the Natchez Trace.

Gerald said, "It won't be our decision to make. TransAtlantic has
leased the land for ten years. Ten years from now, we'll remember what
happened here, but most people will have forgotten who Mickey Joyner
was. TransAtlantic will take the derrick down when it suits them."

Danny said, "And leave a Christmas tree."

It was not a term Gerald knew. "A Christmas tree?"

"It's what they call the wellhead. After they've gone, it's all that's
left. It's little, though, Granddad says about the size of a family cemetery. Ask Kenny. He knows."

But before TransAtlantic could declare their intentions, the derrick
did come down. Partially down. The top half lay hung over the bottom
half, which had been knocked askew on the rig floor, and half the guy
wires had gone slack, while the other half had either snapped or been
stretched to the breaking point. The derrick hung cradled there like a
broken arm in a sling, and when the remaining guy wires snapped, it
was assumed the whole derrick would come crashing down. Police cor-
doned the area off. The three people asleep in the Joyner house, Frank
Joyner, his grandson, Danny Joyner, and Gerald Joyner, a son who had
traveled from the West Coast for his brother's funeral, had all been
wakened by the blast, but it was never a case of them being thrown out
of their beds. The explosion was relatively small, the explosives, presumably dynamite, planted, instead of near the base, where the most
damage could have been done, on a platform just above where the two
parts of the derrick joined. No one had been injured. Whoever had left

the explosives had clearly given himself enough time to climb down the ladder and reach the nearby forest. There'd been a moon, waning, but before it set giving sufficient light so that anyone out walking the road at that lonely time of night might have observed someone up on the platform, not when he crouched to position the explosives, for that platform was three-quarters enclosed by a metal shield, but before, or perhaps later, in a moment of quickened nerves, as the perpetrator stood with his hands on the railing gazing out. But no one was out walking the roads at that time of night. The well site was inactive. Material was stockpiled to resume operations, and tank after tank of fracking fluid was on hand, and the flag still flew from the bird's nest, but after the tragic events that had recently occurred here, the immediate future of the well was in doubt.

The land had been leased and the well dug by the TransAtlantic Natural Gas Company, as the sign at the mouth of the access road clearly indicated. Beside that sign the sheriff's department discovered another. It was hand printed with marker ink on a piece of cardboard and stapled to a stake: LONG LIVE MICKEY JOYNER. THIS ACT OF INDUSTRIAL SABATAGE COMMITED BY HIS FRIENDS. A spokesman for the sheriff's department was unwilling to comment, but reliable sources in the law enforcement community discounted the existence of any organized band of saboteurs. The sign was clearly a makeshift affair and, like the spelling, rushed. More important, it was pointed out that Mickey Joyner, son of local architect Frank Joyner, had not had a numerous group of friends. He was a known loner, with a spotty employment record as a high school teacher in another state. In fact, when he'd fallen to his death a short while before, no one seemed to have been sure he'd been in town. Most likely, the same sources indicated, the group calling itself the Friends of Mickey Joyner consisted of a solitary soul, who had reached out to a dead man in his search for an ally and friend, and, for that reason, police were labeling the partial destruction of the TransAtlantic drilling derrick a "futile and purely symbolic act."

Acknowledgments

Most of the research for this book I did on the ground, wandering around gas drilling sites and through towns that had thrown in their lot with the gas companies, talking to whoever was willing to talk and keeping my senses alert. I also wandered on the Web and was surprised to find that a number of drill floor workers had posted videos. A couple of gas companies were willing to talk to me by phone, but not for an extended time. My real debt of gratitude goes to my agent, Dan Mandel, for insisting that this was the book I was meant to write, so keep at it, and to my editor, Rob Kirkpatrick, who told me that this was the kind of book he liked to read, so why, he reasoned, wouldn't others. And to my wife, Amparo, of course, who's watched me play my hunches for years now and knows the sort of wandering that that entails.